ETCHED

Miki and Garrett Ward

2nd Edition

Ward, Miki & Ward, Garrett (Jan. 2019). Etched: The Ceorfan Gargoyles Series (2nd ed). New cover design provided by Christopher Coyle at The Dark & Stormy Knight Graphic Designs

Cover Design by Christina Schneider - MikiandMine LLC/Editing by Erica Collins/Proof by Robin Lee/Formatted by Zoe Parker

Copyright © 2018 Miki Ward & Garrett V Ward

Published by Miki & Mine LLC

Published in the United States of America

CONTENTS

Note from the Authors
To our Readers...
The World Before...

1. Work
2. Glister Cave
3. Blood
4. Motto
5. Allodium
6. Incursion
7. Scrap
8. Mission
9. Uh oh
10. Teens
11. Hot Tub
12. Firestarter
13. Discovery
14. Home
15. Information
16. Miserable
17. Getting Ready
18. The Party
19. The Bond
20. Dreamwalk
21. Mistake
22. Crying
23. Apologies Hurt
24. Pain Reliever
25. They're Hollow
26. Ready
27. Some Better

28. Urgent Fall

29. I'm Ready

30. Grandmother

31. Despair

32. I Lost Her

33. Ancestors

34. United

35. Sad Tidings

36. Free at Last

37. Reunion

38. Sneaky

39. I Understand

40. They Care

41. The Tunnel

42. Smiles

43. Alive

44. Ready

45. Swimming

46. Arrests

47. Apple

48. Terminus Debrief

A Sneak Peek
Chapter One of Hewn
Glossary
Acknowledgments
Other Books by Miki and Garrett Ward
Find us

NOTE FROM THE AUTHORS

This is a work of fiction. Names, characters, businesses, places, events, locales, and incidents are either the products of the author's imaginations or used in a fictitious manner. Any resemblance to actual persons, living or dead, or actual events is purely used as fiction. We have tried to recreate events, locales, and conversations from memories of them. In order to maintain their anonymity in some instance we have change the names of individuals and places, we may have changed some identifying characteristics and details such as physical properties, occupations, and places of residence.

TO OUR READERS

Thank you for purchasing this book and reading it! We hope you as the readers enjoy this book as much as we enjoyed writing it. We want to make sure you know that we feel this is a serious story about changing a world. It's an urban fantasy, a romantic adventure, dramatic, funny, and sometimes a heart wrenching read. It's full of sex, drugs, and rock and roll. We didn't add a trigger warning in the blurb on the paperback. We added it here. Be warned: this book contains reverse harem relationships, graphic sex scenes, violence, and language.

Sincerely Yours,
Miki Ward and Garrett Ward

The Ceorfan Gargoyle Series

By
Miki and Garrett Ward

We dedicate this book to our baby brother Rob. We love you brother.
You deserve golden apples.
-Miki & Garrett

THE WORLD BEFORE...

Recap

This book picks up immediately after the end of 'Carved' Book One of The Ceorfan Gargoyles Series. Carved begins with David Ross' funeral. His murder was devastating to Kendra Macbard. They had lived, worked, and loved together for seven years.

As Kendra and her brothers, Jared and Dana, grieved the loss of David, a small contingent of gargoyles and a mage, Jericho, spoke with David. He agreed to return to Earth as a carved gargoyle. This process called Resurgere included a gargoyle willing to give a physical piece of himself to David. This binding returned David to life. Then produced a son, in all of the meaningful ways, for Mega—the Ceorfan gargoyle warrior leader. Mega had pressed his king, Findare, to allow this to take place because he was convinced David was such a kind soul he would make an outstanding addition to the Ceorfan. Additionally, he and his race owed an ancient debt to Kendra and her brothers.

Mega and the Ceorfan people had been secretly guarding Kendra and her brothers her whole life. Protecting Kendra was one of the primary tasks of a prestigious group of Ceorfan warriors called the Ducere of the Elite Warriors Guard. She was their charge. They knew she was the descendant of a rare bloodline, which they had been waiting for more than a millennium to see a re-emergence. The Ceorfan Dragons.

Kendra and her new partner, Mica, were soon entangled in nefarious plots, kidnapping, torture, rape, and murder by the notorious criminal Jessup Cartel. Kendra used every bit of her training and called on new found powers to decapitate the head of the Cartel and protect her brothers and the gargoyle nation called the Ceorfan Guild.

Kendra and her brothers spent a great deal of time in the ancient, magical city of Navan, the cave home of the Ceorfan. Their continued presence in Navan brought their powers to the fore. When they were each in desperate situations, they became the dragons their ancestors had intended.

Dragons are matriarchal, and only the blood of the female is magic. Those around female dragons are stronger, keener...and more virile. The blood of the female dragon can heal even the most desperate wounds, in addition to transforming human flesh, if desired.

Kendra, as the only female dragon, was the only hope of the Ceorfan when an ancient, once thought destroyed, foe returned-The Horde of Barat. A sociopathic mage from a time when gods and goddesses chose to play with human life. Baratium crafted an army of evil robotic killers to exterminate the humans of the Earth. Committed to protect the humans and bring equality to the Ceorfan people Kendra searches for answers with Spar by her side... Spar is David returned to her.

Ultimately, Kendra traveled to Scotland to meet with The Alumbradai Sanctuary State or TASS when invited by the humans who are the real power of the human governments. Making allies, the

Ceorfan find themselves embroiled in other fights to castigate certain criminal elements.

Kendra now has two other consorts besides Spar as she becomes deeply involved with Mica Jacobs and Kino Magus. They have met with a dead-end in the search for the Horde.

Their story continues...

1

WORK

Kendra

HERE I AM SITTING in the pristine examination room at Dr. Vargas' office. As he's finishing his exam, I have a good idea he's happy. "Kendra Macbard, I've known you since you were a little girl. If I didn't know how you heal, I wouldn't believe these tests results and would run them again." Doctor Vargas flips through my records. "I think you are more than ready to go back to work at the Ranger's Service. No restrictions. Do you agree, or do you have a problem that we need to discuss?"

"No sir, no problems I'm more than ready to return to work." But I'm also thinking I'll be able to get inside information much more accessible at work; meaning I can protect and care for my people better. On another note, I can't continue to let them down like I feel I have. Having to have two of our number executed for treason in the short time I've been queen is terrible. I think about that a lot. Well, at least they can't call me Bloody Mary—though I've got to do better. I must find ways to improve their lives.

On my way out of the doctor's office, I overhear two ladies in the waiting room gossiping about the Cutter girl. The one says to the other, "Did you hear? She has gone perfectly insane. Spouting that drivel about the devil saving her and that awful Danforth boy."

Oh no, this is my fault. I sigh. I've got to help Vanessa. Gossip—it only hurts people.

I'd made a date with Chris to meet for lunch. Today is her day off, and I'm in the mood for pizza, so we're going to get some. I'll also take some home to the guys too. Wow. I view Navan as home instead of my dinky little apartment. A dinky little apartment that I need to check on while I'm in town.

I get to Mama's Bistro on Main, and there's the always-dependable Chris, waiting for me. I get a hug before we sit. "Well, chica, I've been given a clean bill of health by the good Dr. Vargas. He says I can go back to work tomorrow. Am I back on the schedule?"

"You better believe I put you on the schedule, Kendra. We're so short-handed it'll be a blessing for you to be there tomorrow. Your new partner was back today. Too bad about him losing family and all, but he's back. Did you hear about John?"

Chris tells me all about John selling drugs then getting caught. I act surprised before I ask a few questions to further cement her belief in my falsehood. I am learning to better conceal the things I know from those I care for. Chris and I laugh throughout our lunch. She is such an easy person to talk to I momentarily forget some of the burdens I'm carrying and have a good time. She has a hair appointment, so she needs to go. "Kendra, you look great. Maybe I should get shot, so it'll make me look better." We laugh. I tell her she's a pretty lady and she knows it.

I order three large, thick, stuffed crust pizzas to go for the guys. On second thought, I better make that six and load them with protein, extra sausage, and pepperoni. I secure them in Jasper's back seat, and head to my apartment. When I get there Brian, the doorman, greets me with his usual smile and expression of how beautiful a day it is as he opens the door for me.

I'm disjointed as I exit the elevator, this place belongs in an old movie, not my life. Unlocking my door, I close and lock it behind me. It's different, not like home anymore... no this isn't home anymore. I'll keep it because we need a place in town for a base, but that's it.

I pack a few of my uniforms for work. Check the fridge to be sure nothing is ruined. No, it's empty and clean. Huh, I'll bet some stone dude is taking care of me. I love them. Wait, yeah, it's true. I'm not denying it. I'm not going to choose between them either. I want to love and be loved. I'm going to do my best and see what happens.

I take my uniforms to Jasper, my truck, load up, and drive away pausing to look back at my life. I'll leave Jasper at one of the Ranger cabins that no one visits. Then I'll stop to pick up Mica from work. He won't mind helping me carry stuff when we fly home.

Back in Navan, my room has had a makeover. Yay! Dana is here putting in some closets made of stone—like my cave walls, but more functional. I see Dana's touch in the kitchen too. He's manipulated the stone; I have several gorgeous rock shelves. We spend a lot of time here. I bet that I can fit in more supplies instead of having to go to the lunchroom for everything. He's put up some of the prettiest red glass lights for me. I set the pizzas on my table. Mica gets some out and starts to eat right away.

"Work is going well. There's a lot to catch up on. I'll show you everything tomorrow," he says between bites.

"Yeah, I suspected we might be behind. Get your shower. I'm changing. The others should be awake by the time you're finished. We can go to the High Guild meeting together. If we get it over fast enough, we can get back here, watch a movie, eat pizza, drink a beer, and then go flying."

"Sounds good to me beautiful," Mica says.

After taking care of showers and food Mica, Spar, Kino, and I go to the HG meeting—I laugh at the acronym coined by Clifton—he brings the meeting to order.

Jericho interrupts, "This cannot wait, Your Majesty."

"What can't wait, Jericho?" I ask.

"The crystal cave is lit up with lights, all of its own making. Usually, it's a signal to enter and sleep so I can dream. Do you recollect my informing you of the dreams one has while sleeping in the cave? It would not let me enter today, so I desire your presence, or that of one of your brothers, to ascertain whether it will allow one of you to sleep in the cave. In the past, the dream cave was used by the dragon kings and queens... well at least until I was the only one available to use it."

"I'll go with you when this meeting is over if you don't mind waiting," I plead.

We finish the rest of the guild business in short order after he agrees. Rising to leave, the guys and I follow Jericho to his laboratory. I step up to the little enclave, and its strobing colored lights. My skin thrills from the display. I feel it's saying it needs me. Taking a deep breath, I sit on the smooth stone seat inside the cave.

I tremble as my body understands more than my brain. "I'm here," I say out loud. My mind is captured by a vision. My body tenses as I lean back into nothingness. Suddenly I'm transferred to another space, another time. I am gliding like a bird then abruptly I stop in mid-air. I'm suspended in front of a stunning gargoyle on the side an exquisite palace, surrounded by lofty towers and giant palisades. She—I'm sure it's a she—is speaking to me in my vision. I ask, "What did you say?"

Oddly, I see both her human form and her dragon avatar simultaneously. Her dark face and shoulders show the strength her body held. She stares into me with her crystal blue eyes. Her magnificent orange dragon head avatar seems to radiate energy, strength, and power. Together they turn to face me.

Her voice is a haunting rhythmic whisper as she speaks clearly, *"Kendra, i agapiméni mou kóri, férno tous agapiménous mou gious, ton Jared kai ti Dana, kai érchomai se ména sto Troa."*

I have never spoken this language before. However, I understand it clearly. As a child intrinsically understanding her mother... the caressing tone, the gentle flute-like fluctuations, the love... *"Kendra, my dearest daughter, bring my well-favored sons, Jared and Dana, and come to me at the Troad."*

My heart swells with joy. I know with all my being that I have found my grandmother.

My vision continued, *"My daughter, I have waited for you for more than a thousand years. It is difficult to speak to you from atop my monument. The distance... You must come to me. Your memories are not complete. You must be etched. I cannot reach you as my physical tether prevents me from joining you. You must find me before the next full moon, or the Ceorfan will turn from you. Doing so, they will be destroyed by the enemy. Divided, they will be weak. You must unite the gargoyle clans. Bring the surgeon. I will etch you for your reign."*

My heart is racing. The beating seems to fill my ears and begins to overwhelm the dragon's lilting voice. It fades further replaced by only my breathing and heartbeat as I travel back to my body, back to Jericho's gem-like cave.

I take a few seconds to adjust. "Oh guys, I think we're in trouble." I proceed to explain, repeating every word I heard the dragon queen say in the vision. I'm not sure vision is the right word. It's the closest description I have though. I try to think of a way to explain my emotions to them, the way I felt... feel and I can't. I do feel a sinking feeling and a sudden racing of my heart. Fear strikes me, and I break out in cold sweats and heavy breathing.

Jericho, however, is amazed. He's never seen anyone speak to an ancestor that way from the cave. The cave appears much the way it did the day I was previously here visiting with Jericho. No lights. Again, it's only a beautiful colossal geode, not the harbinger it became.

"Don't worry, beloved we will figure out the puzzle," Kino's calm voice settles me. "Jericho, do you know where a beautiful orange dragon queen's head might be?"

"I am acquainted with exactly where she is located. It is exceedingly difficult to get there. It will not be an easy journey. Turkey is restricted to Americans, and you cannot show up as a dragon in daylight. This will take some planning and quite a lot of luck."

My heart sinks. I must do this. There's no way out of it. Now that I'm out of the vision, the pull of the journey is on me. What am I going to do about work? How am I going to get there? Who the hell is the fucking surgeon?

2

GLISTER CAVE

Kendra

I FEEL LOST IN A FOG. What did I just see? Wait, can I see it again? Did I imagine it? Looking around I see Jericho, Mica, Spar, Kino, Fin, and my brothers standing in a large loose semi-circle around me, all talking excitedly about the vision. I repeatedly tense my body and wring my hands. I rub my face for the fiftieth time. I stand and begin pacing in front of the stone geode where I've just had a vision of my grandmother! She told me to come see her by the full moon, or the Ceorfan will be destroyed. That is only... how many weeks away? Do it, or the Ceorfan will be dest... just then I smack my toe on one of the rock protrusions. Of course, I'm only wearing my sandals, and I yelp as I throw my hands up in frustration.

The guys automatically close around me to offer support. They can sense my tension as well. I brush them off and continue my pacing. I have too many important jobs to fix before I can go! I can't keep up. What am I doing? Who am I kidding, I'm not even prioritizing well right now, I yell at myself in my head.

"It'll be okay Kendra," Spar says in his soothing growly voice.

Each of my guys is telling me something similar. I know I'm panicking. I feel like everything I touch is spinning out of control. How can I ever balance the two worlds I live in? When I leave here, I've got things I need to accomplish. What order I do them in is my quandary. What's most important? The belief I'm going to mess up keeps filling my head. I tilt my head back a little, close my eyes, and deliberately breathe in. Hold, count to five, and slowly release. I open myself to my three guygoyles. I discern each heartbeat, attitude, and emotion as clear as a bell. They're concerned for me. They want to help me. They feel they're not doing enough. Crap, that's not what I want... at all. I need to calm down. I can't do or be everything, but I can affect others by doing better myself. I concentrate and relax.

I pause. I need to relax for a bit of time to loosen up. "Jericho, I've been to your quarters twice now and haven't really seen it all. Will you give me a tour?"

Jericho looks at me with an enlightened look on his face understanding what I need and gives me a knowing gentle smile. He takes my hand and says, "Yes, your Majesty, I would love to show you my laboratory." They move to enter the room and his pride shows as he motions with his hands in a grand gesture.

"My Queen, you may rightly suppose this quartzoid cave is the focal point of my laboratorium. I call it my glister vault. Nevertheless, over the years it has played its role only as I lie dormant. There are times that I repose in my hypnagogic state, or druid sleep and I see realities which are best illustrated not spoken. Utterances infrequently provide proper context and do not convey the depth of emotion that I feel when I lie in that state. The state between wake and dream. The state immediately before I fall asleep. Awkwardly my reckonings are rarely clear. I may envision a glimpse of the tasks in our foretime. Other times I view only people. It was from here where I first spoke with David."

I shoot a look over at Spar, shock on my bewildered face. He doesn't even flinch as Jericho uses his former name; the one he had before he was carved with Mega. He returns my glance with his beautiful toothy smile.

Jericho doesn't even stutter as Spar and I exchange our look. He continues never missing a beat, "My dear, I watched your mother and father from here. I continued to watch over you as you grew. Because of my fantasies and visions of possible tomorrows that I saw from here, Duke Findare sent the Elite to ward off numerous possible ummm... deleterious encounters."

At this, I feel my underpinnings drop from beneath me. My legs begin to shake... No! Kendra, you are their leader, not their lady in distress. Buck up! I remind myself.

Jericho, possibly understanding the power of his last comment shrank into a smaller version of himself. Apparently, he realized he bungled his attempt to help me calm down. "Your Majesty, my dear Kendra, I have only now realized how frightfully difficult this experience must have been for you. I myself have been using my glister vault for many years and have become somewhat benumbed by its... presentations. Might I suggest we continue the tour after you have rested?"

"You're sweet, Jericho. I'll take you up on that offer." I feel I've made it through the worst of the heebie-jeebies though. Now is the time to get organized.

"I've got to make a plan guys, before this spins out of control." Looking around I ask, "Where's Clifton when I need him?" I'm feeling a little stronger now, more settled.

"Jericho, do you know if the surgeon is in Navan—in your hospital? Do you know what an ancient dragon queen might need one of them for?"

"Your Majesty, I know exactly what she needs. I am the surgeon."

Immediately, I feel an enormous burden disappear. I stare directly at Jericho with my mouth open and my eyes wide. I slam my mouth shut. "Jericho, I apologize I had no clue. That knowledge all by itself takes away half my worries. You said you have an idea where this dragon head is located? In Turkey did you say? Am I asking too many questions?"

"Let me put your mind at ease, Majesty. I am aware of where your ancestor's great orange head is located as well as most of the additional needs as well.

"Then I'm not worried about any of this anymore. What could possibly be the problem? Also, you don't have to call me Your Majesty, Jericho. Can we save the 'Your Majesties' for formal gatherings and such?" Softening my tone letting him know I'm not angry.

"Quite right, Your Ma... Kendra, my lady. Though there is a slight problem. Your grandmother's nous is on the Anatolian peninsula in present-day Turkey. I do not believe the country is open to American travelers. If it is, I am sure your State Department is discouraging travel, there. All said we do not have to travel by conventional methods though. I will use my magic to portal us through. The problem is if we get caught in the process... it will take finesse—a little espionage so to speak. Are you up for a little undercover work Your... my lady?"

"Of course, I am. Tomorrow night is good for me, how about you?"

"Let's not get in too much of a hurry Kendra," Jericho continued. "We'll have to prepare."

"Who's been there before? By the look on their faces the answer is everyone except Spar and me. Okay, should have seen that coming. Then who all is going?"

The guys all said, "I am," at the same time, causing me to giggle.

"Okay, two in a row. Anybody want to offer me a question that's not obvious?" I laugh. Now the tired in me is taking over. Mica and I need some rest since we must be at work in a couple of hours.

"I'm going to take a nap, coming?" I ask Mica.

"You don't have to ask me twice," he answers.

"My room or yours big boy?" I ask him with a saucy tone.

We didn't speak at all as we made our way to my room. Mine is more comfortable than his. Mica literally sleeps on a flattish rock!

Nothing compares to waking in Mica's strong arms. His wings buttery soft on my skin. He sleeps so still his face inches from mine. His breath blows across my lips. The tingle it gives me makes me wish for more time. I love breathing his breath. Something about being so close to complete this act and share the very air giving us life. I could look at him asleep for hours. Oops. Getting closer I blink, and my lashes brush his cheek waking him. His golden amber eyes peer into mine. "Princess, if you want to be late for work keep looking at me like that. I'm okay with you getting fired and giving up your day job."

"Not happening, handsome," I say giving his perfect warm lips a kiss and get up to get ready.

Brushing by Spar sitting in our lounge area, I bend and kiss him a good morning before the sun rises and he torps.

"Good morning beautiful," he greets me.

Kino is sitting close to him in my sitting room with his arms on the table. He gets a lick and kiss on the back of his neck. I promptly blow the wet spot, at which he growls the sexiest sound. I can't wait to explore more with him. Spar never takes his eyes from mine. I keep my eyes on his—his interest heating me up.

A million things on my to do list and all I can do is picture them naked. As they say no rest for the wicked, and all that rot, I laugh to myself.

"Kino, Mica and I will probably need a nap when we get home from work. So, I won't have time to stop by the lunchroom. Will you put a message in the B-Board to remind Clifton to provide food at the High Guild's meeting tonight, please? I just hate to disrupt the lunchroom staff by walking in there in a rush knowing the guards will usher everyone out for my privacy."

"Anything for you, beloved," he replies.

"Thanks, I'll owe you."

"Great plan—Edling owing me is something I shall not forget and will remind you of often. By the way, you could leave that job and leave more time for us... just a thought," he said through a smile.

In retaliation, I throw a book at him. He sits as the book sails directly toward his head. At the last moment, he ducks his head ever so slightly and the book hits him straight on one of his horns. It bounces off and lands on the seat beside him. He merely looks at me and smiles with satisfaction.

3

BLOOD

Kendra

I TAKE my timecard from its slot and stab it into the time-clock to mark the beginning of my second shift back from being shot. I hold it briefly waiting for the time-clock to do its thing. I hear the familiar click-clank culminated with the louder stamp sound. "Hey there Chica!" Chris calls out to me.

I look toward her as I put my time-card back into its slot. "Hey there beautiful, how are you today? Ouch! Damn-it-all. You know they have better tech out there now?"

"What's up Kendra?" Chris asked confused.

"I just cut my finger on the edge of the time-card holder. I missed its slot as I said hello to you and... got a tissue handy?"

Chris hands me a box. "You got that good. Need a bandage?"

"Yea, I better, so I don't make a mess on my uniform today." I took the tissue and wrapped it around my finger and put a bit of pressure on the cut. After a few seconds, I took another and wiped up the few drops of blood that dripped onto her desk. I toss the bloody tissue in the wastebasket near her desk. I check the cut, and it is almost healed already. I take the bandage, that Chris left me, and wrap it around the now healed cut to hide it so Chris can't see it's healed.

"Chris do you have information on last week's fire?"

"I do, and it's odd as hell. That's a pun to what I'm about to tell you, sweetheart. Those teens that you and your new partner saved are telling a whopper of a story about that night."

"Do tell."

"The girl, Vanessa Cutter, has given her mother the impression the devil is the one who started that fire, and he's the one who saved her and Jimmy." She cackles long and loud.

"Oh my. Does Vanessa say why she thinks it's the devil, or whatever?"

"Well, she told her mom that the devil—horns and all—flew them out of the fire. She just supposes he must've started it, I guess." Chris finishes and takes a drink of her coffee. "Coffee is good today, Kendra. You want me to grab you and that hulking partner a cup before your briefing?"

"That'd be great." As Chris grabs a couple of mugs and fills them I tell her, "Maybe I'll swing by and talk to both of those teens and find out the real story sometime."

"Well sweetie, you might just find she's pulling her mom's leg. She's mad at her parents you know?"

"I know. Thanks for the coffee."

I grab the two cups and head to the training room. I enter the room from the back door and have a seat beside Mica then hand him his cup.

Sitting beside him with his heat radiating on my arm, waiting on our morning briefing, provides me with an otherworldly feeling. Quite literally, otherworldly. I feel shivers run up my spine as I recap the last six weeks. At Christmas, David and I had our future planned. Today, I call him Spar, and I'm a queen of a magical realm I couldn't have imagined in my freakiest fantasy.

On top of that, I have two other consorts that screw m—

"Kendra, Helloooo," Captain Murphy said, apparently again.

"Sorry Captain. Got lost for a bit. I was trying to figure out whatever the Cutter girl might be on about."

Murphy chuckles and sniffed. "There ain't no telling, Officer Macbard." I wish he would just use the nickname he gave me the day I started working here. Kenns is so much easier to hear.

He's reviewing our dailies, in a prominent adenoidal voice, reminding us there is a pyromaniac on the loose. "Only 25,000 acres were burned, but the arsonist is still at large. Sorry, this is so short. Be careful, Be safe. I'm not well today, I'm going home."

I watch, concerned, as he sits on Chris' desk to review the priorities with her.

I head out to my Ranger SUV and find Mica sitting in the driver's seat. "What, you're the newbie not me," I tease.

"Ah well, I don't mind if you drive. Have you ever handled a stick?" He teased back as he moved to the passenger seat.

For once, in what seems like years, I have an uneventful shift. Mica and I talk about the Crafted, Barat, the orange dragon, and my need for more closet space... that and his whole room.

By the end of the shift, we are excited to get back to Navan and take care of the High Guild issues waiting for us. We quickly finish up our reports and head to the front to clock out and leave for the day.

"Would you look at that, Mica." I point to Murphy standing beside Chris's desk. He sounds much better than he did in the training room this morning, and is he flirting with Chris?" I laugh at this last prospect.

"I wonder if it could possibly be a gift from the dragon?" Mica asks.

"It makes me happy that it's even a possibility," I counter.

After clocking out and giving our goodbyes, we grab our things out of our lockers and head to the parking lot. I jump in Jasper and take off to the old cabin. Mica follows in the patrol SUV. We drive to the cabin as part of our ruse of driving to and from work each day.

The drive isn't that long, but I'm sure it is just long enough for me... the further I drive, the more my anticipation builds. I love flying, and flying with Mica is always a sensual adventure. I can feel the burn deep inside me already yearning for release as I jump out of Jasper.

I hurry over to Mica and meet him before he gets out of his SUV. With my left hand on his chest, my right hand under his chin, I look directly into his eyes. "I'll race you home." I turn and walk a few steps away leaving my eyes to linger on him as I do.

Fast as lightning he's out of the SUV. He's shucking his clothes faster than a teenage boy with a nudie magazine. I stop to watch. He can win I decide. I want to ogle him more than beat him home. He raises his eyes to mine, pale amber in the sunlight against his pale skin is such an opposite from the coal black coloring of his gargoyle body. Those eyes shine no matter. I wait him out, so he continues taking off everything except a pair of tight ass exercise shorts. The shorts are enough to fly in, the wind and fading sun on our skin is a craving, clothes would only flap and irritate. Slowly he folds his uniform placing it on the seat in front of him.

"It's only fair, princess, to return the favor. I love the look in your eyes as you watch me. I'm preparing for the time I can show you more, but this is as far as I'm going for the moment."

No words are necessary. I flick up an eyebrow marginally and then quickly back down with a slight tilt of a corner of my mouth. I turn around flipping my long locks over my shoulder. My uniform is off and on the seat in a flash. I turn without showing him anything, except my butt and black panties. Thank goodness I put on some pretty ones this morning. Haha, he's so cute. Searching his face, his emotion is evident. No one is here or liable to be, we need to get home, but I can surely take a few minutes with him. I continue my turn with my hands on my bare breasts, just a little low... on purpose. Standing across Jasper with both doors open, him on one side, me on the other I take my hands away bringing a finger to my lips I shush him softly. He nods slightly. I crawl toward him on the seat picking up my flying clothes from the top of the seat on the way. I get my face as close as I can without touching his. I press my naked breasts to his chest. Mica is still as if him moving will break the moment. The sound has disappeared too. All that is left is Mica's longing in my eyes. I pull closer to him, my lips near his ear. Just a small nibble. I whisper as I push my top into his hand, "Will you please help me with this?"

Again, he nods a little affirmation, and as he takes my top, he exhales on my lips. I breathe in his air. My eyes hooding. He kisses me softly, then harder. My hands are in his dark blond hair right where his horns are normally. He flips me around, I lean on the seat, he pushes up close to me, so I can feel his hard erection up close and personal. He trails his hands down my sides caressing my back. He shakes out my top wrapping it on and closing the back. It's one of Jamie Serge's creations, designed for wings, more vest in front, velcroed together in the back. I put on my own tight yoga type shorts. Then, I reach out with my senses to verify there are no humans in the area. I bob my head to him, and he pulls me close melding our bodies together. I feel his masculinity, and in one powerful stroke, we are in the air.

We fly, not really going anywhere. Just being. After a few minutes, I feel Mica's hands move, and the gap between us grows. My wings open and I'm flying on my own.

I maneuver as close to him as possible not wanting the sensual feelings to leave too quickly. He pulses an echo to me and says, "You are the sexiest thing I've ever known. I'm making plans for us to be together soon. Until then, the hunt is phenomenal." Oh my, holy crap... the pulse makes his words feel like he's touching me.

Pulsing back, putting want combined with love into it, "I was afraid I had pushed your limits. I need to be closer to you than I'm able to get. You're too hot, no way can I control myself."

"So, don't, I have no limits where you're concerned." He moves closer to me, takes me by the waist and pulls me to him. I fold in my wings, so we are back to chest again. My favorite way to fly. I relax and simply enjoy the closeness as we near Navan. It is the only city of gargoyles, our magical cave home, my home.

"You want to pulse the sentinels princess?"

"Yes, I do." They return the pulse with respect. I smile and do a one nod sort of recognition toward the guards as we enter the cave city. We go straight to nap.

I wake a bit early so that I can see Spar and Kino wake. I'm fascinated by the way it energizes me. I like to watch my goyles a lot. Maybe I can be classified a voyeur, but I love the way their faces relax when they wake.

Kino glances at his chiroptera to be sure I haven't hooked some panties on his chir—his hand wing. Haha, that memory makes me laugh, I have no idea how long he walked around with my panties on top of his wing. He did tell me he, Mica, and Spar are the only ones to see my pretties. Okay, true. But, I'm never going to let him forget it. We'll need something to tell at parties. He smiles at my laughter, understanding at once.

Spar crosses over to me, gathering me up in a hug and kisses my neck. So glad he has a thing for necks. I love the little bites. I shiver down to my toes.

"How was your day, love? Mica? Anything interesting happen?" Kino asks us in his beautiful lilting baritone.

"Not interesting, uneventful, but one thing happened that makes me happy. I cut my finger where we clock in. It bled, and a few drops dripped on the desk. Captain Murphy had been sick and had even told us in our daily briefing he was going home. Right before Mica and I clocked out, I saw him flirting with Chris Danvers. He didn't appear to be sick at all anymore. What I surmise is; dragon blood while a great healer makes people of all walks of life horny."

We all laugh. I'm interrupted by my tablet chirping a notification. Pulling it out of the side pocket of my shorts I read it to the guys. "The High Guild will meet tonight after breakfast. The Guild will be in the Conference room at 8:oopm to wait upon the queen's arrival, at her leisure. The queen's loyal personal assistant -The Count de Treon." Now I'm rolling in laughter. What a wonderful life I have.

"If we are going to fly for our workout let's get this party started now so I can make it to this meeting on time for once boys," I said, while heading to the cave entrance.

4

MOTTO

Kendra

I SINCERELY WORRY about my status as the 'sudden queen.' I am Queen..., Regent by right... chosen overwhelmingly... by the Ceorfan people. I didn't seek this position. Nor, was I prepared for the astonishing level of power I inherited. Most obviously, I certainly was not ready for the degree of hatred directed toward me from my enemies. Those who've plotted against me, sold me to be tortured and raped, and even hired assassins to kill my family and me are beyond anything I could've ever imagined. I can't—I won't take any more chances. My new motto—trust but verify.

Thankfully, Mica, Spar, and Kino had given me this much needed time alone after we returned from our flying training. They must have sensed I needed some space to get my thoughts in order before the nightly High Guild meeting and planned this.

I enter the conference room promptly at 8:00 pm hoping everyone else is already here including my goyles—my consorts—as planned while we were flying. I'd enter after them, and that would give them time to be seated and take the pulse of the room without me. Then I'll come in, all serious like, and slowly scrutinize each member. Maybe, we can make any shifty members nervous... make them wonder what we know. Regardless, we'll all try to get a read on the room.

I'm sure I'll be able to get information from their auras. I'll write it down, and while I'm at it, I'll keep track of their associated emotions. My dragon senses have strengthened my ability to see auras and allow me to match them to the emotions of the individual. For now, I'll only share it with my consorts, my brothers, Mega, and Jericho. Later, I might share with Fin and Clifton—trust but verify. The torture, from my time in the cartel camp, has undoubtedly left its lasting imprint on me. Trusting is an issue.

As I make my way to my seat near Fin, I carefully observe the look on each member of the High Guild's face. It's almost comical. The base of their brains is in control. It's driving them to behave like a bunch of sixth graders as the principal walks through the door looking for a troublemaker. There are a few exceptions. My brothers, my consorts, Fin, Mega, and even Clifton all seem to sense what's going on and appear to relish in my skepticism of the High Guild.

Duke Findare is an imposing dark-skinned man who appears well into middle age. When he lets you see that side of him, you will find he is funny and a fantastic practical joker. Fin, as he's asked me to call him, didn't lose his ability to display as human after the Ruin. The Ruin is what the Ceorfan call the event that changed them, so gargoyles must torpify during the daylight hours. It also took away the ability to appear human without a glamour stone for most Ceorfan. Fin uses his ability sparingly out of respect for the Ceorfan who did not retain that ability.

When he displays as a griffin, he is even more imposing. In this form, he is more protective and wears his loyalty as a badge of honor. As a griffin, his coloring is astonishingly beautiful. His white chest and birdlike head are exquisitely contrasted against the impossible blackness of the top of his wings. His lower half is that of a lion and is a perfect shade of brown. Even as a griffin his half-beak allows his lower mandible to act much like it would on any human. This allows so many human-like expressions, you sometimes wonder if you are being misled and are looking at his real human face.

Fin stands and briefly catches my eye. His eyes twinkle with amusement apparently at the manner which I chose to enter the room.

From all fours, he lowers his eagle head and chest almost to the floor. He holds this bow as he greets me. "Hello, my Queen."

Damn, this goyle is charming! I take note of his use of 'my queen'. He stands on his lion legs and pulls out my seat and seats me. Damn, the only thing that greeting is missing is him kissing my hand. Nice touch Fin, nice touch, and did I say he is charming?

I ask, "Clifton, count de Treon will you please start the meeting?"

"Yes, of course, Your Majesty," he states.

The meeting proceeds in the same manner as the rest of the meetings the High Guild has conducted when I'm present. Same ole, same ole. Not one of the HG proposes a single thing that will help the ordinary Ceorfan. My frustration grows with each passing minute until Clifton asks me, "My Queen, would you like to add to our meeting or would you like me to adjourn?"

It's here that I decide to throw a wrench in the works.

"I'm glad that the action items from our last meeting are mostly resolved. I know it's a team effort getting the medics ready. Dana, I know that you're working in town and extra hours with your team here to correct damage and build rooms. Each of you has my heartfelt congratulations on your efforts as well as my thanks. Duke of Stone, you're building me a chamber for the High Guild to meet near my rooms—an allodium as Clifton calls them. Is it almost finished?" I want to call him baby brother but refrain and wink at him saying Duke of Stone instead. In a few days, he'll be officially recognized as a Duke along with Jared.

"Big Sis, we finished it tonight. I'd like to show it to you before I leave." I smile at the 'Big Sis' since I'm trying to speak more formally for the advisors.

"I'd love that." But the excitement of seeing my new digs builds so much that I want to immediately leave to go and see them. The sensible side of me tugs me back, telling me I've got lots of work to do to help my people first. I won't avoid that responsibility especially when I'm evaluating the HG members for their desire to do the people's work.

He continued, "My team and I are still fixin' damaged backs and other dangerous areas. There's nothing in the living or work areas that's a threat anymore though."

"Dana, just to make sure everyone is on the same page explain 'back'."

"Sorry, Sis... Ken... Queen, whatever. It's the top of an underground cavity. Sorry about the 'Sis' thing."

At my smile and nod of thanks he continues, "I'd also like to hire some of the Ceorfan stone workers if you don't mind them working in town. Being the only stonemason, I have a lot of things I have to do. If I have some of my Ceorfan team, who are gifted in moving stone, I'll be able to be here more. And frankly, these guys are amazing at their job. Another thing, I have some ideas I'm workin' on with Jared to make a better sewage system. That's a project that'll take lots of work from my whole masonry team. Having their help will help me get ahead so I can take some time off to get it done."

"Dana, those are wonderful ideas," I reply. "Though the Ceorfan need to work only at night and inside with the window-shutters closed." Secretly I'm jumping for joy at the prospect of improving the sewage system. This is what I want. Stuff that makes the Ceorfan lives better...

"Mega, is there any news of the Horde? Are we any closer to finding that psychopath and shutting him down?"

"We are still working on it, Edling. Flint is deeply embedded in the underworld and is trying to find any information possible. There is nothing yet. I have been in touch with TASS's Chairman José

Brinker. They are finding only false leads and cold trails. The children from our last encounter are doing well, I am happy to report. All have new homes, and with the money that Jared donated to their care, they will want for nothing. As for their memory, they only remember they were hurt in war and woke up in Scotland. We have scouts in the area where they were found and across the globe. Barat's hidden well."

"Thank you, General," I say.

Now for my information. "Last night, in the Royal Mages' lab, I entered into the dream cave." Breaths sucked in so fast I could hear gulps. Continuing, "I was instantly taken to talk with my grandmother, an orange dragon named Leta." More gulps. They're grabbing their drinks. "She gave me instructions to come to her so I could be 'etched' for ruling as queen. I'm to bring a surgeon and get to her before the next full moon; which is on the thirtieth of this month." Now that I've repeated the information. I feel the pull of the trip even more than I did last night. "Jericho's going to go with me on this trip. We need to go at night to sneak into Turkey. We don't want to create an international incident. No one else need go for that reason alone."

Suddenly, the room erupts into chaos. The once demure High Guild members all shout to be recognized. My heart's racing and adrenaline is flooding my system. I struggle to maintain a calm demeanor, which I do... mostly. I raise my right hand, and the room begins to quiet.

Over the remaining din, I yell, "I understand each of you have something to say. I'll hear everybody—one—at—a—time!" Looking left, I pick the first goyle I see. "Slateri will you give me any information you have, please, and state your concerns? Keep it short. We have a lot of people to get through."

"My lady queen, I know where that grand lady is located."

Slateri is speaking so fast, I must seriously concentrate to discern his message. Has he even taken a breath?

The excited member continues, "It is a travesty that she is still in that castle after so long. I would have you bring her home and put her to rest in the Sacred Queens' Vault in Navan. We have her body. We must now honor her by bringing the rest of her home. My queen, I only know stories of her. But, I'll proudly go to help you bring her home. I have no information why, but you must take the Elite with you. We can't lose you. Losing you would be the end of our people."

Slateri definitely hadn't taken a breath. Still, I'm struck dumb as I assess what he said. I merely stare at him and... well... umm... at least I haven't forgotten how to blink! Damn, was my mouth hanging open again? He said so much so fast I'm not sure I caught it all. Well, one thing is for sure, he's serious. I can't disregard his concern for my safety. Not because I'm worried about me. I am a queen of a people. I must care about what my loss would mean to them.

The rest of the members basically repeat Slateri. All except Jericho who agrees but adds he needs Kino with him to bolster his spells.

Of all members of the HG, only Alexandritana has remained quiet while the rest of the room erupted. As I watch her, her head hangs a little lower, her hair covers her face. Her aura is blue and purple with little black swirls. Ah, she's trying to hide from her pain. I can't let her hide. I know she needs to speak so softening my question with her nickname I ask, "Tana, please tell me what you need to say. This is not a forum where we hold our thoughts."

She slowly lifts her eyes and stares directly into mine. Her eyes bloodshot, and with tears streaming down her face she begins, "My queen, I was a lady-in-waiting to your grandmother. To me, she was more than my queen. She was my best friend. She was the one who saved me when everyone else had abandoned me and left me to die alone in the trash heap outside Sparta. Kendra, I have failed Leta for too long. Please, let me go with you. I'm not a warrior, but I will not fall behind. I will not fail her or you."

I smile and nod to her thinking I'll reach out to her later, so I can learn more about my grandmother.

"Alright, I need a stone mason. Dana will you be able to go with me or do you have someone to send?"

"Yes, I'll go. She's my grandmother too."

"Okay, today is the twelfth we have eighteen days until time runs out and disaster strikes. This weekend we decided to hold a joint party to celebrate Spar's integration as a trusted gargoyle and his inclusion in the Elite Warriors. During this celebration, I'll also formally recognize him, Mica, and Kino, as Prince consorts. Then I'll acknowledge Jared and Dana as Duke of Storms and Duke of Stone respectively. If I can stand to wait, because I'm telling you, the pull is strong. My skin itches from wanting to leave right now. I need to go on the weekend just in case worst comes to worst, and we are detained. I can't miss work so soon after just getting back—neither can Mica. Shall we set the time to steal her home and get me etched on the third weekend of March?"

After a few objections concerning me holding my 'other job', and needlessly putting myself in danger we agreed on the twenty-fourth and twenty-fifth of March just in case it takes more than a few hours to complete our mission.

"Jericho, do you have more information on the area and how to get to her?" I ask.

"Yes, my queen, I do."

"Will you please work with Kino this week to outfit us properly?"

"Yes, my queen."

"Mega, we can't take too many warriors. I'll accept your judgment on who goes but keep your numbers small. Let's get the scouts there as quickly as possible, so we know what's ahead of us. Kino, you will remain with me the entire time. Jared are you free for this trip?"

"Yes, Kendra. I'll be there. I'll be ready."

"Tana you may also go, but I want you to remain in hiding with a few Elites guarding our path. I'll bring her back to you then we'll leave by a portal. I will have my consorts with me, but I need the rest of you to stay in Navan. The Horde is still a threat. We can't find ourselves weak at home and not ready to respond to a threat from the enemy. Thank you all for your devotion to the Ceorfan people and Navan. Clifton, will you adjourn the meeting."

With the meeting over I move to Dana and wrap my arms around my baby brother. He bends to hug me back. It's clear he's excited to show me what he's made me. I smile and leave the room with my entourage. That's so funny, I have an entourage. Funny, but it's true.

5

ALLODIUM

Kendra

ON THE WAY to my new allodium, the guys are arguing. They each think there should be more Elites to go with me to get the Orange Queen.

I ask, "What if there are more traitors in Navan... who would protect the people? While I'm gone, who will supply me with consistent, reliable information about the Horde? I need folks I trust here keeping things safe for our people. We need to do this on the sly, stealth is important, right?"

Grumbling, they agree although, I can tell Mica is upset about it. That broody face shoots hot sparks straight to my core. Spar's not happy either, but I think he'll be more understanding. I'm sure he just doesn't want me to leave without him—that's not happening, there is no way I'll go without either of them.

Stopping outside of the entryway Dana has his Cheshire grin on full blast. "Here we are. Close your eyes," he says.

I close my eyes covering them with my hands. "All right, they're closed," I say.

"Keep walking, Sis, straight ahead."

I do just as he says.

"Okay, wait here while I get the door. Now, keep walking. Stop. Okay, ...you can open them!" he says with his irresistible childlike excitement.

I move my hands and open my eyes. The light is bright after having my eyes closed for a bit, and I squint a little. My eyes quickly adjust, and I see the floor first. It's the most brilliant white I've ever seen. Not a spec of inclusion, or dirt for that matter, anywhere. It seems to be radiating a soft light, although, I can't tell where it's coming from. I look around the room chancing a glimpse at Dana. He's standing there staring at me waiting for me to say something.

It's a vast room, running at least fifty feet in all three directions, front, left and right. The floor and ceiling are made of the same beautiful white rock except for a few areas, the most notable is under the meeting table. It's black. The black basically looks like a three-dimensional square hole with brilliant flashes of blue which contrast nicely with the bright white of the surrounding floor. The meeting table is the deepest cherry-red I've ever seen. It's surrounded by enough seating for every member of the HG. Interestingly each seat appears to have been made explicitly for the guild member who'll occupy it. At some point, I need to ask Dana how he managed that.

I peek at Dana again. This time my mouth is slightly open. I quickly slam it... nope... it stays open. Dana still has that look of 'desperately wanting me to love it,' but he looks as if he has a bit of doubt creeping in.

The table being round has no head nonetheless, it's hard to miss my seat... no, my throne... it's impressive. It's a high-back chair constructed of the same cherry-red rock as the table. The seat looks like it's molded to fit my butt! It has armrests, and the back extends at least a foot above my head... while I'm standing! It is not an overly large seat though. It is only wide enough for my butt and armrest. Damn, it even has a cupholder! I also see lots of carvings. There's one that immediately stands out, it's of the Orange Queen mounted on a stone edifice of some sort. On either side of my seat are similar seats for Jared and Dana.

They're deep blue and aqua respectively. They have carvings too, each representing different victories or tragedies suffered by the Ceorfan. The one above Jared's seat looks like the Trojan horse.

Looking back at Dana his expression has now moved into the 'well, I can fix it' look.

With my mouth fully agape I run straight at him and scream, "Oh my God!!! It's the most gorgeous room I've ever seen. This isn't a cave —it's a palace!" Losing whatever royal dignity I had left, I grab Dana around his neck and jump up and down while I try to hug him. I guess I squeezed his neck too hard, or maybe my shoulder keeps hitting him in the mouth, so he starts to peel me off... whatever, I don't care, I freaking love it.

"I love it. No one better mess it up, or I'll have to kick some ass." I laugh. "Show me everything. I need to know how this works."

"Well, Sis let's start with the most obvious part of the room; the High Guild meeting table. This was suuuper difficult since it was entirely handcrafted. We didn't use magic, ooonly toools, and sweaeaeat." Dana has a habit of drawing out words when he wants me to pay eeeeeextra attention. I can tell he has a great deal of pride in the work he and his men put in.

"My artisans want it to be our skill and not magic you see when you sit in council. They believe that honoring their history is quite important. All the stone you see was found in various places in Greece. They want it to represent the Ceorfan roots. The floor and ceiling are made of marble from Mount Pentelicus outside Sparta. The black under the High Guild table and covering every inch of the wall space is Gabbro. The red granite is from someplace historic too. You'll have to take my guys' word for it because I can't prove it one way or another. I had to mold the gold into the different wall sconces and around the floor color changes."

My brother, Dana, is a master designer. The furnishings here are made of stone but are comfortable. The reds and black blend beautifully with the silver and gold accents.

I sit in my throne at the roundtable—front and center of the room. My brother knows what I like. It's a style of its own—cave to the extremely divine.

"Never have I seen anything like this, Dana, thank you. You're so amazing. Clifton, will you make the next meeting of the High Guild in here, please? I want all HG business addressed in this room while I'm queen."

"I'm writing that notice on the B-Board now, Kendra. Anything else while I'm at it?" I notice he used a contraction and smile to myself. He tries so hard, even in the little things, to make me happy.

"No thank you, Clifton. That's enough for now. Dana, how did you mold this seat to fit me so well?"

"Umm, you need to talk to Spar." Awkward pause...

"Kendra, I know you're busy, so you have a complete kitchen and dining room as well as a seating area just off your room to relax with aallll your consorts." Dana exaggerates all and adds his southern twang to it to tease me.

I giggle like I always do when I'm excited.

"The cafeteria will hold about forty or so people. The kitchen'll be operated anytime you're in Navan."

I give Dana another hug and a kiss on his cheek. He's beaming and is getting antsy to leave. Putting a hand on my shoulder, he says, "I need to show you and your companions one thing then I'm going home. It's a secret only for y'all."

Clifton turns and shoos everyone else in the room out as he leaves. Then, Dana takes me to a beautiful colossal stalagmite attached to a wall on the far-left side of the room. "Do you see anything different here Kendra?"

I look over the formation intently—nothing. I look at the aura. There's a rectangular line; a door opening. I press it. Low and behold it opens. Now that the door is open I'm amazed it was so hard for me to see before.

Dana laughs at me for being so quick to find the hidden door. He hands me a key on a beautiful silver chain. "Sis, this is an escape route. It'll take you to your room and then out of Navan. I thought you might like it, even if you never need it, it's still cool."

I hug his neck again. "I love it. I can sneak away from parties easier now." Chuckling I say, "Have a safe trip home and try to stay concealed. I'd hate to hear more reports about the devil in Cueva Hallow—even a cool aqua colored devil."

When he leaves, I go to check out my tunnel. Ahh, I should have grabbed a flashlight. Nope, there's some fluorescence to the walls, and I can see just fine.

We four, my consorts and I, are left to discover this new passage alone. I quiet my mind. As I relax my shoulders and take some cleansing breaths, I close my eyes and reach out with my senses. I distinctly see each of my goyles' auras in my mind's eye.

I know after they're officially named Prince Consorts, I'll perceive them always and evenly. Yet, for now, I feel Mica the strongest. Maybe because we work so much together, maybe because my blood flows in his veins. Mica is my warrior. His aura is heavy with passionate oranges and the red and yellow swirls of a warrior. Just seeing Mica through his aura ignites inside me a fiery arousal.

Kino's is soft blue with shafts of gold shot in at random places. By being around the musically inclined, I've found their auras to be blue. The gold means loyalty in Kino. He arouses within me a wild stimulation. I sense his desire to let go of his prim mask and fill me with a properly improper evening.

Spar's is yellow with some oranges but different from Mica's. Spar's yellows tell me he is full of wisdom. His orange represents the authority that he has been gifted. Spar's intelligence indicates he can help me look upon messy situations with clarity. In fact, I have the feeling that his knowledge includes a deep understanding of me. With Spar, I don't have to look at his aura. We have such a history, I know what he craves.

I feel a new want welling up... *Wow!* I think to myself. *I really need to watch myself when looking at their auras!*

All three have a layer of pink segregated just for me. This pink says I love you. I inspect my hand to see what my light looks like. Interestingly, I see mostly deep blue, and I see the same pink I see on them.

I stretch the connection deeper to see my goyles better. Their strength, which my consorts each have in abundance, is evident. So is my goyles commitments to our relationship. I bathe briefly in the richness of that commitment. One thing is incredibly clear... we can't lie to each other!

I break away from my thoughts and step toward my suite. The path is flat but not smooth. Thank goodness Dana is always on his toes. If I hurry the floor will not be so slick that I'd slip and fall. After walking through the short tunnel, I take several more steps, and I'm in my sitting room. A few more and I'm near the door to my room.

My donum, or my sixth sense, is tingling—something is off. With a quick glance at my goyles, I stop. They wait patiently but are now on heightened alert. I lean my face on the door and reach out with my senses again. There's someone in my room. Raising up a hand to Kino, who's right up against my back, I point my fingers to the door and motion forward twice then point at myself.

Kino shakes his head and moves in front of me before I can stop him. Whatever, I could stop a train easier. The other two are right behind him. The low dulcet tone of Kino's song hits me as I follow them on my tiptoes. Mica's just in front of me and is clearly blocking anything terrible from coming in my direction. There's an extra-large male gargoyle in my lounge. Kino's put him to sleep with his song. His head is dodling forward and he's snoring to high-heaven.

I look over at Kino smirking. "You didn't have to put him in a coma." I laughed. I almost ask if anyone knows who the goyle is, but I remember him. He's Ore. The one who found Jerome and put his body in the burial grounds for protection.

"Alright, Kino wake him up please."

Kino's voice rings out, this time his deep tone waking Ore in seconds. Ore draws in a deep breath and stretches. "Now that's strange, I don't sleep that way. Was that you Kino?"

"Yes, we thought you were an intruder. We were not here to feel your introduction pulse if you gave one before entering the queen's chamber," Kino warns.

"Of course, I pulsed!" Ore said defensively. "Amber let me in and seated me here. She said you would be here shortly and here you are. I have a message that I must give to the queen and only the queen."

"Oh yeah, Snorlax. We don't leave her unattended. You'll just have to deal with it," Mica challenges.

Ore watches Mica then quickly glances at me before his eyes bounce around the room hoping for help.

"I think we need to hear what you have to tell me, Ore. I trust my consorts with my life. Please, say what you came to tell me."

Spar waves us all to be seated as Ore starts. "I was in the lower caves Your Majesty and heard an unfamiliar noise. As quietly as I could, I snuck up on the suspects. I am very old and I immediately recognized one of the intruders as Gortanik, a mage under Barat."

Ore shortened the sound of the name so that it sounds like B-rat. I kinda like that, Rats-ass is stuck in my mind now. "He was guiding several crafted as they dug a tunnel in the cavern wall. I left and came here to tell you what I saw and to get the Elites."

Mica takes charge without missing a beat. Kino, you stay here with Kendra. Kendra will you tele-speak to Mega? Spar with me. Ore show us the way to the intruders." And just like that they're gone.

"Mega, can you hear me? There's a problem."

"Edling, what is it? I hear you fine. I am on the way to you as we speak."

I tell him all the information I know from the short exchange with Ore. Mega tells me he's sending warriors to the lower caves, some to me, and others to critical areas inside Navan. "My queen, I believe we should place Navan on lock-down."

I am thunderstruck. One minute, I am looking at my awesome new digs... another minute..., "General, lock-down my city. Protect the Ceorfan."

6

INCURSION

Mega

"GENERAL, lock down my city. Protect the Ceorfan."

"Yes, my Queen."

I say out loud so that everyone can hear me, "My first task is to tell everyone in Navan. As always, it is most expedient if I tell them via 'tele-speak' as you call it." Then I continue in a telepathic mode to everyone in the city.

"All Ceorfan, this is General Megahir. Effective immediately, all entrances, as well as all exits to Navan are closed. No one is to be admitted or will be allowed to leave the city until this situation has been resolved or further clarified. Defense and Reaction Team (DaRT), report to me in the Combat Information Center (CIC). Communications, sound the Incursion Alert."

Within a heartbeat, the clanging of the tocsin breaks through any nattering and the general din in Navan. This is the first time, outside a drill, the Incursion Alert has rung-out in more than one-hundred years. The last time being when a cowboy had stumbled onto the entrance of the cave in a drunken fall. I remember when he passed out I took him to a pool in a canyon several miles away and no one was the wiser. This time it is a little more severe someone has actually entered Navan.

The alarm system starts the warning message. "Incursion alert. Incursion alert. All Ceorfan to your duty stations." The backlit red almandine crystals cast a deep bloodstain across the white marble floor and walls as I rapidly descend to my duty station in the CIC.

"Set Condition Modified-Zulu and Weapons Posture, One RED throughout Navan," I order the information's specialist on duty, one red being the highest threat level.

While the flashing red crystals change the mental posture of the residents, or how they respond to the red condition, its primary purpose is really to signify the weapons posture or the weapons we use for a specific situation as dictated by our policies. In this case, the red represents all guns are locked and loaded, all safeties off and department heads have action authority. "All Elite Warriors, not on duty pulse your current location to your division officer. All Ducere, pulse your position to Commander Mica. All nous-fārī, mind-speakers, report to your communications section."

As the alert replays, I tele-speak to Kendra. *"My Queen, the city is closed. I am on my way to oversee our defensive operations; the offensive, tactical situation is under Commander Mica's control. Your Majesty, please remain with Kokkino; I acknowledge your formidable skills, but please restrict your movements as much as you can."* I am reminded and realize from her feelings that she is not just a military mind doing a job, but a woman who is worried for her people. *I add, "Edling, don't worry. We are well protected, and everyone is doing their jobs excellently."*

"Thank you General Megahir," my queen answers.

By the time I arrive in the CIC, the DaRT team has come and are excitedly debating their suspected reasons for the sudden lockdown of Navan. Without hesitation, I end their debate.

"My friends, Ore has reported to the queen that we have one of Baratium's mages along with an unknown number of crafted in the lower levels of the caves in Navan."

Speaking over the top of me a breathless Apex interrupted, "Sir... queen, where? Safe? Who's with her? Where's she?"

Apex is speaking so fast, he is running his words into each other and his thoughts around each other. A weakness in training which I must address in future drills. Beyond the grammatical tragedy, I expect more from my DaRT. Especially given what we could lose if the queen were to be taken—again. The final word added as a whisper in my mind as it races to her recent abduction.

I raise my hands as a call to calm. "Please, everyone, the queen is safe. She is with Kokkino in her chambers."

"My apologies sir. Just... it has been perpetually forever since we have had a queen to protect." I watch as Apex visibly straightens. His posture is coming back to a perfect military pose. "Sir, I lost concentration for a second. It will not happen again."

I take a deep, cleansing breath then look at each member of my team. Apex has put into words my very thoughts. I calm myself and continue in my most military manner, "Apex, do not apologize for your natural reaction in protecting our queen. We all know her importance to the Ceorfan. I require that we attend to the defense portion of this meeting in a more organized manner moving forward."

At this point, Koke, my new aide-de-camp and one of my most indispensable assets asks, "Sir you said we have a mage... who is this mage?"

I glance at him. He returns my glance with a wise stare. Koke already knows the answer to his question. He is asking because he knows we need this information out in the open and dealt with. He deserves an answer especially now that Commander Mica and Kokkino have been chosen as the queen's consorts. I will have to reshuffle my military. Commander Mica and Kokkino, are still two of my most valuable military minds. They technically outrank everyone here, yet they will remain part of the queen's Ducere. Where I suspect they will still set and lead missions. However, the military needs its chain of command. Koke is my new second in command. Apex is third, and Flint will be fourth when he returns from his mission. I will make sure that they are all recognized and promoted.

"It is Gortanik," I say, finally.

The gulps and gasps were almost audible as I search the room for the collective reaction. Most know Gortanik personally and were fast friends with him before his... current situation. I think Dolo, Commander Mica, and Kokkino even trained with Gortanik. All of this would have been before Baratium captured and tortured Gortanik turning him into a savage dupe. Nonetheless, a dupe who is currently helping the crafted attempt to... to what?

"Commander Mica and Spar are being guided to the area by Ore. Jericho has spoken with me via nous-fārī—mind-speak. He has met Commander Mica on the way and is following to assist with capturing the mage. Nevertheless, I do not believe this is a large incursion. I believe the four of them are more than enough to meet this penetration," I say for their benefit. I am very confident and don't see that this situation is a threat as much as an exercise.

Inside the blink of an eye, I read the room. Finally, it appears my DaRT heads are calming and discharging their tactical responsibilities. It took a little longer than I would have liked. Critical in some situations. Although, not this time... hopefully.

"To the task at hand. Communications, report!" My military swagger is now powerfully tangible in the room.

Dolo has his military bearing in full effect and responds, "Sir, Communications has reported staffed and ready. All nous-fārī are in Navan and at their stations except Tine. She's with the Duke of Storms in Scotland. The B-board has the alert flashing on all tablets, verified by pinging. The cameras nearest Commander Mica, are also set to public. We have no word yet from Commander Mica or anyone with him."

"Security, report!"

Angelita, one of the most beautiful gargoyle females in Navan looks directly into my eyes, her glassy blue eyes sparkling, as she responds. She and I at one time had a brief romantic encounter many years ago. We have both moved on and although I have long since resolved my feelings for Angelita, I still sometimes feel that burn whenever she is near.

"General, I have directed three security teams to the area. We have also erected the flight barricades."

"Thank you, Angelita."

Why did I thank her? I don't usually thank my personnel for reporting in. I mentally reprimand myself for the slip. I must not allow my personal feelings to enter this room. Besides, I am with Sondra!

Apex is next, given his earlier mistake, I know I will be able to count on Apex. He will reinstall the sense of professionalism rapidly.

"Operations, report!"

"General, I have directed one of the security teams to weapons locker V then to proceed to assist Commander Mica in any fight. The other two teams will draw weapons from weapons locker VI and then provide a three-dimensional barricade surrounding the area. I have ordered the cycling of all FAF dampers in all caves near and below the location of intrusion." I note in my tablet that the Flood, Air, and Fire systems should be operational.

"Thank you, Apex."

I tell Apex under my breath, "Thank you for trying to cover for my earlier inappropriate comment to Angelita." He smiles a knowing smile. Apex and I have been friends for the entirety of the Ceorfan. He and I were together the evening Angelita and I decided to end the bonding of our relationship.

"Deck, Safety report!"

Charnock, responds with a simple nod of his head before speaking. "General, we have sealed and pressurized the city. The pressure is holding so we don't suspect any tunnels were dug into Navan. At this time, we don't know how they got in."

"Weapons, report!"

"Locked and loaded, General!" Peri reported.

Peri is a descendant of a romance between one of our gargoyle sisters and her Fairy lover. She's always been a vital resource in our relationship with our Fairy family. "FAF is operational and online sir," she reports. Flood, air, and fire I add to my note of systems that are definitely operational. This system can flood any of the lower levels of Navan with water, acidic nitrogen, or fire. Peri adds, "The Last Dance is also online and operational." The Last Dance, our magical last resort test weapon, destroys all life in a given area. Even a gargoyle who is torped would be destroyed. "However, it is still under construction in this area of the city."

"Logistics, report!"

Sandy is a golden colored gargoyle. She loves torping outside, so she spends her days in the sun. She longs for the day that she may lay, once again, on a beach in the sun. Her mother was born in northern Africa and raised her daughter to love the sun and ocean. That pull never leaves her.

"General, everything's good. No problems, except the Duke of Stone. We do not know where he is at this time. Gabbro, I believe, has a report on it though."

"Intel, report!"

Gabbro answers, "Sir, the Duke of Stone is shadowing Commander Mica. I have Mason and Amber with him. Their current instructions are to keep the Duke away from the battle. Reportedly the Duke is saying he can grow a wall around the infiltrators if needed." The room laughs an endearing laugh.

"Well, at least he is not unlike his sister and brother," I tell Gabbro. "Dolo, have communications contact Amber. Her orders are to keep the Duke at a safe distance. I am concerned he may not be able to construct the wall fast enough to avoid a strike if Gortanik is not who we believe he is.

"Medical, report!"

Dr. Ogman of the Fairy responds as professionally as any of the others.

"Mega, I have two medics heading to the area right now. They are prepared for any injury, magic or otherwise. The hospital is prepared for a mass-casualty event, even though it may be unlikely."

"Well done all. Apex, I want–"

"General, Amber is reporting that Commander Mica has made contact with the intruders. They are under a mass attack by Gortanik and the Crafted," Dolo says.

"Apex, take control of CIC. I am going to find Commander Mica and his team." I quickly finish my notes and save them to my tablet. I am possibly the only one who can understand these. Yet, I need them for my reports. I will evaluate this alert later to plan lessons learned and strategy for improving using this information.

Elite Warriors in response to Incursion Alert:
Communications – Dolo, Outstanding (O)
Security – Angelita, Good (G) – work on pheromones
Operations – Apex, G – work on focusing
Deck, Safety – Charnock, O
Weapons – Peri, O
Logistics – Sandy, O
Intel – Gabbro, O
Medical – Ogman, O
Assistant to the General – Koke, O

FAF – ACTIVE AND OPERATIONAL

The Last Dance – ACTIVE IN SUPPORTED AREAS

Kendra – In quarters protected by her guard and Kokkino
Jared—In Scotland with personal bodyguards
Dana—Verified accompanying Amber and near Commander Mica

7

SCRAP

Mica

I LEAD Ore and Spar in a dead run. We are shouting to those in our path, "Clear the corridor! Against the wall! Move!" We resort to pushing at those not listening as we race down the corridors as fast as we can away from the queen's chamber and toward the enemy. I never stop even while listening to General Megahir's mind-speak orders closing the city and activating the DaRT team.

We round the final corner at a dead run into the open and take flight. Flying to the lower levels has always been the fastest way up and down, but it's reserved for use only during emergencies.

We have no sooner taken flight when I hear the clanging of the incursion alert. Well, someone is definitely on point and doing their job correctly. The sanguine light accompanying the warnings are flooding Navan. I can spot the Elite Warriors among the Ceorfan as they move with a purpose to their destinations. Others in the area, take a breath or two, overcoming their initial inertia and begin moving in stunned disbelief to their duty stations.

"Set Condition Modified-Zulu and Weapons Posture One RED."
The alert blasts from the alert speakers.

"Spar, Ore head to the lunchroom, now!" I yell.

"Mica, what the fuck are you talking about? The fastest–"

"Spar! No time! Follow my orders. Move it, Mister!" I roar in
response.

As we drop the last few feet to the walkway in front of the lunchroom the cross-level netting shoots into place. Spar turns to me his
mouth agape. I give him a knowing grin.

"Clearly, my friend, we have some training we still need to
complete!" I say.

Spar laughs his agreement.

"All right, Ore, which direction now?" I ask.

"Commander Mica, it's this way," Ore points in the direction we
need to go. As I follow his guidance, I see Jericho coming to meet us.
As he meets my gaze, I watch his eyebrow lift, asking the question
WTF is going on, without uttering a sound. I quickly lay out the situation to him.

"Jericho, it's Gortanik." Jericho jerks his head up to meet my eyes.
I glimpse the loss in his eyes.

"Spar, Ore, we have weapons free at *my* discretion." I emphasize
my and catch both of them with a glare before I continue, "I want the
mage alive." I've known Jericho so long that I know he'll follow my
lead without my asking. So, I turn to proceed.

"Ore, go!" I yell. Ore guides us toward our prey. We descend
leaving the red-lit bustling Navan behind.

The terminus between the hustling Navan to the bowels of the
city is not a fine line. It's more of a gradient. Like most cities, we have
those who choose to live on the fringes, away from polite society. As
we move through this incline, I think of my childhood. The area we
pass now I remember many scratched out a lonely existence.

Entering the lowest levels of the city after long since walking by the
embedded lighting and the commotion generated by the alert, we pause.

These are the areas of Navan rarely frequented by any but maintenance workers and security forces. The odor of the bat guano combined with the low lighting makes this area more akin to the places the humans visit in the Cueva Hallow Caverns than the last city of the Ceorfan.

We're silent as we move into position finding the Crafted right where Ore said they would be. It looks like a small team, consisting of six Crafted and the mage—Gortanik.

As I turn back to the other three, I spot Amber and the Duke of Stone on a rocky outcrop above us, less than a hundred feet aways. It looks like Amber is leading the Duke in but doing it very slowly and circuitously.

"Spar, I want you to my left. Ore, to my right. Jericho, stay back and take care of the mage. This mage was a friend at one point. He was captured at the beginning of the Mage Wars but was unable to escape. If possible, I want to take him alive and uninjured. If he can be saved, I want him to have that chance. Before Baratium killed his family, he was a good guy."

"I will take care of Gortanik, if he should attempt to use his magic, or if he should seek to escape. I have just the thing too, Commander. The truth be told, it is my chance to verify how well my new spell will work. By a happy coincidence, I recently finished it. I have since been seeking an opportunity to examine it under duress," Jericho answers excitedly to my back.

Nope, I can't have a new magic spell used. Not while we are trying to take Gortanik alive. I turn to face Jericho. "I realize I'm not the expert in this field, by any measure. But I don't want a new spell used right now. Please mage, only use it as a last resort."

"Spar, Ore, ignore Gortanik. He is Jericho's responsibility. You each have two crafted to deal with. Don't let me down," I say with a challenge and a grin.

With the odds in our favor, I relax, thinking this will be good practice for Spar. I give this fight two minutes or less... as long as Jericho takes out Gortanik quickly.

"Move," I whisper to the others.

We spread out as planned. I'm going up the middle but to the side of Gortanik. There are only six, so I don't need to worry about a swarm. We can take them on as we see fit. I reach my first target, a wooden crafted, who hits me dead center of my chest. No challenge here. I land one punch to its head and it's gone. It splinters and flies apart covering Spar. The big blue gargoyle looks at me questioning, with shards of wood shattering further as it falls off of him. I shrug my shoulders at him and move to the next one.

As soon as I do, I catch Jericho casting a spell at Gortanik. I don't know how, but the spell is redirected by Gortanik, and it hits me square in the chest. My body freezes, mid-run, and just long enough to see Gortanik, spin backward and land an amazingly powerful back-kick to my groin. I then have time to see Jericho unleash a white powder on Gortanik which immediately pins the infiltrating mage to the floor. With my testicles screaming their displeasure at me, I now regret my attempt to dissuade Jericho from using his new spell at the beginning of this fight. Note to self, don't pretend to know as much as the mage. Let him protect the family jewels!

Ignoring the pain with a limp, I move on to my second Crafted opponent. This one, however, is not acting like any Crafted I've ever fought before. It's ducking and weaving like a boxer. But box, I can do. Only, jab after jab, hook after hook I let fly and miss! This little shit is much faster than it has any right to be. I rush it. Nope, it moves to the side and jabs me—solid hit. Desperate times... I turn away from it and pretend to ignore it. That's the ticket. Not knowing how to respond—it rushes me. As it does I quickly grab it around the waist and crush it with a simple bear hug, further littering the cave floor.

Spinning around, I ready myself to help the others. I find them staring at me like they've been waiting for ages.

"Okay, so it took me a bit longer. My second Crafted was a loon. Why didn't you guys help? You fuckin' suck!"

They laugh. Spar asks, "How're the balls?" But, before I can respond, General Mega arrives.

"Mica, I want Gortanik to be jailed in a spell protected cell. You are also responsible for his interrogation. Keep him from speaking with the other mage we have detained down there. We need answers from them both. These answers are essential. Do you understand?"

"Yes, sir!" I respond to my general. "Alright guys, let's get Gortanik onto the stretcher and get him to the lower levels on the other side of Navan. The sooner we do it, the less likely it is he will be found by other Baratium allies."

As we head off at a quick-time pace, Spar asks, "Hey Mica, why do we have to hurry? This guy, did you call him Gortanik, is out cold? And, what other mage?"

"Well, we have reason to believe this guy has, at a minimum, a tracking spell and a compulsion spell on him."

"Ooookay..." Spar started. "So, is there something I need to know? Like, how in the magic rabbit would you know Gortanik might have those spells on him. Or, why in the spelunker are we headed to the lower levels on the other side of Navan?"

Judging by his comical questions, Spar still seems to be in a good mood. It's probably because we just kicked some ass and captured the infiltrator alive. The reality of what he's asking for is starting to dawn on me in a very uncomfortable way. Damn it, this is going to be embarrassing. I should have talked to him about this weeks ago.

"Well," I began cautiously, "you remember that mage who attacked you on your final Elite Warrior test?"

"Yep. I should have stomped his smart mage-ass harder than I did!" Spar said with a wry smile.

"We have him," I said this and almost dodged as I did. I decided I'd give him a couple of heartbeats of a pause. I should be able to read his response better...

Spar's reaction... he jogged on. But I could see his face beginning to twist with the absurdity of what I had just told him. Witnessing the judgment forming on his face I now feel the need to spill the beans on the rest of what I know before he can blow up on me.

"You see, we captured him that night while you were recovering.

Kino recognized him. They were friends before the Mage War. His name is Peter. He is locked up on the other side of Navan in a special cell Dana built to contain him," I said hurriedly.

"Wait a freaking minute, you have that mage... Peter... here... inside Navan... with Kendra? What the fuck are you thinking?"

"Spar, give me a second..."

"What do you mean, give you a second?" Spar retorts before I can finish, obviously frustrated.

"First, my friend, it was not my decision. It was Kendra's. Although, I happen to agree with her. We simply forgot to tell you. There wasn't any reason... hell, Spar, you were hurt, and we made some decisions and... well, you know how fuckin' busy we've been. I'm sorry. This one's on me. Okay?" I implore.

8

MISSION

Kendra

I WATCH mouth agape as Mica and Spar run from my chamber. My head rushes as I attempt to keep up with the unfolding events. Suddenly, I hear General Mega tele-speaking to all of the Ceorfan, locking down the city. My mind flies to the average Ceorfan. What is going through their minds? Do they know how to protect themselves? Well, of course, they do, they have practiced—right? Wait, what if they haven't?

I look at Kino. "Kino, did I go overboard in calling the lockdown?"

Before he can answer, I hear a very loud bell. It isn't some bell like you might hear in high school. This is more like a ship's bell clanging loudly and quickly. It tones down a bit, and I listen to the message before I turn to Kino for my answer.

"Edling, we are in a time which delivers to us enemies who are devoid of humanity. They are bereft of empathy. Their callous disregard for human and Ceorfan life cannot be overstated. I cannot imagine a reason to not take these actions. We must act as if this incursion is a preparation for an all-out assault on Navan."

As I start to lower my head onto his shoulder, I receive another message from Mega. "Kino, the city, is closed, and he has restricted me to my quarters! What... why would he do that?"

"Kendra, you must understand..."

"I can take care of myself Kino and what if I'm needed to help with the wounded? How can I help if I'm locked up in this room?"

"My love, I do not believe that the General meant for you to be locked up here. I believe he wants you to stay here and let them handle the situation. That is all."

"How do I know he has this situation under control? Why can't I go with him? If it's so under control, why can't I be there too?"

"Edling..." Kino stops there, and he wraps me in his arms and pulls me close.

Staying here with Kino is even harder now that I have had a chance to argue about it. I'm not afraid that the others can't handle themselves in a fight. I worry that if they're hurt I won't be there to heal them.

As we sit, Kino starts telling me of Ceorfan history, apparently in an attempt to keep me busy. Whatever, my mind is drifting to the battle below me. What the hell am I doing? I'm the fucking queen! I'm going to help my goyles.

I stand and push my big red goyle away, and as I reach the door, I yell back to him, "I'm going to help!"

"Kendra, please. This is not a good idea. Trust them to take care of it. Please, just wait here for them."

"No, it's been almost twenty minutes. Kino what if they need me?" My mind made up, I charge around the first corner in the hall and let my dragon-self take over my nose. I can smell the way they went. I allow a little growl to escape my throat as I run on.

I hear Kino's words again... trust them. Seeing the netting everywhere, running to my destination seems to be my only means of getting there. I hear a noise behind me... Kino is right there smiling. "Edling, I must go with you. You know the rules," he says with one of his enigmatic grins.

"Rules, screw the rules. I'm the queen," I say with a laugh.

I begin to hear a commotion in the distance. I even hear Mica yell something I can't make out. There is plenty of laughing and talking, and it's getting more evident with each step I take. My mood is getting much brighter. Now all I need is to see how it all went.

I turn the corner, entering the hallway which passes in front of the lunchroom. At the end of the hall, my gaze lands on Jericho leading a group of gargoyles. I laugh, who could miss the mage in his tall hat with his goofy waddle walk. They're all moving quickly and excitedly, but not recklessly. I feel excitement bubbling off of them. They're even moving in-step! Even the ever calm Mega is excited... at least for him anyway.

Their excitement is overtaking me, then I make out an overly-large stretcher carrying a filthy mage. They ended the threat and apparently taking the intruder alive. I'm so excited I want to grab Spar and Mica and do some very un-queen like things to them both.

Just then Mega catches my eye.

He yells, "Squad, march!" As one, they stop talking and began a silent, professional march toward me. Their victory display suddenly forgotten, their exuberance lost.

Odd... I wonder what happened? Mega with a perplexed look about him marches the group directly to me. His frown doesn't seem to be angry, but its purpose is lost on me.

Mega bows and states very loudly and pointedly, "My queen."

Uh oh, something is going on. I don't think my general is happy with me. Talking out loud and 'my queening' me is a dead giveaway. His aura is flaring red too.

"My queen," he starts again, carefully gauging his words. "Was there a reason you did not trust your Ducere to take care of this small entanglement?"

"I did trust you." I somewhat lied, Kino's words in my mind, my face heating as I say it.

"My queen. With respect, I must know your whereabouts during these situations. I have a duty to know if you are moving from your specified location. Because when we fight I must factor your location into my awareness."

The looks on Spar and Mica's faces are telling me the same thing. I didn't trust them, and they feel diminished because of it. Crap on a cracker—big mistake.

"I'm sorry General," I say, trying to show him some of the respect I'd taken away. "Please forgive me. I was only worried. I thought I might be useful. I was scared that someone might get hurt. Really, I'm sorry, I wasn't thinking clearly." I was hoping one of my excuses would restore the pride I'd inadvertently taken from my Ducere.

No words. Mega lowers his head and shoulders to me, his wooden bow acknowledges my apology, then he moves on to his destination with the group.

Lesson learned; don't ever do that again! Always trust my general and consorts. Never make them think I don't believe them or believe they are weak again.

"Oh Kino, I think I really screwed up. They're going to hate me. What do you think?"

"No beloved, that would not happen. Mica and Spar are not happy and feel belittled. They will get over it because they love you. Give them some time."

Oh crap, what have I done? I couldn't be more upset with myself if I tried. "Do you think I should follow them and try to talk to them?"

"No, dearest. I think you should trust that your consorts can take care of their business. They will come to you because you trust them to love you as much as you love them."

"Thank you, Kino."

"Well, my beloved, we have some time to wait now. Are you hungry, or do you have something you would like to do?"

"I'm not hungry. I'm going to my room to think. You are welcome to come, but if you have other things to do I understand," I say, hoping he'll leave me to my thoughts.

"I should check on my mother and Sondra. I'll be by later if that is alright with you, Edling."

"Fine, really, I'm just fine. I just need to think some. I'll see you later then. Please tell Gem and Sondra hello for me." I don't wait for his answer and leave him standing there my feet dragging as I move.

I'm drained. I can't believe I've ruined such a beautiful thing. This was too good to be real for me anyway. I'll never be good enough for any of my goyles after what Jessup did to me. Damaged goods are damaged goods.

I walk right past my room. That's okay, I just need time to think and make some decisions. Toughen up. Get some tears out without anyone seeing me cry. As I continue to walk, not taking in where I'm headed, it's a little colder here. Not anything I can't handle, but I should have brought a blanket. The darkness overtakes my vision, my dragon eyes see a ledge in the distance. It's darker still and hidden out of the way of prying eyes. A perfect place to stew in my stupidity.

The dank is more than I expected as I climb onto the ledge. I don't care, it doesn't bother me.

While I sit on the ledge, I pull my legs to me, pressing my back against the wall. I give into my building pity party and let the quiet tears fall. Silence is my friend since I don't want any help. I deserve this soundless punishment.

I have got to do better and take better care of the needs of my people. I'll pour myself into them, build them up. That includes everybody, especially my goyles. That is, if they choose to stay. I never wanted to let them down. Yet, I'm flawed and undeserving of their love.

My mind races from one deprecating thought to another. But, it always comes back to my consorts. Damn it, I let two of them down before we even had a chance to start. I have to own it.

Spar, Mica, and even Kino can do better. If they decide to leave, I'll let them. I won't... I can't make them stay if they don't want me. They deserve better than this hot mess.

While I sit and stew I feel decisions forming in my head, and I stiffen my spine. The resoluteness pushes my legs away from my chest and forces me to sit taller. With a disaffected calm taking control of my mind my body surges with bitter energy.

But... if by some miracle they do want me I'm going to do my best to trust them. I'll trust them, but I'm going to the fights from now on. I'll find a way to be useful and keep myself safe.

Contemplating my decisions, I feel a small touch on my shoulder, with a tiny pulse. The hairy, disconcerting contact causes me to just about jump out of my skin. I laugh to myself as I realize I understand the pulse. It's different, less of a wordy description and more of a feeling. I sense support and love from the vibration. Holy harbinger, its a bat!

I turn my head looking for my little friend. I find him sitting on the same ledge as I am. There's no tension from him when I reach for him. He's so soft! I pick him up, and he nuzzles close to my hand. I hear a small chip and feel his pulse. Contentment.

Wow! What a cutie. I raise my hand to let him fly away. He stays, it's obvious he has chosen to be friends. I place him on my shirt. He moves near my heart and almost audibly decides to stay put.

Funny I don't know why I keep calling him a he. I just do.

"Do you have a name little guy?" All is quiet. "How about I call you Elmer?" I don't know where that came from. I like it though, and he chirps a little chirp in agreement. He falls asleep clutched onto my shirt, and I'm happy with that, so I leave him.

Elmer, coupled with my earlier thoughts and decisions crystalize my direction. I'm ready to go back to my room and start on my plans.

9

UH OH

Mica

SON OF A BITCH! That hurt. I know Kendra didn't mean to hurt any of us... hurt me. Damn it all, it still stings. Spar looks like he's letting it go. I should too. But what if I can't?

If she doesn't trust me to take care of a small pain in the ass like a single scrawny mage and a few Crafted, maybe I should back off. Damn, it wasn't even a challenge. Hell, I've only been fighting like this for a few thousand years! What the hell would I know about it? Was that sarcasm? Yep, I think it is.

Maybe to her, I'm not cut out to defend Navan, or her... protecting her... that's the problem. She doesn't think I'm capable of protecting her. I know she can defend herself. Maybe she looks at it like she can take care of herself. That means she doesn't need my help. If that's the case, I may not be the one for her... such a fierce, strong, beautiful queen.

Shit! I know I'm strong enough to stand beside her! Well, at least I was sure, but evidently she doesn't see me that way.

For fuck's sake... This is just great! I finally find the love of my life... the love of any lifetime... the only one I think I'll ever love... and I'm not enough for her. I couldn't keep Jessup from taking her. Damn it, taking her, my ass, I couldn't prevent her from being tortured either!

The thing is, I love her enough to get out of her way. She doesn't have to take me just because I'm her partner at work. She deserves the strongest Ceorfan. Apparently, it's not me. We're tied together with a tight blood bond. It'll be hard for me to walk away but I don't want to be the weak link either. I'll protect her from afar. That I can do!

"Commander Mica, I need your full attention." Shaking off my thoughts I return to the present.

We're standing in front of the new cells Dana had made for any enemy we happen to capture. Damn it, how did we get here so fast? Mega is looking intently into my eyes. Finding what he was looking for, General Megahir continues, "Commander Mica, after you have dealt with Gortanik, I need to see you in my office."

"Yes, sir!" I respond absently as I turn to Jericho.

"Jericho, when I get him into the cell, I'll remove his physical restraints, and you slap on the magical restraints."

"Yes Commander, I can do that. But, may I suggest I place the magical restraints before you remove the physical restraints." Jericho added a bit of emphasis to make sure I understood the proper order.

Damn it, Mica, get your head into your job! Maybe that's why Kendra's lost her trust in you... I think to myself.

"Yes, yes," I answered exasperatedly. "Will you also, perform the necessary spells to isolate his cell from any magic from the outside, just like we did with Peter?"

"Commander, if you don't mind a small recommendation... Let us put him in the cell next to that mage."

"Jericho, why would you do that?" I ask.

"Mica, I believe they have been struck with the same compulsion curse. I would prefer to keep the blinding spells, which I use to keep the mages from being found or tracked, located in as small an area as I can."

"I don't see a problem with the physical protection if they are close together. Very well, Jericho, let's put them next to each other," I agree.

I put the still unconscious Gortanik into his new home, lock him in, and wait as Jericho adds the magical restraints. Jericho removes the physical constraints from Gortanik as he suggested as well. At least, for now, Gortanik has the run of his small cell.

"I sure hope there's a way to save him. He was a good man before Baratium," the old mage says.

"Jericho, if you don't need me, I have to go to Mega's office," I state.

"I will attend to everything here, Commander."

"Okay, I'll check in with you later. Buzz me on my tablet if you have any issues. Any at all, understand?"

"Yes, yes. I understand the importance of this Mica. Trust me."

Trust that is a funny word right now. I just wish I had earned some from my love, Kendra. I need to get to Mega's office. I bow my head and shake it. On the walk, my mind races from 'what-if' to 'what-if' without any results. No matter what I think, I'm still in love with a queen who doesn't trust me.

I reach Mega's door and announce myself, "Yes, General."

"Commander Mica, thanks for coming up so fast. I need you to assign an Elite to a covert assignment. Please sit and let me explain it."

As I sit at his conference table, he slides a file to me. The data is labeled, SPARK.

"Mica, we have a suspect in the fire incidents which have been plaguing the border states of the United States. TASS has been providing intelligence." Mega looks very intently into my face. He is apparently trying to read... something. "We believe the fires are a result of the drug trade, sex trade, and illegal immigration. The criminals are lighting the fires to take attention from their transport of humans and drugs in and out of the country. It is the ones leaving the country that we are going to focus our attention on. We believe they are being transported for use in the sex trade."

My attention is now entirely with Mega. This is right up my alley. I am a park ranger after all! "General, how have you gotten the information in this file. TASS is good but is the information reliable?"

Mega, eyes me again and seems satisfied this time with what he sees. He continues, "Mica, we also have an operative embedded deep within the coyote's operation. Our scouts have confirmed the suspect, his location, and his henchmen. We need facts that governments can't ignore. Afterward, we will make them public, so the American and Mexican governments will be forced to work together to address this problem. By sending in an Elite to gather those facts we can hopefully finish this quickly."

By now, my mind is spinning. I'm looking at all of the avenues of investigation... Mega continues while my thoughts persist, "Send someone who is good with others." Where will I go first, who will I contact... "and speaks several languages. I believe Jadeite is our man for this operation."

"General, I want this job personally. I'm more than qualified," I say excitedly.

"I am not sure you are the best candidate Mica. What about your job with the park rangers? We have you there to protect the queen while she is away from Navan. Also, you are supposed to be named consort publicly at the end of the week. This job will take longer than that, once you opt in you cannot leave until it is complete."

"I understand. The thing is General, I'm the best choice. This would allow me to protect the queen in the most direct way possible. I can have Dolo manipulate the system so that a federal mandate is applied to my position with the park rangers so I can be replaced. The consort business... well, I'm not sure it's for me."

Without a hint of a question in his voice or discernible change in his expression, Mega responds, "Commander Mica, you are my second in command. I trust your judgment. If you want this job, it is yours."

"Thank you, sir." I stand to leave, but Mega had other thoughts he wanted to convey. I stop and listen to what he has to tell me.

"Man to man, I want you to carefully consider your feelings concerning your relationship with our queen. Mica, I don't believe she thinks you could not eliminate the threat to Navan today. I believe she is a queen who needs to be involved in the fight and fiercely wishes to defend her people. Think about that if you will."

I only add, "I'm sure I am the best man for this job General."

"Then you leave 0400. You are dismissed, Commander."

I turn on my heal and leave. Hurrying to my room, I pack a special duffle bag and include a portal stone. I write a note for Kendra and leave it on my bed. Maybe she'll see it, perhaps not. I can't put anything on the B-board because this is a covert mission.

Finding myself at the jumping cliff in front of Navan's entrance, I feel this is the beginning of a new life. As bad as I feel, I'll just have to bear it. Just... no... not going to feel anymore. I'm gone, maybe I'll be a nomad after this mission is complete. The Hewn might need someone like me.

10

TEENS

Kendra

AFTER I RETURN to my rooms, I wash my face trying to hide any evidence of my sorrow and sulking. I hear a soft, lilting song coming from my living room. I need a hug.

I have such a twisted reality in my self-loathing that I wonder if anyone ever needs me if anyone could desire me at all. I slowly walk toward Kino, wondering if I have chased him away too. He reaches for me. That's what I need to know... he still wants me. I hug him tightly. His spicy citrus scent smells like the calm foundation he is to me. I relax into him and feel movement on my chest.

Oh yeah, Elmer. Smiling I share, "I have someone I want you to meet Kino," picking up my little bat friend in one hand, "this is Elmer."

"Well hello, there my fine friend," Kino says in a soft tone. He pats the top of Elmer's little head with a finger and hums a short refrain. "Where did Elmer come from, beloved? Were you in the lower caves, by chance?"

"I was just walking," I deflected, so I don't have to talk about my pity party.

"Hey, Kino, I've been thinking. Can we take care of some business? It's still early enough that the teens we rescued from the fire might be out and about. Do you want to go to town and see if we can find them? Maybe we can talk them into believing it wasn't the devil who rescued them."

"Of course, let me get my glamour stone so I can be seen in polite society, Edling," he says with a sweet smile like he has a plan. "I'll meet you in your room in about ten minutes."

I pull out my tablet and type a message to the B-Board, telling Spar, Mica, and Mega where we're going and why. Mega will tele-comm me if anything happens—I hope.

I race back to my bathroom and brush out my hair and put on a lightly scented lavender lotion I like, but that Jared always says it smells like purple. He does have some funny ways of identifying things. While I don't know what purple smells like, I do like the lavender.

I finish up with a bit of makeup, and slide a hair tie onto my wrist. I'll put my hair up when we jump to fly. My heart still heavy and morose I take one last look. Strong fingers touch me low on the back. Drawing in a breath and holding it while I enjoy the pressure of Kino's hands on me.

"You are magnificent, you don't need to do anymore. Are you ready, beloved?"

"I am," I say turning into him. He is an unmovable wall of hard muscle. He didn't back up even a little. He's strong, tall, and slim, I breathe deeply he smells divine, definitely not purple. Looking up into his brilliant green eyes, I'm shocked. Seeing him in glamour the first time is crazy good. He's a breathtaking monster, but in glamour, he's just as hot. I guess I wouldn't have thought he might be a redhead, but he has cornered the market on gingers for looks. His eyes are the same, so is the cleft in his chiseled chin. His lips are full and pouty, but not feminine at all. He has a mass of the most beautiful auburn hair reaching past his big squared shoulders. He has it tied back in a low ponytail. He has no stubble on that chiseled chin, different from Spar and Mica. I'm not comparing or complaining, more taking it all in. Starting to lose my faculties here, staring at him.

He is smiling watching me like what I see. "I am glad you like this side of me as much as my gargoyle body, Edling."

"Like has nothing at all to do with it, my foxy singer. It's more of a groveling slobber."

He chuckles and bends to put a soft kiss on my hungry lips. "We could stay here and explore this feeling little one, but I am sure we need to correct the teens as soon as possible. Would you go with me to dinner in town? Show off, my lady."

"Why, yes kind sir, I would be delighted. I'll be the one showing off my man candy though." We both laugh, then hand in hand walk to the hidden entrance of Navan.

Kino and I decide, on the way, that we would first deal with the two teens, then we would find our own little restaurant to cozy up in.

We head over to the mall, our first stop in looking for the kids. Calling this a mall is a little like calling your small-town baseball field, Coors Field. It just doesn't stand up well with the title mall. But we're in Cueva Hallow. It's what we have, and it does serve us.

We're in luck and find the two teens in the middle of a large group of people.

Vanessa is recounting, "He was huge and red."

Jimmy adds, "The other one was just as big but blue." While I am sure the two of them are entertaining this multi-generational, multi-cultural group, I'm equally sure no one believes it was the devil or his ice twin who was helping to rescue her and Jimmy from the fire.

I push through the crowd, Kino close behind. No one challenges his tall, muscular frame as we slide through. I swing around and tell the people that we need to speak to the teens on federal business, and politely ask them to disperse.

Vanessa cocks an eye at me like she isn't going to take any guff from my corner no matter if I have a badge or not. She glances up at Kino and smiles and wiggles a little.

She says, "Well who have we here Officer Macbard? Could you introduce us?" She ignores her boyfriend, Jimmy.

"Sure I will young lady, this is my boyfriend, Kino Magus. Kino I'd like to introduce you to Vanessa Cutter and her boyfriend, Jimmy Danforth."

Kino reaches for her hand and bends to kiss the air above it. Poor girl, I know how she feels, swooning in her little size five Keds. I have idea that her bravado is just a cover and she is a sweet kid, why would a guy like Jimmy like her if that weren't the case.

I save her asking, "We'd like to talk to you about the story you were just telling the people who were here. If that's okay with you? Nothing official mind you. You both can call me Kendra instead of Officer Macbard if that helps."

Jimmy pipes up, "What do you want to know Kendra?" I'm pretty sure he knows, but I'll ask anyway.

"I want to know exactly your version of what happened in the fire last week? You start first Jimmy," I suggest.

"Well," he drawls, "I had a date with my girlfriend." He focuses intently on Kino's face before going on. "We had gone to the movies, then went to Courtin' Canyon up by Deer Ridge to... talk. I guess we weren't paying attention and the next thing we knew the fire'd surrounded us. So, I grabbed an old t-shirt I'd stuffed behind my seat, and cut it in half with my knife. After I'd poured a bottle of water on it to make it a better air-filter, I handed half of it to Nessa and told her to put it over her face. Just then, we heard this loud whop, whop. I figure it had to be the fire getting closer and poppin' trees. So, now I was figuring out how I was gonna get Nessa out of that mess when I..."

Vanessa interrupts to say, "But, the only way anyone could have gotten to us was by flying. That red dude and the blue one had to have been flying!"

Jimmy nods his head intently as his girlfriend spoke trying to show that he and she were together in this. Jimmy continued, "It wasn't the devil though. He looked red, because of the fire, I guess. And like Nessa said, there was also a blue one. And, don't tell me we imagined them. I wasn't getting sleepy yet. They swooped in and grabbed us without a hitch. They were big guys with muscles like the Rock. I heard some really cool singing, and I guess I passed out or something. Because the next thing I know I'm standing there, and you are talking to me with your partner. I know he's the blue one, but I never saw the red one again." Jimmy pauses just a bit to stare at Kino a little harder. "We both saw the same thing, and we're sure of what we saw."

Trying not to chuff or roll my eyes I ask Vanessa if that is correct.

"Yes, but I do think the red one looks just like the devil. Just... he was so nice."

I make a split-second decision to trust these young people. I didn't do so well on that earlier, so I'm trying to do better.

"Can I be honest with you two? I need a promise first that you will never tell a soul what I'm about to tell you. I need your promise before I start."

They chorus, "We promise."

"It's a long story. When do you have to be home?"

"I have until midnight," says Vanessa.

With a hard stare, Jimmy says, "I live on my own. I go and come as I please."

"How old are you Jimmy?" I ask.

"I turned eighteen six months ago," he answers.

"If you need a place to stay I have one. I don't want you living on the streets. No shame, just making sure you know," I offer.

Jimmy looks at his feet. Shifting a little, he says, "I'd be lying if I told you that wouldn't help me, it would."

"I'll make you a deal then. Let's go to the diner, get a cheeseburger and talk. I'll tell you my story then. I glance at Kino, and he nods to me his agreement. I hope he doesn't mind and will make more dinner plans with me in the future. When we get there, we sit in the back booth of the diner away from other customers. Kino, and I tell the teens the story of the Ceorfan. Letting them know not everyone likes gargoyles and would try to demolish them all if they knew. They sit wide-eyed and don't interrupt.

"Jimmy the apartment I have in town is empty most of the time. I only keep it so we have a place to change and to keep things looking normal, so no one suspects. It'd be a big help if you were to live there and keep the place up for me while I'm gone. What do you think?"

The young man gulps. "I'd be honored to help. Thank you for telling us the truth Kendra. Lots of times parents and people older think we don't have brains enough to know what's going on, we do though. I'll try and do my best to take care of your apartment too." He looks at Vanessa and takes her hand giving her the cue to say her piece.

"Kendra, I had no idea," she starts. "I'll do my best to help you too. First thing is I'll stop telling my fire story and take it back. No one believes me anyway. So, do you think we could see this city of gargoyles sometime, maybe?"

I take a relieved breath and smile at the two. Thankful I was learning my lesson about trusting. These two were giving me hope I might be able to do something right after all.

"I'll fly you there myself Vanessa, but it is getting late, and you need to meet your curfew. She nods then looks at Jimmy. He gets out of the booth helping her slide out.

He says, "I'll be right back if you want to show me the apartment?"

I smile nodding to him. That is so sweet how he pays attention to Vanessa.

"I'll be right here waiting," I reply.

In just a few minutes Jimmy is back. Kino and I walk with him over to the La Caverna apartments. Thank goodness Brian is working as the doorman tonight. He's the most helpful and doesn't ask questions.

I greet him, "Hi, Brian. This is Kino Magus and my cousin Jimmy

Danforth. Jimmy is going to be staying with me for a while. What paperwork do I need to fill out for a guest? Do you know?"

Brian helps me through the paperwork and takes my added rent charge for a permanent guest. Before we head up to the apartment, he gives Jimmy an extra key. Thanking him, I take everyone up to the studio.

"It's not much Jimmy, but it's better than nothing, right?" I say quietly.

"Right! Thank you, Kendra. What's your phone number, just in case?" he asks.

After I give him my number, we have to leave, but I let him know that I'll be in touch. Kino and I then head to the roof.

11

HOT TUB

Kendra

ON THE WAY to the roof I say, "We better get him a few groceries tomorrow. I can take care of that while y'all torp. Then when I see the hot tub on the roof, I have an idea, my libido on fire for my hot ginger goyle. I think he'll be happy with my proposition.

I try to flirt. "We have a little bit before we need to get home. Do you want a dip in the hot tub, handsome?"

His eyes spark. "Yes beloved, I do."

He's seen me undressed already. I feel the teasing side of me come out. I run around the hot tub and stand behind a column to take off my clothes. I'm hurrying as fast as I can when I hear something. He's singing to me. What a sexy sound. It's not a song I've heard before. I'm not catching the words, but it's hot on my skin.

I look out from behind the column and connect with his eyes. Watching his face, I extend a leg so he can see it. I can tell his heart has sped up even though he hasn't moved a muscle. He keeps singing to me, and I'm feeling the need for him growing. I extend a hand curling a finger at him to come to me. He doesn't wait, but he doesn't race over to me either. My need increases with each step he takes. His long red tresses are loose, blowing in the wind. He's so sexy! In a minute I'm not going to hold back. His clothes are in a pile on the ground. He is perfection. His body has long defined muscles that gleam in the moonlight. I can see he wants me. His erection is beautiful. I do not want to ruin the moment, but I have to know.

"Kino are you sure you want me? I'm damaged. I make lots of mistakes, and I need to be sure. I love the always kind of love. If we go on with this, I won't recover if you decide you don't want me anymore. I don't want a fling. I want you forever."

He stops singing, a hitch in his voice. A single tear falls from each of his emerald eyes.

"I want you more than I want breath, beloved. You are not damaged. You are flawless in my sight, beautiful beyond words. I make my declaration of love to you this instant. You are mine. I never want to let you go. Please be my lady, my love for as long as we live. I will be true to you. I have never felt this kind of attraction. The women I have known before only wanted me for my position or looks. Someone with true feelings for me has never asked if I will be theirs. I want your love, always your love. I will give you mine in return— forever. I belong to you, heart, mind, body, and soul."

His full, warm lips kiss me. Ahhh, so hot, my body melts into him. He lifts me and sets me in the water. The fresh night air is not an issue, the water is warm but his body covering mine is on fire. "Sing to me Kino, love me with your voice, will you?"

He puts his mouth on my ear and kisses the lightest kisses then sings softly, his breath blowing on my ear. A shiver runs down my spine. At the same time, he rolls one of my nipples with his fingers sending tingles down my body. Cupping my head with his other hand, he sings a song filled with sweetness and love.

Tears are in my eyes. I believe this mangoyle loves me and will not leave me. I have his forever, and he has mine.

My body is following my mind. I reach for my sexy goyle's hard penis, and my body takes over. I have no more control as my hips rock up to his, the friction making me ready, quickly reaching the edge of an orgasm.

My lips open and I groan, "Fuck me, Kino, fuck me hard, make me cum on your big hard cock."

He explodes into action, lifting me from the water and sitting me on the edge of the hot tub he spreads my legs hooking his arms under my knees, pushing them up to my ears. I'm totally exposed to him as he slams into me with his dick, taking my breath away. In about three seconds flat I am starting a ginormous orgasm. I pulse, covering him in it. I shout out for him to hurry, fuck me I'm cumming sending him on his way. Grunting he pulses back making me cum again. The spasms don't stop, even after he stops moving. He stares down at me with a satisfied loving look and smiles.

"Holy fuck, Kino, that was fantastic."

He growls a laugh at me, pulling me into his lap in the water. I snuggle into his chest thinking, I should have figured that dirty language would turn on my singer. Makes sense, sound is erotic to him. I've never done that, I'm going to have to look up some nasty phrases for him. I smile to myself and enjoy being close to him.

He says in his lilting sexy voice, "Come beloved let us dress and head for home. If you don't wish to cover up, I'll carry our clothes." He moves his brows up and down at me.

Laughing at him, I say, "Now that's funny."

We dress and head home. Spar and Mica will be waiting for us. I hope they've forgiven me and are waiting in my room.

12

FIRESTARTER

Kendra

DISAPPOINTMENT... I seem to have it ingrained into my soul. Yet, it doesn't even begin to express the way I feel as I search my chamber once we're back in Navan for my guygoyles, Spar and Mica.

I pause in the wide doorway between my bedroom and the vestibule leading to the lavatory. I search, hoping to find either of my goyles, both of them. I lose strength in my legs as I find neither. I fall against the wall, my shoulders slumping forward. My loss and knowing I am the cause, weighs on me as powerfully as if a megalith had been placed on my back.

Kino, always careful of my feelings, always gentle with his criticisms and ready to give love places his arm, gently around my shoulder. As he pulls me closer, he softly coos to me, "They will forgive you little one. Give them time."

I turn from him in yet another lame attempt at hiding my feelings from someone I love. A single tear rolls down my cheek. As it drops to the floor, I decide I will shed no more. I caused this. I will not let pain destroy me.

I'm tired though so I tell Kino, "Thank you for tonight. It was wonderful. I am so exhausted though. Good torp. I'll see you tonight." I turn and kiss him dolefully on his beautiful mouth. Then turning back, I walk away without another word.

I reach my bed, knowing I need sleep before I head to work in a few hours. I feel like I should sleep forever. But I am so tired that I fall into a restless, hagridden sleep.

I find myself standing in a treeless, rolling field. It has the greenest grass I've ever seen. A large wire fence stands between me and another area. Is it a mirror of mine? I don't think so, but... I watch as a large flock of colorful birds begin a slow trek toward me, on the far side of the fence. No. They aren't birds they're animals. As they close, the details are hard to make out, but I can tell it isn't many animals, it is only one. It is orange and frightening. I run. My life is at risk. The fear is consuming me from the inside. I run. The orange specter is near. I turn to face my death. No, it'll not be my death. Surprisingly, it's my grandmother. I don't know how but it's only her head. She is angry. I stop running and round on her. Not in anger, but with love. I need... it is urgent I touch her. The wire fence is blocking my way. I stretch my arm as far as I can. She has stopped just out of my reach. I push on the fence, hard. There should be enough give in the barrier to reach... almost there... she dissolves away. I'm alone.

Now, a stiff wind is blowing my hair from behind. My hair is loose and freely flowing in front of my face. I smell the salt air of an ocean. I turn to search for the sea. As I do, the green meadow dissipates, and I now see a rocky crag spread out before me. I don't know how I know this, but it's not an ocean I know, it's a strait. A sea pressed between two lands. Waves are crashing on the escarpment below. I run toward the edge of my precipice, my instincts pulling me toward the other shore. I must reach the bank on the far side of the narrow channel. There I will find... what? As I throw myself into the zephyr, my wings fail to lift me. They are there, but they aren't functioning. As I fall, I feel no fear, although, I know death is nigh. I failed, and a grave is my dowry for my new consort, death. I see the ocean, the rocks, and the

waves. In the instant, before I plunge into the boulder-strewn water, I
turn my head and see it...

Jerking, I wake. My breathing fast and heavy, my heart racing to
catch up. Slowly, I pull myself out of bed. As I rise, ready to tidy up
my room, my subconscious begins to chastise me. You are only doing
this out of habit. It doesn't have a point, why do I care?

I stand in front of Kino watching him. I can't see him breathe. Of
course, I shouldn't with him in his torpified state. But I know he is
awake. I kiss him on his unmoving, cold, stone lips, instead of the soft,
warm, fat lips of yesternight.

Elmer is still sleeping in a crevasse high up in my room. I'm sure
he'll be safe up there while I'm at work. I still don't know where Mica
is. I reach out with my senses to see if I can find him. Nothing. I can't
even find his heartbeat. I'm pretty sure I'll be on my own today.

After I get dressed to fly, I stop by my dining room for some
breakfast. A few of the Ceorfan who don't have to torp are awake and
have food ready for me, just in case. I talk to my kitchen staff for a
few minutes before I beg my leave and head out to the jumping off
point.

I stand there in the fresh morning desert air thinking. The
preponderance of my thoughts dwells on what I need to do to get my
family back.

The flight to Jasper was quiet and passed quickly. My mind so
lost in my thoughts, I don't even remember the trip. I've gotten so
used to flying with Mica, it is hard without him. The fun is lost
without him.

I make it to work a little early when it's still pretty quiet in the
office. No Mica yet. I have a terrible feeling he isn't showing today. I
sit and drink my coffee, silently watching as other rangers clock-in,
beginning their day. I've waited too long and finally get up and head
into the briefing room.

Before the briefing, Captain Murphy asks to speak to me
privately. He says, "Mica was assigned by my boss to take an undercover job. His security level makes it classified and confidential so I

can't give you any details. Kendra, I didn't have any input. Do you want a different partner assigned?"

My answer is unequivocal. "Hell no! Just, please let me do my job without someone acting as my nanny. I'll wait for Mica to return... or not."

Murphy listens to me and pauses. After a bit, he seems satisfied with my answer. Then in a loud, commanding voice, he orders, "Rangers, please be seated for today's orders."

Murphy waits for the room to quiet, then begins his brief. "The arsonist who has been starting fires in the park and surrounding land has been dubbed by the news media, 'The Firestarter'. How original," he mumbles. "We need to exercise special care and report anything that might be linked to the fires. Remember, the fire threat is extreme throughout southeastern New Mexico," he finishes.

The rest of the briefing was rout assignment and special duty assignments for today. I ignored every bit of it. I follow that statement on my professionalism by walking to my patrol car in a fog. I miss Mica. Is he even thinking of me? Yeah, I bet he is, and it's not good. I feel the strain of the blood bond, sure he is far away and satisfied to be so.

I have been on my patrol for more than an hour. I've also been stubbornly sticking to my 'I got to feel sorry for my dumbass' plan. So, I've done my best to have no idea where I have been or what I've done. Dumbass! Kendra, get your head out of your ass and into the game.

Suddenly, a lightning bolt of pain sears through my head as I see my grandmother, the orange dragon. The pain makes me slow and pull off the road. I never get headaches, but this stabbing pain is ripping into me. I don't have time for this. But, now I have an over-whelming feeling to turn my car around and head in the opposite direction. Maybe I'll just continue on for a few miles. Finally, I give in and follow my feeling.

The pain is still present but lessening. Interesting... maybe I am heading toward my grandmother's head now, and less strain is my reward. Well, that's my first thought anyway. Whatever... it's stress Kendra, I tell myself, hoping it isn't related to my treatment while imprisoned by the cartel. Arden, my doctor friend, had given me a thorough check-up, as did my hometown doctor. They both told me I was amazingly healthy. Maybe I'll check in with Jericho later. He might have an idea or even a stone for headaches. Not that it matters now, I feel better.

I smell smoke. Rolling down my window so I can get a better idea where it is coming from I take a deeper breath. I travel over a hill to verify what I believe to be the area the smoke originated and see a raging fire covering an entire ridgeline. I call in a 10-70, *fire alarm*, and scope my surrounding area without getting any closer. This fire is starting to burn higher and is moving fast in the desert winds. I better get out of here before I can't. Calling in a status of the fire mentioning the 10-72, *fire progress*. I smell a chemical smell. Concentrating for a few seconds to be sure. Then I speed toward the main road to get to safety faster. I stop at each camping spot in my designated area as I leave.

The animals are running away from the fire. Rabbits and mice run across the road in front of me, so I slow some to not run over any of them. Just as I begin to slow, I see a large hawk swoop in and pick up a rabbit and carry it off. Wow, I sure hope that isn't a sign for what's to come in my future.

Maybe it's a representation of my wounded psyche. I'm incomplete without Mica. I don't want to get tough or learn how to live without him. It's close to how I felt when I lost David, but I'd known that I would never see him again until I got my miracle in Spar. I'm in limbo with Mica gone. I can't force him to care for me if he doesn't, but this bond makes my skin crawl without him close. Should I fight for him, find him, go to him? Groveling on hands and knees, yeah, I'm pathetic. I'm not groveling! Not unless he says he'll forgive me. I'm crazy.

I'm going to chomp this elephant one bite at a time. First, I need to finish my shift. After that, I want to check on Jimmy and Vanessa.

Making lists in my mind is what I do when I stress. Maybe if I write it down, I'll quit going over it over and over.

Parking in my regular spot at the station, I get out, I can smell the smoke even here. I walk up to Captain Murphy's office, where seeing me, he waves me in. "Captain I wanted to give you some information before I write my report. I think it might be important. When I came upon the fire in Sage Canyon, I'm sure I could smell an accelerant. I know that sounds strange, but I'm sure it's acetone." Working in politics, I ended up on several tours in facilities where they used acetone and alcohol to clean parts. I would know it anywhere, keeping the dragon smeller to myself.

"Macbard, I know you, do figure on investigating off the clock? Because I want you to know I will not cover for you if you get yourself in trouble. I want you only working during work hours. Your job is reporting and the fire chief takes it from there. Do you understand?"

"Yes, sir I do. I'll see you later I've got to get my report filed." He waves me off with his fatherly warning.

Finishing up at my desk, I clean up a little then leave. Jasper is waiting as always. I look around, then get in my truck and head toward town.

13

DISCOVERY

Kendra

TODAY, the trip to town seemed to take forever. As I stand in front of my apartment, I feel a little conflicted. Do I knock, to show respect for Vanessa and Jimmy's privacy... what if they are getting busy? Do I walk in, like I live here? In either case, I know standing here is not the right answer. But I can't seem to get my decider operational.

I finally choose. I'd rather not take a chance of embarrassing them. "Well, great decision Macbard. Now what, dummy?" I mumble to myself.

Just then, a hand reaches out of the now open door and drags me inside. Vanessa says, "What are you doing? You'll give us away doing stuff like that."

"Oh sorry. I was trying to respect your privacy," I said sheepishly. Her lips quirk.

"Whatever... we have bigger issues. We'll be sure to not play naked Twister in the living areas if you'll just come in like it's still your apartment. Deal?"

"Deal. I was really stopping to check on you and make sure you don't need anything that I can help with. I also wanted to invite you to a party tomorrow night in Navan."

"Wait, did you say Navan? That's the gargoyle city, right?" Vanessa interrupts giddily.

"Yes, Vanessa it is." My confirmation must've been something they both have been excitedly waiting on. As they looked at each other, they seem to resonate the same excitement a child would have after being told they're going to their favorite theme park.

"It's in honor one of our soldiers, Spar," I continued. "I'm also naming my consorts. As queen, I have that privilege and responsibility. But..." I duck my head and speak softer getting them to lean in a little, so I can play with their emotions a bit. "It might be boring come to think of it. So, you don't have to come unless you really want to."

"No, I mean, yes! We want to come with you!" Jimmy blurts out. "What time and what do we wear? Do we need to bring anything?" He fires off the questions at me like it's normal to have more than one consort. Maybe he doesn't understand that part... yet. I'm sure Vanessa will tell him though.

"No, don't bring anything. You can wear whatever you want, but it is St. Patrick's Day and I'll be wearing green. I'll be dressing formally, but most of the guygoyles just wear pants, sometimes less." I give Vanessa a side glance and see just a hint of her wry smile. "Girl-goyles," I continue as if I hadn't seen a thing, "wear skirts or pants and wrap tops. Having wings makes us unable to wear stuff that people without them like to wear. Likewise, if one of us were caught out in the open when they turn to stone... well, most statues don't wear many clothes. Especially ones who look like monsters. But, our battle gear is different than clothes too. All of these elements make for a diverse kind of wardrobe, you see?" They nodded their understanding to me.

"Kendra, do you guys make your own clothes or do you all buy them at the gargoyle mall or what?" Vanessa asked.

I laugh as I tell them, "A little of both. I have a wonderful tailor named Jamie Serge. He makes me some amazing things. In fact, he will be making my dress for that evening. Most Ceorfan don't use Jamie, they buy their clothes from a tailor inside Navan. You see, we are such a small community, we don't have a need for a full store with lots of choices. We just have what we want made. There are times, like when Mica is working at the ranger station that he or others will buy the appropriate uniform or other items they might like from a store you might visit. Anyway, I'll send someone to pick you up at eight pm. The ceremony starts at nine pm, is that alright?"

"Yep. Nessa's parents are gonna go to Paris for the weekend. They never check on her. We can be gone all weekend if we want. Well, if it's ok with you?" Jimmy looked hopefully at me.

"Jimmy, I wouldn't want either of you to do anything illegal, or dangerous. Other than that, Vanessa's parents seem to be ok with her decision making. I'm not going to be talking to them about the Ceorfan. So, I guess you two get to decide. Except, you both need to be in school on Monday morning. Fair enough?" I finished. I'm thinking, *No wonder Vanessa acts so brash with those she doesn't know. I'm glad we are getting to know the real Vanessa now. She really is a sweetheart.*

They nod in assent and Jimmy changes the subject. "Also, we both heard some stuff at school today that you might wanna know about. I kinda think it's common knowledge at school now. They're saying the fires are being set by some of the drilling companies."

"What? Who are 'they' first off? Then tell me what you know." I can remember it wasn't too long ago I hated the—who are they—question because it always seemed so obvious. I used it as in, everyone I knew. What could be more understandable, I used to think to myself.

"They, includes everyone we know at school, even the teachers. It seems like one of those things that's like—what is said at school stays at school—and nobody on the outside seems to have a clue. I think people are scared to have their name associated with it. For a few days, it seemed more like a rumor. Today, it's more like what everyone knows to be a fact. That's why we'd thought we'd better tell you about it."

"Are they saying why the drillers might be setting the fires, Jimmy? Is there any one particular kid who seems to know more about it?"

"Yeah, I heard from Joe Keet, his dad's a lead-man for one of the drillers. Joe said that Mr. Keet's gotta do what the company says, or he'll be fired. The Keet's aren't rich. In fact, since Mrs. Keet got cancer, Joe said they had to go on welfare just to have enough money to buy food. So, Mr. Keet really has to have his job. I think they get their insurance through the company too. They need it for her chemo treatments. Well, Joe said the owner personally told Mr. Keet to cover up the mess they'd made starting that fire on Deer Ridge."

"Time out Jimmy. You're telling me that Mr. Keet's company is responsible for the fire out on Deer Ridge?"

"That's what Joe told me."

"Jimmy, tell me about this company, please," I asked excitedly.

"Well, it's a new company in town, and it's called SpotOn Drilling. Right now, they are taking over the area right and left. The other drillers are making money hand over fist, so these new guys want all the work. Joe said they are burning down the other companies work sites or starting well fires. It costs a ton of money to fix you know. So, I'm guessing it isn't worth the risk to the smaller drillers. Some of them are leaving already."

Vanessa adds, "We can let you know if we hear anything else at school too."

"Thank you both. It'd really be a big help if you would keep telling me what you hear. Heck, you've helped me a lot already," I say. Maybe the problem is half solved now that these two have let me in on the secret. "Kendra," Jimmy asks, "will Joe's dad get in trouble? He hasn't started any fires or done anything yet. Joe said they all talked about it at the table last night. Mr. Keet doesn't want to do anything illegal. He just doesn't know what to do or how to get help. Will you be able to help him?"

"Yes Jimmy, I will be able to help them," I state categorically. While I am secretly thinking, 'But I'm not sure how!'

"Can you both help me with something totally different? You can say no," I mention.

"Whatcha need Kendra," Jimmy asks seriously.

"I want to do something cool for my brothers and consorts at the ceremony I told you about. If I order a few things for them from Traders Jewelry, will you pick it all up and bring it to me in Navan?"

"No problem," Vanessa says, "the owners are friends of my parents."

"Thank you," I say as I rub my forehead and squeeze my eyelids together. Pausing, my headache reasserting itself, I tell them, "I'll be right back." I remember I have some ibuprofen in the bathroom, so I stand up to get it. After I reach the washroom and swallow a couple of the pain relievers, I check the other cabinets. *They're going to need shampoo and some bathroom cleaners soon. The towels are all washed, and the room is spotless. This was a wonderful decision on my part*, I think to myself.

Coming out of the bathroom I ask, "Jimmy do you have anything with caffeine to drink."

He says, "Yep, it's in the fridge." Opening it up to get something the coolness wafting out feels good on my face. Oh good, he has some soda and energy drinks. I take one of the energy drinks thinking it should help kick my headache. Hopefully, it doesn't make it worse. *Well, he has this fridge stocked, so I'm not going to bring him food, he's got that covered.*

I shut the fridge door and take a big drink. I turn as I take the bottle and stumble on my own feet. Vanessa is right there to help steady me.

"Kendra are you okay."

"Yeah, it's just that I have this monster headache. I took some ibuprofen in the bathroom. If you run low tell me, okay? I'm just a klutz. Thank you, I better get home. Now, remember eight pm tomorrow, I'll send someone, or I'll get you myself. Bye, y'all."

"We'll be here and ready Kendra, bye," Jimmy says. Vanessa waves.

"Sounds good, I'll see you soon." I leave the teens and head over to Traders Jewelry. I want to be sure to get a special something for my guys to mark the occasion this weekend. I know Traders is just the shop that can make it for me. After ordering my items, I head in the direction I had parked Jasper.

I need to get home. I want to see if my relationships are in the dumpster forever or not. Then I need to figure out how to fix it!

14

HOME

Kendra

NOW THAT I'M home I feel like dropping into bed. I'm tired, not just trying to avoid reality either. I go to my chambers, fall into my bed and shut my eyes. "I'll just shut them for a short nap to kick this headache," I tell Elmer. My body relaxes into my bed. *I think, damn, this is comfortable as I fall asleep.*

I see a light growing larger. I'm beginning to recognize it as a dream as I move toward it. I know, technically, I can fall into the dream, or reject it. But, I am learning, painfully, that not accepting my responsibilities leads to unpleasant side effects. I choose to accept this dream and fly on my great dragon wings toward it.

I look around, and I find myself standing, as a human, on the high walls of a great and beautiful city. Twin towers, more than a hundred feet tall, guard the splendid gate, opening toward a large green plain and ultimately, the sea. The place I stand is built on a large mound with a sharp drop on one side. This mound dramatically exaggerates the strength of the city walls.

It's daylight, and under the bright blue sky, the city is full of joy.

Children are playing with wooden swords, reenacting battles both they and I have seen. Older children are tending to their garden or the livestock, and their mothers tend to the weaving. Men are gathered around a large pit where sizable animals are being spit roasted. They are drinking and having a good time. Near the king's residence, a troupe of actors play out a scene concerning Paris. Everywhere I look, I see jubilation and rejoicing. I see these same dramas being replayed throughout this beautiful city.

A small gust of wind makes my white and blue dress puff out in front of me. The breeze is blowing in the salt air from the nearby sea. As I turn to look out over the crystal blue sea, I see a thunderstorm billowing in behind me. This storm nears this wondrous city, threatening to tread on the celebrations below me. It isn't my worry. I'm here, and I'm ecstatic. Although, I'm not sure why.

Another gust of wind catches me from behind. This one is much stronger than the first. Unprepared, I stumble forward, only slightly. It's then, I hear the first roll of thunder. Its closeness is odd given how far away the storm was... curious, it's now mysteriously above me. I search what my dream self believes is my mother's felicitous city. The streets, once teeming with pomp and circumstance are now empty. The rain falls.

Unperturbed by the rain, I continue to stand. A solitary sentry watching over my children in the houses below. I'm at home here. The storm, abnormal as it seems to be lasting, so far for fifty-two days, it's powerful. I do understand that no rain could possibly last that long. Though, as suddenly as it arrives, the storm's fierce winds and destructive lightning pass. The walls have withstood the fury of the storm, standing the lonely guard with me, and remain unharmed.

Success we have withstood all that the storm had to offer and are victorious. Yet now my once beautiful dress is aged and in tatters. At this time I see the impenetrable gates now standing open. My eyes follow the road through the gates and into the center of the city. Terror grips me as I look from home to home, searching everywhere for my children.

Finally, I see a group of women in chains being led from the city. I also look at the bodies of those that have been slaughtered. My children are destroyed. Their blood runs in the street. Blood I could have stopped... I should have stopped.

Suddenly, as if waking from the dream, a mist clears from my mind. I see the city in its actual state, a ruin. The conflagration which once burnt throughout the once great city is extinguished. The reprehensible hoard answerable for razing the walls is long dead. Taken and still dead are many of my children, slaves to their dead masters. Men who were murdered by the sword search for their families. Now, only the rocks can tell their story.

A thousand ships are leaving. With them go the treasure of this great place. Left behind under the pond near the king's chamber lie the sorcerous treasures of past kings.

My eyes snap open. Spar is holding me close rocking me as I cry.

"Kendra, are you awake, are you okay? You were screaming. In your sleep..." Oh my God, Spar is here with me! I grab him hugging him to me tight.

"I thought you left me and hated me. I mistakenly thought I would never see you again," I blurt out in one breath. Pulling his face to mine with both of my hands on each cheek, I kiss him softly. My head is still aching but better now just knowing he is here.

"I will never leave you, Kendra. I was a little upset, nothing to leave the most beautiful dragon queen in the world over. You're mine, I totally belong to you. Never worry that I'm leaving. I'll always talk our problems out. We were given another chance when it wasn't a possibility. No way in hell am I ever going to give you up without a fight."

"That's what I need to know." Kissing him again but with more gusto this time. Smiling even though I wonder about Mica. I'm not ruining this moment by asking if he knows anything. If he does, he'll tell me, if not I'll figure it out.

"I have so much to tell you. Where is Kino?"

"I'm right here beloved. Glad you two have made up. I've been studying some spell songs. These songs are wonderful. I am trying to adapt them for general purposes so I can sing them in public and private settings without the magic being overwhelming. What is your news, Edling?" Kino asks.

"After work, I stopped in town to check on Jimmy and Vanessa." I stop to catch Spar up on the situation with the teens. Continuing, I say, "I wanted to be sure that Jimmy has groceries. Which he does, by the way. Those kids told me some interesting stuff about the Firestarter. They said it's common knowledge at their high school that the fires are being set by a drilling company called SpotOn who is trying to take over the business in the area by burning out the other drillers. I'm giving this information to the High Guild in a bit. Maybe we can shut this problem down quickly.

"Interesting that the kids know this information. I think you made a good decision telling them the truth," says Spar

"I think so, plus we get to help an otherwise homeless young man. But we have lots of time, what I want, Kino, is to hear a little of your new song."

He smiles that million-dollar sexy grin at me and I'm lost. He picks up a guitar that I had not seen before and starts playing. He has no embarrassment and does not stall. He plucks a pick out of the strings and begins a soft melody. Of course, his skill is precision. However, the song weaves around the room with a life of its own. He sings me a love song similar in style to Irish folk songs. My headache is gone now. I can't take my eyes from him. I thought he was gorgeous the first time I saw him, actually his torped form on the roof of my apartment building, but watching him now... I've fallen for him. My heart is fully engaged, and he's playing it like a violin. Bending over the instrument with his long red locks covering half his face. I'm sure Kino has no idea how attractive he is and if he does, it isn't something he capitalizes on. His long sexy legs stretch out in front of him. Ha, I just figured it out. He's still in his human glamour. I don't even notice when any of them switch anymore. Crazy. They are the most handsome beasts ever, no matter how they choose to appear. *I wonder if he plays that guitar as comfortably with claws as fingers? I bet he does.*

His song ends, and he looks up at me with gentle pleading eyes. I know he's questioning if I liked his song. The request isn't just in his eyes or manner it's in the air like a wave asking me.

"Kino..." I raise from Spar's arms glancing at him to be sure he is alright with my actions. He nods at me with a slight smile, so I proceed. Touching the side of Kino's cheek with my hand, I kiss him on the corner of his mouth softly with a little growl. Oops, I'm definitely starting something...

We can get ready for the Guild meeting in a bit.

15

INFORMATION

Kendra

MY HEADACHE IS GONE. I'm smiling on the way to my sitting room for the HG meeting. Everyone is here as Spar, Kino, and I are seated. I note that Mica's chair is empty. Tele-speaking to Mega I ask, *I've evidentially lost Mica. Is he alright? Please tell me."*

"My Queen, Mica has volunteered for a mission and is not here. He is currently in Mexico gathering important intelligence regarding the fires which are being started in the mountains," he tele-speaks back to me.

"I have some intelligence of my own to share on that subject General," I say.

I start, "Hello, everyone. We have a great deal of information to get through tonight. Clifton, if you would, please begin this HG meeting."

He nods and starts the meeting by having the minutes read from last night's meeting. Not much has changed, and all of the significant actions are yet to be completed. "Your Majesty, I have the party for

Spar, the recognition of your consorts and acknowledging the new chain of command well in hand. You have a fitting and lunch with Jamie Serge tomorrow while most of the Ceorfan torpify."

Clifton pauses. His eyes darting quickly from face to face around the room. I see the sweat building up on his forehead and watch as he takes an utterly uncomfortable drink from his human-shaped cup. All of this is almost as if he didn't want to say what was next.

"Majesty, you must be required to have a guard for this trip. The High Guild has requested the Duke of Stone to accompany you as a guard."

"Wait. No. Wait just a minute, can I have the floor? Never mind can I... I'm taking the floor," I state with more intensity than I intended. "I don't need a guard. I do fine on my own. I don't mind spending time with my baby brother, so I'll let him come along. But don't make a habit of assigning me a guard moving forward. I don't appreciate being treated like I can't take care of myself," I counter.

"Your Majesty," Tobert Reyder, the Marquis de Roat, and one of the members, begins.

I catch Clifton taking another drink of water and taking a deep breath, obviously glad Reyder is helping him out. Well, I don't like the idea of having a guard. Nevertheless, watching Clifton has been fun.

Reyder continued, almost as if he had no idea I was processing things while he spoke. "We believe you are extremely competent in self-defense. You are both, a strong woman and queen. Please understand our point of view. We almost lost you once to an evil madman. That was beyond all of our control, even yours. If we must take extra measures to end any and all attempts on your life, please consider them."

Now, I'm getting just a bit pissed the fuck off. How dare any of these people think I'm incapable of taking care of myself! I have to calm myself and speak low, so they don't see how angry I actually am. "Marquis Tobert Reyder, I will consider them. However, I neither have the need, nor the desire to have a glorified babysitter follow me around."

"Your Majesty, if you please and with all due respect, you must know that since your coronation, the strength of the Ceorfan Guild has grown significantly. Your presence is intrinsically secured to the health of the Ceorfan. Majesty, there is a pregnancy!" Reyder is almost pleading with me to listen to him at this point.

"Wait! Again, what? Who is it? Why didn't I know? We meet every freaking day for a half hour. I live here! How do you guys keep this stuff from me?"

"Just before this meeting, she mentioned it to me in passing, Majesty. She is planning on telling you personally. I don't feel it appropriate for me to speak the details in public. My queen, the point is we are stronger with you as queen. We have not had a pregnancy in hundreds of years. I only mentioned it because I believe it absolutely necessary. Now, seemed a good time to... what is it, let the kitten from the knapsack. Majesty, we implore you. Let us help protect you. We cannot lose you again. What do you suggest if not to be guarded?"

"I concede the point, Tobert. What if we establish a human Ducere team? They'd be more covert than a bodyguard while still providing appropriate protection in situations beyond my control. The question is where I would find this type of protection, much less pay for it?"

Slateri pipes up, "I understand the Duke of Storms has many security personnel. This is only a suggestion, but what if we ask him to supply the talent and we supply the training? Would you approve that my queen?"

"That could be the answer. I'll speak with Jared tomorrow when Dana and I visit Jamie for my fitting." We have a compromise that seems to make everyone happy, so I move on.

"The incursion yesterday resulted in the capture of a mage and the destruction of six Crafted. I would like to give my thanks, as queen, to Ore, Mica, Spar, Jericho and to all others involved in the protection of Navan. Knowing we are protected by such warriors, allows me to sleep much better."

The room applauds, and Spar tilts his head, first to me, then Mega. I know he's going to tease me about this. He hates being told what a good job he's doing! That's ok because his teasing usually leads to wrestling which leads to... well, you know.

"It also appears, like Peter, this mage is known among our people. His name is Gortanik. Jericho has him spelled like what was done with Peter. There are both physical as well as magical protections. No one may approach the cells without the General's, or my permission. We will not withhold our permission unreasonably. However, Commander Mica must be present for any interview. Since he is not available right now, please hold your requests to visit until he has returned."

I pause, as is my habit, waiting for any questions or comments. This is how I feel the most comfortable moving from one topic to another. Plus, it also gives me time to read the room and get a drink of water. I can't ever drink enough water.

"To the subject of the fires. I have some compelling information which I need to share. I've spoken with the two teenagers about the Deer Ridge fire. Kino and I chose to confide in them. They know about the Ceorfan, and they intend to keep our secrets. I'm letting the young man, Jimmy Danforth, stay in my apartment in town. I believe that'll help both of us. Him because he needs a home. Me because I don't need to look like I fly off to live in a cave, in the center of the desert, with a bunch of gargoyles. Oh, and on the side, fight a world-wide battle to defeat an evil mage bent on destroying the world!"

General laughter and some murmured genial comments wander through the room as I pause for a second.

"I believe Jimmy and his girlfriend Vanessa will be wonderful allies. They've already helped by telling Kino and me what they know about the wildfires in the area. They hear all the gossip from school and share it with us. Long story short, they told us a drilling company called SpotOn is starting the fires to run-off competition. They also said they know that the Deer Ridge fire was set by a father of a schoolmate. We already know the man dubbed by the media as the Firestarter. I don't want his name out, so please be discreet with your use of it. He is Mr. Patrick H. Keet."

"Majesty," said a somewhat abashed Mega, "if I may beg your pardon, why do you wish to keep the name of Mr. Keet private?"

"Yes, thank you, Mega. To that point, according to Jimmy and Vanessa, the Keets' are seriously struggling financially and as a family. Mrs. Keet was diagnosed with an aggressive form of skin cancer. Mr. Keet has been unable to find another job with health insurance which can cope with his wife's illness. He feels as if he is trapped in his job. As you can imagine, this has caused many problems within the Keet household."

"I understand Edling. Thank you," replied Mega.

"I would like to make a motion. I would like to give shelter to the Keet family, in Navan. Mr. Keet would then be free to tell us what we need to know regarding SpotOn and I would be free to heal Mrs. Keet. More importantly, I believe this could be the first step, albeit small, toward reintegrating the Ceorfan into the larger world community."

Mega responds, "I second the queen's motion to give refuge to the Keets until this fire situation is sorted."

The good Count de Treon, always on the ball, is quick with the yeas and nays and tallies the unanimous vote into the record.

"It is Mr. Keet's son, Joe who is providing Jimmy and Vanessa this information," I continue. "Mr. Keet works at SpotOn and has spoken openly with his family regarding the lack of ethics there. Maybe, General Mega, that'll help you find more information," I tell the General this while I still feel the sting of his cold shoulder after the capture of Gortanik. All right, if the excellent General wants to be formal with me then so be it. I'll now require of him, the respect befitting a queen. I'll also need to revisit the idea of having such an open relationship, as friends. It must be put aside for now.

"That is interesting Edling," stated Mega. "Right now, I have men in the field whose job it is to find those starting the fires. So far, our intelligence indicates that Edomants, the lawless humans, also are playing a role. The Edomants continue to deceive their own countrymen into paying them to provide illegal transportation into the United States. These victims are looking for jobs and homes in a better environment than what they are currently in. They save their money and then sell all they own to give to the criminals in hopes of being transported to the U.S. These Edomants start the fires to draw the attention of the border patrols away from the caravans making it possible to enter undetected."

Then the General pauses to look around the room and to take a quick drink of water. His tankard is quite large and seems as if it will hold at least two gallons of water!

"My queen, with this new information, I would like to refine our intelligence gathering to ascertain if the Edomants and SpotOn are working together. I'll assign additional personnel immediately after tonight's meeting, with your permission," the Mega finishes.

"Yes, General, run those leads down. These Edomants are some of the foulest, evil animals. The vile things they do to their victims during the crossing is beyond reprehensible."

"Does anyone have any other information concerning the fires," asked Clifton to move the meeting along.

No one did. Then Mega apparently sensing my feelings begins a tele-comm, *"Edling I apologize for my shortness after the battle and before the meeting. It is not the way I should be treating my queen or one I consider as close as a daughter. I was frightened when I saw you were not where I thought you were. This is my problem, not yours. Will you forgive this old gargoyle?"*

"Of course, General, forgiven," I say out loud. I'm still not ready for him to know how much I have been hurt by their reaction. Yet, I know he can read my mind and all my feelings in a heartbeat. My first task is that I should toughen up and act like a queen. "Please let me know of any updates concerning Commander Mica. I turn and leave but not before I notice a frown on Mega's face. I can feel sadness from him that I will have to find a way to alleviate without sharing my own regret.

Since the meeting was wrapped up Spar, Kino, and I went flying. I can use the exercise to clear my mind and plan.

16

MISERABLE

Kendra

THE THREE OF us flew hard pressing the pace to exercise our wings. In my dragon form, I use my pectoralis major and supracoracoideus to fly. I use other muscles of course. But, these are the two that, if I don't regularly exercise them, the muscles will atrophy and that could make it so I might not be able to fly as long or as well. If I let them atrophy too much, I could even lose my ability to fly altogether. Like I'd ever let that happen.

Anyway, I've not neglected it, per se. Yet, I haven't placed a premium on exercise either, at least not lately. My simple flights to and from work are great for what they are. But, they're not enough to give me the stamina needed during a pitched battle with, a psychotic, maniacal lunatic narcissistic misanthrope like Baratium.

When I train in an exhaustive manner like this, my endurance in my dragon form increases way more than what I would see from similar exercises in my human form. Interestingly, my flying training also helps me in my human form's strength and endurance. I've even had a few comments from some of the ladies in the office about the fantastic muscle tone in my arms and... umm, around my breasts. Suck it up, ladies. A girl's gotta keep toned for her hunka-hunka-guygoyles!

I savor my time with Spar and Kino right now. Yet the blood bond with Mica, the string that I recently tugged on, is exerting a maddeningly large amount of control over my thoughts far more than should be possible. Well, at least it's more powerful than I think it should be!

Spar, Kino, and I return to the city at 1:00 a.m. sharp. They have Ducere duties to perform, and I need to get some sleep for my shift in the park tomorrow.

After a quick shower, I fall down naked on my bed. I pull Mica's pillow, first to my face, then to my chest where I draw it to me as tightly as I can. Mica's intoxicating scent is so strong, I imagine him behind me, pulling my still wet, breathless body onto him. His smell makes me believe I would do anything to feel his hot skin next to me again. But, he has to want me. I can't force him.

Although I am dead tired when I hit the bed, sleep runs from me. When I finally catch it, it darts off again, and I wake. I awaken in the morning, frustrated with another fitful night sleep. I can't even seem to sleep correctly now. Add to that how broken I feel. Damn it, it's disheartening how little control I have over this situation. I feel like a ghost moving through the world unable to interact in any meaningful way with my loves.

It's becoming increasingly routine for me to wake early and slowly pull myself from my bed. My movements now seem more of a chore than an act of living. I move from one task to the next, getting dressed, on to making my bed, then tidying my room, all the while, questioning the what and why of my upcoming day. I wish I had someone who could give me any answers. I'm the one in charge, so I'm the only one who can't ask for help.

After I dress, I trudge to my cafeteria off of my allodium to grab something to eat before heading off to work. As usual, Lesham, the cafeteria manager, is awake and has a menu of my favorites ready to be freshly made. He also has some grab and go grub for me if I'm in a hurry. "Lesham, will you please give me a blueberry muffin for here and one to go. A giant cup of coffee, a couple of power drinks and a BLT sandwich with chips?"

"Yes, my queen."

I'll give a muffin to Chris. She's always bringing us doughnuts, so, this'll be a small payback. Then I'll have the BLT and chips for lunch with the power drinks to keep me awake.

As my food is being made, I sit at the bar and pinch off parts of my blueberry muffin to eat with my coffee. Damn, these gargoyles can cook! As I wait, I ask, "How are you doing, Lesham?" After that, I let him guide the conversation. I genuinely want to know what the Ceorfan think about all that's going on.

He says, "I'm happy that you have chosen Spar, Kino, and Mica as your consorts Your Majesty, I don't remember a time that the Ceorfan felt this powerful. It isn't just that we have the mighty new members with you and your brothers. That's great and all. But, there's capabilities within the Guild, or our race, that I'd once thought were gone. We're so much stronger since you arrived. Thank you, Kendra. We love you very much, Your Majesty."

I merely stare at him for a second not sure what to say. Fighting back the tears I say, "Thank you, Lesham. Knowing that means a great deal to me." I pause for a heartbeat then ask, "Lesham, would you please make a point of telling me what your friends and colleagues tell you about life here too? I don't want the life of the Ceorfan to get lost in some of the other issues which seem to be consuming my day. Somehow I've got to make sure I don't neglect what is important."

"Yes, my queen, I will," he says with an adoring smile.

Lesham has the rest of my food and a thermos of hot coffee ready for me. I grab it and head off to the jumping off point.

The flight to Jasper was cold, cloudy, and a slight rain was falling. If Jared were here, I would think he was upset about something. He isn't though, no, it's just like the way the pieces of my life are falling right now.

With the morning flight not reinvigorating me, I arrive at work and plod to the morning briefing. As I slog past, I drop off the blueberry muffin on the empty desk where Chris Danvers is usually seated. I allow myself a brief little smile, knowing she will love this treat.

The daily briefing is the same as it has been for the last few weeks. Find the Firestarter. Well hell, I know who that is, but I'll be damned if I'm letting him go to jail because some piece of shit found a way to intimidate him into causing the Deer Ridge fire.

The day started cold but heated up fast. The light drizzle I flew through on the way to work is entirely gone by ten. By noon, the heat had taken over and the day turned in to just another day filled with dust and boredom. Oh, and don't forget, for the second day in a row... no Mica.

I return to Navan full of intentions of getting ready for Dana to take me for my fitting. I'm so tired. I'm not sleeping well by myself, and with the strange way I sleep anyway, I decide to take a quick nap. I take my blanket to where Spar and Kino are torped on the stage and lie down under their raised wings. I get as close as I can to them, so I can touch both of them at the same time. Then, it's lights out. I only wake when my two goylehunks bend to touch me.

Kino rubs the back of his hand along the side of my cheek. Spar kneels beside me and takes my hand in his, raising it to his lips. Concern shows on their faces. Well, that's mine to erase, so I smile at them and act excited about my trip with Dana. I laugh even if all I really want to do is cry about Mica to them.

They seem to accept that I'm okay as Dana arrives to take me to see Jamie. Since Jamie will work his magic on me anyway, I don't really care what I look like as I prepare to leave. "What are you two doing while we're gone tonight?"

"Training." Spar laughs. "It's what we do and, according to our red friend," he pauses and pokes at Kino, "I have lots to learn. Kino's gonna be teaching me some new moves. Anyway, we have to keep up our strength. No telling what our lady love will get us into next." He finishes with a smile.

"Oh phoo." I see Dana smirk, so I say, "Get me out of here before I have to whoop up on these two will ya?"

"You bet, Sis," he says as he pulls out a stone and opens a portal. We enter through the aqua colored supernatural horizon and exit in a cold, wet and dark alleyway directly behind Jamie's shop.

"That was good Dana, you got us to the perfect spot. "How'd you get so close."

"Well, I've had to come over to help Jared a couple of times. I guess it's starting to sink in."

"I guess I should practice. I'm not sure I can even operate my portal stone half as well as you." I grin at him as I enter Jamie's shop.

"Uh oh, Darling! What could be the problem? Do you want some tea? I could put some mint in it. It tastes really good with mint. Come here and tell me what is wrong? Jamie has big shoulders to take any problem." His sing-song voice reaches me the same time as his hands to draw me in for a hug. I sink into my friend like he is the only life-line I can ever expect.

Dana says, "This looks like it could take a while. Hey sis, Jared's personal squad is on duty for you right now. They'll stay with you 'till you're done. Jamie I'm going to leave my sister in your care. When should I be back?"

"Oooh my goodness. Dana, you get better looking every time. I miss you. I won't need long to fit her dress. But Kendra love needs some TLC. Give me two hours at least."

As Dana kisses me on the cheek, Jamie pats his butt lightly. Dana swats his hand away. "What's it with my butt lately? Hey Kends, I'm meeting up with Jared. We'll be close if you need us." Then Dana backs out the door, keeping his butt out of Jamie's reach. Jamie for his part laughs and gives him a little tiger growl and claws a wave at him as he leaves.

As the door closes, I feel the weight of the world jump off of my back. I finally feel free to express my feelings regarding Mica to another person. In fits and starts, I try to explain my situation with Mica to Jamie all while he adjusts the green dress he's made for me to wear to the party tomorrow.

Clicking his tongue as his intro, Jamie starts, "Darling your Mica is a man, erm, gar...hunk of goyle in love. He'll come around and if he doesn't then good riddance. Don't worry so much over the ones who don't want you. I think he does though. But really honey, don't waste your life being sad. Find the good in this situation, even if it's just that you know what you want, better now than before. Life's too short to waste. So, if you want that hunk of a gargoyle, fight for him. Otherwise, let 'em go. Phhht! You decide. Use that decider God gave you and make your choice. Then... be happy with it. My sweet Kendra, don't you control the air around you? Don't answer me. Yes, yes you do. Well then, do you like everyone else to feel bad because you feel bad? No, I don't think so. You don't need fake feelings, but you be happy and find the positive."

I touch Jamie on his hand. "Jamie Serge you are my voice of reason. I needed that so much. Sometimes I have a lot going on in my head all at once. I just can't figure out what I want to do with it all. You are so right. I want him. I'm going to fight for him. Maybe he feels just like I do and isn't sure in himself. I can change that. I breathe deeply and smile. I love you, thank you fairy godmother!"

"Of course, my little Kendraella," he says with a big toothy grin.

Jamie has been pinning and cutting this whole time. He looks at me and says, "Ok, I think you look amazing. Look at you, don't you think you look amazing? Yes, you do."

"Jamie, it is beautiful!" I exclaim as I look in the one hundred eighty-degree mirror. The green dress shimmers with gold, silver, and ruby highlights playing with each other. The dress hangs from one shoulder with a slinky quarter sleeve falling down into a ruby red sash across the front from my armpit, under my breasts, across to my hip. The dress is cut straight across my breasts, lower than my mom would have liked, but exactly where it will cause my consorts to drool. The dress is floor length in the front and a small train in the back and with a cut, up each side to show plenty of leg, should I choose to stand that provocatively. The gloves that Jamie hands me are a perfect fit and really tie this ensemble together. Well, I may not pass for the queen of England, but I'll damn sure pass for the queen of the Ceorfan!

Dana plows into the shop his curls blowing in the wind. He shuts the door and walks in, and he evaluates the surroundings. Pinning me with his crystal blue persuasions he cheerily asks, "You ready Sis, I found us a place to eat if you're hungry. Jared's there. He rented the whole place, so you don't have to worry about drama. You can come too if you want pin cushion."

Haha, now everything's funny to me. We both take Dana up on the invite going to a little place up the street. Jamie tells me this place is known for its breakfasts. While we sit and eat our meals, I remember to ask Jamie to come to the party tomorrow. He says that Clifton invited him too and he'll deliver my dress in person. Dana takes care of the bill when we finish and gathers up two boxes of chocolate desserts that he ordered to-go.

We walk Jamie to his shop and tell him goodbye. Then we leave through his back door. Dana opens another aqua colored portal. This time, we go from the rising sun of Scotland and return to the bright lights of my bedroom. Once there, Dana hands me one of the boxes of the chocolate desserts he brought back. Laughing as I take it he says, "That should buy me some points in my favor for a while." He hugs me and says, "I'll see you tomorrow."

"Goodnight Dana. I had a great time. Thanks for lunch and the cake."

Dana laughs and leaves. Just as he walks out my door, I hear him say with one of his 'I got you' laughs, "That ain't no cake."

17

GETTING READY

Kendra

TODAY IS PARTY DAY. I'm sitting in a chair getting tortured by the best. Three people surround me, and my friend Jamie is keeping everyone in line and on time. The noise is crazy! I'm being pampered more than any typical day because this is how a queen gets dolled up. It's special all right, we're to host the party that I've been waiting on for forever and a day. This party will be the honoring ceremony for Spar, and I will name my consorts.

The lineup of workers on me today is staggering. Sunny Carnack is a guygoyle who helps me when Amber can't help with my hair. He's doing my hair today. He runs a salon in Navan called Perruquier and Claws and is the best claw-tender in Navan, so they tell me. I'm partial to Kino myself. Then we have Maddie one of Jamie's helpers to do my makeup. Trent Jay, one of the orneriest men I've ever met, is doing my nails.

"How did you start doing nails Trent," I ask shifting in my seat. I'm really stiff and tired of just sitting here.

"That's easy to answer Queen Kendra. I have two daughters that got me interested in manicures. My oldest daughter constantly bothered me until I finally got certified. With the help of my youngest, I finally completed my certification. I argued about it at first, but I love it," Trent tells me with a sly grin.

Jamie comes over as the manicurist finishes and says, "That's gorgeous! You did superbly Trent. Remind me to set you up with the Princess of Wales she loves that color." Then to me, he says, "Come, darling, I'm so excited, it's time to squeeze you into your new dress."

I tell him, "I'm so ready! Calgon take me away!" We both giggle as we make our way to my closet. With all of his extra help, Jamie had loads of time to sort out my clothes and change my damn closet! "What the hell? It's nice in here but holy crap there's tons mirrors and the lighting. I love it, Jamie Serge," I exclaim hugging my friend.

With his help, I'm able to get into my dress. He makes sure all of the seams are in the correct places then tells me, "Bend over so I can be sure there isn't any danger of accidental spillage!"

"I'm afraid to, I might split this tight ass dress up the back." I joke with him as I bend over. He whistles at me when the girls stay confined making me smile. He primps me a little more then moves so I can see myself. Standing in front of the mirror I feel like a queen. I gulp. That can't be me. My dress has actual gold, silver, and a green metal from a meteor comprising the structural the material of the dress. It is much more substantial than any other dress I've ever worn. The experience is more like a treasure has wrapped itself around my naked body with lots of skin showing at the waist. The cloth feels like silk yet moves like spandex. I'm sure that magic is involved. The bright shimmer is impossibly scintillating. I have never wanted to be in front of and around people more than I do at this moment.

Wait, I think. How in the world... "Jamie, how can I ever afford to pay you for this?"

"Don't worry darling, you just go be the queen tonight. The rest will work itself out. Oh, you are so much my Kendraella. I love you to little pieces and beyond!" He's talking with his hands excitedly and scrunching his eyes tight.

I turn to face the door to the sitting room, and I spot my great red goyle. Kino is standing there ready to escort me to the ceremony, his mouth agape. I look into his eyes and giggle to myself. I walk to him and gently close his mouth as I get close to his sexy form. He smells like home. When lifting my arm for him to take, I growl to him, "Careful my magnificent Rockstar, if you leave that open too long you might forget where it belongs and what it should be doing."

I guess his thoughts and hormones are rushing through his body so fast his brain temporarily turns to mush. After a second he regains his composure and places my arm on top of his. He shares the briefest impish smile before he steps forward and flirts back, "Your Rockstar will never forget what his mouth should be doing, beloved."

Leaning on his arm, we walk to the vestibule outside the throne room where my brothers and Spar are waiting. Kino is at my side, followed by Jared and Dana who lead the reception line which includes Duke Findare and Flint, my Ducere. Spar is the last in the line.

This reception line isn't like any I've ever witnessed before. As usual, the guests file past in front of us. But instead of pausing to shake hands and say hello they pulse their greetings and venerations. This way each Ceorfan who passes is able to express their feelings be it excitement, happiness, love, respect... whatever. Most pulse more than once and sometimes, several times. My whole body is glowing with the love of these people and tingling with emotion. The entire room is tinged with a pinkish haze, which makes me feel so very happy.

After what seems like a few minutes but is more like half an hour the final guests pass through the line and are taking a seat. This party is primarily to introduce Spar as a full Ceorfan because of that he's the last to enter the room as the rest of us go in. We are now in the front of the room and face the entire Ceorfan Guild. We take a second and pulse our love and admiration into the crowd. Mason and Fin guide first Kino and Spar to their seats nearest my throne then Jared and Dana sit together to the right of Kino. Duke Findare and the count de Treon are seated to the left of Spar. I'm left to stand on my own for a bit.

At this point the room fogs around the edges. I'm not dizzy or lost per se, but the adrenaline's now pumping so furiously through my body, I feel a slight buzz. It makes me laugh as I realize the immediate karma return for my earlier teasing of Kino.

Mason and Flint now flank me and lead me to the elevated staged where my throne is. Looking out over the Ceorfan, I feel a great pride swelling in my chest and an even greater need to care for them. It's a humbling feeling.

Mounting the stage, I glimpse a table where Amber has set out six small emerald green pillows each with a chain and pendant that Vanessa and Jimmy must've brought with them. I've gotten each of my consorts a thick gold chain with a dragon holding a large ruby on it with a banner that says, Chuisle mo chroi, pulse of my heart, bordered in diamonds. Jared's and Dana's pendants look similar but with stones matching their dragon color with rubies around the banner. The banner on the bottom says Duke of Storms and Duke of Stone respectively. Flint's pendant is different. His is a replica of the flag which Kino had designed with fire opal representing the fire element, sapphire depicting the water, a cognac colored diamond embodying the earth, and finally alexandrite portraying magic. The banner above says "The Queen's Ducere" with a small ruby in the bottom center. Money well spent. I'll never tell that I drained my IRA, used my entire savings, and took out a loan to pay the rest. I want this to be special for them all.

18

THE PARTY

Kendra

MY HEART IS GOING to beat out of my chest. It's surreal. I watch as Mason and Amber take their places in front of the stage armed with what looks like pikes. Jadeite is acting as herald tonight and brings quiet to the pulses and voices of the crowd. Kino stands, takes my hand, and escorts me the final few feet to my throne and seats me. He bows as he steps back to take his seat.

Without even a hint of notice, Jericho begins the ceremony with a magical chant. He is mumbling so low I bet few can hear him. The room is already magical, but to my ear, Jericho's mumbling amplifies the grandeur. Shofars and panpipes sound from the back of the room then fade into a soft continuous melody.

Jadeite stands then calls out crisp and loud, "Clifton Danby, the Count of Treon and personal assistant to the queen."

At one time, I would have thought it odd that after someone was introduced applause didn't follow. I don't find it odd any more especially not here or now. This is a solemn occasion for the Ceorfan. Too since being in Navan, I've learned that sound's a big deal to the

Guild. It reverberates in the caves of the city. Sound can give away your location, but pulses can't, and they're used to welcome the count. My skin warms with the pressure of the many gentle pulses. *I'm still getting used to the Ceorfan culture.*

Clifton starts the award portion of the ceremony with Flint's promotion by explaining the depth of his heroism. I stand to wait in front of him. When Clifton finishes, I turn to retrieve the pendant from Mason, but I see Jimmy standing there with it instead. I smile brightly at him and he winks in return. I take the jewelry from the pillow, and my young friend disappears behind me. I feel pulses messaging my entire body. I want to say awww, but I say, "I proclaim Flint that you are my Ducere. This day I recognize your bravery and diligence above and beyond the call of duty. The Ducere are my Elite force, and not many can aspire to become part of these warriors. I name you...

Megahir tele-speaks, *Fourth in command of the Ducere.*

Thank you for that General. So much better than the queen's badass. He chuckles in my head, and I smile, repeating Mega when I continue... "Fourth in command of the Ducere." I place the pendant on him. He stares into my eyes, and I pulse my pride to him. His eyes water just a bit, and he pulses back. I'm not surprised at the fervent devotion he has for me. I lower my eyes to dismiss him to his seat.

Now the elegant Duke Findare moves to the podium. As he arrives and Jadeite calls, "Spar, stand before your queen."

I watch my handsome goyle as he moves forward. The light around him shines with the yellows I'm used to seeing. His optimism and intelligence glow from his character. When he looks me up and down I see a bright flare of pink. I smile knowing how much he loves me.

The Duke speaks, as Spar stands in front of me, "Spar Megason you have proven your merits, both with your savvy competencies as well as your placer le Ceorfan sous votre, placing the Ceorfan under your protection. You have proven yourself to the Guild by passing all required trials and giving understanding to all that you will protect the Earth, Ceorfan, human, and beast. You are our champion. Kneel."

I place a hand on each of Spar's broad shoulders while the Duke continues, "Spar Megason, I hereby announce to the Ceorfan Guild and to the world that you are Ceorfan. You are wholly integrated with us without reservation or hesitation. You have proven yourself in our eyes and in the eyes of your queen. I introduce you as Elite Warrior Guard. You are hereby named to the Ducere of your queen."

Spar stands, and I lift his hand, as far as I can reach, he had to raise it the majority of the way. He just winked at me and laughs as the guild pulses their approval covering us in praise. He takes his seat.

Fin still standing at the podium announces Jared first then Dana as Dragonlords of the Ceorfan and brothers of the queen giving me the pleasure of naming them Dukes. Jimmy once again brings their pillow and pendant to me to place on them. I lift the necklace over Jared's head, he bends, somewhat stiffly for me to reach. I make a note to ask him why my tough brother is stiff. When he raises up, I notice he too has wet eyes. "I name you Jared Macbard, Duke of Storms. You are part and blood of the Guild from this day forward dragonlord."

The pulses are astounding in their love and respect for Jared. They know the role he's playing in hunting Baratium. I hear, "I love you, Jared!" shouted from the audience. I look out across and see a beautiful redhead. I recognize her as the same redhead I met in Scotland. Well, that is something else I need to ask him about.

Holding Dana's pendant, I glimpse that Cheshire grin of his and him standing straight as an arrow. I wrinkle my brows at him and make a little jerk with my chin. He chuckles mischievously as he bends letting me put his pendant on him. I say, "I name you Dana Macbard, Duke of Stone. You are part and blood of the Guild from this day forward also dragonlord." Then add in a whisper, "I love you both like no tomorrow!" A giant pulse covers them and knocks them back a step. They return the love with a pulse of their own.

Looking out with my brothers, I see a people who are proud and strong. The joy, the happiness, the love they feel is immutable. I scan the room trying to reach into each eye looking at me. *Wait, who is this beautiful brunette? She's with Dana! Well, you just wait for one-second missy, that is my baby brother.* "Not until you convince me," I say.

"What was that," Jared asks.

"Nothing, sorry," I answer.

Now to the part of this ceremony that I'm most involved with. Clifton returns to introduce Jericho for the final part of our celebration. Jericho comes to stand in front of me and announces, "I call forth Spar Megason and Kino Magnus. Queen Kendra, I call forth your innermost chord of love and call forth the heart string tying you and Mica." I'm not sure how but I see a beam of light shoot from my heart into the blackness to my right. In the darkness, I see an apparition. In my heart I know it's Mica. I'm going to pass out from joy.

I'm reeling from seeing the spectral form of Mica, but I stand Kino to my right, Spar to my left, Jericho in front, and the trace of Mica lighting up the darkness. Like a minister at a wedding ceremony, Jericho begins booming forth, "Kendra Macbard, granddaughter of Iphigenia the Firstborn of our Guild, daughter of Leta who's sacrifice saved our Guild, reverent queen of the Ceorfan name your beloved consorts before the Ceorfan and all who are witnesses here. We shall bear witness to your eternal bonding."

My turn. "Tonight and all nights forward I name Spar Megason my consort. Tonight, and all nights forward I name Kino Magus my consort. Tonight, and all nights forward I name Mica Jacobs my consort. With all of my heart, body, and soul I will love you, cherish you, and bind us for eternity."

Jericho speaks, "Spar Megason, declare your intentions. Kneel at the feet of your sovereign and then stand beside your consort or depart this room without shame or retribution."

Immediately, Spar kneels at my feet, and after a heartbeat of a pause, he stands beside me.

Jericho speaks again, this time to Kino with the same results.

Finally, he speaks to Mica. The apparition naturally kneels then rises again.

Jericho's intonations grow louder. I watch as he removes his small stag knife from its scabbard. His words become clear to me, "Heart, mind, body, and soul. Be bound in the magic of Navan forever and a day. No separation shall be possible for the four of you."

I blink and gasp at the reality of this statement.

"My queen, I must make a small incision on your head." I assent. He does the same to Spar then presses our foreheads together. When our blood intertwines, power beyond anything I have ever felt melts through us... MIND, we are dragon bound and heal instantly.

"My queen, now I must make a small incision on your abdomen."

I ascent, thinking I wonder if this is why Jamie made my dress with the cutouts at the waist. He repeats the process on Kino and presses us together. Again, when our blood mingles, another bolt shocks me... BODY, we are dragon bound.

Finally, Jericho says, "You are dragon bound to Mica by heart. Reach for that string and pluck it, my queen." I reach for it. It's right in front of me coming from my heart. I grab it using my undoubted love for Mica, and Boom! HEART, we are dragon bound. We were bound before, but the binding is different from the magic of the Consort Ceremony.

I hope Mica can tell I love him and I'm fighting for his love in return.

"I'll not live without any of you," I say aloud for all to hear. Amid the pulses is the roars and shouts of approval thick with applause. It's a gift from our people who agree with the bindings.

I laugh, swaying with glee. Clifton takes the podium and releases us all to the reception hall for our party. A sea of green-clad party-goers takes off for the food, drink, and dancing.

The party is fantastic, lots of good food, music, and dancing. Wondering where Kino is, I look around the big room for him. Just there, I catch a glimpse of auburn hair with the band. He's up in front with them. I feel a gentle warm pulse. Pretty sure it says, please let me speak. The way you would with a look or a touch on the shoulder, without words. Everyone, even Vanessa, Jimmy, and Jamie turn toward him to give him their attention. The band begins to play a mellow seductive tune. He raises his eyes, moving up slowly to meet mine. He stares at me and shares with us his beautiful voice. I'm captured by him. That voice calls to my body as well as my heart. No one on Earth has a voice as magnificent as his!

I feel someone take my hand. It's Spar leading me toward Kino and the stage. I know it's Spar without looking because he's the only one who could touch me right now—besides my sexy Kino or Mica. Oh, I'm so glad he's all mine.

Never taking my eyes off Kino, I find myself just feet from him. He reaches for my hand and Spar places it in Kino's. I glance at Spar, and he smiles a tender smile back at me as he bows backing away. This is Kino's moment, and he's respecting that. I step onto the stage as Kino draws me near with a warm hand on my waist. As he does, he begins to dance slowly, hardly moving. All the while he continues to sing me his love.

I keep watching him, I couldn't stop even if I tried. He bends closer to me and whispers, "I love you, Kendra," in my ear with his warm breath blowing over it. He hands his microphone off to one of the band members asking them to keep playing.

Kino lifts my arms for a spin, so I walk under and lose my balance, so he pulls me all the way into him and off the stage to finish our dance. I see him look up and nod imperceptibly but think nothing of it until I feel more hands on my back at my waist. Deep breath, I know it's Spar. He leans forward putting me between them squeezing me a little tighter he whispers, "Thank you," into Kino's ear. Oh, bloody hell, a girl can only take so much. I can't think as we finish this magical dance. Kino spins me, a final coup, ending as I fall into Spar's arms who holds me tight and dips me, bending over me as he does.

I tell them straightening up, "I'll never forget this night. If only..." Well, maybe I can include Mica by tugging on my heart string to him. I blow a kiss down the line and then kiss Kino and Spar.

"Thank you for the song, Kino. I loved it." Taking his and Spar's hands in mine I say, "I think we should call it a night or I won't get a minute alone with you. Let's make our way around the room to say goodnight. I need to tell Vanessa and Jimmy I'll show them around in the morning. I'll also have Clifton get them some rooms." Smiling they both agree.

I also notice my brothers are waiting to leave, so I go to them. "I love you two. Tomorrow, I'm going to be showing the teens around Navan. You two, take some time off. I'll see you both on Monday night at the HG meeting."

"You bet Sis," they both say at the same time. Then they both take off so fast, I'd bet they have hot dates waiting!

I make sure and give Jamie a big hug and tell him I love him. "I hope you have as good a life as you are making sure I have my friend."

"Kendra, my darling, you are a gift to me too. Of course, I have a wonderful life. You are in it!"

"Goodnight then, this Kenderella is weak and exhausted. If I don't see you tomorrow, I will soon." Giving him an air kiss, we finally leave the party.

19

THE BOND

Kendra

TONIGHT, I have Spar and Kino both with me walking to my chamber. The intimacy they convey burns so sincerely. I ask quietly, "Do you guys feel like this is our honeymoon?" I can't believe I just blurted out what I was thinking.

Spar laughs and says, "That is exactly what I was thinking. How about you Kino?"

"Without a doubt, this is our honeymoon. Too bad Mica is going to miss the best sex in the world. Serves him right," Kino declares.

The power of their sexuality is irresistible, and my core is melting. "So, let's hurry up then," I say breathlessly as I take off running in my heels. I'm going nowhere fast, and they notice, so Spar scoops me up and runs the rest of the way home with me laughing in his arms. He sets me on the bed and Kino bends to remove my shoes.

"I can do that," I start, but he moves my hand away with a soft touch.

He declares as he takes both heels and sets them on the floor next to him, "No beloved, let us show you how a gargoyle loves his mate."

Spar looks into my eyes and asks, "Honey, if you aren't okay with this that's okay we'll stop. What I want to know is can you handle us both at the same time or is that asking too much?"

My pulse spikes and I can just make the words, "Kiss me I love you both and don't want either of you to leave me tonight. Make this the best honeymoon ever for me." I add a pulse that says I want you now and they get started. They take off my dress hanging it over a chair then let me watch them both strip for me. I laugh as Spar does a little dance making his dick jump. Then laugh harder when Kino sings them a dirty song and joins in. We are all laughing when they join me on the bed then start to touch me. Not laughing anymore my body is straining for them as they kneel on either side of me. I reach for their penises and slowly moving my hands to make them feel good.

Spar puts his hand on mine to stop me. "Hun, I can't wait long so go real slow and stop a lot." All I can do is nod. My voice isn't working at all.

I'm not at all surprised when Spar kisses me but when Kino gets close to us and takes over not caring that his mouth is so close to Spar's I melt. He doesn't stay and moves lower to my tight nipples, reaching under Spar's chest to massage one while he sucks the other. Spar is keeping my mouth occupied and cups my pussy with his large hand and puts a finger inside my wet center. I'm in heaven, and my body is on fire. Kino moves down and brings my legs up over his chest, and my golden boy moves to my breasts. The last thing I see is my redhead lapping at my sensitive center, and I tilt my head back and close my eyes. I pulse my sexual climax to them as I come. Then I feel Spar roll over, putting me on top of him and Kino stands beside the bed while I maneuver Spar's dick inside of me balls deep. I reach for Kino and put what I can handle of his big boy in my mouth. Now they are the ones pulsing, and the bond hits us as they come. Sizzling our hot bodies in even more satisfaction. I think of Mica in that second and tug on my heart string to give him this feeling if that even works maybe one day he'll tell me. We all fall together exhausted and rest. I snuggle between my two bad boys who are so good and sleep.

I wake before dawn with them lying on either side of me and whispering. Sex like ours is more than romance it's real and blows my mind. It figuratively transports me to a time and place where the pleasure of love knows no boundaries and love is the glue of the universe. Staying up all night is much easier than it's ever been before, and I think I can't wait to do it again. The things we did still fresh on my skin and in my mind. I kiss them both good morning and get up so I can watch them torp. They move over to the pedestal stage where they sleep.

I say, "Hey aren't you going to put something on first?"

"Why, you want us this way anyway, right beloved?" Kino asks, but I know it's not really a question. I hurry and kiss them as they pose and turn to stone.

I pick up the room and notice Elmer in his favorite place to sleep. After my bath and when I am dressed, I go to him. He wakes just long enough to climb down my outstretched arm and onto the front of my shirt. There he snuggles down and goes right back to sleep.

I'm ready to show Vanessa and Jimmy around Navan. I guess I should've asked Clifton where their rooms are. Now I'm going to have to figure it out. Oh well, good thing I'm a dragon. Before I leave I plant a sweet kiss on each of my goyles lips and tell them thank you for a beautiful night.

I reach out to feel for Jimmy first by concentrating on him. I look for his face, and then I find a light that looks just like him. There is another bright luster with him. I look hard into that spot, and just as quickly I find Vanessa with him. While I was searching for them, I was able to see all of Navan in three dimensions. I didn't see lights everywhere because I was only looking for Jimmy and Vanessa. The way I found him also built a 3D map of how to get to him.

When I arrive outside their room, I wait in the hall. It feels like when I went back to my apartment after they moved in. So, if I pulse will they know and call out or something? Or should I holler at them?

I think I'll pulse. They'll get used to the gargoyle ways faster that way.

I pulse a hello to them and tell them I am waiting at their door.

Immediately Jimmy says, "Come in Kendra we're decent."

"Let's hope so, I'm not running a brothel for mischievous kids wanting to put one over on their parents. Didn't Clifton give you each a room?" I immediately regret my choice of words since Jimmy didn't have anyone taking care of him when we met. Okay, Kendra a bit more tact.

"Yes, he did," Vanessa tells me then continues, "But what we... I didn't want to be alone." I raise an eyebrow at her. She keeps trying to explain, "We didn't tell you because we didn't want to ruin your party. But, yesterday was my eighteenth birthday. So really, I'm legal to decide who I sleep with, right?"

"What?" I almost screech. "Are you telling me your parents are in Paris on your birthday? You should have told me. That was a combo party anyway we could've had a cake!"

With tears in her eyes, she reaches to me for a hug. "That's so nice Kendra. Jimmy's the only one who ever pays attention to stuff like that for me. My parents will give me something nice they find in Paris. But they say I'm too old for a birthday pa.... Is that a bat on your shirt?" She asks backing away.

I chuckle. "Yes, his name is Elmer, and he's asleep or I'd let you hold him. Don't think I forgot about the who you spend the night with stuff. Yes, you're legal to decide. But you might want to consider that while you live with your parents, they might not be happy with this decision. They might even have some solid advice. Talk to them so that trouble doesn't come out of this, okay? Then I'll support your decision."

"I can do that," Vanessa happily replies.

"Good, let me show you the cafeteria, and I'll make us some breakfast."

After we eat, we spend several hours wandering around the caves. I show them how to use the formations as guides to the rooms they are looking for. I also, somewhat jokingly, let them know I won't leave them alone to get lost. We talk a little about the fires again, and they assure me they'll be quick to relay anything they find out.

"Are you both ready to go home? I can take you anytime you're ready."

They both nod that they're ready. Jimmy says, "We both have homework we need to finish before school tomorrow."

"Oh, awesome, I'm glad you're keeping up with it. If you have everything, we can go right now." They both nod their approval, so I pull out my portal stone. They've seen a portal stone and know what to do.

When we exit on the other side, we find ourselves right on the roof of the La Caverna in the middle of a sweltering afternoon. "Take that Dana," I say.

"What was that Kendra?" Vanessa asks.

"Oh, nothing." I give them both hugs and tell them to be safe before I leave.

20

DREAMWALK

Kendra

I HEAD straight over to the Blake House Bakery on Main Street where I pick out a triple layer chocolate cake with bright pink strawberry frosting. The silver and gold decorations are reminiscent of exploding fireworks. 'Happy 18th Birthday Vanessa' is written in big block letters across the top. Barry, the chef, is, to use his words, older 'n dirt and he uses lots of vintage phrases like dagnabit. I get a chuckle on every visit with his unending torrent of them.

Barry says, "I will deliver the cake along with a half-gallon of homemade strawberry ice cream on my way home from work. If that's okay with you Miss Kendra?"

I need to let Jimmy know to be sure to be home to receive it. I hope it makes Vanessa happy. My work for the day done and I'm dead tired. I head up to the roof of the La Caverna to open another portal this time to my room. I need to get some serious sleep, so I'll be ready for tonight's High Guild meeting.

Maybe I missed because I'm tired. Perhaps I just need to practice more. Whatever the reason, my aim is way off, and I exit the portal just outside the main lunchroom it's the middle of the day, so no one is around but me. Still, that is messed up. By the time I arrive at my chamber I'm positively knackered! Elmer is still sleeping nicely, so I lay on my bed with him snuggled on my shirt and my hand around him. He's not Mica. But at least I don't feel so alone while Spar and Kino are torpified.

Despite how tired I am I have trouble falling asleep. Finally, I do reach a state which could generously be described as sleep. It's still somewhere between awake and asleep, but asleep nonetheless. I know this type of sleep well. I'm usually here when I have difficult decisions to make or other pressing matters in my life. I developed it when the boys were young, and I couldn't pay for something they needed. Entering this semi-lucid state, I can let my subconscious help me solve my problems. I talk to myself, and on odd occasions I even dream. But the dreams are more like movies where I'm the star and director simultaneously, I can do just about anything, and change it if I don't like it.

Even though I'm in a light sleep, I still feel the pain burning through my head. "Damn it, what is that?" I yell then notice a bright yellow thread of light leaving my chest and going... oh, wait! That's the light which connects me to Mica. I focus on the thread to follow it. Since I already know where it'll end up, I can jump to the end or take the trip I'm thinking.

First thing, I need my wings. Poof! Wings attach. "Dragon form Kendra, dragon form," I tell myself. I'm off to see the Mica the beautiful Mica I love.

Ok, I admit, this dream walk is not like my normal ones. And maybe I'm a bit punch drunk from not resting over the last week. But I'm so excited to see my love, my heart... Well, crap if I can just get there!

I fly fast, close to the string. I see the vista changing around me, yet my excitement to see Mica has me paying them little attention as I race forward. Beautiful! That's White Sands.

Nice, I see the end of the string. I'm almost there. There it is the end, and there he is—my love, my heart.

I reach out to touch his rugged unshaven face. As I do, I call out to him, "Mica, my love, I'm here." He opens his eyes, looking at me, both surprised and happy.

"Kendra! I love you, Kendra."

"My name isn't Kendra, but you can call me that if you want to," says a girl lying next to him.

I jerk backward. The traitor reaches for me, but I fly away faster than before. This time back to my own heart the one that's breaking with every stroke of my wings.

I wake in a start. Tears flow down my face as I take Elmer and put him in his alcove on the wall. I can't even think my head hurts so much.

Maybe Jericho has something that'll help the pain, help me sleep, and maybe forget what I just saw. On the way to his lab, I've time to think about what just happened. Why am I so broken up about it? It wasn't a dream is why. Why did he say he loves me and have someone else in bed with him? I don't even care. If he doesn't want me, he doesn't want me. I need to just get over my schoolgirl feelings for him. I don't think that's going to be easy for me though. That's my plan, and it'll be for the best. I can't stand in the way of his happiness. It looks like I have decisions to make. Fuck! I don't want to think about it. I've got to forget this and get it off my chest. It's not like I can really sleep now anyway.

When I get to Jericho's laboratory, I start to pulse an admiring hello to him. I try to pulse hello and how tired I am to him, but I'm pretty sure it came out as nous knackered quietus. Which is like saying my common sense tells me I'm so tired and I feel like I'm dead. Which, isn't really that far off in reality. I lurch my way into his laboratory, and he's suddenly standing right in front of me. "Edling are you alright?" he asks. Worry lines creasing his already deeply creviced forehead.

"I'm not sure I'll ever be alright again," I tell him, and I spill the whole story about finding Mica with another woman. Rubbing my head the entire time.

"Kendra, I am sorry for this. However, all may not be how it looks where Mica is concerned. Communication is key. However, I want to address the reason you are rubbing your head first. Do you have pain?"

"Yes, that's what I was paying attention to in my sleep before I went to see Mica. I don't understand it, Jericho. I've never had headaches like this. Tonight, isn't the first one over the last few days either. Ever since that night in your crystal dream cave I've been getting them. This one's the worst one."

"Just as I suspect. You are having symptoms from the strain of not being etched. I fear it is affecting your health. We are going to have to keep an eye on this Kendra to make sure it does not get out of control before we leave next Saturday for Anatolia. I think we should change to Friday night unless you can get some time off of your job earlier would be better."

"No, Jericho I do have some vacation coming, but we're very short staffed with Mica on the Firestarter case and the other park rangers we lost. They won't be able to let me take any leave right now. Friday'll be fine. I'll make it 'til then."

"Kendra, if things change, let's leave early. In the meantime, drink this." He hands me a beaker with a brown and gold looking fluid in it. "It should help with the pain. I'll make you up some more to take to your room. If it is not enough let me know. I can always make more. That's going to make you sleepy now let me walk you to your room."

"Thank you, you're right that drink is kicking in and I'm ready for a nap right now."

As we walk to my room, he tells me, "I think you should leave a note for Clifton that you need a night off too. We have nothing pressing in the HG tonight. If something happens, I will make sure you are notified." I giggle because he said HG.

Jericho helps me to bed and tells me, "Sweet dreams, Edling."

"Sweet dreams to you too," I tell him in my drugged state. "Oh, you better write my note to Clifton I can't keep my eyes open or even think straight right now."

I don't know anything after that. It's been so hard for me to sleep and I want to avoid it even more now that there's a chance I could see Mica. Be that as it may, that's my last thought as I drift off. I sleep like a baby from sheer exhaustion, and my goyles let me.

The next day, with effort, I pull my tired ass out of bed and drag it to work. Another long, feeling lost, non-productive, hot, dusty, time sucking, soul-draining day. And did I mention, there's no action either. I sit at my computer and fill out my daily report. It's got a few little items. I guess I can say I stayed busy. I helped a camper find his keys... they were in his car, on the dashboard. In the most exciting call of the day, I had to direct a vehicle full of travelers back to highway 285. When I told Chris about it, we agreed that it was probably the most interesting call so far this month. It turns out that a group of Chippendale dancers were in from Vegas to do a photo shoot and got lost. I swear to all that is good and holy hell they were hot... They wore no shirts, had dark tans, large muscles. If I hadn't known better, I would've assumed they were a plant from Jericho to get me past my waking dream yesterday.

I clock out and stop to talk to Chris on my way out passing her desk I'm almost weaving. I run smack into the tall shelf she has next to it. Rebounding I do a comedic slow-motion turn, and I fall flat of my face. Well, it must've been comedic because Chris can't help but laugh at me. I was anything but ladylike in my landing.

"Let me help you up, hun," she chuckles. "Are you okay? I noticed you're really quiet today Kendra." Putting her arm under-mine she does help. I need her help too. I'm just very uncoordinated today. *I must've slept too much. I better fly fast and hard home to exercise this off.*

"Well, obviously I'm not, Chris. I've forgotten how to walk," I quip a little embarrassed that I need her to help me up. I'm just a little weak.

"Did you party too hard this weekend? Or get totaled because your hunk of burning love partner is still on that mission for the feds? You miss him, don't ya sweetheart?"

"Yes, I do. Crazy, isn't it."

"I don't know Kendra. I only knew my Sonny for two weeks before we married. We were together for twenty-one years. We'd still be married if he was here and hadn't passed. It doesn't always take ages to figure out you care for someone. Sometimes you just know in your knower. I'm not saying it happens to everyone, but I for sure ain't gonna judge you for that."

"Honestly I'd like to lie about it. Body language is an amazing thing. Most people can tell what others are feeling anyway, especially me. You know Chris not to change the subject, but has any more information on the Firestarter surfaced?"

"Not that I know of, I guess maybe in the daily briefing in the morning Murphy might have something."

"Yeah, maybe, I'll see you tomorrow then," I say as I slap a hand on the counter as I leave.

"Anything you need Kendra, I'm here, just ask. Maybe a girl's night this weekend?"

I turn back to her and say, "Might have to wait for that I've got the stuff to paint my bathroom this weekend. We'll talk about it, okay?" I walk out the door as she agrees.

As I drive to the old outpost to park Jasper, I think that was a close call. No way can I spend any time with anyone outside of the Ceorfan this weekend. Not just for my health but for my people, I must go to my grandmother in Anatolia.

I reach the outpost and walk around to the passenger side of Jasper to change. There, I catch a scent I haven't smelled here before. I think I'd better look around. My donum is tingling strongly on this too. I let my dragon out just a bit, I don't feel any danger, but I'm sure I should investigate.

I start for the little cabin that the Park Rangers have been using for storage as long as I've worked here. On the way to the door, I see dusty footprints leading all the way to the doorway. Too big to be mine and too small to be Mica's.

Before I go in, I check all the windows and the back door. Just what I thought the back door's jacked. I can't see anything looking into the windows. It feels safe enough, so I swing open the door standing off to the side and call out. "Federal Park Ranger, is anyone in here? Hello?" I repeat, "Federal Park Ranger I'm coming in." Drawing my weapon, I enter back of the shack. Damn! I smell the strong smell of acetone and gasoline.

It's pretty dirty in here. We should have done a better job of maintenance. That hot, dry New Mexico dust covers everything in here. Everything except that! Fuck me sideways. There are several fifty-five-gallon LDP plastic drums with ACETONE written in large white letters on their sides, a couple of red, plastic five-gallon gas jugs, and a pallet full of ANFO—ammonium nitrate—a blasting agent.

Holy fucking firetruck! We should have been checking in on this site. We're just spread too thin. It looks like the same footprints have been in here as the ones in the front. I holster my gun and take out my phone to take pictures of the scene.

After I am done with the pictures, I head back to the Ranger's Station and straight to Captain Murphy's office. Thank goodness he has an open-door policy. If ever there is a time to use it, today is the time. He waves me in as soon as he sees me.

"What's up Macbard? I thought you'd left already?"

"Yes sir, I had." Then I tell him about the supplies I just found and where they're located.

"You go write a report detailing your investigation, and I'll call the ATF and FBI."

Sitting at my desk, I pull my phone to send the pictures to my work email. As soon as I sit, I think of Jared and Dana. "I'd better call my boys," I say out loud. I call Jared first and get his voicemail. That's different. He usually answers. My second call is to Dana who answers immediately. He's in his truck headed home. "Hey baby brother, don't worry but I've got to work a little late."

"Sis, do you think that's a good idea being how bad you've been feeling?" he asks.

"Yeah, I'm okay Dana, I'll only be here a little while longer. Who told you I've been sick anyway?"

"Kendra you slept all day and all night yesterday. You never sleep more than a few hours at a time. It doesn't take a genius. Just don't over-do it until we figure out what's wrong okay?

"Jericho has figured out what is wrong, and he has made me some concoction to help. Hey, I tried to call Jared, but he didn't answer. Is everything okay with him?"

"Jared's in meetings all day. I think he's buyin' another small security company to get more bodyguards. You know since Mica is MIA and all. I'll tell him you're good if he can't get through to you though."

"That'll be good, thank you baby brother. I love you."

"Love you too, Sis." With that, we hang up, and I start uploading the pictures of what I've found in the old shack and write out my report.

While I'm writing, I wonder, why the explosives? You can start a fire here with a single stick, it's so dry. The accelerants will make it easier to start and grow it faster and bigger. But what is the ANFO for?

21

MISTAKE

Mica

TRUST, that's the fucking word of the day! Well, at least it was when I first arrived in Barrio de Chabolis. That was five days ago. Five days that I've had to sit on my decision and let it dance on my brain. It seems the longer I sit on it, the more it chaps my ass. This is one of the worst decisions I've made... and I've made some doozies in my ultra-long life.

My decision is even more fucking-fucked up when you consider where I volunteered to go. This shit-town is put together with sticks, mud, and blood. Yes, yes, I know most of these people are merely trying to get by... trying to stay out of trouble. Those who run the town have got a different idea of staying out of trouble. Every day here life starts by forcing you to answer a simple question. Do you work for the suppliers or not? Simple, right? Except, if you don't work for them you're considered a potential problem. Cause too many issues, and you become a torso-up target. The easiest disposition of which is a bullet to the back of your head.

Okay, I have this pain in the ass proclivity of charging ahead without thinking, all the while believing I'm doing the right thing. Sometimes it's good, other times not so much. This time... definitely not! Just like Thersites from the Trojan war, I say and do what most are thinking but are afraid, or too smart, to say. Yet Kendra isn't most people, she's a queen. More importantly, she's my queen. I owe her the respect of me rising above most people, not her. I owe her the ability to grow without throwing my temper tantrums. She above anyone I've ever known deserves that. I need to learn to control this part of my somewhat one-trick personality.

I know I messed up majorly. I miss Kendra with every cell in my body. Sometimes I can almost feel her touch. There are times at night when I'm so lost in my thoughts of her, I actually believe I can feel her kissing me and other stuff. Like last night, I swear I could hear her telling me she wouldn't live without me.

Damn, this hurts me to my torpis, the innermost portion of my being... my core. I'm done, I quit, and like the genie says, I'm outta here! I'll finish collecting as much data as I can, as fast as I can, then— back to Navan!

To do that I gotta get my ass in gear. I've been posing as a traveler. I've let people know that I'm interested in documenting the area for a small indie film. I know I'm too big to hide, and lots of people notice me... meaning everyone. I could've come in disguise, but I'm glad I didn't. I prefer using my human looks. I see them as an advantage. These locals are used to film scouts anyway. There's always a studio looking to make the next action adventure in the jungles of South America. I speak the language fluently, yet I don't let these guys know it...

I've heard the locals talking about some 'hijo duro', tough son, since I got here. The conversation goes something like this 'where's the pickup' and 'El Jefe said he didn't pay, so hijo duro should talk to him.' Sometimes they just give Hijo money for playing songs on his guitar. I've been following him, and the kid's a certified badass. He's looks to be about fourteen and skinny. He'd be no competition to anyone in a fight, but his fighting skills aren't what makes him a badass. He's got a wicked tactical mind. Yesterday, I watched as he gave a quick jerk of his head toward a small, blue and green building, laughingly one of the nicer buildings around. With that twitch, three beefy men leave a nearby cantina, enter the building and drag some guy out by his bare feet. After they cut his clothes off and steal anything of value, they flog him using a shalalee, a thirty-inch piece of fire hose with six inches of rolled tape on the handle. They swing the weapon with devastating results and pay extra attention to his feet and legs. They want him to survive but live his life a cripple. The kid never looks up. It's as if he has no idea what's going on. He just keeps counting his money then stands and walks away. Nobody lifts a finger to help the man before, during, or after the beating. They leave him in the mud and sun.

After watching the kid for the past three days I know he's the one in charge of this town's sex and drug trade. Hell, you don't get your splinter fixed at the doctor without this kid's tacit approval.

This little village has twelve cantinas. They're a great place to hang out, have a beer and listen for information. Most people here don't think the big, blond American would know any Spanish. That makes it easy to listen in. Especially with the way I can speak my Spanish. I do it in a way so they think I only know a little.

Tonight, I'm having a beer at the bar in the Urraca Borracha when I learn something that has me shaking to get out of here. A conversation starts between Hijo and this prostitute I've seen around town. The prostitute, a short woman with black hair and dark eyes, gives him some money for a song. As she hands it to Hijo, she tells him, "That big American, he wants to talk to El Jefe."

The kid points at me followed by "pinche pendejo". She nods to him. Hijo shakes his head, and the prostitute comes over to check me out. Her features are reminiscent of a smaller Audrey Hepburn during her glamour days in Hollywood. Her dress is deliberately designed to portray a stereotypical cantina girl from the old American western movies. It's cut from the bottom, all the way up to her waistband on both sides. It makes for a terrific effect as she walks, one leg or the other always standing as an eye-catching advertisement. This girl exudes sexuality, but this sexiness seems designed to hide something. She knows how to move, keep her balance, how to carry herself. I think she has some severe hand-to-hand and grappling training. I teach it, I know what to look for. She has it in spades. When she reaches the bar, she leans sideways onto it, holding herself with one elbow on the bar and her other hand hanging onto my shoulder as she does. She tilts her head to look at me from the corner of her big brown eyes and in her broken English asks, "Hi muscles, how long you in our village? I will find anything. I get you anything you want. You want me, sí?"

Trying to get people to say things in public almost never works, so I'm not surprised when she says, "I have a room. It is private. We talk, sí?"

I want to know what she's hiding behind that sexiness, but there is no way in hell I'm going to her room. It would be a perfect place for an ambush. Maybe similar to the naked man in the mud. So, I reply, "That sounds like something I'd like little lady. Would you like to have a drink in my hotel room?"

"Yes, sí!" she replies eagerly.

No one in my hotel lobby even looks in our direction as we make our way to my room. They must know her, who she works for, and what we are doing plus the people here stay out of other people's business. When we get to my room, I offer her the promised drink while she turns on some music.

Pushing the drink away and pulling me to her she whispers in unbroken and perfect English, "I don't have time for a drink. I will take it with me. The hookers here charge by the minute. My name's Sofia, and I'm with TASS. I know who you are from the Scotland bombing. I know you're good, but you can't help here. I've got very little time to give you anything useful."

"Do you have information on the fires that have been started in the border states of America?" I whisper back as I nuzzle her ear.

"Yes. But first, give me a hundred dollars. You hired me for ten minutes starting when we left the bar. I have to give the money to the kid you saw me with. People here call him Turtle."

Taking my wallet, I pull out a hundred-dollar bill. She takes it and tucks it between her braless breasts. Then, she pulls me close, unbuttoning my shirt and kissing my neck as she does. She whispers, "We need to pretend. Take your shirt and pants off." I do as she says while she unbuttons her blouse and takes off her shoes. She pulls me to her again, her bare breasts hot on my chest, and with another whisper, "Don't talk, listen. You must leave tomorrow. Go back to the gargoyle queen and tell her TASS is embedded deep in this jungle. I'm not the only one. But I promise you, I'll get you all of the information you need just give us time. I've gone through too much to take any chance on it getting screwed-up—even by someone as good looking and talented as you. They're not paying any attention to you... yet. Don't let them.

Before you leave tomorrow, find Turtle and slip him a hundred-dollar bill. Ask him for help making your film. People have already seen you taking pictures of the rainforest. He'll tell you no, but you don't care, you just need to leave. Other than Turtle, don't ask anyone any other questions, then go home—tomorrow, first thing! I'll get you the information you need as soon as I can. I have to filter it through TASS for my safety. I've been around long enough to be trusted as much as possible. I have to go now."

"Thank you, Sofia. If you need me, just ask."

She leaves holding her top together and her shoes. With a wink and swish of her skirt, she disappears, leaving my door open. I go to close the door, and I see some muscle standing in the hall. When he sees me, he turns and follows Sofia.

Yes! I see a light at the end of the dark tunnel I created by running away. Now I've got the perfect reason to go home, and we know TASS really is working on this issue for us. I collect my stuff and pack it, leaving out one pair of pants, a black tee and a book I've been reading. I'm going to portal home, but I need to catch a little sleep. I'll have a lot to do when I get there. Including apologizing to the only girl I'm ever going to love.

After this excitement, I read my book for a bit, so I can relax some and hopefully fall asleep faster. My book's about a group of kids who fight demons and such. Demons aren't very realistic, but I find it interesting. After a couple of chapters, I start to get tired. When I lay down, I fall asleep quickly and with a smile.

I feel a feather soft touch on my cheek and open my eyes. I see Kendra. She's dreamwalking, and I can feel her in my heart. Light is all around her. My god, she's beautiful.

"I love you, Kendra," I tell her without waiting.

A voice beside me says, "I'm not Kendra, but you can call me that if you want to."

I see the hurt look on Kendra's face as she jumps and leaves like she can't get out of here fast enough. I jump out of bed.

"Who're you and how did you get in here? Forget that, just get out!" The woman gets up without a stitch on and walks over to me.

"What? You don't want to even get to know me? You didn't have a problem with Sofia being in your room."

"No fucking way, out now!"

She huffs over to a pile of clothes on the chair on the other side of the room and gets dressed before she leaves. The whole time, she is cussing me.

Jolted awake, I decide it's time to get the hell out of here. "Motherfucker! I'm in so much trouble! I'm going home now," I say to the back of the woman as she leaves.

I get dressed and gather up my pack and walk near the Barrio de Chabolis cantina on my way to find the kid. I find him sitting on the curb out front.

I ask him, "Hey kid, you want to work in a movie?"

"No."

"Why kid? Why not?"

"Because el Jefe didn't tell me too." Then he stands and walks away not even bothering to look at me. Damn, this kid is tough.

I shrug my shoulders and walk in the opposite direction. I go far enough out of town to ensure no one sees me open my portal. Excitement seizes me as I reach a point I feel safe. I open the portal to my room in Navan.

I set my stuff down and check to see what the Plan of the Day is and what Mega's orders are. I hit up Dolo to get him to change my orders at the Ranger's Station. I want to be back at work with Kendra tomorrow. What was I even thinking? I wasn't thinking I was just reacting... again. The fact is, Kendra is it for me. If she still wants me that is. I better get flowers, chocolate, and diamonds!

She's already gone for work, so I'll have to wait to talk to her. After writing out a detailed report for Mega, and one for Dolo, I send Kendra a message. To my chagrin, she doesn't respond. I guess I need to rethink what I'm doing. So I head over to Kendra's rooms to check on Spar and Kino. I've missed them too. My rash decisions are going to stop. I hurt myself and at least three others. From now on I'm going to think before I act. I hope that's possible at least where my family is concerned. I raise my wings and torp beside my brothers. I'll be right here with them when we wake and apologize first thing.

22

CRYING

Kendra

EVERYTHING'S finally finished here at work well... at least my report is. I even explained why I was out at that location. I thought I saw flames in this area that should be believable. With my report filed the pictures of the accelerants uploaded to the supporting documents file I can finally leave.

Walking through the parking lot to my truck is hard work. It's like I have on galoshes three sizes too big and I'm walking through the clay after a rainstorm. I have to concentrate just to get one foot in front of the other. If I can only make it home and rest I'll feel better, I tell myself.

I meet Murphy leaving at the same time as me. He smiles a little and says, "Good job, kid. Thanks for your hard work. It should get better around here soon. The Feds just released your partner from his mission. He's traveling today, but he'll be back at work tomorrow. I'm glad, we sure can use the help."

"Thanks, Captain that's good to know. See you in the morning. Have a safe trip home."

He nods his head at me waving. "You too kid."

Shit, what in the hell is going on. I catch Mica with another woman this morning, and this afternoon he's coming back home! Damn, I pause to think for a second he's probably already in Navan.

I finish slogging my way over to Jasper and hoist my unbelievably heavy ass into the seat. My legs feel like I've run a marathon... no energy is left in them whatsoever. They're numb and racked with cramps. I try to rub the pains out, but my hands and arms feel like I've been lifting weights, heavy ones, nonstop for a month. My body hurts... everywhere. My headache has even returned. It feels like I'm wearing a steel band around my head that is being tightened. The pain... it's a horror show made real.

Now, I have to figure out how to deal with Mica and his betrayal. I wish I knew how this was going to play out. I rub my head my headache matches my heartache. I'm not even sure which one hurts worse. Yes, I am.

I check my tablet before I start Jasper and discover a message.

Mica: I'm home, Kendra. I need to talk to you. I need to apologize. I was wrong. Please, can I see you tonight?
Me: I need to think. Not tonight.

I CAN'T EVEN THINK ABOUT WHAT MICA WANTS. I NEED TO FIND a better place to park Jasper. The old cabin is out for sure. For now, I'll just go to the apartment. *That's it Macbard, you can do this one step after the other.*

The drive to the La Caverna is utterly forgettable. I can say that for sure because I did. I have no idea how I got here but I'm glad I'm in one piece. I stop and park as close to the front as I can. The fewer steps I have to take the better for me.

I hit the front doors with all of the grace and power of a typical garden slug. As I try to push it open and walk through my arms collapsed and I run face first into it. The doorman hurriedly opens it for me. I give him an embarrassed wave and then head up. Who was that guy anyway? I've met everyone but not him. I'll save that for a different time when I can actually think and don't have to explain why I can't properly operate a door at my age.

I enter the apartment the way we agreed and just unlocking the door walking straight in. Jimmy's sitting at the table doing his homework and looks up as I enter. With a tired look, he says, "Hi, Kendra."

"Hi there yourself. I just came in to check on you and let you know I need to be parking and leaving from here for work for a while. Have you heard anything else about the Firestarter today?"

"Only that the kids at school are sure the fires are almost over. Joe said his dad thinks that SpotOn has all the profitable rigs now."

"That'll be good if it really happens. Let me know if you hear more about the fires. Anything you think is important, okay?"

"You bet I will, Kendra."

"Jimmy, do you need me to get you anything?"

"No, ma'am, I'm doing fine unless you have pull with the city and can get me a job that pays at least the minimum. Thank you anyway."

"I might have an idea about that give me some time and if I forget remind me. By any chance, have you met the new doorman?"

"Nope, I didn't even know there is a new doorman. Also just so you know, Vanessa is really happy about her cake. She cried. No one pays attention like that to her except me these days. Thank you for that."

"It's my pleasure. You and Vanessa are part of my family now. We take care of each other. I guess her parents are home from Paris now, aren't they?" I ask.

"Funny you should ask, they aren't. They called her and said they are taking another week away. Vanessa is home doing her laundry. I'll call her later and tell her you said hi if you want."

"Sure thing. Why're Vanessa's parents gone so much, with a teenage daughter at home?"

"Yea I never have understood that, and I don't know either. Her parents and I don't see eye to eye on almost anything. They don't like me to be around her at all," he says scratching his head.

I say, "I never could leave my brothers. It would have torn my heart out to be away from them like this. I'm going to portal home from here. I'm just too tired to fly today. I thought I was building up my muscles, but I'm really not feeling well."

"Hey Kendra, can I ask you about something before you go?"

"You know you can, Jimmy."

"You know that cake guy, Barry?"

"Yes, I know him well. Why?" Wondering what Barry may have done.

"Well, first off he's a nice guy... I think. But, we're not sure. What does gadzooks mean or even grumption? Well, he said a bunch of things we didn't understand. Like, when he first got here, he said, 'Gadzooks, that wind's got me worn slap out.' And then, he was talking about you trying to find the fire starters, and he said, 'That Kendra, she's got grumption. She can do it 'cause she knows, can't never could. I don't know what gadzooks, grumption, or 'can't never could' mean. I mean, are they nice?"

"Let me put it this way Jimmy, Barry is a nice guy. But, he learned to speak English before there was any dirt," I said with a wink. "And, the word is gumption. It means determination. I need to get home and get some sleep, okay Jimmy?"

"Sure, thing Kendra. See ya."

I open a portal and wave at Jimmy as I walk through. I go straight to my room, and there's Mica. He's hard, torped right beside Spar and Kino on the platform. Tears leak out of my eyes. I'm too worn out to hold them back. As much as I want him here why would he be here when he knows I saw him with that other woman. I don't care. I can't care. I really do care. I don't want to think about it. I can't think about it now I feel sick. I grab one of the blankets and toss it over Mica, so I can't see him then I lean back on my bed ball up into a fetal position and cry myself to sleep. At least Mica can't see me cry is my last thought.

KINO

I see my beloved come into our bedroom and watch as she sees Mica beside me. I recognize the disappointment on her face. Tears fall from her beautiful green eyes. The redder they get the greener they look and the madder I am. I was planning on talking to Spar about how we think is the best way to handle Mica's callousness toward our beloved. But this is terrible to watch her cry when I am torpified and cannot hold her or give her comfort. As soon as I revert, I will punch Mica in the face, then I will hold my beloved.

SPAR

Fucking firetruck! That bastard has Kendra crying. As soon as I revert, I'm going to beat him like he's a one-legged man in an ass kicking contest. Then I'm going to pick up my beautiful girl and hold her, so she knows my love's never a contest.

MICA

I'm not worthy of the most beautiful dragon queen ever. I hate that I'm the cause of those tears. The pain on her face is a dagger in my heart. My fault... all my fault. I'm guessing that Spar and Kino are pretty upset too. I hope they don't plan on trying to beat my ass. If they do, they'll have to at least wait until I talk to them and explain what happened. But whatever punishment Kendra chooses I'll take it without complaint—including the blanket over my head. Fuck!

23

APOLOGIES HURT

Kino

I'VE BEEN awake for a while now and thinking about what I need to do when I revert. I have thought of one hundred and one ways to punch, choke, kick, headbutt, elbow, or plant a knee to the balls of Mica. The problem is Mica is a far better warrior than I am. Whatever I do must be fast and clever. That is the only chance I have to get some damage in early. Maybe then, Spar will be ready to assist me, and we can pound Mica.

I can feel the change coming. My plan... after planning for the last hour... is that Mica is to my left, so I will bring my left hand near my right ear and backhand Mica by spinning backward and toward him. I will use the rotational energy generated by my spin along with the power generated by me flinging my left hand away from me directly into his face as hard and as fast as I can. After Spar and I beat him down some, then we will question him at length about what he did to Kendra and why he did it. If he cannot offer sufficient reasoning for his abhorrent behavior, we will be forced to beat him some more.

Mica must convince us that he is one hundred percent dedicated to our mutual relationship or he will return to whatever living accommodations he had before joining Kendra in hers. After he is gone, I will work every spell I know to ease their binding and her pain.

I feel my skin starting to tingle reminiscent of how I feel when my lady touches me. I am ready.

As the crackling starts, I prepare to spin. I ignore the crystal crunching sound that I usually love, and I burst through the final stage of my torp. I begin my spin... Mica is always prepared as a warrior. He calmly grabs my arm as it inexpertly flies by him and uses my momentum to continue my turn and throw me off balance and straight into Spar knocking him backward off of the stand. Now that I've knocked Spar over I am unprepared for what is happening. Mica has an easier time pulling me back into him painfully and wrapping me with my wings effectively turning me into a giant red ball. He pushes me with little effort back into Spar knocking him down yet again. This time Mica expertly jumps onto Spar, as I am consummately out of the fight and very dizzy.

Spar growls, "Get your fat ass off me you treacherous botfly."

"Okay, but only if you listen to me—for just a minute. Then we can go to the training field, and you can whoop my ass there, so we don't hurt or wake Kendra," he replies begging. I think he is desperate to tell us his side, so I sing a spell under my breath to calm my brother and even myself from the rage at the ass who abandoned us.

Spar looks at me, and we nod our assent to each other not even looking at Mica. The ass, seeing that we agree and that my brother has quit fighting him, lets Spar up.

The three of us get up and walk to the sitting area. None of us wants to wake Kendra. She has not been sleeping well. Also, when she wakes she does not have any feeling of being rejuvenated as is needed for proper sleep. Her health is worrying me to no end. I sing a peaceful sleep over her then I sit in my usual seat. Our blue gargoyle stays standing motioning for Mica to sit first by pointing to a chair near the table, I feel he is doing well waiting to kill the traitor.

Spar starts his words pricked with passion and anger, "You prick! You left us! Fuck that, you left Kendra! Do you have any idea what she's been going through? Do you even care? Why did you bother even coming back, anyway?"

"My thoughts exactly," I back him up. "I too wish to know where you stand on this relationship—if you want to be in it or not? Or even if your fragile ego can handle thinking of someone else first. You have hurt my beloved to an incredible depth of pain." Lowering my voice and adding a threatening tone to my most minacious voice, I add, "Now speak, before I spell your dick into nonexistence!"

Mica looks up sharply at me, with shock on his face. Ha! I was able to punch him... just had to do it my way.

He looks down into his hands, searching them for any help. Then he bends over and brings them up to rub his face roughly. Much the way Kendra has done as of late. "Guys, I'm so sorry. I'll never be able to make this up to either of you, much less her. I was just so upset that I left instead of facing her and talking things out. I know that I'm the problem. I let her get abducted. I didn't protect her, and she's still suffering from it. I know she can't trust me. I deserve that. I didn't want to admit it while I was trying so hard to make it up to her. I thought she would see that, and when she didn't trust us," poking his chin at Spar, "to take care of Gortanik and six Crafted, I did what I always do. I ran. I'm a failure, I know it. When I took the assignment, I thought that she deserves someone who is strong enough to take care of her, to protect her and never let her be hurt again. But being away from her... from you all... has been a wake-up call to me. I can't live without her. She isn't just my love, she's part of me. Please, what can I do to make you understand and forgive me? I'll let you beat my ass into the ground if you want. Just forgive me, please."

I respond, "That is all well and good, but you have really hurt her Mica. She told me that she loves you so much that she can let you go. That way you can be happy. She doesn't think you love her and the pain is making her ill. What did you do that could make it that bad?"

From the bedroom door, Kendra says, "He has replaced me with a blond. I saw her in his bed. She was naked. She was with him when I dreamwalked to him yesterday. He's moved on guys, and I'm not in that picture. Mica don't listen to these two. You don't have to stay here. You can go to the one you love and have the life you want. I'm good with that. It's not fair for me to ask you to be faithful to only me when I have Kino and Spar also."

I get up and reach for her. Her little-defeated body slumps into my arms. She tucks her head into my shoulder to hide the tears threatening to spill from her eyes.

Now Mica will be dead to me. The anger that I was letting go of flares back to life. "Mica just go. There can be no reason for you to be here if that is..."

He buts in, "No, no, no, please... please, listen to me. I don't know who that woman was."

Now Spar is sputtering, "Sppptt, Wha...What? Another fucking woman. You piece of shit. That doesn't make it better. Just get the fuck outta here."

Mica tries again, "Guys, you have to listen. Please, listen, baby, let me explain." He comes close to Kendra and reaches for her hands. If she pulls away, I will fold her into my arms and sing a song of relief to her.

She just looks at him and waits. As he touches her, she immediately retracts her hands... but just a bit. I can see she loves him terribly. It shows in her eyes. "Kendra, my love. I didn't even know that woman was in my room. I had never seen her before that minute. I was asleep until I woke, feeling your presence. It shocked me as it did you when she spoke. I made her leave the second you fled. I haven't wanted any woman other than you since you gave me a chance. I don't think my dick even works for anyone else anymore."

I feel a microscopic up-turn of her lips on my chest while he is giving his speech. I think for a split second I might sing a calm, forgiving song over her, then think, nope he can suffer a bit.

The deserter continues, "You're it for me! I love you. I'm the stupidest guy in the world for messing up with you. Please, I'll let you do anything you want to get back at me, and I'll be okay with it if you'll just forgive me and let me back in your lives." His pleading eyes look much like hers, but a few tears spill from the sides of his.

"Yes, Mica. I forgive you," she says. "I want you in our lives. I'm glad you're home." Then she turns and goes into the bathroom to get ready for work, surprising us all. Although, we all notice she doesn't touch him.

The three of us just look at each other for a second, not sure what to do. I break the spell when I pat Mica's shoulder and tell him, "Give her time, it is obvious she loves you. I, on the other hand, I might love you, but I still want to kick your ass." Feeling proud of myself for using their vernacular.

Spar says, "So do I, what do you think when y'all get home from work, maybe we can go fly, then find a spot to get out some of this anger so I can let it go. Mica, I might not be able to kick your ass, but I know I can get in a few good shots before it's over."

I watch as Mica laughs, a combination of relief and laughter. Then Spar continues, "Never treat her that way again, or I'll shoot you in the ass when you're hard, and I will chip it!"

I am not sorry in the least when I laugh!

Mica says, "Guys, that's fine with me. I need to leave too so I can get ready for work."

After Mica leaves, I look at Spar and ask, "Well, do we want to forgive him or make him suffer?"

Shaking his he says, "Make him suffer, then forgive him!"

He bumps knuckles with me. We both turn to prepare for our own days. I must work with Jericho today. He needs to know how my bard spells are evolving. If they aren't, he needs to work with me on strategies. I understand being with Kendra is affecting me in all ways, but even my speaking voice is having unusual magical effects on those around me.

24

PAIN RELIEVER

Kendra

I CAN HEAR my goyles in the sitting area when I wake. I hear Mica ask Spar and Kino for forgiveness. I don't get it. Maybe he needs his friends.

Kino is speaking, "She doesn't think you love her and the pain is making her ill. What did you do that could make it that bad?"

I walk into the room, and I can't hold back answering the question instead of letting Mica. "He has replaced me with a blond. I saw her in his bed. She was naked. She was with him when I dreamwalked to him yesterday. He's moved on guys, and I'm not in that picture. Mica don't listen to these two. You don't have to stay here. You can go to the one you love and have the life you want. I'm good with that. It's not fair for me to ask you to be faithful to only me when I have Kino and Spar also."

At this point, my instinct was to protect myself through grand statements which I didn't mean. My emotions have been raised to insane levels since the party and even further at seeing Mica in my dreamwalk only to be crushed when I found him in bed with that woman. I felt my family was coming back together only to be defeated at the last second. Waves of panic born from re-experiencing the loss of my parents, the loss of David, crash into me. I don't want Mica to see my tears though, he can't see them. I must let him go... I'm ready to do that for him.

Kino is always so good at reading my emotions. He must sense that I need some protection and comes to hold me. I lean into his strength and try to hide my face from the near tears. It's okay now, I think.

Then Mica apologizes followed by a clumsy explanation, the relief that washed over me was almost incomprehensible. From the highest of high to the most desperate of lows and back again in about twelve hours. Holy shit, I don't recommend doing that again. Combine that swing with the pain from not being etched and the lack of sleep that has left me nauseous.

Mica has a habit of running away. That gives me pause as to how much I'm ready to invest in trusting he won't leave me again. He is reaching for my hand but I can't yet, I am just not healed up enough, but I'm over the moon he loves me. All I want is for us all to be happy together. "Yes Mica, I forgive you. I want you in our lives. I'm glad you're home." Then I turn and head for the bathroom... and yes, I can see the surprise on all their faces as I do.

As I said earlier, I'm feeling nauseous, and I need some room to breathe as well as some time to recharge, just a little before I've gotta go to work. I'll take a few minutes to think while I get ready. My headache is still in full force, so I take some more ibuprofen and some antacids. I'll need to stop at the market in Cueva Hallow to get some acetaminophen after I portal. Something's got to work better than what I'm taking. After going to the market, I'll head over to the La Caverna to talk to Brian really quick... if he's the doorman today.

After I finish getting ready, I portal straight to a small store near the La Caverna where I grab some extra strength acetaminophen. Then I cross over the four-lane street called Channel St. It also doubles as part of the nearly eight hundred and fifty-mile-long Highway 285.

I get back to the apartments and stop at the door to throw the security wrapping from my pain medication into the trash can. After I pop a couple of the pills into my mouth, I fake a smile at Brian. "Good morning Brian."

"Good morning Ms. Macbard!"

"Brian, I noticed a new doorman last night."

"Yes, ma'am. That was Loren Kirks. Was there a problem?"

"No, nothing like that. I was just wondering; do I need to introduce myself and Jimmy? What is the protocol? I've known you since the day I moved in. I'm afraid I don't know what the procedures are so Loren will recognize us. He didn't stop me last evening. In fact, he opened the door for me and let me in." I left out the part of me running into the door... face first.

"Oh, I understand. Well, Loren said he already knows you and Jimmy, so he didn't need an introduction. Should I report that difference?"

"No, I'm sure it's alright. I might know that doorman and have just forgotten. I'll talk to him this evening if he's here. Have a wonderful day, Brian." *Maybe Jared has put protection in place for me without me knowing or talking to him yet.*

I leave and head over to Jasper. I love my truck. Luckily, he is parked near the door, so I didn't have far to go. With my energy level as low as it's been, I'm glad for the welcome non-walk. I climb in and lock my doors, buckle up, and start him up—sounds like my sex life, I laugh to myself. A knock on my passenger window snaps me out of my reverie. Oh damn, it's Mica. Yep, I slam forgot about him. He needs a ride, and I'm it, so I unlock the door, feeling just slightly ashamed for overlooking him. How did he find me anyway?

"Thank you, princess, is there a reason we're leaving from here instead of flying to the outpost building we've been using?"

"I have a lot to tell you." That's precisely what I do. I tell him everything. Hopefully, I'm not going over information that he's already a party to. The look on his face says to me it's the first he's heard of most of it, so I plow on through it. The recap made the trip seem very short. The acetaminophen has lightened my headache some. Good thing for me I got the large size of the brand-new bottle of pain relievers.

Mica is out of the truck and opens my door before I blink. He pulls me toward him and leans in for a kiss. I give him my cheek instead and push on his chest a little and continue to get out myself. As I look up into his impossibly golden eyes, I see his hurt expression. Damn it, did I forgive him or not?

"Mica, I love you too. The start of this, it's my fault. I know it is. I should've trusted y'all and stayed put. But," I jab two fingers, hard into his sexy chest, "from now on, I'm not staying put, no matter what. I'm going and if I gotta fight, I will. You can tell that to everyone in Navan, and they can put it in a giant pipe and smoke it." I ended with a grunt that took almost every drop of energy I have.

His face breaks into one of his amazing grins, "Fuckin' A Batgirl, roger that. It wasn't all your fault. I don't want you to feel that way. I should have been able to protect you from Jessup and failed. Then when I actually did protect you in a way, I thought you didn't notice and I wasn't good enough for you. Forgive me babe, please?"

"Of course I forgive you," I mumble then take a deep breath and blow it out. As I do, I see him staring at a spot on my chest. I look down, and there's Elmer attached as pretty as you please. Using my hand, I encourage him to a new location, and he moves up and settles in the back of my neck under my hair.

Murphy starts the review of the dailies with the team. "The explosives have all been moved from the shack near the old ranger station. The ATF is investigating and has the scene closed off. We don't have a need to be there, so let's stay out of their way. Macbard, good job on finding this one. This could be the break we need.

As always, if you see anyone or anything suspicious radio it in and investigate. There's another new fire so we might see some activity with the firefighters. They have helicopters in the area too.

Keep everyone out of Washburn Canyon 'cause we have some spot fires near those camps."

Just the thoughts of that canyon reminds me of the hole in the wall cave where Spar made me a picnic after we first got back together. I hope my thoughts aren't showing on my face. Mica's quick squeeze of my hand told me I probably wasn't. I drag my hand away slowly so not to offend, I'm just not ready for the touchy thing yet.

The rest of the briefing was just more of the same. Nothing specific but loads of keeping your head up and protect yourself or, don't be a hero injected in random spots.

Leaving the meeting with our instructions for our tour, Mica and I walk past Chris's desk on our way to our patrol SUV. I hang a half a step behind Mica and watch as Chris gives me a big smile and thumbs up as we pass. I can't help myself, I give the same back to her, but in my head, I'm still a bit wounded. I'll get over it.

As we get to our unit, I can definitely smell the smoke from the fires. There've been so many fires, and they've been so near, I don't need to use my dragon sense.

25

THEY'RE HOLLOW

Kendra

I SMILE as Mica doesn't even try to get into the driver's seat of our patrol SUV. Our tour begins like another dreary day when we start out. But not for long when the radio comes to life, and we hear Chris's calm voice, "Lima 26 respond."

Mica keys the mic and responds, "Lima 26 available."

"Lima 26, we have a 10-38 Vandalism call at the main cavern in the King's Throne Room. The tour guide, Officer Vaughn has three perps cuffed and prone waiting for Federal Rangers to take control. You better hurry."

We smile at each other knowing that it's the queen with the throne room in our cavern. Mica answers, "Lima 26 in route. ETA seven minutes."

As we arrive on the scene and I see three people lying face down on the ground in front of the King's Throne formation. Their arms are cuffed behind them. Standing above them strutting like the rooster in the hen house is Officer Vaughn he is the skinniest man I can ever remember seeing. I don't mean to be disrespectful, but his head is precariously balanced on his long and improbably thin neck, looks like a bowling ball sitting on a tall drinking glass.

I look at Mica who is walking beside me, his grinning mouth opens wide. I quickly jab him in the ribs and straighten my own face.

I ask, "Officer Vaughn, what seems to be the problem?"

I know he is also an older gentleman, but he looks well for his age. He straightens his back throwing his chest as far out as he can and with one hand pushing hard into his lower back and spins on one heel. His gawky turn leaves him with the three perps on the ground directly behind him, a major no-no in any kind of police work. However, it does lighten my mood, and I have to hold back a giggle.

To be abundantly clear Chris' job, in this case, was to relay information from him to us. She was probably laughing about the perps comment as much as we were. She knows his job is a tour guide.

The fallen man rights his awkward turn, sees me watching, and takes his campaign style hat off and offers a "Ma'am" to me with a slight bow. Then he sees Mica. The officer's mouth drops open, and he stumbles backward as his eyes open wide enough that I had the impression they might pop right out of his head. At this point, he somehow loses control of his hat. He tries three or four times to catch it before he finally does. Once he eventually does catch it, he tucks it under his arm like nothing had happened, and he meant to do it the whole time. Except, he crushed his felt hat flat... this is kinda fun, I think.

Here Vaughn regains his composure but without losing his bug eyes and obviously still unsure what to do about Mica. I honestly think he believes my partner is a bear. Officer Skinny's job now is to make himself look as big as possible. Well, that's going to be tough. I've seen sticks bigger than this guy.

Vaughn's new course of action is to puff his chest out even more than ever. He has his arms away from his sides, and his elbows pushed back. Damn, how far back can he pull them without hurting himself? All of this in a feeble attempt to thrust his teeny chest out further than he had it before he saw Mica... the bear. Yet, this is the pose he attempts to maintain as he begins to tell us what has happened.

"I was in the queen's ante-room," he begins in a somewhat loud high pitched officious manner, "when I heard loud and somewhat raucous laughter. I entered the area to restore order and to tell the offending individuals that they happen to not be the only visitors we have in the caverns. So, please be respectful of others who are touring the cave. As I entered, I saw said perpetrators," pausing he dramatically points to the three individuals cuffed on the ground, "they were breaking off soda straws from under the Hanging Man Formation." The last three words were each pronounced in a more reverent tone and with the emphasis of a Perry Mason courtroom.

Then Vaughn turns and looks at us. "Ya know officers those soda straws took thousands of years to grow. It takes about one hundred years to grow a little one that is only about an inch and a half long. These speleothems are hollow!" Almost whining the last sentence to me. Then, leaning in close, in a conspiratorial manner and he says, "They're hollow..." Quickly standing back up he resumes, "I mean they are easy to break because they're hollow." His hand points to the long delicate straw formations hanging in a large cluster over the unfortunate men on the floor. He is getting excited as he tells us what happened and is getting way off the subject.

Gently, I guide him back on track, "They are beautiful. So, you saw them breaking them off, officer?"

"Yes, ma'am," he screeches at me. "I saw each of the perpetrators break off some of the formations and put them in their backpacks as I was arriving here to stop their illegal behavior. This part of the room is restricted, and they aren't supposed to be here at all. The soda straws are hollow..."

Mica butts right in this time, "Thank you, Officer Vaughn we'll take it from here." He places one of his big hands on the excited man's chest. Skinny looks down at it seeing that Mica's hand is nearly as big as his chest deflates him and he backs out of the way.

Mica looks at me, and I know he's going to proceed with the

arrest. Winking at me, he Mirandizes the perps sitting them up. He informs them that we have probable cause to inspect their backpacks because we have a witness. They say they understand their rights and speak anyway and my partner starts emptying the packs onto a nearby table.

"We're sorry officers. We didn't know it was wrong and just wanted a souvenir," says the one in the front of the other two. He chuckles a bit too and says, "What is the harm anyway there are lots of them." He has a German accent, so I ask, where are you from are you US citizens? Do you have ID and passports?"

"We are all from Frankfurt, Germany, and our passports are in our packs. You can get them out," he says.

"Officer Macbard," Mica says. "Come look at this." He has at least 10 soda straws lined up beside each backpack and various pieces of drug paraphernalia with a bag of some kind of stuff that looks like angel dust. Then one last item a bag of rolled... what seems to be joints, and there are amazingly a lot, I would guess at least fifty.

"Well, I'll call the sheriffs in. I'll bet they are going to need ATF and the U.S. Marshalls on top of Homeland Security," I tell him.

I get on the horn, and the Sheriff's office lets me know someone is in route. While we're waiting, we check the ties that the park tour guide used to restrain the three vandals before we search them.

"Well, it goes from bad to worse," I comment as I pull out a folding knife from the first one's pants pocket.

"I have two more; they each had a pocket knife," Mica says. "You want me to radio our progress or do you want to?" he asks.

"Go ahead, I want to look at something over behind the Hanging Man. There's a brown thing sticking up, and I want to make sure it's kosher." Moving to the formation, I see that it is not good at all. "I figured out what the ANFO is being used for. I'm not an expert, but unless I miss my guess, this is a bomb. Let's get these guys above ground and call for an evac."

Mica is on it and calls in the evacuation of the Caverns. It's at the end of the day, and most of the tourists are leaving anyway. When we get the suspects out of the cave, we're met by Officer Jerry Gonzales and his bomb squad. I take him to the site while Mica oversees things on the surface. After a couple of more hours, we are able to turn the investigation over to the Sheriff's Department. We roll back into the Ranger's Station to start the required mountain of paperwork.

"Mica do you want to come with me to talk to the Captain or would you like to get a jump on the field report?"

"You go ahead and talk to Murphy, and I'll start the paperwork. We may be able to leave on time that way."

"I like it. I'll be back as soon as I give him a first-hand account."

"Well, would you look at that," I say as I round the corner and see Chris just leaving Murphy's office. His door is left wide open. She smiles a shit-eating grin and says under her breath, "I'll tell you about it later hun."

I give her a half cocky, side grin and continue into Murphy's office since he had waved me in.

"Well, I understand you and Jacobs had an interesting day up at the King's Throne Room today Macbard. Have a seat and tell me about it. I'm guessing your partner is filling out the report as we speak?"

"Yes sir, he is," I reply and continue telling him about the vandals and finding the ANFO bomb. It seems to me Captain that we know what the ANFO was intended to be used for, but not who the perpetrator is. Do you have any information or is ATF and Homeland Security not sharing yet?"

"You are correct on the not sharing, but they are saying they have some promising leads they are following up on and will give me a detailed report when the matter is closed. Good job Macbard tell that giant of a partner I said so and get out of here. Get some rest, you look like toast," he says and dismisses me at the same time.

When I get back to the office pod, I find Mica still typing out the report, so I don't bother him. I upload the pictures we had taken of the arrest and the bomb. While I'm going through the photos, I notice that the wires are all over the place and some are not even attached.

They are just laying out on the ground beside the taped-up bags of the explosive fertilizer.

"Hey Mica, I start walking over to his desk and pull up a chair to sit by him. "I note that not all of the wires are attached to the bomb in some of the pictures that I just uploaded. Did you by any chance add that in the report?"

"I'll add it now. That makes me think maybe someone got surprised and had to stop but intended to finish later." Mica finishes the report and attaches the photos. The next thing I know we're out in the parking lot getting into Jasper and headed to the La Caverna.

26

READY

Mica

KENDRA IS SLEEPING SO DEEPLY that she doesn't move when I get out of bed. We'd been snuggled so tightly, she was using my arm as a pillow and holding my other arm as it draped across her chest... okay, I'll say it, we were spooning. We just fit together so well. I can't say how beautiful it is to hold her like that when I was so afraid she wouldn't let me ever again. She is physically very fit, and her butt... never mind. I'm getting off topic.

She should've felt me get up, but she didn't. I know she isn't feeling well, but damn it, this has me worried.

I need to talk to the guys about her health. I'm sure something is wrong. They might know more than I do and if not, we need to decide what to do—together.

But first, the correct phrase is 'butt first.' Meaning I've gotta get cleaned up before I do anything else. Yesterday was a long day, and Kendra fell asleep with me holding her. I locked up Jasper and went up to her apartment at the La Caverna where Vanessa let me in. From there, I opened a portal straight back to her room in Navan.

I can't quit thinking of how I got her undressed and how beautiful she was, is. I mean how beautiful she is! It was a trick to get undressed and keep holding her. I just didn't want to let her go. The point is, I didn't have a chance to clean up last night. So today is Butt First Day. I'm not doing anything else until my butt and body are as clean as a baby's bum... well, after the baby has had a bath. You know what I mean!

I step into the main room refreshed from my bath. I'm still wet, and my hair is dripping down my back as I comb it out. I smell coffee and can hear the guys talking in the kitchen, so I walk over to them. Silence.

"Okay guys, I guess we need to get to the training field." My statement sounds more like a question. I do say it as gently as possible, but I didn't want to sound like a wuss. That bit of sophistry would have likely pissed them off more than they already are. "After, I need to talk to you about Kendra and what's making her sick."

They both get up, and Spar says, "She's still sleeping. So, you're on lightweight. Let's go!"

Kino says nothing. He just follows Spar out the door. I follow Kino. The three of us make our way down to the sand pit where we train. They both stand on the far side of the field, me on the near side, closest to the door. I wait on either one of them to take the first swing.

Both Spar and Kino know my skills. They know that if they try to attack, I could just stand here all day and deflect anything and everything they had. Them attacking first won't work, and they know it. I think they know if I attack first, they can't deflect what I bring. This leaves them in an awkward position. They want to beat my ass for what I did. Yet, I can tell that they aren't really that mad at me anymore. Maybe I should provoke them to get this over with.

"I don't know why I bother, I've done my best, and you two still can't fight your way out of a wet paper bag." Then just to force it I add, "You dickheads do something, that is, if you aren't scared little pussies!"

Something in there is enough of a trigger for Spar. He doesn't hesitate and runs straight at me, spinning two times as he comes at me and then throws a wicked roundhouse kick. I see it coming and let it land. Damn, that boy has some power.

I stay up but just barely. I feign a wobble and drop down, spinning to take out Kino's feet. That should get him started. One thing about Kino, he's a very efficient fighter. No wasted effort, ever.

The fight's on. I'll take whatever my brothers give me and only return enough to keep them going. I know these two need to get their licks in or they're gonna stay pissed.

We've been at it for a good hour, and they have long since figured out I'm not really fighting. None of us admit what is going on, but we continue... you know for practice.

"Spar, you keep raising your wings just before you throw a punch. Dead giveaway brother. Try and keep 'em locked low. That way you won't telegraph your punches, and it'll also keep them from being such a target."

Spar pulls his wings lower and locks them using the fantastic back muscles he's built. On his next punch, he succeeds in not telegraphing it.

Kino is already one of the best fighters in Navan. He has other tools to use besides his strength. Tools that are growing stronger since our new queen has arrived.

"Guys we need to stop and..."

As if they'd planned for this, as soon as I dropped my guard, they rush me. They both land a solid blow on either side of my chin... in an uppercut fashion. What a dumbass! Why would I ever let my guard down around these two buttheads? I fly backward, just like you see in the movies, into the sparring weapons closet. Of course, this tears open my side.

Neither one flinches, nor helps me stand up. I refuse to just lay here and let these goyles stare at me. So, as quickly as I can, and ignoring the piercing pain in my side, I stand straight and tall. As a consolatory gesture, I reach out my hand.

Kino is there first. He takes my hand and looks directly into my eyes and says, "Never hurt my lady again. Mica, we are brothers to the end. Don't leave us again. We must work out our problems together, as a family. If you leave again I will not be so agreeable."

"Deal. If I ever leave again without talking to you, it will be because it's beyond my control," I reply. Kino pulls me to him for a bro-hug. But, Kino, Spar and I are more than friends and brothers, much more.

Kino steps aside, and Spar takes my hand next. "Mica, you hurt us all by leaving. But honestly, Kendra's been losing it. She's sleeping more than I've ever seen her sleep. But, her rest is more like she's passing out and less like falling asleep. I think this is because of her fears from the abduction haunting her. Before you ask, she doesn't complain about it—but it's there if you're looking. She's got headaches and nightmares like crazy. See that you keep your word, she doesn't do well without you. Do you understand?"

As Spar pulls me in for another bro-hug, I answer, "Yes, I do understand."

I stand tall as they both stare at me. If I wait for even a second, this will get awkward. Instead, I ask quickly, "Is this enough? Is it over? Can we please get on with our lives now?"

"Yes," they both answer.

"Let's get back and check on our dragon. Then we can talk about how to battle the problems with her health." I feel better than I have in days.

When we arrive in our suite, we find Kendra up and dressed for work. I grab another quick shower to wash off the ass-whooping sweat, then get myself ready. I don't put on my shirt since I need some help slapping a bandage on the wound in my side. I guess I'm hoping Kendra will take care of it for me.

I follow her to the sitting area where the others are waiting. My side has stopped bleeding but still looks nasty. Kino's got a bruise shaped like Texas on his forehead. Spar's got a scrape from his forehead, down his nose, and across two ugly blimp-like lips. Well, at least they are uglier and fatter than I usually see them.

Kendra climbs onto Spar's lap. As she does, she looks into his eyes, and he returns the favor by not breaking eye contact. She rewards the blue guy with her signature cuteness and gives him a sexy little pout as she bends to kiss said nose and ever so gently, place several soft kisses on each of his grotesque lips. Her hands cup his face, holding him in place... like he'd want to move. She lifts her gorgeous head and smiles at him.

She turns her attention to Kino. Just like Spar, she straddles him, then gently but firmly holds his head in her hands. Instead of the cute little pout she gave Spar, Kino is treated with one of the dirtiest sexy looks I've seen in... well, for a long time! She pulls his face to her chest, where she can reach the bruise on his forehead. After kissing the injury, she moves to his eyes, then his lips. Which by that time, seem to be begging for her to do more. You can see the love pouring off of him as he stares into her eyes.

She gives Kino a saucy lick on his lips before she sits at the table to drink her coffee and have some breakfast. She finally looks at me.

I wait, not knowing if I have the right to say anything right now. I wait. Each heartbeat feels like a day, each blink a week. I wait. I'm sure she's saving something special for me. And I wait...

"Mica will you hand me one of those scones. I'm so hungry I could eat a horse, hooves and all." I smile, a little uncomfortable, and give her the plate of scones. Suddenly, she jumps and says, "What the bloody hell happened to your side?"

"Ummm, I fell into one of the weapons lockers. It's okay, I'm alright." She sets a hand lightly on my chest. It's so soft I hardly feel it, other than the tingles it sends through me making my stomach muscles flutter. As she bends down toward my waist, my mind does what anyone would do when the love of their life lowers their face into that area. When she blows on my cut, I only wish I had a way of cutting my other side too. She kisses the cut. I swear, I can feel it healing, pulling itself together. Maybe that is something else growing. Yep.

I know the guys are watching, but right now, I couldn't give two shits. I'm in heaven with her touching me. I start to imagine exactly how I want to touch her back when she snaps me back to reality by handing me my pack and saying, "Come on let's fly to Jasper this morning."

I answer in a gravelly voice, "I'll come anywhere you want me to princess—anywhere." I break out of my fog and look around at the others. Those two dunderheads have shit-eating grins pasted on their ugly faces. I pause. "Damn it, you two. That's not how I meant it." I stop, again, this time I look directly at Kendra.

"Oh, really Mica? You won't come with me?" Feigning hurt on her face and exaggerating pain in her chest. I can't believe I chose that word, 'come' to use. My dick's already reacting on its own. I can't control it with her or them in the room.

"Fuck! I've turned into a satyr-goyle!" I lashed out good-heartedly at them. Then to Kendra, "I mean, yeah, we better go now if we intend to be on time."

She looks at me and kisses Spar and Kino goodbye. Telling them, "You two have had enough practice today why don't you go have some fun while Mica and I are at work? Love you, bye."

27

SOME BETTER

Kendra

WHILE WE'RE FLYING to get Jasper, I recognize how much clearer I'm thinking and how much more energized I am. Relief has made its way through to every cell in my body. I know I'm a changed person from who I was when I first met my goyles. It was especially apparent when Mica was gone. He told me that he would always be here for me and then wasn't. Now he's telling me he'll go anywhere I want. I want to believe it. I need to think about it, but I must also protect myself. I decide when we get in our patrol car, I'm going to bring up the subject of our future. Just to be sure he knows how invested I am.

I hope breathing on my goyles has them healed up already. That's a nasty cut on my contrite goyle. I smile to myself thinking those butts were fighting and each got hurt. I'm sure it won't last past today, and I doubt there'll be anything more than the bruises and scrapes I saw today. Mica had taken it easy on my loves. Yes ma'am, and a dippidy-do, I do feel better.

I fly hard pressing as fast as I can to beat Mica to Jasper.

Mica picks up on my game, then disappears from view. I don't hesitate and take the shortest route I know. I'm going to get there as fast as possible.

Once I make it to the La Caverna, I quickly land on the roof, the darkness shrouding my descent and landing. I don't even bother to go to my apartment to change clothes. I do it right there on top of the building. After I finish, I race to the first floor before slowing and walking respectfully out the front door.

As pretty as you please, there's Mica dressed and ready for work talking to the new doorman. Mica looks up and waves. I am so surprised that he beat me here so that we can drive to work. I haven't check the new doorman Laren's aura so I'm checking it now out of curiosity mostly. My donum is not up, so I concentrate on Loren's aura. Clear. Red is prevalent with a dark blue which is similar to what I see on Kino but still different. There's a white bubble close to his shoulder... wonder what that is, I ask my inner voice, what are you telling me with this aura?

He's an adventurer and a great cook. The red and the blue show that his donum is very intuitive and he uses it.

Great cook! What the crap! My inner Leta voice is getting even more specific and clear.

The bubble is a guardian with him, I hear. This man intends to protect you dragon daughter, as does your consort beside him.

I switch my gaze to Mica and see yellows and his abundant orange with some places that are blue. Awh daughter, he is also hurt and has sorrow in his spirit for nearly losing you. Even though he did it to himself. It makes me feel better knowing. He's a grown ass man for crying out loud. I am too, and I still doubted him and the others I guess that's something this grown ass woman will need to work on also.

Later as we start our patrol, I tell him, "Mica, I have really missed you." I pronounce each word to allow me time to search for the next word. The next word that I don't know... I stop reaching for the words I can't express.

"I missed you too. Kendra, I wasn't thinking straight. I know I can't go back to how things were before I left. But, I'm willing to do whatever you need me to do so I can prove myself to you. I was thinking of myself and my own shortcomings. I believed you deserve better than me, it made me run." His deep rumbling voice stops.

"If anyone can understand that kind of thinking, it's me. You don't have to apologize anymore. What I'm struggling with is..." I pause then move right on before he says anything, "I want to love you and want to be with you. I want to be yours, and you be mine; and never worry that you won't be there for me again. I'm not saying you have to be perfect, just that we will always be together. I'm one hundred percent invested in this relationship." I can't even look over at him. I'm looking at the dirt road, driving slowly and watching each pebble. Reacting, not thinking, I decide to pull off the street and park.

"Do you think you can be that invested. Can you do that? Because I really need to know before I get any deeper into this relationship. It'll tear me up to end it, but it'll be easier now than later. No fighting, if it's better for you and what you want we can stay close friends." I added the last sentence quickly, knowing I can't ever stay entirely away from him.

I wait, hoping with every atom in my body that he won't take the freedom I just offered him. I wait. I hold my breath, afraid of letting anything go right now. I wait. I'm sure he'll love me even if only from afar.

I wait...

"No! Never say that to me again," he said forcefully.

I look up and see the pain in his shining golden eyes. He reaches for my hands, and I let him take them, feeling the calluses from his training. One thing, he may be gorgeous everywhere, but his hands are amazing.

He continues, this time stronger and with all of his conviction, "Princess, my love, I promise, since you're giving me another chance. I won't fuck it up. I'm in one hundred percent too. I'll be yours forever, and you will be mine."

The same emotions pulse from his body into mine, and I know without a single doubt he'll be true to his promise. I revel in the warmth of his pulse for a few seconds, the heat filling my body with, I don't know how to say it other than to say, that pulse of warmth felt like everything. I lean into him and kiss him softly.

28

URGENT FALL

Kendra

I GUESS the attempted bombing of a National Park location has finally gotten the attention of the Feds in a big way. *As if the fires alone didn't warrant this type of response.* However, since Mica and I seem to have been at or near the nexus of many of the essential evidentiary discoveries, we spend the next few days in a blur of meetings with the ATF, Homeland Security, FBI and a few other three letter agencies which I can't disclose in this book. Add to that, my need to update TASS and the High Guild, and... well, you can imagine.

The blur of meetings causes our days to meld into visions of chairs, whiteboards, bottles of water and lots of blank stares. The only thing changing is the person asking us the same questions we've answered seven other times.

Very little else happens during this time to break the monotony of the endless meetings. Oh, wait... I almost forgot... we did give directions to a couple of lost visitors. This has been our life for the last few duty shifts.

Mica and I are getting in our patrol SUV when Mica commits the unforgivable curse of grumbling about boredom. As if on cue Officer Andy Vaughn from the caverns radioes me. "Officer Macbard, this is Officer Vaughn." We all know Andy pretty well. He's a stickler for rules, and his skinny body and big nose are hard to forget. He's also, not really an officer, he's a tour guide who gets paid accordingly. Overall, he's helpful. Yet, there are other times where he is most certainly not beneficial.

Today his voice is exceptionally high and manic, so I'm guessing this will be one of those 'is not' times. "I have a 10-31, a 10-15, a 10-10 and possibly a 10-51!"

I look at Mica and restate them to make sure I heard them correctly. "A 10-31 is a crime in progress, a 10-15 is for a civil disturbance, a 10-10 is a fight in progress and a 10-51 is a hit and run... did I get that right?"

"Yes, yes you did! It's a madhouse down here! I also need assistance with an emergency evacuation of an elderly person in distress. She, I mean the perp, has a broken arm and ankle as well as a bloody nose. Furthermore, I am issuing multiple citations to her," big nose Vaughn wails.

"Vaughn, this is Officer Jacobs. We've received your call. ETA four minutes. Andy, don't issue any citations. Do you understand me?" Mica orders.

"Okay," Andy answers Mica with a definite note of disappointment. Luckily, we're near the entrance to the cave and are able to get there quickly.

We arrive and find a red-faced Andy Mirandizing a woman who is in obvious medical distress... lying on the cold ground... on her back... crying. I kneel down to examine her for signs of shock. Mica gives me the field medical kit and the wool blankets we'd grabbed, then he pulls Andy away to speak with him.

"Andy, what in the hell happened?"

"The perpetrator," he pointed two of his long skinny fingers at the lady on the ground, "stepped in a location which was not expressly contained within the well-established path! She then continued off said path directly into that stalagmite." Again, pointing his fingers... "I am issuing citations for the following: walking off the path; touching the stalagmite as mentioned earlier; a third for causing a disturbance in a National Park; and finally, a hit and run."

"Andy, what hit and run are you talking about?" I know Mica regrets asking the question, but I know he had to. You see, Andy is well known for getting out of hand at times. It's usually best to not ask him why. Just don't let him do anything and everyone is better off.

"Well, she hit her face on that stalagmite and her husband, Ralphie..."

"Andy stop. No citations. Do you understand me?" Andy grudgingly agrees.

While Mica is speaking with Andy, I speak with the lady on the ground. As soon as I do, I figure out she isn't crying, she's mad as all get-out. She's going on about that "skinny little butthead." Her name is Veda Jenns. After I set her up just enough to get her head off the ground, she pointed a surprisingly steady finger at Andy and said, "If I ever catch that squirrelly little toad, I'm going to stick him, butt first, on top of the stalagmite I fell into! You understand me you... you... well, you butthead?"

In his frenzied high pitched nasal tone, Andy sputters out a response, "Now you see here! You two are my witnesses. She just threatened a Peace Officer. That's the second time. I'm afraid I'm going to be forced to arrest her."

"Hang on, Andy. You're not arresting anyone," I say.

"Awe come on Ke–"

"Andy, stop it," Mica says, complete with a hint of his gargoyle growl.

Evidently, Veda had stepped wrong and fell. As she fell, she hit the stalagmite face first, breaking her nose. She had also broken her leg and arm in the fall.

"Officer Vaughn, you will not be issuing any citations either. Ms. Jenns didn't willfully leave the path. She simply fell off of it. And this business with the hit and run... Andy, you have crossed a line with that one. No more! You'll apologize to her and let us take care of this."

"But Kendra, she..."

"Andy, don't make me talk with your mother again," I tell him.

"Awe, alright. I'm sorry Ms. Jenns." Andy hangs his head and drags his feet as he leaves. I shake my head at Mica as he walks away. Ms. Jenns watches him go and calls him a "butthead" to his back.

We check her for other injuries before Mica picks her up and carries her to the waiting ambulance.

Veda is so sweet, she hands me a hundred dollars for Mica and me. She said, "Young lady, I would gladly pay twice that amount to be carried around by that hunk of a partner of yours." She giggles. I tucked the money right back in her giant-sized flowery purse when she wasn't looking.

With the great Veda Jenns Saga behind us, Mica and I head home. I drank a little water and had a quick meal... Spar insisted. Then I fell asleep leaning on Spar while Kino sings a relaxing song to me.

29

I'M READY

Kendra

IT'S FRIDAY NIGHT. Damn, I finally made it. I'm so excited to finally get on with our travel plans to my grandmother. I feel a little worse every day, even with Mica home. I also want to see my grandmother very much. This time for real. This'll be a solemn trip but a wonderful one nonetheless.

"Beloved are you ready for this trip?" Kino asks. Spar and Mica each intently watch me, waiting for the answer.

"I need it like breathing. Besides, I don't think I've got enough energy to wait any longer," I reply weakly.

Spar laughs and as he looks at me flips out his trademark question, "Well, what can happen?" I relax knowing they'll take care of me.

The three of them walk close to me as we walk through the secret tunnel from my room into the Allodium. Here we will meet the others traveling with us to Turkey.

I see Alexandritana. First, she is unusually somber. She wants to go now and is having a difficult time waiting. My grandmother was very special to her, and she's been thinking of bringing her back here for burial for a very long time.

I get close to her and say, "Tana thank you for what you're doing honoring my grandmother this way and helping me."

She shakes her head. "My queen, I have wanted this ever since she was put on that odious wall. It's a fact that I can't be any more prepared."

"Well, you're about to get your wish my lovely Tana. We only have to wait for the surgeon." I force a laugh at that remark, and speak of the devil, Jericho walks in as if summoned.

"Edling, I can see from your aura, you are greatly diminished. You should eat before we leave. Better yet, let me brew something for you to drink?"

"Stop fussing mage. I'm fine. Do you think my goyles would let me skip many meals? Not likely! Let's go, I need to get there," I said a little testier than I should've. Jericho seemed to understand. With a look of compassion, he merely bowed to me.

Jared and Dana are both happy to be going. But you can tell by the way they act, they're apprehensive about me. Every woman should be loved this much. I guess, if I had three wishes, everyone being loved as much as I am, would be the first of them.

Jadeite is with our group too and is standing in front of me. His great green wings curl around his chest. Seeing him is a reminder for me to do my best for my people. They're doing their best for me. Flint is also with us. Since Mega is staying home. I feel safer having these two Ducere with me. Neither would ever let anything hurt me. Well, I guess that goes for every person on this trip.

"Flint, I'm happy you're coming with us. How're you able to, given your current mission?"

"It is an especially long tale, my queen. Suffice it to say, I've been sent to gather intelligence about you," he says with a lopsided grin.

"Well, that's very good for me then. I'm glad you're going with us. Jadeite, thank you for coming too. Is everyone ready?"

"My queen, if I may have a moment?" Mica asks.

I nod weakly at him, giving him the floor.

"Alright everyone, for today's mission, we'll be using our new earbud communications system that Dolo has secured for us. It's called Operating Radial Communications System, or ORCS for short. Let's put it on channel three. This system will allow all of us to talk to each other. It will work as long as you are within one hundred feet of another ORCS earbud," Mica finishes.

Jericho, who has been watching me starts in again, "Kendra, may I please get you–"

"Jericho, let's just go. Now please."

Jericho simply smiles at me as he opens the portal.

Our small party finally arrives on a plain, several miles from the Castle Ilioilion. The ground is flat in front of us except for a small bluff, less than a mile away, but still in front of the distant castle. The castle itself sits on a mound, some one hundred feet high, and we landed west the castle. I know my grandmother's head is fixed to the western wall of Castle Ilioilion. So, from this vantage point, I can finally see where her great orange dragon's head is located.

The moonless night combined with the low reflection of the city lights on the horizon, make flying the quickest and safest way to travel the last bit to the castle mound.

As I wait on Mica to review our path with the team, my skin starts itching like a dry scab. I flex my shoulders attempting to alleviate some of the irritation. It doesn't help.

Dana is sitting beside a little scraggly apple tree and talking with Jared. I watch as he reaches out his hand toward the apple tree. In seconds, the tree grows into a beautiful apple tree full of lovely apples. He picks one and takes it to Tana. She was surprised at the kindness shown by Dana. Gently, she takes his forearm in her two hands, and she tugs him down to her where she softly kisses him on the cheek, thanking him for the apple, but more for caring about her.

Dana knows, hell we all know, this is a stressful day for Tana. The last time she was here, she was the lady in waiting for my grandmother, her best friend.

"Come, Sis, let's go see our grandmother," Jared tells me.

"Wait a sec, Jare. Sissy are you sure you're okay? Maybe you should stay here and let us bring Leta to you," Dana says quietly.

"I'll be okay. If I'm not, I'll let you know okay?" I reply.

"Go on ahead Dana," Jared starts, "I'll stay by her just to be safe."

Mica looks at him with an over my dead body face which is hard to miss. It was matched by an equally intense glare from Jared. *Well, shit on a shingle, this isn't something that'll end well. Both of these men are among the most stubborn beings ever to inhabit this blue ball. Well, next to me...*

Spar, sensing the same thing says, "We'll watch over Kendra, Jared. You and Jericho help Dana. We'll be right behind you.

Dana nods and is off first, Jared and most of the others right behind. Into the moonless night sky, I watch them as they quickly clear the first bluff. Only my consorts remain with me. I wish we had time for us to stay here and just let the night and location take hold of us.

Mica touches my arm, returning my gaze to him and asks, "Are you ready? We can wait if you need a minute we don't need to rush."

"No, I'm ready. Let's go."

30

GRANDMOTHER

Kendra

MICA LEADS us skyward followed by me, Spar and Kino take up positions by my side. The fresh night air feels good as it slides over me, easing the itching sensation that's been bothering me.

The flight is exhausting. I can't find an air current like I'm used to near Navan. This makes me rely entirely on my muscles. I press as hard as I can, and still, I have to stop on the bluff less than a mile from the castle. I can't seem to catch my breath. Mica is right beside me with a creased worried forehead. Spar and Kino land beside us looking just as concerned.

"I'm all right. I just have no stamina right now. It's a good thing we didn't wait any longer." I pause, hating what I'm about to do. "I'm not sure I can make it."

"Come here honey," Spar is behind me and draws me in close. Reminding me of the first time he flew with me. That small bite...

I notice Mica nod at him, and off we go into the air. I tuck myself into Spar's tight chest as he carries me the rest of the way up to the castle. He has to work at it, but the climb isn't beyond his ability.

"Not much further, how are you, babe?" he asks.

"My head hurts, and I feel weaker by the minute; like if we had worked out hard and haven't recovered yet. I'm okay. We're almost there, Spar. I feel her." Tears start leaking from my eyes. Not sad tears, but relief and happiness... that this is a good cause.

"Can you hear that?" I ask Spar.

"The birds? That's all I hear. What are you hearing?"

I cock my head concentrating, then close my eyes.

"You make me so happy daughter. Almost here, have faith, you can do this. You can accomplish so much more than what you give yourself credit. Just a little farther." The echoed words of my grandmother fade off into the darkness surrounding us.

"It was my grandmother, Leta. She said we're close and to have strength," I tell Spar trying to summarize the important part since I don't have the energy to tell him all of it.

We land in an area below what Jared calls the Dardanos Gate as he did our walkthrough on the map. The gate is on the southeastern corner of the castle wall. From where we land it's a short walk up and to the entrance. Spar continues to carry me despite my protests. Here Mica starts arranging our forces and reviewing our plan.

"Alpha Team, Tana I need you, Jadeite and Flint to stay here and protect Station One. It encompasses this corner of the wall, that small area of the eastern wall, as well as the path leading to the gate. You'll also have a great view of anything south of the wall. You three, stay concealed." Mica pointed to the areas he was talking about.

Flint answers in his usual military manner, "Yes sir. What would you like us to do if we are spotted and attacked by Crafted?"

"Sing out and hold your position. If you risk being overrun, fall back to Station Two with Dolo and Apex."

"Beta Team, that's Apex and Dolo. You'll take Station Two about halfway between here and the Holy Place Gate. Your job is to find cover and observe both directions along the wall as well as the alluvial plain south of the wall. Should danger arise, sing out. After you receive confirmation of your warning hold your position. Remember, it's the fall back for Alpha Team. Alpha and Beta Teams, you're falling back to Station Three if anything happens that you cannot handle and are overwhelmed."

"Yes sir," the two friends respond excitedly.

"The rest of us will go to Station Three near the Holy Place Gate. There we will protect the queen and her brothers."

"Hey Mica, we can take care of ourselves," Jared added. "Just watch out for Kendra."

"Jare, I know. But we don't know what'll happen to the three of you when you take the orange head. Jared and Dana both nodded their acknowledgment.

"You two, your sister, and Jericho will be Omega Team. You'll be stationed on the western side of the wall with the orange dragon head. Kino, Spar, and I make up Charlie Team. Spar, you'll hold Station Three. Kino and I'll patrol from the Omega Team to Beta Team."

Set up like this, we'll have complete control over the only side of the wall open to attack. The majority of the rest of the walls of the castle are immune from a Crafted ground attack because of the high cliffs at the base of the other walls."

In our planning sessions, we decided to take control of the entire southern wall because it's the only area that can be attacked by Crafted from outside the castle. We believe it's possible Baratium's stationed Crafted inside the fortress too. That's why we're taking control of the only two gates in the wall.

We thought of opening a portal to get here but ultimately decided against it. If we'd tried to portal in, we could've opened the portal right into the middle of a bad Crafted party. Multiple portals also wouldn't work this close together. Jericho said it has something to do with magic being warped by space-time. Anyway, the portals would interfere with each other and knock off the targeting.

I watch as Jadeite and Tana take cover near the gate. I only know where they are because I see them take cover. Gargoyles are very good at concealment. It'd be challenging for any human or Crafted to find them. Dolo and Apex are equally adept at concealment near the middle of the long southern castle wall.

At the Holy Place Gate, in the shadow of two very tall towers, each standing more than seventy-five feet tall, Spar hands me off to an on-edge Jared. This is Spar's post at Station Three.

I watch as Jericho is slowly looking around, almost searching the Holy Place Gate. After about a minute, and for the first time since we left Navan, Jericho speaks. "Mica, I apologize. I did not know I would need to adjust your carefully devised plan until this particular point in time. Even so, the three of you, Spar, Kino as well as yourself, must accompany Queen Kendra. I do not know why. I simply know it must be."

"Got it. Let's hustle up. I'm starting to get some bad feelings crawling up my butt. Spar, get Stations One and Two up to date. Station One is to collapse to Station Two on contact with an enemy. Station Two will then protect our rear."

I looked at Mica adoringly. "My love, I'll guard your rear, don't worry about that."

There was a murmur of a laugh.

After Spar returned, the seven of us move together toward the western portion of the wall where Leta is located. We reach the curved area of the wall, leading from the southern side of the wall to the bedrock situated on the western side. Here, I ask Jared to set me down.

My bare feet touch the cold earth. Huh, I lost my shoes somewhere. I look up and see the crenellations atop the massive stone works making up the castle wall. I also see her. As my feet touch, I walk forward as if I'm a dancer walking across a stage to her partner. I feel I'd know precisely where my grandmother Leta's head is even if I were blind and unable to use my dragon's senses.

The ground in this area has built up over the centuries to a point, we can walk up to the grand head. Jared, Dana, and I pause together, transfixed by what we're seeing. As the three of us have a familial love, intrinsic within us after our dragon transformation, we linger, a moment of respect and love as we change into our dragon forms to fly up to the roof of the castle.

Finally, I can wait no longer. I walk up the incline to my grandmother's stone head, and I reach for the etching stylus in my belt. I know, instinctively what I need to do. I don't hesitate. I just touch her elegant forehead with the stylus.

Abruptly, I'm back in suspended animation. It's just her and me. Then I hear her spirit.

"Granddaughter with all my heart and all my love I offer this gift of my memories of my life and those of your great-grandmother Iphigenia. I do not know how your human side will fare, consider that. I had to fight for my own existence when Mother etched her memories into me. It is something you must defeat before the fates release you back to your body after the trial. It was a great test for me, and I was proud to have been able to survive it. Before you touch your stylus to your own head, you must have the surgeon remove the stone from my forehead and hand it to you. Then you use the stylus. I believe in you and that you are able to do much good for the entire world—not just the Ceorfan. If you choose to not take this gift, the world will change and go on. You may not survive and must move on to the spirit realm if you don't accept. I cannot know. Fight and be changed."

I'm a lot like Mica and charge forward telling the mage, "Jericho, we need to take the stone from her head first, then you need to give it to me before I touch the stylus to my own head. She said it'll be a fight for me and I need to consider that, but if I don't do it, the world would change and go on." I leave out the part about I may not survive. I don't want them to try to stop me or make me wait. I can't wait. It is too hard on me, and my decision is made.

Jericho walks up the grade to the top of the wall. I watch as he begins mumbling another spell. I see the shiny purple stone leave her great head without leaving a mark and float gently into his hand.

I hear it calling me, softly, constantly. I listen closer. Nothing more. It is calling me. It glimmers in the moonlight as Jericho puts it into my hands.

Instantly the world blows apart in a shower of sparkles and light. A gust of wind tosses my hair back, and I blink to see better. The stone tells me to press it to my head the way Jericho did the deep green one when I first went to Navan. I hold back.

"I love you with all my heart, you are mine." I look directly into Kino's gaze while I say this, then turn to Spar.

"I love you, you are my everything."

I touch Mica on his hand and indicate to them all with a slight motion. "Come with me please." I can just hold off the plaguing desire to touch the stone to my forehead. It's a struggle, and the lights are blinding me, but just in case, I have to make sure they know what they mean to me. We four are in front of my grandmother's beautiful face, now hovering in the air.

"Mica hold on to me please, I'm weak. I love you. I will not fail or let you go."

Feeling his strong arms gather me to him, I touch the stone to my head, and it sinks in. I start to dream walk the same as I did when the green stone healed me.

I ask the stone, like it's sentient, "What is your intention concerning me?"

There are no words, but I understand that this stone is magic incarnate and wants to now make my grandmother's magic mine. I'm sure that's what it wants *"I accept, but I have to stay awake and not dream walk. I must be etched."* I'm awake, and in control of my body so I touch the stylus to my own head. I feel my body falling and then... well then, I start the fight.

31

DESPAIR

Mica

I FEEL Kendra go limp in my arms when she presses the purple stone to her head, so I hold her tighter. The stone becomes part of her fast. She's aware and sighs as she touches her stylus to her head to begin the etching process. Boneless, she relaxes into me like a dead man. Kino's eyes go wide, and he starts to sing, reaching for us both.

Spar yells, "Get 'er back to Navan!"

I yell at Jericho, "Mage, what is this? What do we do? Help her!"

I feel Kino's song trying to calm me. Kino is far too good at this I think as my shoulders relax... a little.

"Jericho," I tell him, "open a portal, we're taking her home, now!"

Spar is close to us and enters the portal to our rooms just in front of both princes and Jericho. I lay her down gently and comb the hair from her eyes before I let Kino in to help. He and Jericho take over. Kendra's pet bat lands on her chest, chirping and will not be moved.

"All of you, please, go wait in the sitting area. I will inform you of the queen's condition after I examine our Edling," Jericho says matter of factly.

Spar says, growling between clenched teeth, "Okay, but do it now and do it right mage! Kino, you watch and make sure he does, and she's all right. I'm trusting you." Then he stomps off to wait. My roar backs him up as I follow him to the sitting area.

Mega pulses. Without waiting for a return pulse, he enters Kendra's sitting area and is heading straight for us. He asks, "What happened and where are the others?"

"Oh shit! We forgot! We left them sheltering in concealment along the southern wall of the castle. Come on Spar, let's show Mega where they are and go get 'em."

"Slow down just a minute Mica. Tell me first what made you leave them there in the first place," he states with a bit of fire in his voice.

I tell him the whole story, and just as I finish, Flint, Amber, Mason, and Ore come into the room. Damn, this room is turning into Grand Central Station. But, I know they are all rightly concerned. From experience, I think Mega has asked them telepathically, to come with us. That's when I add, "Dana I'll take you back, so you can get the dragon's head removed from the wall too if you are ready."

"Give me a few seconds, I've called in some extra help, so we can get this done quicker," he says as he puts away his tablet. While we're waiting on Dana's team, Jericho comes into the seating area from Kendra's bedroom where we're gathered. Since his back was to the door, I tug Spar aside, so Jericho can enter unobstructed.

Jericho shakes his head slowly, a grim visage spreading across his face. "I have tried all means within my power to reach our queen. She is in an unknown discontinuity, suspending her between worlds. I cannot contact her. She is not dreamwalking. Her body is not injured, and she is breathing nicely. There is nothing wrong with her. She is not in danger of having her physical being... lost. Yet. I believe the best course of action is to do... nothing. At least for now. Kino is with her now. If her suspended state lasts for more than an hour, we will put in an IV for fluids and nutrients, so her body does not degenerate."

"Fuck that mage," I growl, "use magic. I've seen you use magic to heal others plenty of times, use it to heal her like you did when she was shot."

Spar put out an arm to hold me back. What the hell? I'm not going to hurt him. I guess it might look like it though, so I try to calm down some.

"I have exerted every type of magic and used every appropriate spell in furtherance of your goal my dear friend Mica. All forms of magic dissolve around her. There is a magical field of force surrounding her,which is simultaneously protecting her as well as preventing my ministrations. I believe it is up to her to quit this discontinuity," Jericho ends gloomily.

"General, I'm going to see my lady. Then when I get back if Dana's men are here, we will go. If you are ready."

"Yes, young prince, we are ready and waiting," Mega says.

Dana says, "My men are minutes away. We'll be ready too."

Spar comes with me over to Kendra. Kino is sitting in her bed with her. He lifts his head as approval for us to approach.

"She is not here, and yet is here, my brothers." The sorrow in his voice hurts my heart. I grab him in a fierce hug. Spar puts his hands on each of us then goes over and starts telling Kendra we are going to go get Leta's head now and how much we love her.

I let go of Kino and lean down and kiss her.

"Kino, watch over her we'll be back soon," I say.

We walk back to the others, and Dana's crew is with them.

"Alright everyone, earbuds to channel three. Jericho, will you please open the portal for us. I've got my stone and can get us home if you need to stay here."

"There is nothing further I can do for her. I can be of more assistance by going with you," he says as he opens the portal.

We step into the portal, this time he opens near Station Two. We find that those at Station One had already fallen back here when they saw our evacuation portal open. Jared walks up to the ones we'd left and tells them what'd happened. They're all slump-shouldered and looking grim as Jared finishes delivering the news. That's when Jared and Dana excuse themselves and head out with Dana's crew to begin the process of collecting Leta's dragon's head with as much respect and speed as possible.

All I want, and need is to get back to Kendra. *Typical Mica attitude... I'm never satisfied with where I am and what I am doing. Damnit, Mica. Get your head in the game.*

As we settle in, and the others begin talking, telling stories and asking questions... all about the queen. It is here that the quiet Tana starts a story to take our minds off of the wait.

"When I was a girl," she starts, "I was the fifth daughter of a poor warrior who was gone most of the time on the queen's business. Even when he could be home he wasn't. Queen Leta was walking through the market near the Dardanos Gate. There," she pointed near the apple tree that Dana had grown. "she saw me, a dirty little urchin. My queen walked straight toward me. I was afraid I was about to be punished. She had an apple in her hand and asked me if I wanted it. I had never seen one before and quizzically asked her what it was. She bent down to me and looked into my eyes blowing her dragon's breath on it and passed it to me saying, 'It is food, and you eat it.' I was planning to take it home to share with my sisters and my mother, but she waited and urged me to take a bite. I took a small one—it was the most wonderful thing I had ever tasted. She could tell I loved it and gave me two more saying, 'Come to visit me in the castle Tana. I want to spend some time with you. Will you do that?' I could not have imagined that it would be the beginning of the best friendship I have ever known. Her decisions were always made with others in mind, even to the blowing on an apple for a skinny poor child in the market. Does anyone else have a memory to share on this monumental day of this great lady?"

As Apex began his story, I decided to check in with the recovery team. I'd been listening to parts of what was going on with the Duke of Storms and the Duke of Stones throughout Tana's story. It seems the recovery attempt is moving along well.

I really need to pay attention to them, I decided. Kendra will kill me if I let anything happen to them. On the other hand, they'll be equally as pissed if they think I am babysitting 'em. My compromise was to use the electronic earbuds that Dolo had supplied. These allow me to hear every word and keeps me out of their way.

I see a bolt of lightning behind the group seated along the center of the southern wall of Castle Ilioilion. While they continue the storytelling, I decide to take a closer look. The lightning may be noth... nope, it's something 'cause there's another one.

Not wanting to interrupt, yet, I fly up behind everyone to get a good look at what is going on with the Dukes. What I see isn't very good. Things are about to get busy.

32

I LOST HER

Mica

"ALRIGHT EVERYONE UP AND READY. It looks like we have some Crafted in the area. Dolo, Apex take flight with me. The rest of you move to Station Three, the Holy Place Gate. Hold that gate. It's our only way out."

Dolo, Apex, and I fly toward the Dukes. What we find is more interesting than we would have imagined. It appears as if one of the castle walls collapsed. Out of the opening, crafted are pouring... hundreds of them! "Well, if this isn't a bloody bag of dicks!" I yell to no one.

Not surprising, Jared and Dana are doing quite well against the hordes of Crafted. As I fly as quickly as I can, I watch as dozens of crafted are fried by each of Jared's lightning blasts, one right after another. Beside him, Dana has manipulated the earth to form a giant hole under dozens more. After they're in the hole, Dana crushes the trapped monsters with a massive rock.

It looks as if they are holding off the masses of crafted to allow Dana's men to remove Leta's head. In such close quarters combat, I wouldn't have expected them to be this successful against such a mobbed attack. I direct Dolo to help with Leta. The Dukes look like they have a weak spot forming. Apex and I swoop down to fill it.

Crafted have never been particularly good warriors. They're effective only because of the numbers they can bring to bear. Also, if they do happen to get hold of you, they're quite strong and can hurt you quickly.

Apex and I aren't taking out the numbers of Crafted as are Jared and Dana. We have effectively plugged the leak they had on their right flank though. As the destroyed Crafted pile up too much, the Duke of Stone opens another hole to let the remains fall into.

The four of us seem to have gotten into a rhythm. There is the flash, boom from Jared, the gravely crunching from Dana, and the bop, pow, bang from Apex and me. Dramatically, I hear Dolo yell, "We've got her!"

Jared yells to everyone, "Alright, we need to clear a path to get out of here. I watch in amazement as Dana builds a wall of sand which is then hardened into an amazingly strong stone by the lightning from Jared. Within less than thirty seconds, the two of them built a path for our escape.

I yell, "Everyone, run! Now!" I see Jared take his grandmother's great head and gently wrap it in a large brilliant orange silk cloth. The embroidery on the fabric is very intricate and recalls the wonderful days of her childhood spent living in early Greece. Tana had made this for her friend and queen to be used at this time. It is obvious how much Jared cares about the Ceorfan. With all of the fighting, running and so forth, he still took the time to honor Tana and Leta.

Since I want to cover our retreat, I'm the last one out. The crafted are beating against the wall, like waves on a rocky outcropping. But they aren't getting through—yet. Suddenly they seem to find purchase... I watch as they pour over the wall by the dozens. I let everyone know they are on our tail. "Jericho, I need you to prepare the portal. Everyone else, prepare to evacuate quickly. I mean it, be fast!"

I can only imagine the look on everyone's face as we round the corner. We had to looked ridiculous. Sprinters, we're not. The others have cleared the gate in the castle wall, so I fly ahead to defend them as they pass.

When I look back, I see the ferocity in the looks on each face. Each person convinced they will not let this mission fail. I hear lots of yelling, but I can't understand it. It just adds to the general din surrounding us.

"Jericho, open the portal now. Come on Ceorfan—let's get out of here. Hurry! Hurry!" Everyone starts toward portal except Tana. She's headed toward Jared and Dana.

I notice now that the Crafted are now much closer than they were. I quickly spot the problem. Another breach has allowed Crafted to exit the castle almost on top of us. As soon as I see how close the enemy are to Jared and his group, I take off toward him. Flint and Jadeite stay with me. Apex and Dolo turn and now move back to support us.

As the retreating group is close to passing me, I point to the portal shouting, "Go." Then I flip my stone to Dana, so he'll close the portal after us. He's at the tail end of those running for the portal. If I weren't so busy, I'd laugh because he reminds me of Fred Flintstone on steroids. He even gives me a little grin as he passes me.

I catch up to Tana as she bashes the first of the Crafted with a big rock. The thing splinters to shreds, but there are dozens more to take its place. I grab one closest to me and use it to bowl down several others at the same time. I see Mason close behind me bashing the ones who are still moving.

I keep going, but I am getting surrounded. The wooden army may not be able to think on their own, but the one controlling them has them ganging up to take me out. I could avoid them by flying. But I can't leave the others. Behind me, Jadeite stands after fighting his way through and pressing his back to mine.

He says, "Three-four-butt-kisser."

I got it. We move at the same time, and my green soldier's momentum lets me flip him over my shoulder and onto a crowd of the Carved while he hangs onto my hands my head level with his butt—hence the name. Within the confusion we created by clearing a path forward I see a dark mage. Huddling over a large staff like the one described as the staff we had remembered as the Caor Thintri, or the ball of lightning.

I shout, "Take out the mage." Who I think is Barat. Only then, do I see how close Tana is compared to me. I watch as she reacts instantly. She screams as she charges Barat.

The only thing I have time to do is fly up to present a target for the mage, other than Tana.

He sees me, and without ever taking his eyes off of me, he shoots a ball of fire at her. The blast just misses her. Particles from the rico-chet hit her as she snatches the staff out of his hands and turns to run with it then falters as I speed quickly at them both.

I don't change my course. I will take this motherfucker down. I see Tana near him. She is down. I press toward him, then watch help-lessly as he waves his arms over his head. Then he along with all the Crafted are gone. I slam into the side of the bluff leading up to the castle, right where Barat was, less than a second ago. Turning and getting my bearings I find Tana.

She's still breathing and asks me, "Did the others get away? Are they all through the portal? Did they get my queen home, Mica?" She puts my hand on the staff she has stolen back from the evil villain and quiets. I tuck the staff into my belt behind my back.

"Yes, noble lady they are all safe, and Queen Leta is home. That is where I'm taking you now, just hang on." I lift her easily in my arms and walk to the ruins where we'd be hoping someone is on the way to open another portal for us. As I close the distance to the spot we had been waiting just minutes ago, I see Dana standing there waiting for us. The portal had been closed, but he's opening another. I feel Tana slacken in my arms. Looking at her, I know she's gone from this realm. Flint sees and gently closes her eyes. Not a bird chirps or a cricket sounds. All is silent as we enter the portal. Dana looks around making sure all our remaining number have come through and then closes the opening.

I take Tana to the medical facility in Navan hoping just maybe there is a chance. The medical personnel responds as soon as I'm through the door. I lay her on one of the floating stretchers, and they begin to examine her. So, I walk over to the waiting area and sit down with my head in my hands.

Mega reaches for me with his tele-speak and asks for a report. I'm lost. All I can think back is; *"She gave her life, so the others could take the old queen's head to safety with themselves. She fought valiantly, then that motherfucker hit her with fire from his hellish hands and killed her. The doctors are just coming to talk to me Mega, stay linked with me."*

Flint says, "I am so sorry Commander Mica, there is nothing we can do, she is gone. Is there someone we should call to come help you?"

"No. Please call this brave lady's family. I will speak with them later. They have the right to know how she died."

"Did you hear that Mega—Tana is dead."

"Come to my office and debrief before you go home, Mica. I will have food and drink for you here."

When I get to Mega's office, Jadeite is already there with all the Ducere except Kino. I step to Spar, and he puts a hand on my shoulder. I look into his eyes and see that he is here for me, understanding my pain. I take the lightning staff and hand it to my commander. He takes it from me, then pauses for a few seconds to tele-speak to someone, I guess. I hope it is Jericho to come and dispose of the hateful relic.

"Commander Mica, your report please," Mega states.

"Yes, sir. You know that we were on a mission to retrieve Queen Leta's head from the Castle Ilioilion. Queen Kendra was there to be etched. After accepting the jewel from the old queen and being etched, she fell into a coma-like trance state. In the heat of the moment, we opened a portal to bring her home to safety as quickly as possible—as is our policy. After she was settled and found to be living but not waking, and knowing there was nothing further we could do for her, we returned to finish the mission.

When we arrived by portal, the Duke of Stone and his team started the removal process while the rest of the Ducere stayed with the High Guild members who were positioned in the ruins of Diana for concealment. The Duke of Storms was with his brother. We didn't expect any large-scale entanglements, but we remained concealed to keep the Ceorfan secret and cause no international conflict.

We had been in the area approximately an hour when the Duke of Storms started attacking a large number of Crafted seen swarming their location. The Duke of Stone began helping his brother. Apex, Dolo, and I went to their aid. I asked everyone else to stay behind, partially for their protection.

After a brief time, where the Dukes destroyed more than a hundred Crafted, Queen Leta's head was freed. During our escape, and as we neared those who remained behind, High Guild member Alexandritana ran toward the Duke of Storms and indeed, she ran past him. That is when I noticed the Crafted hot on the heels of the escaping Duke of Storms and Duke of Stone.

Tana was in combat mode and destroyed several Crafted before I arrived on the site with Jadeite, Flint, and Mason. We were being overcome by the sheer numbers of Crafted when Tana charged the mage Barat. I acted for a distraction but wasn't quick enough. She was able to seize the staff but lost her life as a result of mage fire." At this, I turn and ask the others if they have anything to add.

Hearing no one speak Mega says, "You and your team have given the Ceorfan a great victory today commander. Please sit and eat while I question the others."

Dolo was in the debrief room and was filling out the reports. I'm relieved because if I have to write it all before I go rest, it'll be a real chore. I'm tired. Even so, what I really want to do is plan tactics for Barat's demise. That's just what I'm mulling over when I'm snapped out of it by Mega saying my name.

"Commander Mica, you and your men are dismissed. Get some rest we will meet with the High Guild tonight to plan our retaliation tactics."

"No Mega, I'm all right. I need to call TASS and get this information..." I'm stopped when he places a big meaty hand on my shoulder and says, "Mica stand down son."

I turn to Flint and nod to him. He dismisses the Ducere and leaves.

Mega says, "Mica I understand how you feel. This is the moment that the welfare of the men needs to be addressed, you among them. You need to rest. TASS has a representative who already is with them and reporting as we speak. We will have more information tonight when we wake along with a new perspective. Now leave, check on our queen and sleep so I can get some responsibilities taken care of in the few minutes I have left before I torp."

Dismissed I get up and head to Kendra's room in a robotic style not thinking just moving by muscle memory. It's killing me that she is laying there so still.

"Kino, how is she?" I ask.

"She has not changed my brother. I have an inkling that she is dreaming, due to her eyes moving like she is in a REM cycle. When I am touching her, she is calmer. It is getting time to torpify will you stay and sleep beside her? I am sure it will only help you both. I know I will feel better if you are here with her when I cannot be."

"Yes, that is what I really want. So there is nothing we can do?"

"We have discovered no way to wake her brother. She is far from us. I expect she will wake when she is ready. She is strong and will make it through this. I decree it and will it to be so with everything in me."

Right then Spar enters asking, "Well?"

"No changes brother, she seems well, just asleep. Let's make a pact," he says, reaching for us with both hands. We take his hands in ours, and he says, "One of us will stay with her at all times, but we will continue with the plans she was working toward and go forward knowing she is going to recover. Deal?"

"Deal!" We both say it at the same time a pulse covering us all and sealing the oath. They move across the room to the posing stage. I think it is bigger than I remember. I wonder if the room adjusts for us on its own? We smile slightly when we all say, "Wings up," for each other, at the same time.

I lie down and softly touch Kendra's hand. Folding it into mine. Her little friend Elmer is still perched on her chest as still as she is. I'm afraid to cuddle too close in case I hurt her while I sleep. She smells so good and looks so beautiful. Kino is right she seems like she is dreaming. Those are my last thoughts as I slip off to sleep myself.

33

ANCESTORS

Kendra

I'M FALLING. No Mica has me. Again... though he isn't here with me. I'm falling back, then suddenly I surge forward. The stop isn't jarring. But, it is sudden and takes me to a tunnel filled with very thick heavy air. It looks like a massive fog bank is surrounding me as I walk through the tunnel and out into a place I don't remember ever being too. Especially in the area of Turkey where we are so that my grandmother can etch me.

I pause for a second and look around. As I do, I come to one inescapable fact, I am not in the same place as I was. No one is here with me. I'm alone. While that's different, I don't feel my donum warning me, so I continue looking around.

Without any clear idea of where I am heading, I start walking. I'm actually on a path, a rocky little roadway. I don't remember any road that looks like this. I'm pushing forward more as the ground inclines in a steady upward slope. I decide to just go with my gut. This must be the right way to go, so I persist in this course, then I see it.

A stone compound, attractive but still a compound, is close and before me. But now my donum is starting to nag me. I stop and look around for cover. This area is mostly a vast plain with little cover. I take my only option and hide behind a cluster of large boulders to take stock of my situation. I start to turn and sit. As I do, I have just enough time to dodge a sword strike headed directly for my head. But... by a stranger. A stranger who looks vaguely familiar to me. One who nonetheless has it in his mind to do me bodily harm it would seem.

The fact that it's a little chilly here has no effect on this guy. He's dressed in little to nothing and looks much like my goyles in build, broad and muscular. His, I don't even have a word for what to call it, it's little more than a breechcloth, just much nicer. Black leather with decorative studs, belts crisscross his body holding sheaths full of weapons including a sword.

At this point it's obvious he's a gargoyle, and he's trying to talk to me. The problem is on my end I can't understand a word. I have lots of voices speaking in my head at once, and pictures of places and things are zooming around in there too. I'm getting woozy while I'm concentrating on figuring out what he is saying; I feel a sharp pain in my head, and I fall forward into the blackness again.

I wake when a hand touches the tender part of my head. That must be where he hit me. That man... that stranger who used my head to stop his sledge-hammer or whatever it was he hit me with.

"Leta, darling, are you awake?" says a soft melodic voice close to me.

"I'm awake, and my head is killing me, but my name's Kendra. Where am I and what is that buzzing sound?"

"Darling, you are home in Troy, where do you think you are? Kendra... hmmm... Leta let me see your head. The stunning woman who's speaking reaches for me. I catch her hand before she touches me. I see the surprise in her beautiful hazel green eyes as if she has all the rights in the world to touch me. But I'm looking at my own hand.

It isn't mine. This hand is too pale and larger than my hands. What the hell is going on here?

"Who are you? What's going on? I am Kendra Macbard, queen of the Ceorfan, and I demand some answers," I say.

"Now that is a fun new game Leta, but I assure you, I am queen—a position you are just training for at this time. I can tell, daughter, that you need some rest. That bump that Traver gave you has not changed your ability to joke with your mother."

Mother? Sensing that I should go with the flow, I ask, "Traver why did he hit me in the head... ummm... mother?"

"He saw someone he says was attacking Krag and didn't realize it was you, with you being so far from the castle. I have warned him against trying that to your face. Try to take it easy on him if he does, but give him a good lesson for us all, Leta dear."

"Oh, you can be sure of that," I tell her.

She laughs and says, "You are so like your father. Sleep sweet girl. I will send you something to eat in a while. Jewel will want to see you are well too. She has been waiting so patiently for you to waken."

I nod my head at her, causing what looks like ripples in the air, making everything vibrate with a hundred thoughts going through my brain at the same time. When she's gone, I scoot to the edge of a very soft bed and stand up on my feet. I'm steadier than I thought given how dizzy I am, so I walk around the room seeing if I can discover where I am.

I see a mirror on the wall... a beautiful white marble wall. Interestingly, it looks like the walls in Navan. It seems like... Stop it, Kendra, focus. You are going to look in the mirror! When I glimpse into the mirror, I'm flabbergasted. I'm not only not where I think I am, now I am not even who I think I am. That person's not also me. It is someone who has beautiful orange-red hair...

"Grandmother, can you hear me?" Nothing.

Well, these people here think I'm Leta. That's something. Nonetheless, how am I going to get home? What do I have to do? She told me to fight to survive. Who do I fight? If things stay the same, my life seems pretty nice, no fighting involved. I return to the bed and lie back to think. So, if I'm here with Leta's body where is my body?

There's a quiet knock at my door. A large woman smiles at me coming near and sits close to me. She moves a strand of my hair behind my ear and says, "Leta, I was so worried. Are you feeling all right or do you think I need to send for a healer?"

"I'm just fine. Don't worry. Are you Jewel?"

Shock shows on her kind face as she replies, Leta you have known me all of your life. I'm calling the healer." She runs out of the room before I have a chance to stop her. I guess I'll have to come up with a plan. What kind of story can I tell the healer? I'm going to try the truth.

It doesn't take long, and a mage knocks on my door. He's dressed pretty much the same way Jericho dresses, but he isn't human, he's a different kind of being though. I don't understand how, but I know it's true. One who looks mostly human shaped but bigger. He has skin that looks like coffee with lots of cream, is that a shimmer on his skin? His hair is a little past his ears and curls at his neck. The top is pulled back in an ornate clip with the rest down.

He sits on a stool near my bed and looks at me silently. I ask him, "Aren't you gonna do anything?"

He replies, "Edling Leta, My name is Gortanik. I have been instructed that you have lost your mind. I was summoned to mend it. Given your peculiar way of running words together maybe they have a point. What is going on with you? I wonder, is it at all possible that the bump on your head has addled your brain?"

"The truth is, I'm Kendra, and I'm not from here. I'm not even from this century. I went to my grandmother to be etched and fell into this dream where I'm in her body. I have no idea what's going on, or where my real body is at the moment. Everything is out of sync, my mind has so many voices. It has music too. Can you help me? Please?"

He waits, puts a hand to his face and scrubs up and down a few times in delay, searching her statement for deceit. Not finding any, he says, "I know you are not lying to me. It is my gift—to tell if someone is lying. Let me get you some food, and then we can talk about how to help you get back into your body."

"Okay," I tell him, relieved that he actually believes me. Again, I fall forward into the darkness as time does this odd skip forward. I groan as it squeezes my head in a tight grip of stabbing pain. Gortanik is with me still, no that's not right, again. We are in a different room, and he is dressed differently. I know he is trying to help and will keep me safe.

Another skip forward and my whole body is tortured by the pain. I don't even care what is going on around me. I notice other people are trying to help me. I'm holding onto Gortanik's hand for dear life and he's letting me. He's my anchor. I'm fading out trying to deal with the pain. I vaguely hear him talking to someone and telling them he's not leaving me. The pain is all I can handle it's getting so bad that I just can't... then I remember... fight. I won't give up I have too much that needs to be finished. My people need more, my goyles... I need them.

Suddenly, I find myself in my own head again. I reach for one of the pictures spinning around. When I do, it dissolves into my hand giving me a high feeling of happiness. My hands are hot from feeling the memory. Deciding this is the answer I reach for another memory. Agony, the pressure of a deep wound. Sucking in my breath, I hold onto the thought, and it too dissolves into my hand. Shaking from the trauma of that memory I brace myself for more.

Turning my hands over as I look at them I see they are getting redder from the heat of the visions. *I'm still me at least. I'm the one living, or is it re-living the memories. Maybe it is both.*

The lifetimes of not just Leta, but also her mother Iphigenia are swirling around in my head like a tornado. I think I might lose myself and fade into them. *There is so much to deal with. How do I get through this confusion? I just have to keep going until I can't. That's my decision, and I'm going forward.*

No sooner than I made the decision, I grab the next event and watch, as it too dissolves into my hand. The next one takes both hands, it's life-changing it takes my breath away. The wonder of having a child. The love is so big it bursts from the recollection into every pour of my being. I understand more about life. There's so much more than I could have possibly known.

Yet, I feel myself weaken as each memory melts into me. Both my hands and arms are burning. The heat is far beyond what I can take. Exhaustion is taking over as my hands begin to shake. I'm so drained.

Panting I pull another vision into me. Ahhh, it brings me to a knee! This makes some of the worst things I have ever faced seem like just a growing experience. Collapsing to both knees, I think I have overtaxed my body, and then I know it. "Arghhh," I roar and keep pushing and grabbing more of the images. Even my scream is weakening as I fall forward.

Just as I decide the pain is too much, I feel the presence of my consorts. They're all with me! I have no doubt they're helping. I have no doubt who they are. They are part of me, and I'm trusting them to help. Their energy is filling me up, and it gives me a much needed second to think.

"No! I will not give up!" I scream into the void. I square my shoulders and push myself up again. I roar, this time using my dragon voice. It likes this feeling, this heat. It's enjoying this experience immensely. I do feel stronger.

My dragon side is the key! It must be. So, I push my dragon blood forward and change to my red dragon shape. I feel my goyles even more pronounced as soon as I change. They're adding to my strength. Oh, how I have missed you all! I think.

We're a team, and this is bringing us closer than we've ever been. I sink into my loves the way the etched lives of my grandmothers sank into me. I'm safe now, I do trust them! They are mine! I fall and rest in them, closing my eyes, I will call myself into my body.

34

UNITED

Kino

I FIGHT to forget the previous days in which I had remained awake for the entirety of my torp period. Yet my mind is drawn to it, akin to a princess, to her lovers. I cannot but remember the day my Queen Leta sacrificed herself for us. I was not there, but her gift got me released from a madman.

It is not possible for me to rest or relax while my beloved drifts, alone in her suspended sleep. Her beauty, her healthy appearance belie the perilous state of her stillness. I wish with all my being that she is just sleeping in Mica's arms.

Throughout our time of rest, I am envisioning every spell I know, to sing it over her. There is nothing. Nothing I know will obviously help. The old mage had said she is unreachable. Possibly. More probably, she must fight.

As I am the elder of our family, I feel I should take watch over and guide the others. They are also mine to protect. I must find a way to remedy this situation.

I know how strong of mind and body my beloved is. I have faith she will rejoin me. She will return. I cannot tell what will happen or how I will go on if she loses this battle... fight... battle... Maybe we can help... but we must work together. If we unite as one, we can will our strength into her. We can only see what it brings. Night time cannot come soon enough so that I might try to see if my idea has any merit.

The daylight is waning. I start to feel the tingle as my body returns to flesh. There is a soft crackle, and I am free to move about. Spar breaks out of his torp and rushes to say, "Kino I have an idea."

I wait for him to voice his thoughts before I tell him mine.

"What if we all put our hands on Kendra and you sing our power into her?" he says, his voice excited with the idea.

I smile to myself so that he will not think that I am laughing at him or not taking him seriously. I am happy though that we think alike after only being bound to Kendra for a few days.

"I believe you might have something there. I would like us to break our fast and let Mica also have food then try this experiment, so we are at our best to start. I also would like to invite mage Jericho for safety measures."

My brothers and I each check on Kendra. We each take our turns with her. I have to touch her. She looks to be concentrating, and her body is tight like she is in a fight. Otherwise, she seems much as she did yesternight when we laid her here after the etching. It must have worked. Mayhap there is something which she must resolve herself.

I touch Mica on the shoulder to wake him and tell him we may have an idea which will help. He instantly pops up and takes a swing at me. I quickly duck out of his way. I know he doesn't like to be touched to wake, so I am ready for his combative response.

"We have a plan," Spar says as he starts for the kitchen area.

The chefs have started on the breakfast foods and are setting it on the buffet. Spar and I do not wait, energized by the thought we might be able to help our lady. Mica is dragging up and sits without getting food. Spar tells him that we want to try giving Kendra some of our power, so she can wake up.

I push my plate over to Mica and get up to get me another. He is more awake now and starts eating without a complaint. When we are almost finished, we feel a pulse asking to enter. Mica is the first to pulse back. Mega walks into the room with Jericho.

Mega asks, "Is she any better? Are there any changes?" His head is wrinkled with worry, and his shoulders are tight.

I answer, "No, but we have decided on a path forward. We believe it might be possible to share our strength with our beloved. We plan to lay our hands upon her while I sing strength to her and see if she can wake. If you have anything to add, this is the time mage because we do not feel inclined to wait much longer."

"Might I suggest that you all tighten your hold on the cords that bind you together as well. I will also perform a spell so that you can see the bonds to help you fortify them. Shall we try it now?" Jericho says.

"Of course, we do not wish to wait," I answer motioning them all to join me as I walk to Kendra's bedside.

Everyone positions themselves around her. Mica sits at the right of her touching her and holding her hand to his heart, Spar is close to the head of the bed with his hands on her head, I am on her left side holding onto her hand too. I start a low silky smooth melody.

Jericho is singing beside me. His tune getting louder as the room seems to change. The lights darken, and the blood bond threads are brightening. I put my other hand on the one connecting me to my beloved and sing strength into her.

Our bonds pulse with energy from us. Our strength moving to our lady as we each meet her needs. Mica is pulsing his bright orange passion and his fiery red warrior energy. Spar's is pulsing his yellow wisdom and burnt orange authority. And mine is pulsing the azure blue of my determination and my aureate gold of my longing for my beloved.

The others are standing, eyes closed. I watch, joined with my family, as the light from our bonds grow. The power transfer is immense and is radiating to her. To her head. To her heart. To her body.

We are connected, the four of us. Here I see a very tiny, but non-trivial intense pink pulse of energy coming from the spot on Kendra's chest where Elmer is laying. As I know the effort that Elmer is putting in, my heart is buoyed. We must be on the right track.

I see Mica and Spar open their eyes in shock. Simultaneously, the three of us feel it... we have lost control of our energy. No, we did not lose our control, Kendra's dragon self has taken it over, and she begins to roar.

Relief floods my body as I realize she is waking. She pulses a booming pulse which shakes me. It tells me she is aware and loves me and she is happy I sacrificed for her. Thank the creator!

I nod to the others who also know she is all right now. We all gather her to us in a big happy family hug carefully of Elmer who is pulsing wildly. My beloved cups her hand over him and pulses a little pulse to him. Satisfied, Elmer takes wing and flies away, while we continue touching and greeting Kendra.

I am not holding back the tears and have to stop singing to say, "Let us not do that again, beloved. I do not think I can stand another such occurrence!" We all smile nodding our heads in agreement.

"Damn straight, Hun. This has got to stop, you about gave me a heart attack!" Spar tells her emotionally.

Mica is rubbing her hair back from her face and keeps repeating, "I thought I lost you."

I just gather them all closer squeezing with my big arms the ones who I will not do without. I breathe in their smells and make a note in my head to pay special attention to each of them. I am not trying to be self-serving, but I need my beloved to myself soon!

35

SAD TIDINGS

Kendra

THE FOG BEGINS TO CLEAR. The grey-black edges moving slowly away from the center of my vision. The brilliant white light replacing it overwhelms my brain, flooding it with more sensations than I think I'm ready for. So, I close my eyes.

With everything I am, I know that my dragon was the catalyst which allowed me to burn my way through the memories and etch them. It's as intrinsically clear that without the supercharge added by my consorts, I wouldn't have made it through the etching process. I need some time with my three goyles to thank them properly for loving me enough to save me.

The pull is powerful for me to see my goyles. I missed them. I must've been gone a very long time... days or even weeks or longer. I distinctly remember multiple events where I experienced joy, pain and yes, the sickness. I know for sure that these events aren't part of my recently etched memories. I lived them with the associated time seeming to pass routinely. Whatever, whether it's been three minutes or three years, I've got a deep longing to see my goyles and be home.

So, it's understandable how happy I am when I slowly open my eyes for the second time, and my first sight is a wildly chirping and bouncing Elmer. I pulse to him that I'm okay and I want him to go eat. As I watch him fly away, I notice Jericho and Mega in my room with the most handsome of prince consorts ever. I smile at the two of them and say, "Give me an hour, and then we will convene in the allodium to share the information that I've discovered." They nod and back away out of my room.

I feel sure that I'll have a long life with my goyles, so there's nothing to rush. Nope, no rushing, I want each moment with them to be special. I'm not going to waste time either! Mica has been so crushed, so I pull him to me first.

Pressing my lips to his neck first so I can say, "I want you to know how much you mean to me. Give me your best, I'm going to give you mine." I feel the others behind me start to back away to give us some privacy.

"No, don't leave us." I hold up a hand, so they will stop, and say, "I just need a minute with you all. We haven't much time and need to get ready for an HG meeting. I tug on Kino's hand then Spar's and put them on my body. Leaning forward, I kiss Mica softly breathing in his breath as he sighs into my mouth. I don't know who did it, but clawed hands make small work of my clothes. I adjust and sit strad-dling my big amber eyed goyle's lap. Kino is kissing the back of my neck sending chills down my spine. I arch, and Mica holds me by the waist and kisses down my chest. Spar takes my now free mouth with a deep kiss, thrusting his tongue deeply into my mouth rubbing up and down on my side I can feel his erection hard and needy. Hands on my face turn my head, and now my singer is fucking my mouth with his. He holds nothing back as Mica lifts me and turns me around with my back against his front, his hands kneading my sensitive breasts. I hear him sigh as he takes a deep breath smelling my hair. I lift into Kino's hand as he reaches for my throbbing center. I bite Mica's arm which is crossing my shoulder. Spar is kissing me when I pulse to them all and orgasm on Kino's hand. They all stop with a deep sigh highly satisfied that they could do that to me. I want the same for them. I'll give them a minute for their own satisfaction of taking care of me. Now for them...

Right then someone pulses a greeting from the doorway intending to enter. My rooms are one big opened cave concept, even though the bedroom area is farther away from the door than the living space, we would be seen easily. Every one of us takes action. Kino jerks up, starting for the opening when Mica scoots out from behind me and shoots into the secret entrance. Spar jumps up and is standing on the bed. I use the momentum of Mica shifting me to twist through the air, land on my feet, and throw my arms out in front of me pointing a finger at the entrance to the chamber.

With a commanding voice, I say, "No entrance."

A flare of purple magic weaves a net of light on the doorway. Whoever is wanting in will definitely have to wait.

"Wow, that's so cool! Did you guys see that? Haha, I love it," I say.

They must have because of the shit-eating grins they've got plastered on their faces. We can all see now that Jadeite is outside of the doorway, but it is apparent that he can't see in. Kino asks him what he wants, and he says, "I want to be sure my queen is all right and to tell you all the High Guild is meeting in the queen's allodium."

So, we can see and hear him. He can't see us or enter the room but can hear us. I walk over to Kino and put a hand to his stomach leaning into him as he wraps a muscled arm around me. Jadeite, I'm just fine. Thank you for asking. I'll meet you in my meeting room in fifteen minutes. I watch as he leaves then I smile up into Kino's face. Haha, that was fun! He smiles back at me with joy.

"Are you all okay with that? Can you wait for your own gratification or shall we run away and join the Hewn?" I ask.

Kino laughs with gusto and Mica joins him in glee. Spar has a questioning look on his gorgeous face.

I try to explain, "Spar, the Hewn are Ceorfan who for many reasons do not live in Navan. Some are pirates, some outlaws, some just can't stand the confining space. They're mostly nomads who survive on the bleeding edge of life. They'll..." Seeing his serious face, I chuckle and say, "It was funnier when I thought it." The other two laugh again.

Mica says, "Soon we'll take you to meet some of the Freebirds we call the Hewn. We do have business now though. Princess, let's send a family pulse to the people right now and let them know you're all right so they'll know and not worry anymore."

"Good idea, handsome." We pull each other together in a big huddle and pulse a happy message to the Ceorfan. I get up on wobbly feet, unsure if it is from my etching, or my... celebration. Spar, Mica, and Kino each reach to steady me at the same time, causing me to laugh again. Now everything is funny, and I am snorting I'm giggling so hard.

Hugging them all, I say, "I know you were with me and gave me your strength. Giving me your oomph made it possible for me to continue to fight and to get back to my body. Thank you, I couldn't do any of this without you."

They tell me in varying ways that they're here for me and love me before I head to my bathroom. When I get back, they're there in my sitting area joking and talking to each other. This is special, I take just a second to relish the family closeness they're displaying. This is what I want. This is why I keep pushing through the awful times. This... it's more than just a reward it's precisely the way I want to live. I jerk myself out of my thoughts and walk up to them with a bounce.

I quip, "Ready to start? We have lots to share with the HG." I'm going to have to thank Clifton for dubbing them that. I like it—it's more my style. We almost skip through the secret tunnel to the allodium.

Mega is in his large, carved seat already, but many of the other members are milling around the room. I take a minute to decide if I approve. I conclude this is very much what I want. I walk over to the coffee maker sitting on the bar in the kitchen area and pour myself a cup. Then I grab a jalapeno-cheese bagel. I'm not bothering with a plate, and I just sit my bagel on a napkin in front of me as I sit. I know the reaction I'll get, and that's what I'm going for—a more relaxed atmosphere.

My people have been too tightly strung, and I know I've played my part in it. I'm sure it was stressful enough for them to fear to lose a queen they hadn't thought they'd have to begin with. The members follow my lead and quiet and wait while they break their fast.

I use the quiet to start. "This meeting of the High Guild is come to order," I begin. They seem surprised that I start instead of asking Count de Treon. Let them wonder, it's time they see the leader, not the organizer.

"Continue eating while I give you my information and perspective on the events of the past day. Then I need to know what happened here. I know from my grandmother's memories that there have been only two previous Ceorfan queens."

I look around the room and watch the heads bob up and down. "I have lots to tell you, so please be patient with me. Some of this may seem unnecessary, but I assure you it is." Again, I pause and watch their head bobs...

"Part of the information which needs etched in Navan is that when a queen is etched the process is a test of both strength and will. I'm sure I wouldn't have survived if the prince consorts hadn't given me their strength when and how they did. It was a gift that the timing on their part was spot on. Also, if I hadn't known my dragon-self, I wouldn't have survived the encounter at all. I'll go into more detail and etch the story in the Halls of History later, so we don't lose the lesson." I watch as a few guild members acknowledge my consorts and Dana slaps Spar hard on the back. *David and Dana were very close, and that closeness continues with Spar,* I think to myself.

"The more important part of what you need is... when I touched the stylus to my head, I was taken back in time. I entered my grandmother Leta's consciousness. She wasn't queen at this time, her mother Iphigenia still was. Even before I absorbed their memories, I could see they were women to admire and love. During this time, I grew very sick. A mage was sent to tend me. He's also one part of why I was able to survive. He, above all others, chose to believe me. He and I became friends, and we need to get him out of our prison. His name is Gortanik."

The phrase 'quiet as a tomb' comes to mind. There was complete and utter silence. The mirthful look turned to absolute shock on the faces of everyone, and it's priceless. I don't even try to hold back my laughter.

"I assure you, I'm not crazy. I do have the memories of my grand-mothers, but I'm still very much Kendra Macbard. I just have loads more experience to draw on now. I believe that with Gortanik's help we'll have a better chance to find that rats-ass Barat." I try to say his name the way I'd heard Ore say it before the etching trip, making the name sound more like brat and not the b-rat Ore says so well.

"Also, I understand why some jokes are funny that I never got before," I add, attempting to return the mood to its pre-Gortanik relaxation. My attempt went over like a fart in church. It didn't work. All right, I can understand their feelings. Still looking at the disbe-lieving faces around me, I decide to move on. "I also need informa-tion. Did we succeed in bringing Leta's head home? Where is she if we did? Were there any extenuating circumstances which I need to know about? And... while I'm at it, is Tana preparing a ceremony for Leta's body? Is that where she is?"

The room remains silent. However, the mood changes instantly. It grows cold and unreadable. I look around the room and not a single person, except for those closest to me, will make eye contact. All eyes are cast down, shoulders rolled forward. Instantly, I know why Tana isn't here, and the room is deadly silent. I see and feel. I know already she's not okay.

Quietly, I ask, "General Mega, will you please answer my ques-tions. What happened while I was being etched."

My consorts come close to me. Kino gets up and kneels beside me and puts a hand on my knee. Spar and Mica stand behind me, each with a hand on one of my shoulders.

Mega nods at my consorts and starts his tale. He tells me everything which transpired including what happened to me from their perspective. He tells me that Tana is a heroine and snatched the Caor Thintri from the villainous Barat before he killed her with mage fire.

Now it is my turn. I sit in silence. I can't help myself as tears stream from my eyes. I watch Mega, so he'll continue.

"Her body is in the Queen's vault as we speak, Edling. Now that you are awake, what are your instructions concerning her?" he asks with respect.

This isn't the first time I've had to deal with loss. It always hurts. The instructions I give for my friend come from deep feelings. Having known her through Leta and Iphigenia's memories, I want her to have a most amazing send off as a celebration of her life. I want it to be in a style she'd never imagined when she was a deprived child surviving on the edge of life on the streets outside of Troy.

Tana was a member of my High Guild. She is now a heroine who has given us a tremendous victory which may well give us the ability to capture Barat and destroy the Horde.

"Clifton, I need volunteers to give Tana a hero's send off—a real celebration of who she was. Anyone who wants to help get together with Clifton.

I stand, and Kino stands with me at the same time. I turn into him pressing my face to his broad chest. He holds me close with his arms wrapped around me in a way that covers me from any who might be watching us. I calm and look up into his beautiful face. Raising my hands, I press a soft kiss on his lips as he bends to let me reach him. I wipe the tears away and I notice that Mica and Spar are standing in front of us, sort of in an on-guard position. My hands reach to touch them, and they turn at the same time. Maybe my own senses are not the only ones that are stronger now. I rest a hand on each of their chests with Kino at my back and give a small nod. They understand. I'm okay.

Turning I watch as my brothers get up and step toward me. I ask,

"Jared, this is the end of the HG meeting. Will you be sure to report what you have witnessed to José Brinker?"

"Yes Kendra, I will," he says as he gives me a hug before he leaves.

Dana asks, "Are you sure you're okay Sis?"

"Yes, Dana. I'm better than ever."

"Well, tell me if you need something."

"I will." I have wonderful brothers. To me, they are priceless.

"General, will you join the princes and me? We're going to the cells," I say.

"Yes, Edling, this way," he replies and motions toward the doorway.

36

FREE AT LAST

Kendra

I FOLLOW ALONG WITH KINO, Spar, and Mega as Mica leads us lower into Navan along the path to the prison cells. As we walk along the recently renovated path, I feel calmer than I remember feeling in a long while, sad at the loss of Tana, but nevertheless, peaceful.

The Ceorfan have never had a great need to lock up any of its citizens. Recently though, there have been an increasing number of run-ins with Hewn. Still, even accounting for the problematic Hewn, there's almost no crime in Navan. However, at my request and supported by the HG, Dana did add this half dozen or so cells. So far, we've only locked up two mages. One mage is the Hewn who attacked Spar during his final test. The second is the one who caused me to close Navan due to his infiltration with some crafted... Gortanik. Well, I guess that isn't the whole truth. Since the Hewn are more... combative, security has used the cells a few times for short visits by a few belligerent Hewn.

We enter the the detention area, which is nestled in a previously unused cave in lower Navan. Its shape is so reminiscent of the face of a golf club head, the security personnel has named it 'The Club.' The entrance to The Club is located at the point where the shaft of the club would be. This makes this room a perfect place for the detention area because it's out of the way with only one way in or out. Four of the six cells are situated in the middle of the room. Two much larger cells are on the far back wall, near the head or toe sticking with the golf club head analogy.

Gortanik is being held in the second of the first two cells and stands as he sees us enter the room. His six by eight-foot cell is the far one in the room but still faces the door. His clothes hang off of him as if he were a child wearing his father's robes. His face, a mix of morbid meditation and dark impassivity rakes me from head to toe. He is studying me. He tilts his head slightly as if he is working out some intrigue, or I hope to myself, he is trying to remember me.

I use the thick silence in the room as a shield to stare at him at length. I take in every detail, every wrinkle, every freckle, searching for him. I'm reminded of a movie I saw as a child. A child actor was seeking the face of another, much older character, pulling, pushing, and stretching it. Then he exclaims, "There you are Peter!"

Even in this tattered, ruined persona standing in front of me, I find Gortanik. I guess it was easier since I was with him earlier today. Well at least in my thinking I was.

Although now, his hair isn't the neat coif of curls, smoothed into a half up ponytail like when we met. It's shoulder length now and a tangled mess. The color is still the same inky blue-black—that's the only thing which is the same. His sparkling dark eyes are now sad. He's skinny now, where he had once been a big man. I feel anger at his diminution. He's still tall, but now lanky, where in my grandmother's time he was a robust warrior mage. I can see something attached to him. He continues to stand quietly.

"Mega tele-speak to Jericho. We need him here—now. There's a tracking spell, an epoidai attached to the mage. It is almost undetectable, but my magic knows it's there and is warning me," I tell him.

Not seconds later Jericho's in the room. I know he moves stealthily and is very good at it, but I was able to notice a little itchy feeling with the slight breeze he created with his entrance. His robes swish louder than any noise he makes when he moves.

He starts, "Your Majesty, please do not be alarmed about the epoidai on the interloper. Any magic attached to him is contained while he is in the cell. His master cannot find him here. What I want to know is how much you're able to see now and do you know how to rid Gortanik of this spell now that you have your ancestor's knowledge?"

Well, that's a thought. "Let me think a sec," I say.

It comes to me quickly. The same way one of my own memories comes to mind when I'm thinking. In Iphigenia's life, she was given the purple stone, which is now part of me, as a reward for helping the Fae in a desperate time. This stone provides us with magic to wield through me. *Of course,* I think, *the rocks... they do different things for us. The green one connects me to the Earth, and I have used it for healing; that's why only the female dragon's blood can heal! The purple stone gives me magic! Okay, I know what to do now. I'm going to provide some flare to the occasion,* I turn toward the prisoner and let my arms fly out from my sides as I do. I purposefully walk, no, I strut toward him. His eyes get bigger as he watches me come toward him. I do this all hoping that Gortanik is still a friend.

"Jericho, please expand your protections to encompass me as well as Gortanik. After you do, please open the cell for me. I'll be safe and will stop this quickly," I tell him.

I feel the magic containing Gortanik spread over and pass me. As I feel it move beyond me, the cell door opens wide. I act fast and fling a hand toward Gortanik and push the energy contained in my epoidai, saying, "Den magikó. Ta xórkia dialýontai, poté den epistréfoun se aftón ton ánthropo." This roughly translates to "No magic. Spells dissolve, never return to this man." Immediately, a greenish brown haze flakes off of him like peeling paint.

The tattered mage takes a quick and deep breath and falls

forward, landing face first. Everyone stands there in amazement, no one attempts to catch him.

"What the hell, guys?" I drop to the floor and pull his head to my lap smoothing his curls out of his face. He's breathing and seems to be alive. At least I didn't kill him. I'll have to think about whether the person is strong enough if I ever have to do this again.

The others in the room continue to watch me like I've turned into a crazy cat lady.

"Come on y'all. Remember, this guy was your friend. Can't you see he's been tortured and compelled for too long? He helped me while I was being etched when I was very sick and not likely to survive. He also believed my totally unbelievable story when no one else could. I want him to be cared for, he's my friend," I explain.

Spar comes over and lifts the mage as if he were a child. Jericho tells him to take him to the medical chambers. He'll care for him there. I watch as Spar and Jericho leave.

"Well, I have to get ready for work." I hear the groans, well maybe I imagined hearing them. I don't intend to give up my day job. Mica is standing near me, it's still dark and we have plenty of time. But, I feel, I feel the need for speed. My dragon wants to spread her wings and fly!"

Mica just grins at me and says, "Yeah, baby."

We go back to our room and get into our flying clothes and pack our work uniforms into a pack Mica wears. Kino wants to go with us this pre-morning. So that as soon as he wakes he can check on the teens and talk to them. They might have new information concerning the Firestarter.

Spar comes home right as we are leaving. I give him a quick kiss breathing in the smell of him, then tell him I'll see him tonight. He slaps me on the butt as I walk by to start the day. Oh, fuck I will never tell him that's a turn on!

37

REUNION

Kendra

WE FLY fast and hard and make a circuitous route to the apartments, making it before sunup. Kino will pose here, and we put his ef, as we call gargoyle effigies, in the storeroom. When we've dressed and are ready for work I give Kino a little kiss and tell him, "Wings up, Rockstar. We'll be here after work."

The guard who's posing as a doorman has made coffee, and it's calling me. I hope he keeps making it every morning, and I tell him so as I pour Mica and me a cup. He nods and gives me a slight grin then is back to his doorman posture. I kinda like the fact he's in on the situation, so I don't have to fake the story that I still live here in front of him. The other doorman, Brian, I bet isn't fooled either, but he's very trustworthy. He never says one way or another what he knows, he just helps if I need it.

Mica and I make it to work and clock in as usual. We see that Murphy must have gotten some funding because there are a few new hires in the daily briefing this morning.

No warning tickle from my donum so I believe that they are all going to be good officers, but I will check with Dolo on my tablet when we are on our watch. Someone brought donuts and muffins this morning, and we all grab something on the way out to the patrol vehicles. I grab a donut wrapping it in a napkin for Chris. She isn't at her desk, so I leave it in front of her keyboard with a post-it that says— have a wonderful day, love K.

Buckling up I notice I got into the passenger side automatically. I think I like it, not having to drive, that is. While Mica drives us onto the unpaved road, which is the beginning of our patrol, I shoot a message off to Dolo to ensure the newly hired park rangers are legit. Then I begin to read the messages which have built up in the inbox of my tablet. Wait, what's this... I read out loud to Mica as we drive down the dusty dirt road.

"Listen to this... it's from José Brinker, he says TASS has found some information concerning the fires and maybe a small lead on the Horde. What do you think? Shall we hide the patrol SUV and go see Brinker? We can forward any calls to our tablets and be back in seconds by portal."

"Let's do it," he agrees.

I type in a quick message to José to tell him we're coming to see him in minutes. He replies with a thumbs up. I laugh and tell Mica, "Damn that man has come a long way since we first met him."

We portal right into José's baronial reception office. I've never really taken the time to appreciate how opulent his office is. The entire effect is what you would imagine being in the halls of Windsor Castle in the early sixteenth century. Well, José is a Baron, so it fits him to a tee.

Cecile is sitting behind her desk as we portal directly in front of her. I notice my portal target is perfectly precise this time. I wonder if it's an effect of being etched. Cecile stands without any hint of surprise. Her face brightens, and she smiles broadly when she sees us step into the room.

"Kendra my dear, should I message Tito to bring you something to eat or drink?"

"No thank you, Cecile. We only have a few minutes. But please let him know that I said 'Hi'."

She sees us to José's door and lets us in, as she says, "I will tell him." And in an almost conspiratorial manner, she lowers her voice and tells me, "You need to keep an eye on that Jared. He has found himself a wonderful woman, Jolie, and I believe their relationship is moving very quickly."

No wonder I haven't seen much of him here lately. Before I even have a chance to register my shock at what she just told me, José grabs my hand and drags me to a seat in front of his desk. Then, with a point of his chin, he indicates the place for Mica to take near me. As he starts a machine on his desk, he begins speaking to me in low tones, "This device will interrupt and intercept signals which are not part of TASS systems Kendra. I believe this increase in our security is warranted with... well, with what is going on with you, to put a very fine point on it. Our regular systems are still in place. But the security personnel which your brother has brought in, are... well, they are the finest in the world. They are bringing our security up to scratch which I was falsely under the impression, was already top notch."

I'll have to have a conversation with Jared about a couple of topics now, I think to myself.

"I have a better understanding of the dreadful ordeal you have been through. How are you, my lady?"

"Today, I'm very well José, thank you,"

"Initially we were in the dark as to what was going on with you. Jared would provide me a public big picture discussion of your situation. However, he was unwilling to provide us much in the way of any details regarding your personal health."

My eyebrows rise somewhat knowing Jared.

"I had to threaten to personally go to Navan to better understand your situation. His response was along the lines of, you could try. Tell me, are both of your brothers so protective of you?"

Laughing a little harder than I should have, I answer, "José, they've always been overprotective of me. You'd think they didn't believe I could care for myself. I'll have him tone it down. Although, I may receive the same comment as you did." I laugh.

"Well, I will say the United States President could only hope for such security... and devotion. Nonetheless," the TASS chairman says in a much happier and an I'm moving on tone, "your brother and representative has informed me that your etching was a success and that you are healthy and doing well. I couldn't be happier to see you."

"Thank you, José. I'm doing fine now. I'll have to come back and have dinner with you some time and tell you about my latest, I'll call it,adventure. As you say, we completed my etching. I have the memories and experience of my ancestors to draw on now even though I do not understand how. I'm putting things together and will certainly share if I find a way to help any of us in any way. For now though, I need to know what you've found out and what you can share about the fires and the Horde?"

"Well, I'll get straight to the point then. We have an operative in a small village in South America who has provided significant data as well as the needed proof that the fires in the state of New Mexico are being set and controlled by an oil company called SpotOn. We have also found out that the same company is collaborating with the drug cartels who bring illegal immigrants over the borders in your area. Our agent has provided information regarding the schedule of the fires. Our agent was unable to acquire a copy because it is in the hands of the oil company in the States. Our agent is embedded deeply; to leave now would compromise said agent's identity."

Inside I am laughing since Mica was with said agent only a few days ago. Well, the least I can do is save José a few words and worked over sentences. "I understand the need for secrecy José. However, please understand, I know who the agent is. We had an informant," I pause and look at Mica who is sitting stoically beside me, "who met your agent."

José rolls his eyes and smiles at his slip of not recognizing Mica as being our asset. "Umm, sorry Kendra. It is out of habit which I speak in great generalities regarding assets of her nature. I meant no disrespect. Also, I am not sure how I missed remembering Mica being there. He's so big..."

This time, I laugh openly as I respond to him, "José I only told you so you'd be able to speak easier regarding her. In fact, we follow the same procedures as you. Please, I felt no disrespect, kindly continue."

"Thank you, Kendra. I should have known you would have already been completely briefed on the situation. Still, we can use your help. Is there any way you can find the file or schedule regarding the fires?"

"Yes, there is," I tell him. "We'll start on the solution right away. Now, what about the Horde? Have you anything that can further our cause there? I assume that Jared was able to give you information concerning a few things that have happened in our favor involving the shithead in question? If not, I'll fill you in."

He responds, "Jared did report, in great detail, this morning. We realize we have great cause to celebrate the victory which the Ceorfan have brought us. I would extend both my felicitations as well as my profound grief at your loss, Kendra."

I nod my head, knowing José is on a roll and will continue.

He stands and turns toward a painting on the wall behind him. " We are still pressing on in the search for the Horde and Barat to put an end to him. The information we have is sketchy. But we did an on-ground investigation this morning." He swings the picture outward. "In the area of, and surrounding the castle you call Ilioilion, we found an item." In true spy fashion, he opens the safe hiding behind it and removes a box. He hands it to me as he takes his seat.

I tilt my head and still myself, opening myself to my donum before I open it. I feel nothing terrible, or even good for that matter. There's no spell which I can detect, no smell, or even sounds. Sure it's safe, I open the box carefully. Inside I find a kilt pin. I raise my brows as I wonder, now that's crazy, and I haven't the faintest idea what this could mean. I really do need a little while to think on this to figure out this piece of the puzzle.

"Well, José I have no idea what to make of this. Do you?" I ask.

Mica takes the pin from me and looks it over. He says, "I don't know what it is, but I bet Kino is our guy to figure it out."

I nod thinking I agree. Mica continues, "Chairman Brinker I'd like to thank you and your agent Sofia for the help she gave me in South America. I was able to leave safely only because of her being there and us being able to trust the information she's supplying."

Jealousy rears its ugly head then I get it under control with a thought. *He's here with you stupid!*

A slight wily grin on the chairman's face gives away his pride as he says, "Of course, that's what we do, isn't it." It was more statement than a question.

I add, "Yes, thank you for all your help. We must get back to work before they miss us. Please greet the Collins's for me, José. Do you mind if I take the pin and bring it back later?"

We get up and move toward the door. "We have all the information we can glean from the pin. You may keep it."

Just then, Mica opens a portal, and we step through, right back at the patrol SUV. I stay still verifying there's no one in the area before I move again.

I'm deep in thought as we're driving down the road when it hits me like the turkey at Thanksgiving. "Mica, that kilt pin could belong to another prisoner of Barat's who is trying to give us a clue!"

Mica and I talk over the possibility and conclude that we need to speak with Gortanik. He should be able to fill in some of the blanks we're bumping into. We decide that when we get home, we'll check on him before we go to sleep. First, we're going to find out from Jimmy if he's heard any more information at school and find out the location of the offices for SpotOn Oil Company.

When I get back to my desk at the end of my shift, I find a Butterfinger candy bar taped to a card. When I open it and read it,

I'm not surprised it's from Chris. It says, "If you're not makin' it with that stud you call partner, I wants 'im."

Yeah, over my dead body! The answer is—hell no! Friend or no friend I'm definitely not sharing. In fact, I'm not sharing any of my goyles. This is, by thousands of years of tradition, a one-way street. I intend on keeping up the tradition!

38

SNEAKY

Kendra

I DON'T KNOCK before I enter the apartment, but I do listen carefully to make sure it's... umm... safe, before I barge in. I use my dragon hearing to monitor the situation. Jimmy's typing on his computer. My bet, homework's getting done. That means it is safe for me to enter.

When I walk in with Mica hot on my heels, Jimmy looks up, surprised to see anyone, much less me. He looks pretty ragged tonight too. Instantly, concern flares in my mind. Is he eating? No, maybe he and Vanessa broke up! Damn Kendra, you do seem to enjoy jumping through all of these conclusions instead of the simple route... I ask him, "What the hell happened Jimmy?"

"Nothing happened to me. I'm fine. Why?" he asked the question but could have cared less what my response was as he just plowed on through the rest of his response. "I've just been studying like a madman for my tests this week. Next week is spring break. I'll rest then. I really need to do well because I'm hoping for a scholarship. Right now, I have a 3.8 GPA; but I need it to be a 4.0 to get noticed."

"Sorry Jimmy, I sort of panicked when I saw how worn out you look. I understand it though, I was the same way. I'm glad to hear you have goals. Do you have time to take a break and talk to us?"

"Sure, I've got time Kendra." Then he pushes his papers and his white TI-84 graphing calculator aside. *Ok, Jimmy is a nerd. What kind of math is he working on?*

"Jimmy, have you eaten yet? Let's go get something to eat. What do you say? We've got lots of stuff we really need to discuss with you."

Like most teenagers, he's hungry and says, "Heck yes!"

Since I didn't feel like walking anywhere, we decided to hop in Jasper and drive over to the Sun's Up Diner. Seriously, not only is the name one of the best names for a diner but the food is good too.

During the drive, Jimmy says, "Joe, my friend who's been telling me about the fires, well, he's not had any new news for a while now. I'm not sure, but his dad thinks it's because they don't trust him and are cutting him out. Joe said his dad is scared too and might take the family away soon."

I really didn't know what to say. There're so many moving parts to this activity now, it's hard to keep it all straight. Fires run off all of the competition for SpotOn. They also cover for the human and drug trafficking. Top it off, Jimmy's friend and family seem to be in even more trouble too. I had forgotten that we should offer them a place in Navan. We need to get on that offer.

Without giving me a chance to compose myself and respond, Jimmy continues, "I also found out where the SpotOn building is."

Dang, that kid. He's helped us as much as any one of the three letter organizations that the Feds have sent in. He also adds that we should check out the building and maybe we can come up with something more that way. What a genius kid.

On the walk back to the apartment I invite him and Vanessa to stay in Navan during their spring break. He really looks like he could use some rest and we could make sure their visit is all about rest. He says he'll text me when he finds out if it's okay with her. But as far as he's concerned, the answer is, "Yes."

When we drop him off at home, I sneakily make sure he has groceries by asking for a bottle of water for the road. Ok, so it wasn't that sneaky. But, I did see that he's got a full fridge. I feel better knowing he isn't going to go without a meal.

"Jimmy if you need something just let me know, okay? I don't want you to do without. You can always ask me for anything, and then we'll work out how to get it done."

"Thank you, Kendra. I'm fine though. Don't worry, if I need something enough I'll ask for sure."

Mica pats him on the shoulder. "Jimmy we like to see that you are all right. You're family. Got it? See you in the morning, if you're here when we go to work."

Jimmy smiles and shakes his head a little, not quite looking at Mica. "Thanks for the warning, see you in the morning." I catch his sideways grin as he turns and shuts the door behind him.

Mica takes my hand as we take the stairs to the roof. Mica's big rough hand envelopes my entire hand in his. He makes a fist, teasing me about how small my hand is.

When we get to the garden, Mica sits facing west, watching as Apollo drives the sun behind the plateau which protects the western edge of Cueva Hallow. He waves me over to sit beside him. I snuggle into his strong embrace watching the sunset and loving the feel of him. I relax like I haven't in a long time. I might need to do this more, it feels nice just to be here with my partner doing nothing but enjoying the present.

I can feel his heart beating in his chest. I put my hand on it playing with the buttons on his shirt. He doesn't stop me, so I unbutton them to touch his bare chest, "I need to change, but I really would like to stay and snuggle with you. This weekend, do you think we can find some time for just us all alone?"

"Baby, that is a dream of mine." He emphasizes the word 'is' to make sure it has extra meaning, I guess... anyway, he continues, "I'll do my best to make it happen, as long as nothing else changes our plans. Would you like to go back to Oahu with me or do you have something else in mind?"

I tell him, "I know you think I judge you when you pick a place. I don't. You seem to always have amazing ideas for us. So, whatever you think, is just fine with me."

We sink into silence. As we watch, the prismatic bursts of yellows and reds contrasting with the brilliant blues, shift into the darker burnt oranges as the blue sky turns to darkness. There's something special about a high desert sunset. As a little girl, I remember sitting outside and being excited as the sun disappeared behind the same plateau I see now.

Today was a warm eighty-four degrees. I have lived here so long, I can feel the weather turning. Tonight, will be cool and tomorrow will be at least ten degrees colder than today. But, in Mica's arms, it doesn't matter. I feel nothing but serenity.

The last of the sunset sinks behind the hills, then the distant horizon when I feel the tingle of my gargoyles waking up.

"Do you feel that tickle on your skin when everyone wakes?" I ask Mica.

"Never have, do you?"

Letting go of Mica, I say, "Every time one of you wakes. Do you mind? I motion with my head toward the now awake Kino, and he lets me go without hesitation.

My sexy red goyle smiles at me with the most sensual smile. It's kinda devious looking, making me wonder what he's been dreaming while torped. I run at him, and he clutches me in a tight embrace. I'll never get to touch him enough. He bends toward me, his face so close I can feel his hot breath on my lips. It makes them tingle, then he kisses me deeply. My body responds in kind and presses closer to his. Pretty sure I know what he's been dreaming. He pulls his lips away just enough for me to see his entire face and smiles.

"Now that's the way I like to wake up. How was your day beautiful lady?" he asks.

"It just gets better and better," I reply.

Then I let him know we've taken care of getting the information from Jimmy and, by extension, Vanessa when we took Jimmy to eat at the diner.

"Oh, I love that place!" he says.

I ask, "Is it okay if we go home by portal because I'm exhausted and need some rest?"

Neither Mica or Kino have a problem with using the portal stone. After all, they're still concerned I'm up and about so soon after being on the edge of death during the etching process. We replace Kino's ef on the edge of the building before we head home.

Prior to stepping through the portal, I take a brief moment to just be with two of my goyles. I hold them both and stare at the waxing moon which is almost overhead. Finally, I duck my head and step into the sitting room of my chambers.

My chambers... that sounds very natural now. I've just spent a very relaxing few minutes with Mica watching a beautiful sunset. So, you'll understand why, when I see Spar sitting at the dining table eating with his mouth open, I have cause to laugh out loud, maybe too loud. But, he's so cute!

I sit on his more than ample lap and kiss him on the cheek, so he can finish chewing his bite of chicken. When he finally swallows it, he leans his forehead to mine and says, "I missed you today."

"I missed you today too." Exhaustion I rarely feel takes over, and I ask, "Will you please message Clifton for me and delay the HG meeting tonight? I need to sleep. I really am dragon-ass tonight." I smile at him over my intentional mispronunciation.

He smiles back and tells me, "I'll take care of that. Go get some rest, honey." He kisses me just a soft touch on the lips as he lets me go. David, or Spar, those lips still make me tingle when he uses them that way.

Mica and I walk over to our sleeping area in the back of this giant room where we fall into bed. Pressing up against his warm chest, I'm out like a light. Sometime later, I feel Elmer snuggle in between us in my sleep, so I put a hand on him... jealous little guy, ha-ha.

When I wake, I look at Mica who's still fast asleep and snort as I laugh. Elmer is asleep on Mica's head with a wing draped over his forehead. If I didn't know better, I'd think Elmer was dead. My laughter wakes them both and Elmer chitters his displeasure flying off to find his nightly repast.

Mica pulls me into him and laughs himself.

"What's so funny, princess?"

When I stop laughing, I say, "Elmer was asleep on your head, and it just hit me funny." I snort at him again, and he grabs me with a chuckle and tickles me until I beg him to stop. Then I start giggling still unable to remove the comical scene from my mind. In fact, I believe the thought of Elmer on Mica's head is going to make me laugh all day.

He draws me in for a few minutes then I say, "I feel much better. We need to get up and let the others know what we've found out and make a plan."

"I feel better too princess. Okay, I'll get up, but I'd rather stay in bed with you," he says with a horny growl which makes me want to stay with him. Nope, we've got work to do.

I throw on some sweats and saunter into the dining area where Spar and Kino are sitting. I casually watch them with their tablets open working on something.

I can smell breakfast! I'm so happy that these guygoyles like to eat. But, I am even more pleased that they've thought to get me some chocolate chip pancakes. They have them waiting in a warmer for me in our seating area. Spar tells me they just canceled the HG meeting hoping I would sleep longer.

Well, skipping an HG meeting isn't a crime, but I like the way I sleep... a few hours here and a few hours there. I have a schedule for the most part. I'm healthy and to be honest, I don't think dragons need much sleep. I do think I should check with Jared and Dana and make sure they're getting enough rest. Pulling the big sis card is my specialty.

While we eat, we fill Spar and Kino in on everything we found out earlier today. That's when I remember to take out the box that José had given me. I show it to Kino. He says he'll work on figuring out the clue and without missing a beat, he says, "Gortanik is awake." He looks over at me out of the corner of his eye, watching for my reaction.

"What? We should go see him now. You coming or do you want to work on the plan to break into the oil company's building?" I ask them.

We finally decide that Spar and Mica will start the draft of a plan while Kino and I go to the medical unit.

39

I UNDERSTAND

Kendra

ON THE WAY to the medical facility I hold onto Kino's arm, and he strolls so I can keep up. We would probably hold hands, but claws are involved, and it just isn't the same unless we're both in human guise.

He pauses when we get to the little bench where we first kissed. I sit thinking, believing that is what he wants from me. Then I remember we both don't fit, so I get up and let him sit first, and I sit on his lap. Same as before.

I ask, "What is it? Do you need to tell me something? Talk to me, Beloved." using the same endearment he uses with me. It doesn't even feel strange to me.

Looking back at me he says, "Beloved, I will support you in whatever course of action you decide upon, but if you decide to trust this mage you must know more. Beloved, I remember him from the dark times long ago. Gortanik was a warrior mage, much like me. He was an acclaimed mage and well known as one who could be trusted. Yet when the Mage Wars began, and he was captured, he chose the other side. My beauty, I do not wish to further pain you. I hesitantly recount this only so you understand the root of my unease.

Kendra, I am one of the Cursed. One of those who was captured and held by Barat in prison and tortured. Leta died freeing us, I am not sure you know of the Cursed from your grandmother's memories. None of the mages locked in our prison were with us when we were released." Here, I see a pained Kino pause. I can't tell if it is because of his discussion of him being a member of the Cursed or talking about Gortanik.

I place a gentle hand to the side of his face and lean in to kiss his lips. As I pull away, I pause to look into his eyes. Satisfied that he wants to tell me this story, I tell him, "It's true that neither Iphigenia or Leta knew of the Cursed, so I don't have those memories. Please tell me your story, my love."

"Edling, when the Mage Wars began, I had recently come into manhood. I was cocky knowing I was a good warrior as well as a mage. The evil mage Barat, as we call him now, also knew and took many of us prisoner including Gortanik. To make a Crafted, Barat had his mage carve pieces from us. He placed the carved pieces into wooden forms, and used some dark magic, not of this world, to bring them to life and create the Crafted. It was through my torn flesh, and others like me, that numerous of the wooden enemy were created.

Beloved, you should know the Crafted are not people and have no soul; they only do what the one who made them demands.

What you may also not know, is why I and many others like me, became willing donors. We were forced to give our flesh to the monsters, so that they could create more minions for Barat's army. In the beginning, because of the immense pain we suffered at each muti-lation, we fought. You see my love, Resurgere is a painful process as the cut flesh must come in the moments before we torpify. However, we soon learned that to fight meant death. Yet not the death we longed for. If we resisted, the evil mages employed by the enemy would destroy someone whom we cared for. I only attempted to defy these mages once. In that defiance, I honestly did not believe the horrid mages would kill as they had warned me... I quickly found they would. Most horrifyingly, they restrained, tortured, and murdered my own father before my very eyes. After his death, I willingly suffered the pain to protect the others I loved including Gortanik.

Beloved, many mages participated in cutting pieces from my body. One of those mages was my friend Gortanik."

The shock must have been evident as Kino quickly began singing a song of reassurance. My mind flashed to my own torture at the hands of the Jessup Cartel, and my anger boils. Kino's song is a little louder in my heart. But I'm rethinking any friendship with the sick and injured mage. My rising pulse isn't lost on Kino for a second.

"Pulse of my heart, I do not tell you this to set you against this man. I tell you, so that you will have the information you need to make good decisions concerning him. To find a way to help another who has been used and manipulated. I did not want to make Crafted or to be responsible for so much torture and death, yet if I had not, I would have endangered the lives of Sondra and my mother the way I had my father's. When the queen, gave her life for the release of the Ceorfan I went home with a chip on my shoulder. I was angry and lashed out at others until the love of my family reminded me who I am. I was able to deal with the anger and be the man who I should be only after I forgave myself, something which was and still is tough to do. I am asking you to consider Gortanik's anger and the chip on his shoulder so that you may help him remember who he is. He was a good man, or you would not have removed him from his cell yesterday. Trust your instincts and be the queen I know; the lady who helps and finds the best in all. One who knows when to heal and when to harm."

Taking his face in both of my hands I, once again, look into his eyes. "I'm not sure how I got so lucky to have you. You're so amazing, and I couldn't be happier with the person you are. I'm never letting you go. Thank you, Kino, for trusting me with your secrets. Will you, please, tell me any information that you think I might need to know.

It does help. I have my grandmother's memories to draw on, but I'm still learning, and sometimes I need to be reminded what my goal is."

I get up from his lap, which is the last thing I want to do. His body under my hands has my mind blanking out as it is. I better get moving, or I won't get anything done tonight.

I do have a goal for my people. Iphigenia saved the unwanted and made them into a people. Leta sacrificed herself to free the Cursed. I must ensure our people's happiness and acceptance in the human world. They must be cared for and loved. I'm convinced we can make this world better. I want everyone to know we have something to add to the betterment of our land. Great, I sound like a politician—stopping now. We get up and continue to the med facility.

The first of the medical personnel who sees us enter waves us over and bows, "Your Majesty."

I let him. It wasn't too big or ostentatious, and I'm not shaming him by rejecting the respect he's showing us. I do want to soften the situation, so I reach out and touch his lower arm asking at the same time, "We came to see Gortanik. How's he doing doctor?" As I ask, I notice he is neither gargoyle nor human. I need to remember to ask about that one of these days.

I'm not sure why, but I can tell he's surprised by my question when he answers me. "My queen, the patient is awake. That is the best I can say, he is not accepting treatment well."

"Are you telling me he is hard to handle and has a lot of anger?" I wink at Kino.

"That is what I did not say and is exactly the truth. I had heard you were a discerning queen. I am happy it is so. Would you like to speak to him? I will stay with you if you want, with prince Kino I believe you are adequately protected. He tends to throw things."

"I'll be fine, thank you anyway Dr...?"

"I am Ogman, Your Majesty. If you need me, I will be near."

Kino hooks a big claw on one of my arms, and we mosey over to the area of this medical chamber where the beds are. Gortanik is laying still, but I know he's awake. There's a chair at the end of his bed, so I pull it over to his side and sit. As I wait, I can't help myself and reach for his hand. He squeezes mine and takes a deep breath but says nothing. I just wait in the quiet room.

After a drawn-out pause he says, "Eíste Kendra, étsi den eíste?"

With my grandmother's memories, I readily understand him without any translation. He is asking, "You are Kendra, are you not?" He still speaks like he did in my grandmother's time giving me a clue that like many of the Ceorfan he has not been around humans often. I might be wrong.

I reply, "Yes Gortanik, I'm Kendra. Thank you for keeping me alive when I was in my grandmother's head. Just believing me was very important to me at the time. Now, I see it as something that without it I may have just given up, but you gave me hope. I was able to fight until my princes could help and I drew on my dragon blood to survive. I won't forget what you did, my friend." I speak in English, wondering if he would understand me.

Tears roll down his face, and he raises his other hand and covers it to hide the tears. Well, it puts that to rest, he definitely understands English.

I put my other hand on our joined ones and glance up at Kino. Without being asked he begins a low assuasive melody as he walks up behind me, he places his hands on my shoulders.

I notice that Gortanik is breathing deeper and drinking in the magic of the beautiful song my beloved prince is blessing him with. Taking his hand from his face, he looks at Kino and nods an acceptance of the spell.

Calmer now, he speaks in English. "Your Majesty, there is much to tell. I am not sure I have the strength to say to you all I desire before I must rest. Be assured I will tell you as much as I can. I will start with... I'm delighted you are alive and well. You have been on my heart for a very long time. I did wonder throughout my... if you were alive. If you made it back to your own time. I never did give up hope for that, even though there would be no hope for me. Your Majesty, Barat is not in this world. He is hiding in the Fae realm. To get to him, you are going to have to have their permission to enter, or you will not be permitted to leave there, ever.

Well, I didn't see that coming. I think to myself, *There's a frickin' Fae realm?*

His lips are dry, and he begins to fall off to sleep. Before I let him sleep, I hand him a cup of water that's sitting on a tray near his bed. Gortanik looks at me before he takes it. It is as if he sees something he hasn't seen in years. He takes the cup and doesn't stop drinking until he's finished it all.

I take the cup back from him and realize I've got an idea which I'll need to ask my goyles about first. I refill his cup, and he drinks this as well, but slower this time.

I say, "Gortanik, we'll return later, go back to sleep." He clutches onto my hand, obvious desperation in his eyes.

So, I add, "You'll be safe here. Would you like me to send you one of my personal guards to stay and watch over you?"

He nods his head, yes, trying not to look weak.

I tele-com Mega and ask him, *"Is Jadeite free to stay with Gortanik for a while."* He lets me know that he'll send him straight away.

In the few seconds it takes to concentrate on my tele-com to Mega, Gortanik is asleep. I pat his hand and let it go.

Kino and I are talking when Jadeite enters. After I ask him if he'll guard the sick mage, I make sure that he knows Gortanik is not a prisoner but is a friend who's afraid of an enemy, being us. He needs to be assured of his safety.

Jadeite acknowledges my words and says, "I'll do my best because I remember him. When we were young, we trained together a few times. Our training master taught us the art of hand to hand."

"Thank you, Jadeite. I'll see you later," I say.

Kino and I are walking out when I remember that I had an idea I wanted to talk over with the doctor. So we stop, and I immediately start when Ogman looks at me.

"Doctor Ogman, I had a thought and have wondered how we are handling emergencies. We may not even have any. I have no idea. But if you did, how do you plan to get in touch with me? I can't give you any dragon blood if I don't know. Right?"

The shocked look on his face speaks volumes. He says with a squeaky shaky voice, "Your Majesty, I had not dared to consider you would give of your blood so willingly to save someone outside of the battlefield." Almost immediately he recognizes his words may have painted me negatively without meaning to. I watched as his face contorted trying to find a way to take back what he had just said. So, I stop him.

"No, it's alright. You now have new orders from your queen. If you need life-saving measures for our people, you will contact me. I will come twenty-four/seven no worries. Don't hesitate. Do you understand me?" I asked the question softly, so he would understand I had no animosity toward him in any way.

"Dr. Ogman, I also wonder if you'd be willing to do some testing on my blood if I gave you a sample. We should know if we could make a serum which could heal the way my fresh blood does or if only the blood works. There is so much we could do if it works. Many other questions to answer too."

I see the excitement take fire in his face and he becomes animated.

"Now? Would you mind giving me a sample to start please, I mean... my queen."

"Now is just fine," I reply.

He sends his assistant to get the syringes and supplies needed. When he returns I sit so they can do a blood draw. I plaster a grin on my face, so they won't be nervous. The assistant's name is Limon, and he tells me the standard, "This will sting just a bit." However, as he pokes the needle in my arm, really, that was the intent. The needle broke, he tries again, so I change to my human form and once more the needle breaks. Limon gives the next needle to Ogman. Again, when Ogman tries the needle breaks.

Looking sheepish Dr. Ogman tells me, "I guess we know that dragon skin is too hard to get blood with an ordinary needle. My queen let me have some diamond needles made. When they are ready, I will call you to provide the sample."

Let's see if I have this right, "You're telling me I have tough hide?" There is a strained look on the doctor's face.

To which Kino states, "Well beloved, if the hide fits."

We all get a good laugh, and the physician relaxes some.

I wave at Jadeite who's sitting and reading beside Gortanik as we leave the med facility. We want to get back to the others and find out the plan for getting the information on the schedule for the fires from SpotOn.

40

THEY CARE

Gortanik

SEVERAL PEOPLE WALK into my captivity area and now stand before me. I stand in shame and fist my hands. It takes all my strength to remain standing as they watch me. I recognize one of them, he was my friend. He was my best friend who I was forced to wrong. My breath hitches and my heart squeezes painfully in my chest remembering Kino's pain. I carved him for Barat endlessly for... well, I don't know for sure. I was so sure it was to his death. It can't be him, yet it must be. His pain at that time was unimaginable. Yet without hesitation, I continued to carve him. I had to cut him. If I didn't many would die. He would die, and I loved him. I love him still.

Do I recognize any of the others? To my undying shame, I do. The massive blue-grey Megahir standing behind all of the others. I cut him deeply and often. He was so large, he was ordered to be carved by many mages at the same time. With each piece of flesh torn from these men and others, my flesh was ripped from me. The horror will never leave my eyes. The screams will never leave my ears.

For most of the entirety of my life, I've chased a phantom. This haunting queen regent was never my queen and yet she was always my queen. I've longed to meet Queen Kendra for millennia. Her strange words, her fantastic story, and her powerful persona have long pulled me to this place in this time. She is one I've wanted to meet forever and a day. I've never met her, but I know it's her. With all the pitiful worthlessness of my soul, I hope this is Kendra Macbard. With all of the pieces Barat cut from me I want it to be her. My search is ended, but my pain is not stopping. She is surrounded by her retinue, and I know I can't speak to her. My long-awaited questions will go unanswered. I can't so much as groan my pain to her because in doing so I will bring ruin to the queen of the people I love. The people I was forced to torture for so long. I will live in silence hoping for death. I strengthen my resolve squaring my shoulders and promise myself I will not betray her. The traps which the vile Barat has placed on all his slaves including me are clever. If I make one sound, it will blow this room and all the occupants into dust. His traps are not as clever as I am. I stand in silence before this queen. I vow not to bring her harm.

I remember her strange speech as she spoke to me through my princess Leta when Leta was so young. Kendra was understandable, but her words were fitted together in ways which made my heart leap in joy. In all these many hundreds of years, I've never forgotten.

I've dreamed of how she would look. My dreams remind me now of how ineffective they have been at imagining her beauty. It is possible that I've built a picture in my mind of a woman transcending all portents of grace. I remember all the women of legendary beauty. I knew Aphrodite, Hera, and Helen. Yes, their beauty crosses time, but this queen has no equal. Yes, I will undoubtedly stay silent to not bring harm from the maggot who is master of my pitiful life.

The destruction of my life is so complete, I've long known I was past the lustful thoughts of youth. Yet to be confronted by such beauty I find my manhood stirring with a purpose of its own with just her standing before me. Her strength fills the air. She holds herself with confidence and speaks with the same strong voice that she used in the past.

I watch her watching me. Could I only plead this one hope, have her look upon me as I look upon her. Yet, I don't deserve even this most pitiful pleading. I could never expect to have... My manhood stirs further at the thought she might be as attracted to me as I am to her. That is not possible. I am wretched, ragged, and dirty. She must believe me to be an enemy. I have embodied evil for far too long. I have no hope. She pauses her study of me and turns to the largest of the gargoyle men with her. Without a movement from her full lips, an old mage enters. I wonder, is he using a jump buoy? I barely feel the tingle of the energy as he enters the room. The woman before me, the one who I hope is queen of the Ceorfan, listens to this old mage as he explains about the epoidai which has been placed on me by Baratium. I find immediate relief as I hear him say, "Any magic attached to him is contained while he is in the cell. His jailor cannot find him here." Joy fills my soul. As long as I am behind this spelled wall created by this Jericho, this queen and her people are safe from any spell attached to my worthless hulk.

As I am ruminating on my discovery, I hear the end of her shocking request, "...please open the cell for me. I'll be safe and will stop this quickly."

Wait, no! Please, my queen. I want to scream at her. Yet I dare not. I must only do what I can to contain the spells, so she is not hurt. I start to wave her away but immediately as the spell encompasses her and my cell door flies open and she without hesitation dissolves the spells which have cursed me for the last millennia. I can't help, but I still whisper a spell of protection around her. I'm too weak. Protecting her might be the last thing I ever think to do as I finally fall into the blackness which I've longed for.

I WAKE IN A MEDICAL CHAMBER. PAIN FILLS MY BODY. THESE

doctors are helping me. The old mage Jericho is also here and helping with my healing. He was one of my teachers. I'm too weak to care. If this is my end, then I am happy. I've seen and protected the one I have dreamt of for so long. I have lived in pain, slave to a madman for too long. I fall back into darkness.

I hear a voice, a voice which was just a dream. Not a dream. I saw my queen, didn't I? No, this must be another of the fabrications which my malevolent enemy is using to hurt me.

I recognize the voice of the doctor who I threw the cup of poison at, calling to her. He called her, "Your Majesty." That would not happen in Barat's controlling visions. I feel someone take my hand. That certainly wouldn't happen either, this is real. It must be her, beyond all hope she's touching me. I squeeze her hand, so she'll not let mine go.

I finally speak. "Eíste Kendra, étsi den eíste?"

"Yes Gortanik, I'm Kendra."

My impossible dream has come true. I might have actually done something right in my lifetime. The raw emotions of loss, hate, love are too much for me. Tears leak unwanted from my eyes. I don't wish for her to see me crying like a child, so I cover my face.

I've not felt the simple touch of a caring hand in so long. I am crushed by these feelings. The care this woman is showing me is more than I can take. I must take my hand from her. I must hide. No, I must run. I am not worthy of this simple care. I hear another voice. Another voice of someone I know. This time, it is from one I tortured for so long. I feel his singing spell of comfort. Oh, creator, I am home.

I accept the gift and open my eyes fully to the giver. As I thought, I do know him. Kokkino Petra. I thought he was taken from me and killed. I am glad he escaped.

I feel my strength waning when I tell her of the dangers of finding Barat in Faery. I was trying to say that maybe with a jump buoy we might pull it off, but my strength falters.

As she stands to leave, I grasp her hand tighter so that she will not let go. I'm sure she thinks fear is that which causes me to hold tight. It must be so as she offers me one of her personal guards to watch over me while she's gone. I agree to hide the fact that it's not fear, it's the desire to not lose her touch.

I know I'm not good enough for her. I wish I were. I'll keep this to myself. I hope it was different though. I'll still protect her if I can prove myself to her and she lets me stay here with her and her people. My eyes close and I drift into a tranquil slumber where my dreams are all of her.

When I wake, there's a warrior gargoyle beside my bed. He strikes up a conversation making me feel at ease quickly. He said his name is Jadeite. I knew his parents. Both were some of the first casualties of the Mage Wars. I tell him a little about them, and he has many questions. They were killed long ago by my vile master. Wait, no longer my master.

I answer his questions as I can, and he answers mine in return. He tells me about the city where we are and then asks me if I am hungry. I suck in a breath thinking I haven't had these basic human kindnesses in so long that I am shaken to be the recipient.

He must read my body language and gets up, telling me he'll be right back. Upon his return, he has brought us a feast for many. Yet he tells me it is only for us two. He sits and eats with me. A part of me which I'd thought I'd never feel again finds purchase in my being. I might have a friend now too. Jadeite understands me well. Being gargoyle, he's prone to that, but this warrior is much like me. Now with a full belly, I feel the pull of sleep, despite my efforts. Jadeite removes my uneaten food and sets it aside. "Gortanik, I'll stay with you while you sleep." The comfort of knowing I am safe, for one of the very few times in my miserable life, I do just as he suggests and sleep.

41

THE TUNNEL

Kendra

WELL HELL, I couldn't give a blood sample to the doctors. That's a new development. I'll have to remember if I'm ever in the situation, to not volunteer to give blood in a blood drive. I do want to ask my goyles if they approve of me giving Gortanik blood though. I remember that I gave a drop to John Collins and in a sideways way to Captain Murphy and it didn't seem to make them bound to me. I also used a regular pen knife to cut myself for John. Maybe something in the etching process has cemented my dragon self to me, and we are indeed one is why my skin can't be easily pierced now. I'm going to ask for a diamond bladed knife. In fact, experimenting I stab one of my own claws into my hand and sure 'nuff I do bleed, wiping my hand on my pants I keep walking with my red rockstar to our rooms.

When Kino and I arrive in our chambers Spar and Mica are not there with food this time. I'm starving. Maybe they're in the allodium. With the kitchen in there, I'm hoping the cooks will have something fixed, so I can eat.

"Let's go through the secret passage and see how fast they notice we're there. What do you think?" I say with a smirk.

"I think you are a beautiful, scheming girl and I love it!" He touches me lightly in the middle of my back making me stop breathing. He notices what that touch did to me and watches me for a few seconds. I take the hand that gave me the heat wave and lift the digit that has the filed off point and run my fingers over it. I didn't look up any dirty talk to use for him, but I do have lots of memories to draw on now.

"Can I suck on this?" I ask.

Now he's the one who stops breathing.

"I love how your breath pauses when I flirt with you. I want to have you fill my pussy in the secret tunnel. Is that something we can do?"

He says with a deep sexy tenor, "Your wish is my command, beloved." Then he pushes out a little pulse just for me, full of his lust. It thrills my skin.

I pull him toward the secret door opening, looking back to give him my best come hither look. I smile as he raises a wicked eyebrow with a tiny lopsided grin. Entering the dark area lit with the soft glow of the algae I turn and back him against the wall and put the finger I had been holding in my mouth. Sucking and feeling with my senses his passion. *Oh, that makes me really hot. He's really into this, so I think I'll just make it worse.*

"You are better than any fantasy I've ever had Kino. I fucking love your hands on me, treat me like your toy." Oh hell, his temperature just went up five hundred degrees.

"Take your clothes off then, doll," he says as he steps back leaning on the opposite wall.

"Will you sing for me? Your voice makes my pussy wet," I ask him as I start to take off my top. He starts a melody full of want and desire. I begin to sway to his tune, removing my top and dropping it at his feet then I unbutton my pants and take them off quickly, wild with passion for giving him the idea I want him fast. He gets the idea! He flicks off his own pants swiftly and moves to me, lifting me up pressing my back to the wall.

I wrap my legs around his sexy abs while he leans into me. His song cuts off as his tongue enters my mouth in the most fuckable kiss. I'm so gone, but I notice that his hand is behind my back not only holding me but protecting me from the rock wall.

"Pull my hair."

He groans, a killer sound taking over my body. He grabs my hair with the hand behind me and shoves his cock powerfully inside me. I scream, not caring who hears. His mouth crashes back on mine, and all the sound is his now because no way can I be quiet. When he moves and puts his head against my temple picking up the beat for the fuck of my life. I put my lips close to his ear and manage to say, "I'm coming." He speeds up to meet me as I tighten on his own orgasm. We slide to the floor together breathing hard. He pulls me close.

I burrow into him for a few minutes before I say, "You are so good at that, it makes me feel very loved." My senses tell me this is something he needs to hear, and it makes him happy, so I add a little pulse for him alone.

"I think I'm going to start to talk like you beloved." I notice my goyle said I'm. "You know how to make a gargoyle feel like a fucking strong immortal."

Haha, now that is funny. Hearing Kino say fucking undoes me and I giggle making him smile at me.

"I could stay here until I torp. Do you want to get dressed and proceed or shall we stay, my lady?"

"We have a break-in to plan. Let's get going Rockstar. Did I tell you that you rock my world? You do!"

He picks up my clothes and hands them to me before he picks up his own pants giving me one last view of his fantastic ass. Feeling very happy I get my own clothes on then walk with him into the allodium.

Dead silence greets us. Findare is sitting straight in front of us eating, and yeah, they knew the minute we came into the room. I'm sure we weren't that stealthy—at all. Seeing his grin and looking at the rest of the occupants of the room staring at us, makes me think maybe next time I'll close the door.

Spar breaks the silence by saying, "Have you worked up an appetite hun? We have lots of good food."

Everyone laughs, and Kino leads me to my seat. Which I take as he tells me he'll bring me some food if that's alright.

"Yes please, I'm starving," I answer. No use denying anything, that's not my style anyway. I'll just let it be and start my questions for this group.

"Did y'all draft a plan for the break-in? Are we going tonight?" I ask.

"That is the plan, Your Majesty. We would like to convince you to stay behind for deniability's sake–" Duke Findare starts.

"Nope, stop right there, Fin. I don't like being out of the action. Stuff happens when I'm not there that causes rifts in my relationships. I'm not doing it. I'm the one who asked if 'we' could do this. You all should be happy that I'm asking instead of just taking off. In fact, if I have to keep defending my right to do my jobs then maybe I should just quit asking."

Mica says in a gentle voice, "I agree with our queen. She is more than capable of taking care of herself. We have upped the security around her. I for one think she's an asset. Kendra will be able to tell us if there is anyone in the area faster than the rest of us because of her dragon senses. And no Kendra, please don't quit asking, we need to know where and how you are. I apologize for ever excluding you and making you feel that you are not an asset."

I reply, "That's settled then, and I will do my best to make sure you know where I am. What is the plan?"

Findare starts again, "This is what we have so far. We will fly to Cueva Hallow tonight land on the roof of the SpotOn company building. Spar will use his gift to go through the door to open it, remaining in his 'flex state.' Dolo will enter as soon as the door opens to disable any alarm system which might be in place. Dolo will also disable the surveillance system. Then Amber will go find any and all schedules we believe they have for the fires and illegal trafficking. Since the night is half gone already, we will portal to the location. Any thoughts?"

No one says anything. We just look at Findare. Wow, where to begin? I'm trying to come up with a nice way to say—you left out most of the right stuff in a proper reconnaissance for a stealth mission.

Before I get anything out, Fin asks, "All right then General Mega, do you also agree? Is there anything you want to add?"

Mega says, "Yes, and it is not going to make anyone happy. I know you all would like to get this completed so that we can contain the possible danger to others, including the wildlife. Jumping into an ass-baked plan is not what I recommend." I almost snort laugh. He glances at me with raised eyebrows, not knowing what's funny. I'm pretty sure he was going for half-baked or half-assed. Valiant effort trying to update his vocabulary, in my thinking, still amusing, at least to me anyway.

"I would like to take a day to gather proper intel. A week would be better. However, I understand the need for this information. We will need the property to be analyzed. We need to know all entrances and exits, where the electrical boxes are located, and how many guards there are on duty at night. We also need to know if the guards are armed and plan how to take them out if they attack. Is there a need to take weapons ourselves? Do the Ceorfan who do not appear human need a glamour? Above all what is the escape and evade routes in this area."

While Mega is rolling through the stuff we need to do like a checklist, my mind is wandering... I come back when I hear him getting to the meat.

"When we have this information, we can make a plan which will end with a better chance of success. One thing which is part of the plan will be that the queen's Ducere will provide several Elite warriors to contain the perimeter. This will let the Ducere concentrate on the queen and her location at all times. I want security around her tight, but not so much to hinder her. Also, I want Mason with Amber and Dolo on the inside so that he can also reconnoiter while they are both completing their tasks. Questions?"

"You are right General. We need to collect information. I was wondering though if it might be possible to collect the schedule by hacking into their system? Dolo, you had information about one of my reports from work concerning Jerome. Is it possible to hack into the system and get the information?" I ask.

"Yes, my queen, it is, but the risk of being detected is high, and we still need to keep our people secret and safe. In the case of your report, we have access because we have people on the inside feeding us information by way of TASS. I have tried to do a quick sweep, and their system is very well protected," Dolo informs us all.

We spend a few hours revising our plan. Mega gives orders, and in a few short hours, we conclude with a much safer strategy. Mega gave each of us actions to complete. Mica and I are supposed to see if one of the teens will be okay with going into SpotOn and asking for an application with a camera on them to see if we can find information on the lay of the room. The video will hopefully show us where the security panel is located and where the guards are positioned. Then to verify the doors and windows and escape routes during the day. Mega will have looked at satellite maps but needs to be sure the information is current.

Clifton adjourns the meeting in time for me to get a short nap before I need to go to work. I need some rest, but I want to ask my goyles what they think of me using dragon blood to heal Gortanik. And wow, his name, I have to figure out a good nickname for him. Gortanik is a great name I guess but hard to say, in my opinion. Usually, I don't think I would ask about giving someone blood, but this is not an emergency, and although he is not healthy he can still recover in time.

"What do you guys think about me healing Gortanik with dragon blood? He is my friend, and his healing is going to be a process because of the ordeal he's suffered from Barat. I did it for John Collins, and it didn't seem to bind us together other than friendship."

"It shouldn't be a problem, and it is what we do, right? Help people?" Spar says. "I don't have a problem with it, go for it, honey."

"I also approve, beloved. Destiny takes care of what we are fated." He kisses me softly and steps onto the torp stage. Spar beside him they harden to stone. The pain on their faces still hurts me to see.

Lying down I wiggle into Mica's arms.

He says, "Thank you for asking us first. I'm guessing you wanted to be sure just in case it creates a bond?"

"That is exactly what I was thinking. But there is really only a friendship that is mostly in my mind. It might even be a little bit of a Florence Nightingale effect from him taking care of me. I don't see it happening, but magic is crazy stuff..." and Mica is snoring. Laying my head on his chest I fall into a comfortable slumber too.

42

SMILES

Kendra

I WANT to see Gortanik before we leave for work so after goodbyes Mica and I head to the medical facility. I think I'm going to have a drawing to rename the place. The medical facility is too impersonal... what if we dedicate it to Tana. I love that idea. I tap that thought into my tablet and send it to Clifton before I forget.

When I get to where the mage lies asleep, there's a gargoyle I can't remember meeting. I do know him however from Leta's lifetime. His name is Malachite, but he goes by Mal. He must've taken over for Jadeite but was he awake all night. Is his gift the same as Mica's?

"Good Morning, Mal I'm glad to see you here. Is your gift that you don't have to torp?"

"Yeah. It's way cool. I don't have to torp but for one day a month, different from like the prince dude Mica, I mean, um. Like, I don't have a glamour like he does either. Also, so Jadeite told me to like apologize to you since he didn't stay all night. He said he wouldn't be much use if he was hard as a rock." Here, Mal laughs a low "Hua, Hua" I remember the laugh from my new memories from Leta. He continues after I smile at his laugh. "I told him I would like to help out."

"And how is our patient?" I ask.

"So he's been sleeping like the dead since I got here. Oh sorry, hua hmm, I didn't mean anything. I just meant... like well, the doctors gave him a shot for his pain or somethin'. Well, that's what Jadeite told me. Anyway, he's out cold, isn't he?"

I say, "Thank you."

He nods and looks at Mica then says, "How ya doin' sir?"

"I'm fine. Thank you for staying here and giving up your free day. I know you enjoy your time in the sun," Mica responds.

"Yo dude and dudette, I really do enjoy the sun. So next month better get ready 'cause I'm a gonna have twice the fun! Hua hua ha! Anyway, I didn't mind staying to make sure Gortanik is taken care of. After all, he took care of you, Queen Kendra. Like when you needed it. Besides, I like to think we take care of each other in this city," Mal finishes.

"Mal, thank you for being that way. We just came to check on him before we go to work. I also want to help him heal and don't want to cut him. I wonder if he has a wound that I can use to give him a little dragon gift? Have you noticed anything that might be like an open injury or sore on him?"

"Well my queenliness, he is way beaten up under those covers yah see. I saw this area on his chest that's all cut open and stuff. The nurses gave him a bath while I was here. He is pretty torn up. I don't think he'd want you seein' all that, I mean... Your Majesty."

I reply in a whisper, "Maybe if we're cautious, he'll not wake and be shamed by his appearance." It'll be a good day when no one is ashamed of how they look. "Would you hold the blanket, so I can get some blood ready to give him." When he nods his assent to me, I use one of my own claws and puncture my finger with it.

I suck in my breath when I see the mage's thin body. My anger flares. He's been severely abused. I hold my fury and find the wound Mal was talking about then I drip in a couple of drops of blood and watch as it seeps into the cut with a life of its own. I shiver, see a flare of light, and a feeling of caring is amplified in me for this man. I can also see a binding thread cover his whole body. I can't possibly have another man in my life. This is just a deep friendship. That is why it is all over his body. Right?

He groans and turns over but stays asleep and looks more comfortable.

Mal remarks, "That is like totally way cool. Thanks, my queen. Er, umm..." Mal straightens his shoulders and looks at me carefully and seems to choose his words. "Loads of thanks for the care you show for your people. I have to say that even if you weren't my queen, I would give you my protection and my heart. Like, I didn't know I'd feel his healing too. It sure got hot in here. Did you know you are, like really hot? Woah." He wavers so I help him sit in the chair he had been in earlier.

I turn to Mica. "Did you feel anything Mica?" He gives me a goofy grin and slurs his words, "I tink it made me drunk." He hiccups and continues, "How'd you do that, babe?"

"I didn't do anything different from what I do for others. But it does feel different from when I gave you dragon blood." I look around the room to see if anyone else is affected and yes, many are sitting with their heads between their knees.

"Okay, Mica let's fly this off. You can't be drunk at work. Mal, I'm going to send Jericho a message to check on you. I walk over to the coffee bar and pour a cup of hot chocolate for Mal and take it to him. He drinks it and puts the cup down. However, he only sets it halfway onto the tray, and it rolls into the floor with a clank.

"Hey there dudette, I'll be fine my queenly. You can go. I'll protect the city."

I laugh and tell him just to protect the area around him right now. He smiles and agrees.

I swipe a quick message to Jericho telling him we need to investigate the difference in this healing from the others I have done. Mica and I hurry to leave and enjoy a good fly before work.

Clocking in I notice Chris isn't at her desk again. This is getting to be a habit. I'm used to seeing her and think I might just ask where she's been. Then I see a message on my notifications that says no daily briefing today. If there's any pressing information on the Firestarter, we'll be notified while on patrol. So Mica and I take off to start our tour. That solves anyone noticing his 'relaxed state' right now. It's starting to wear off some now, but not so much that someone wouldn't notice he's sloshed. I'm definitely driving today. Mica is giggling so much, I can't help but laugh too.

"It's nottn so much that I freel drunk but vrery happy... and carefree. You're purddy!" he slurs.

"Well Mica if you want a nap, I'm going to be driving around, and I'll wake you when we get a call."

"Well, maybe not..." up ahead is a somewhat minor accident and we need to look in on the occupants of the vehicles. Mica tries to call in the accident. But he grabbed my makeup compact instead of his phone. I let him continue trying to 'call' in the accident, and I pick up my phone and call it in, all the while listening to Mica cuss about his phone not working correctly. "Damnit, Athena..." He was so mad, he was cussing out his old friends.

He does sober enough he is passable as help with the accident. When everyone is cared for and the EMTs leave with one of the drivers. We start back on our regular tour. The wreck was the highlight of this shift. Now that it's over we need to fly to the apartments.

Mica and I have plenty of time to talk during work and decided we want to ask Jimmy and Vanessa if they'll do us the favor of investigating the SpotOn company right away. When we enter the apartment, the teens are watching a movie. They stop it and greet us with smiles. So, we lay out our plan for our little espionage. Jimmy goes to the table and gets a form then hands it to me. He explains to me that it's the guard schedule that his friend's dad gave him when he was told Jimmy has friends in high places who are investigating the fires.

Vanessa wants to be the one going into the oil company's building to ask for the application per Mega's plan. She has college prep classes that require research in the application area, so it'd serve two purposes. I show her the camera that we'll use to collect the data on. We decide together that if we put it in her hair, clipped to her headband no one would even question that it might be a camera. She's excited that she gets to help this way.

Jimmy is going to walk around the building and verify entrances and guards. We think since he is so young he could get away with it. If someone does stop and question him, he can always say he is bored and looking around because his girlfriend is inside filling out an application. In turn, I hadn't expected, Joe's father to give us a list of the guard rotations and shift changes. While it didn't provide us with everything, it did tell me he was on the right side.

Mica and I plan to get coffee and sit on a park bench across the street and appear like a couple relaxing after work. That's the plan anyway.

The teens get a head start on us, but we keep them in sight. Every now and then I glance at my phone to see how the camera is working. I can hear every word clearly in my headphones. It was just fine, even as Vanessa enters the building and walks up to a sophisticated looking bleach blonde receptionist. When she asks for an application though the blonde turns into a snide bitch.

"Do you not understand that applications are taken online these days? Hasn't anyone ever taught you anything about getting a job in the twenty-first century?" the blonde sneers.

I'm so proud of our girl when instead of wisecracking back a clipped retort, she says, "Why no ma'am, I didn't understand that at all. My friend Sherri said if I came in, you would be here and that you were so much help when she came in asking for work." That girl is on her toes and spins around slowly seeming to look around confused, giving us a great picture of the entire area.

The blonde responds to the flattery and softens her tone replying, "Oh, well, that is my job." She hands Vanessa a business card from her desk and continues, "Go to this website and fill out the information and if we have need of someone with your experience someone will call you."

Vanessa thanks the lady and leaves the building and heads straight for Jimmy who just came into sight from the side of the building.

As they take off toward the apartments, I hear her say, "I really am hungry. Would it be okay if we go to the diner?" She's asking us while acting like she's asking Jimmy. I tell Mica what she asked, and he nods taking my hand and crossing the street, so the teens are sure to see that we are headed in the direction of the diner now. I hear Vanessa say, "Thank you, see you there."

We ask for a booth for four when the waitress asks us how many in our party. No sooner are we seated than Jimmy and Vanessa find us and sit with us. We laugh and are being a little loud with the greetings and hugs. Then more quietly they ask if we got the information from the inside that we need.

"Yes, you did that so perfectly we got everything we need. What did you see Jimmy?" I ask.

"There are only two sets of doors in the back of the building and none on the sides. I saw a guard at each door and one on the roof. They were talking, so I think they have some Bluetooth earbud communication device connected to their phones. They didn't put their phones up to their ears but were looking at them and talking some. One of them did stop me and ask why I was back there. He took the 'I'm waiting on my girlfriend' excuse as gospel. They were all packing heat and wearing body armor."

Taking off her headband straightening her hair and putting it back on I watch Vanessa slip the tiny camera under her napkin and slide it toward me. I wait a little bit then fold it up and put it away in my pocket.

"Now, body armor brings up some questions," I say. Mega was right to have us wait, unless I miss my guess there's more going on than what they want us to know. "Thank you two very much. I think we can do the rest with ease now. I want both of you far from this side of town tonight, and I'm not even kidding."

They both agree telling us they'll be studying at the apartment. When we finally get back to the La Caverna, the kids go to the apartment, and we keep going and leave from the roof as usually. What a day. I'm worn out.

43

STEALTH

Kendra

I TALK to Clifton and let him know that the meeting with the High Guild will be canceled tonight. If we need their input, we'll call them after the mission, if it all goes as planned. Now the team for our incursion to retrieve the schedule gathers in my allodium. Mega is giving information and orders to everyone.

"Does everyone understand their jobs? Questions anyone? Then let us be on our way," he says.

Kino opens a portal, and we're all on the rooftop of SpotOn in seconds. Dolo makes a scuffing noise scraping his feet on the roof. Mica turns to him with a finger to his lips. He motions for us to stay put and sends Spar forward with a flick of his hand.

Spar, already knowing what he needs to do, creeps to the edge of the roof. He listens for a minute before lowering himself over the edge. We're quiet. Just squatting in the dark, behind the tall facade on the top of the building. Since the moon is almost full, there is quite a bit of light. So, us staying undercover is essential.

Spar floats back up where we can see him, his head just over the edge of the building, and waves Dolo to him. Dolo shakes his head and puts up a finger for him to hold off. Dolo's job is to be sure the security cameras and alarm systems are offline while we high-jack the Firestarter schedule. His team is relaying information to him right now. He nods his head as he taps at his tablet then goes to Spar, and they both disappear.

The rest of us are on sentry duty. Our job is to warn Kino of any guards in the area. Once he is notified, he'll put them to sleep quickly and quietly. Just then, Mica touches him on the shoulder and points, Kino capers away and is back before I even miss him. He nods to Mica. We all understand that the guard he was sent to put to sleep is out.

Since we have the roof covered, my job is to use my senses. I search in other ways to 'see' if anyone else is here. I feel someone is close and behind our position. I reach for Mica and at the same time, I tele-speak to Mega.

"General, will you please tell Mica and Kino there's a group of people coming from the east side of the building."

"Done, Edling. It would seem that several of the employees of this company are working late."

Mica and Kino, along with several of the Ducere, leave to take care of employees and make sure they do not interfere or know what has transpired tonight. Jadeite is with Mega and me and is ready for whatever could come our way it appears.

"We won't need it, but did you by any chance bring a knife with you, Edling? It would be a good practice if anyone were to be injured severely on any of our missions," Mega says.

"I have my new diamond-edged knife in my boot all the time now. I thought of that too. Claws sometimes leave a jagged cut that doesn't bleed as well. I know that sounds bad, but I heal so fast that it helps if my wound is straight and deep.

We hear a scuffling noise and turn toward it just in time to see the

Ducere running toward us at a fast clip. Kino opens the portal at the same time as he arrives. We rush inside and wait for all the others.

Spar and Dolo are last. Spar has a shit-eating grin plastered on his face. I can't wait to hear what has happened.

Jericho has our portal direct us into my allodium. There, Mega takes charge as everyone sits. "Dolo, was the mission a success? Did you collect the schedule we want?"

Dolo replies, "Yes General, we were able to get the schedule for the fires and a little bit more. Let me read through this for a second, and I'll send it to your tablets. It seems that we may have hit a gold mine."

All of our tablets ding simultaneously as we receive the documents. I immediately notice the information he's referring to. Not only is this a detailed calendar of planned cartel trafficking fires, but it also contains the names and places of each of the persons involved. Bingo, it has details of the precise illegal actions that have been undertaken as well as those that are to take place. It seems that not only drugs, but people are to be auctioned off after each fire. The fires just take attention off the route used to carry the people and drugs into the area. There's also a map with labels of places I don't recognize or understand. Yes, it's a gold mine.

Mega starts again, "I need a report of each of your activities from the minute we stepped onto the roof to when we returned here. Starting with Spar."

Spar responds immediately, "Sir, as soon as I stepped off the roof I checked for people in the area, when I was sure it was clear I returned to the group to get Dolo. I intended to reach into the door of the building to let Dolo disarm the alarm. But, as I was standing on the ground, the door opened hard and slammed me back against the wall. Dolo was crammed in with me behind the door. A couple was making out, and they had pushed the door open. They never saw us. After they left, I stuck a claw in the seam of the door so it wouldn't close all the way, and it didn't. He lifts up a bent claw with a satisfied grin. Dolo went straight in and disarmed the system and cameras. Amber and Mason were in with him. I waited at the door, guarding them while they completed the mission. Then about ten minutes or so later I heard what sounded like Kino singing and a thud. My best guess was he put someone to sleep. Then Amber and Mason came out with Dolo behind them. He said he was ready. I held up for a second because I had heard a commotion. After it stopped, we hurried to get back to you and Kendra on the roof.

"Dolo what can you add?" Mega asks.

"When I went in the door to turn off the system, I found out that there is a keypad and a box, but the alarm was not on. Crappy security if you ask me, but I was happy to be able to take advantage of it. I interrupted the cameras and sent the others to retrieve the information. When they came back, we met Spar outside, and I made sure the door locked. There was quite a bit of noise so after making sure the way was clear, we hurried to get back on the roof and through the portal. When I got here, I made sure to turn the cameras at SpotOn back in operating status. Then I found the file you need and sent it to the team members."

"Commander Mica report, please." Mega orders.

Mica starts, "Sir when you had told us that Kendra found people in the area, on your orders, we investigated and found them. It looked like several employees were having a small party. A few were wearing birthday hats and laughing and stumbling a little on the way out of the building. We saw Spar when we peeked around the side of the building and to make sure that none of the people saw him, Kino created a... diversion. As soon as the people were concentrating on the distraction. We started back to the roof.

"Commander Kino, what kind of diversion did you create?"

Kino looks at me with a pleading look of innocence then answers Mega. "Sir, there were only two women in the group of nine. The women were walking in front of the men on the way to the parking lot. Seeing Spar, I knew we should do something so these men would not see him, so I created a breeze and blew their skirts up and tucked them into their waistbands." Kino smiles a wilted looking smile my direction, blinks and continues, "It worked, not one of those men looked Spar's way. When they all gawked at the women, we took off back to the roof quickly."

Mica laughs out loud, then notices the look of shock on my face and shuts it down. Amber speaks up, "When Mason and I were inside and downloading the contents of their programs. I noticed a phone that had been left on a desk and snagged it." She starts to hand the phone to Mega who points with his chin to Dolo, so she gives it to him.

He says, "I can check this out and get it back before torptime.

Mega then says, "Thank you all. You did well tonight. Everyone is dismissed."

I begin, "Mega, with this information I think we should involve TASS. Mica and I can fabricate a reason to be late at work, so we can discover the one starting the fire and nab them, but the trafficking of people might take a bigger operation. If we do it, I'm sure the Ceorfan will be compromised. I want to take no chance that we'll be discovered right now."

"I agree with passing the intel, but I do not think you should call late to work. It might draw unwanted attention. Would you like to call the Chairman now or do we want to visit?" he asks.

"It's going to have to be a call because they'll want to review all of the information and make sure their operatives are safe. Then they will need to have a meeting. We'll be there and can supply any information they need then."

The guards to the allodium are letting in the chefs to prepare our meals, so I invite Mega to stay, and he could sit in while I call José Brinker from here. He declines with his impeccable manners and leaves me and my guygoyles some free time to talk.

After a bit, I excuse myself to call Jared and tell him what we'd found out. I also had to make sure he has the fire schedule, so he can go through it. He has this uncanny way of picking up things that everyone else misses. He also has a bit of news and says, "Kendy... Sis, I love it when he uses my old nickname, so I listen carefully. I'm getting ready to purchase a large estate here in Scotland. I'm going to get Dana to help with some of the redesigns. You know so I can have dragon and gargoyle parties in private!" *That's all!?* I'm kinda let down. I thought he was going to say he turned purple and is dying his hair to match or something really life-changing.

"Are you serious?" I laugh as I ask my question.

"Yea Sis, why not? Anyway, I need a bunch of efs in storage."

I just laugh at him again then I sober a bit and say, "I'll have the artisans in Navan start making some."

"Kendy, I've got something else, something important to tell you..."

For Jared to use his nickname for me wasn't unusual. But anytime he said Kendy and important in the same paragraph, I knew to listen.

"So, I just need you to know I have a girlfriend."

You might think, "Duh, he is a multimillionaire playboy, of course he has a girlfriend!" but, that isn't my Jare. He's never treated women like that. He doesn't really go for the ones who throw themselves at him either. So, if he says he has a girlfriend, I should really take notice.

"I think you met her once. You wouldn't remember though because it was... well, it was *that* night."

I didn't have to think even a second to know what "that night" means. It was the night a hole was blown in the TASS headquarters, and I was kidnapped.

"Anyway, I thought you should know her name is Jolie Woods. You probably have seen her in the movies. She's going to help me with the manor here."

Well, at least I know that the information I had regarding his redheaded girlfriend was correct. I was told they were getting serious. So, if he is telling me she's a girlfriend—it's serious!

We finish our conversation with a bit of brother-sister stuff, and I let him go since I needed to call Dana.

I call him and ask him about Jolie. He tells me she's a great girl. He said it in a way that I wondered if he had something to say to me. He wouldn't budge, so I move on and update him on what happened at SpotOn and the information we recovered. Dana isn't one who likes to talk on the phone, so the call ended pretty quickly.

After the calls are finished, and we all get our fill of the delicious meal Chef Morgan had prepared I ask, "Do we get cable in the cave?"

Mica laughs and says, "We have movies if you want to watch something. Are you up for that?"

"That sounds good where do we do that anyway?" I wonder out loud.

Mica answers, "I know you didn't know 'cause we've been so busy, but over here in the sittin' area's a big screen. All you've got to do is press this button." He shows me a little cubby with a remote that he pulls out and uses. As he presses it, a television comes down from a section of the ceiling that I hadn't noticed before. I find a comfortable place on the couch and sit, Spar on one side and Kino on the other. Mica is seated in a chair close to the sofa searching his tablet and scribbling in a notebook.

When I look over at him, he raises an eyebrow and asks, "Is it okay if I study this information that we collected tonight while we're watching?"

"I don't mind at all." Then turning to Spar, I ask, "What movie are we watching anyway?"

"We picked this new vampire flick featuring Donna-Stasia Green, but if you want something different just say so," he says.

"Nope, it's one of my favorites as you well know."

Kino jumps up and tells us he'll be right back. He comes back with the claw files and starts on Spar's bent cartoon claw as the show begins. He takes care of all of our nails during the movie. When he's finished with mine, I scrape them down one of his arms. Unfortunately, I'm so caught up in the movie that I totally skip the sexy part.

It wasn't lost on him and chortled at my lame attempt. When I look away from the screen for a second, he's looking completely satisfied. For once it feels like family business tonight. I'm thrilled as the show ends.

I remember to tell my princes that the weirdest thing happened when I gave some blood to Gortanik. I stumble over saying his name, and Kino says, "Love, maybe you should ask him if you can call him Kick. That is the name we called him in training when we were young. He was deadly with his feet in man-to-man combat."

"Thank the creator of all things! I've been trying to decide on a nickname and ask him if it's okay, but Gort just sounds terrible," I laugh when I explain it to them.

"Also, Mica told me about the effects of the dragon blood magic when you gave some to Kick. The drunkenness usually happens to and around the Fae. Maybe his lineage is from them. I never knew his parents. We can find out in the Hall tonight if you want to when you get home from work?" Kino says.

"Sounds like a plan Rockstar, consider me down," I say.

Sunrise in nearing. I can feel the warmth in my blood. Both Spar and Kino tell me good-torp and head to the platform. Looking toward them, I watch and start to say 'wings up' when they lean on each other and touching the sides of their heads together making fish lips and blow me kisses. Awhh, that's so sweet! Then they harden to stone. Damn, they are so cute!

"Are you ready to sleep, princess, or do you want to stay up and rest later?" Mica asks.

"I'm not really tired, and you're working on those forms. Do you mind if I go to the medical facility to see how Kick is, now that it's been several hours since I got them all drunk?"

"No, I don't mind at all. But should I go, I'm not sure if I like you being alone?"

"No, stay here we're in our home. I can defend myself pretty well these days. There isn't much chance of danger anyway. Here, I have this app on my phone I can link to yours. I'll put my finger on the button, and if it comes off it'll signal your phone instantly, then you'll know I need help. Is that good enough?"

He repeats my earlier statement to Kino, "Consider me down, beautiful."

After adding the app to his phone, I show him my finger on the button. I kiss him before I leave.

44

ALIVE

Kendra

QUIETLY I ENTER the medical facility and see Dr. Ogman. "Hello, Doctor. How are the diamond needles coming?

"I am sorry, I don't have them ready yet. They should be ready any day now." Then he returns to some experiment he's in the middle of conducting. I've been politely dismissed, I guess.

I take my finger off of my safety app and message Mica that I'm safely in the medical room.

As I walk over to the mage's bed. He's sitting upright and playing cards with a nurse who looks like a pixie, but the closer I get the more she looks like a tree elf. A real lady, small with green looking skin. She laughs and looks up when I move closer. She immediately stops playing cards, closes down, and backs away stammering inaudibly.

"Please, don't worry. I'm not mad. You're doing a wonderful job," I say in a rush. She scoots away from me like I'm a leper and disappears.

Kick says, "Please, don't worry, Your Majesty. The nurse is a pixie, and it's her nature to move quickly."

"I just don't want to upset anyone or have the ones who're caring for you, not doing their jobs because I'm here. I don't want them intimidated by me. How are you Gortanik?"

"I am fine, Majesty."

"Please, when we are together like this, you may call me Kendra. I also heard you have a nickname. May I use it, Kick?"

He makes a face which tells me he's wondering how I could've found that out. But he doesn't look upset. I wait only seconds for his answer.

"Yes, my lady, you may. You may call me anything you desire, and I'll answer you with gladness. It's been so long that I have even thought of being Kick. I have been another man, living a nightmare. I don't even remember yet who I am. It does make me happy to think that I can be as free and happy as when I was called by that name. Majesty, today I feel like a new man. I know you gave me your blood. Since that time—I am a new man. Thank you, for your gift. It is the most caring thing that's happened to me in a very long time. Still, I have had a lot of care since I have arrived here. Even in my jail cell. My body is recovering wonderfully." Suddenly, Kick seems to remember himself. He slowly and with difficulty, rises to his feet and begins what looks like a very deep, down on one knee bow to me.

"Oh no, I won't have that Kick you're just recovering. I know you intend to respect me, but no. No bowing while you're recovering." I hop up and take him by the arm and very gently push him back into his bed. He's so emaciated by his torture, I am able to lower him without much effort.

This is the minute that Dr. Ogman decides to come over to us. "Queen Kendra."

He calls me Queen Kendra as a compromise I'd asked him to call me Kendra, and he wanted to call me "Your Majesty" or "My Queen" every time he saw me... so, Queen Kendra, it is.

"Our patient, Gortanik is well enough to leave the medical facility."

Without another word, I understand the unsaid problem. Since our new citizen has no home and everyone is torping, I am responsible for his care. I take him to the lunchroom above the sparing area, so we can have some breakfast. I type a quick message to Mica, so he comes to join us.

When I introduce him to Kick, they're quiet but cordial to each other. I can tell they'll need to get to know each other better before they let their walls down. I hope, not without reason, they'll become friends after that.

After a few uncomfortable minutes talking with Kick and Mica, I explain to Kick that Mica and I must get to work. We escort him to my rooms and, along the way I tell him that Mica and I work during the days as Federal Park Rangers.

"This... this isn't a good idea. You are the queen. What about... you have to remember you... you must... well, umm... Mica, tell her. Wait, what is a Federal Park Ranger's job?"

I happened to be taking a drink of coffee from my thermos when he asks that last question. Unfortunately, hot coffee doesn't feel any better being sprayed out like water. I covered my little accident by pretending to cough... "Well Kick, a Park Ranger is basically the same as the police. We enforce the federal laws on federal lands. In our case, Mica and I work in the Cueva Hallow Caverns National Park."

"What? You carry a gun? That means you could have people shooting at you. No, that isn't acceptable. Mica please..."

"Kick, I understand your thoughts. Please get to know our people and me. You will know that this is part of who I am. I love my job, and I am very good at it." I see Mica nodding his head, chin down looking at the floor, in agreement with me. "Despite what anyone else wants, I'm keeping my job." Here, I almost laugh at seeing Mica shaking his head vigorously no at this point. I guess he has heard this argument too many times and knows what the outcome will be every time.

We manage to find Kick some clothes, so he can change out of the tattered robe he is wearing. One of Spar's old black hoodies that zips up the middle and some black slacks, that are baggy on him, seemed to fit the bill. "It'll do for now," I tell him.

Beaming with joy, he tells us, "It's been so long since I've felt any type of compassion. Thank you both."

I leave the two of them, so I can get ready in my bathroom. When I come out, I find that Kick and Mica are talking like old friends. That's good, and I'm happy about it. I have to butt in, so I can show our new friend the bathroom and tell him to stay here and explore Navan. On our way out the door I say, "Get lots of rest, and we will be back before sunset."

When we walk into the front doors of the Ranger's Station Chris is sitting at her desk working. I walk over to her and say, "Hello Chris."

She remains very serious and just nods hello to me. Maybe I shouldn't pry, but she is my friend, and I want to help her. I take a deep breath and ask, "Chris... what's wrong?" She breaks down.

She explains that she and Murphy have been getting close and she's started caring for him. He told her this morning they can't be anything but friends because they work together and he's her boss. What can I say to that. Technically, he's right. I give her a huge hug and let her know I love her and wait for the tears to stop.

Mica has already gone to his desk and clocked in, gotten his gear on, and now is waiting for me so we can get to the daily briefing. Chris notices him and says, "Dear you had better get your butt ready too. I'll be right as rain. You'll see."

I'm reluctant to leave her and whisper, "Chris, we can talk if you need me. You have my cell."

When we get to our daily meeting with Murphy, he's in worse shape than Chris. Not crying but really destroyed and looking like a rumpled mess. Okay, this isn't making any sense. I've got to find an option for my friends and my other colleagues. None of us want to see these two like this. So, on the way to our patrol SUV, I snag a handbook, so I can find a reasonable suggestion that may help them be able to be together and still work.

Mica, being totally sober today, drives as we talk about Chris and Murphy. I review the handbook and find that not only can they not fraternize and work together, but Murphy can also be brought up on charges for harassing a government employee and sexual misconduct if anyone reports this relationship to the higher-ups. If he weren't her boss things would be fine. Now that I'm back at my desk, I think I'll check to see if there are any openings in other departments. Maybe one of them can change to a different department or get promoted away from the other. Then they can see each other and be happy. That's my logic anyway.

I'm working on finding other options when Mica starts to talk about the plan to find the Firestarter.

He says, "You know I think the schedule's right when it says that the next fire is supposed to be started today. But all the fires have been started at night. So, I think maybe I need to check the fire times against different time zones when we get home."

"Why would you think that Mica? The time zones across the US and Mexico aren't different enough to account for that many hours."

"I think whoever made the schedule doesn't live here. I think they're sending it to the oil company and the cartel to use. That means another layer of criminal activity."

"We need to get this information to TASS. I'll call Jared."

"Bossy girl, I can give you more ideas of what to tell me to do," Mica flirts.

I already hear Jared's phone ringing. So, I don't want to be caught saying something enticing to my boyfriend. So, I wait until he looks at me and I wink at him instead. He smiles at me and then makes it a goofy grin while he continues to drive our beat tour.

Jared answers, "Hey Sis, how are you? Is everything all right?"

"Yes," I tell him, "but I need to give you some information that Mica has been mulling over, and I think it might have some merit."

After telling him what we had been thinking he says, "We've been assigning agents all morning and fine-tuning the sting for the capture tonight. We have surveillance of the area as we speak. We only need your Ceorfan in the background to back us up. Your people do not even need to show themselves unless they see some danger which we don't have covered. As to the higher ups in the crime, Sis, you know it's always that way. We can try to get one of the criminals we catch tonight to roll over on their bosses, but it may or may not happen."

"Okay little brother." I like to call him that but he's not little, and I know it. "I just wanted to tell you what we'd thought of this morning. I'm sure Mega has some of the Elite picked out to back you up tonight. I wish it were me. I worry about you, but I'll make sure after sunset. If anything happens before, then call, and Mica and I can back you up with Dana."

"I'll talk to you later then, Sis, if you need me, I'm here," he says hanging up.

I ask Mica if he could hear that conversation or should I tell him what Jared had said.

"No, I got it. He's right it's a turkey shoot whether a criminal will spill on his boss or not. Most cases with the cartels they don't. You understand why."

"So true my handsome man—so true."

We spend the rest of our shift helping drunk vacationers find their way back to their families and verifying campers know the fire danger and that they are obeying the campsite rules. When we're filling out our reports I have a thought; I might just check, while I'm on the computer, to see if the Park Service has any job openings on the board. I get excited when I look at one in a managerial position equal to Murphy's in another department, so I print it for Chris. Whoo-hoo! This might just be the ticket, and a better paycheck for Chris if she gets the position. Feeling good about myself, I clock out and stow my gear in my locker. After I close up my locker, I stop by the printer and pick up the job opening I had printed out for Chris. I see her, head down, and working. She is so oblivious, she doesn't even notice me standing there... so I clear my throat.

She slowly looks up and, in a most un-Chris like way mutters, "Hi Kendra did you have a good tour? Not too many crazies today?"

Smiling, I answer, "No ladybug, not too many. But I noticed that there's a job opening in the Human Resources department. You've been working so closely with them for so long... I just thought it might be a great opportunity. What do you think?"

"Let me see that," she says taking the paperwork from me.

She is smiling now showing a visible lift to her spirit. "You know Kendra this might just be what I have been looking for. Why on Earth didn't I think of this first," she squeaks. She jumps up and hugs me tight, and I laugh with her.

When I back away from her I say, "I'm keeping my fingers crossed that this works out then. We'll figure it out if it doesn't. I'm happy you're better too. I'm going home, see you tomorrow." I leave her as she starts to fill out the job application online from her computer.

45

READY

Kendra

AS WE STEP out of Jasper, the illustrious south-eastern New Mexico wind is starting to blow. We hurry to the front doors getting peppered by sand along the way. Brian holds the door for us as we enter the lobby. I tell him hi and thank him as I move on to what I think of, now, as Jimmy's apartment.

I smile to myself as I pause at the door and extend my dragon senses into the small apartment. Mica nods and grins at me until I know it's for sure safe to go inside. After we walk in, we see Jimmy and Vanessa sitting on the couch watching television. They seem pretty comfortable and not as stressed as they had been earlier this week.

"Well, you two look comfortable and happy as clams. What's up?" I ask.

"We both just aced all of our midterms! We're celebrating with a movie. We don't have to do anything at school tomorrow but check in and then leave because we're seniors. Then it's spring break for a week. Hey, we're going for a swim in the river later do you guys want to go with us? You can bring everyone and make it a party."

"So, what you are saying is that you're going skinny dipping and it's just you two so it's okay for the Ceorfan to show up because no one else will be there?" I laugh.

"Ermm... uh..." Jimmy stumbles over his words, so I decided to save him.

"I'll think about it. Where is it? The Hitchin' Hole is used too much."

"Okay, not the Hitchin' Hole then. How about The Rope then, that's at least twenty miles from there?" Vanessa asks.

"I haven't been there in years. Have you ever been there Mica?" I ask him with a little tilt to my head looking through my lashes.

"No, is it fun?" he asks us.

"Yes!" We all say at the same time.

Vanessa, the ultimate control freak, says she'll bring the food and drinks if we bring towels and blankets to sit on. Also, she wants us to bring another rope just in case the one that is usually there is worn out, or someone has taken it down.

Sounds like a plan for our evening and night then. TASS and Mega can handle the arrests. That'll be better for us all, and we can be sure that Jimmy and Vanessa are safe at the same time.

We portal home from the roof. Kick is waiting in the sitting area of my rooms and greets us as we get home. *You know he's really a good-looking man.* Shut-up I have all the handsome men I need. He is going to be a good friend.

"Hello, how was work today Your Majesty? Mica? Or should I say, Commander Mica?"

"We had a fairly easy work day. Not much happened. What were you up to?"

"I went to the Halls of History and studied for a few hours today. My strength is returned, and I thought I would learn some about this city and about the people. It's fascinating."

"Kick, do you feel strong enough to give some information to the High Guild tonight? We'll meet about thirty minutes after sunset."

"Of course, Your Majesty, I want to help. I will be able to help you find Barat and the Horde, so they can be wiped off the face of the Earth," he says passionately.

"That's the goal! Now, for my own goal. I need a nap. I do not mean to be rude and leave you when I know you've been alone all day, but I really need some sleep." Mica and I leave to sleep. I crawl into my bed still dressed and snuggle up to Mica and am dreaming about my goyles in seconds. Somehow Kick also made it into my dreams. There, he was so full of information I feel an even greater need to make sure he gets to tell his story in the HG meeting tonight.

Stretching as I wake it seems that I'm all alone here for once. I can tell all of my goyles are close by, but not with me. Elmer is attached to my top and stays there as I get up and head to the bathroom. I decide that I'm taking a shower and shaving everything, before our swim at The Rope. In the shower, I have the best idea. I'll invite any Ceorfan who wants to go. They might like to get out of the cave for a swim.

I dress with my bathing suit under my clothes and put on a pair of worn tennis shoes. Not real queenly but I intend to leave the HG meeting tonight and go straight to The Rope.

All my goyles and Kick are ready to get going so I ask, "Hey guys, do you want to go to the allodium with me to see what chef Morgan has ready for us to eat?" Everyone quickly agrees.

Chef Morgan takes his job seriously. But, he's so happy to do it. He says it's fun, and I relish doing it for you my queen. Pun intended the good chef tells me.

It always smells so good in the allodium, and we go straight to the buffet. I tell my goyles all about my idea of inviting all the Ceorfan while filling my plate full.

Mica says, "It's a great idea, we should pulse the invite. We just need to make sure they bring their own food and towels and such. No one lives in the area for miles so we shouldn't be caught in the open.

If you don't object, I would like to have the area scouted before you pulse the invitation."

"Good idea Mica." Then we sit and eat. We are digging into a feast of breakfast foods when the rest of the High Guild members start to filter in for breakfast. After everyone is finished and taken their proper seat, I nod for Clifton to start the meeting.

Overall, the meeting is more on the information sharing side and less on the decision-making perspective. We have got quite a bit of information about how TASS intends to apprehend the Firestarter and any cartel members if a fire is started. There'll be Elite warriors in the area unseen for back-up. They will get involved only if needed. The HG members are happy that I'll be away with my Ducere swimming with Jimmy and Vanessa. They also approve of inviting whoever wants to come. But Jericho also cautions, "Please do not be too let down if others do not join you. Remember the Guild have remained in hiding for more than forty generations."

Clifton added, somewhat dryly, "Introvert is not a good enough description for our solitarian ways."

Clifton wraps up the remaining business in a matter of minutes. The most important topic is the schedule for Tana's funeral. "We are going to celebrate her life, tomorrow night, by placing a statue of her at the library in town. Then we will have a reception here in Navan. My queen, members of the High Guild, I have one final issue before I close the meeting—Gortanik."

The entire room quiets as all eyes turn toward our new guest. Since he is sitting near me, in Jared's spot, I have an excellent view of each face. Most in the room have an intrigued sense to their gaze, others the look of antipathy is obvious.

Clifton asks him with an ease and confidence which he has generally not had until now, "Warrior Mage Gortanik, I see you are feeling better. I hope that is the case."

"It is Count de Treon," Kick replies. If Clifton were taken aback by Kick knowing him he didn't show even the smallest intimation.

Clifton continued, "If you please, this is a forum for an exchange of information so that our queen may rule the Guild as wisely as she is able. She makes most of her decisions, only after much input. She excludes no one from adding to her understanding. Warrior Mage Gortanik will you give us your story?"

Kick stands and bows his head saying, "I thank Queen Kendra for rescuing me from my torment. I have much to tell, and I hope that the information I provide will assist in your plan to capture or kill Barat and the Horde of Crafted. I will be as concise as possible, but I must tell a part of my own story together."

His delivery is sober, and his speech is eloquent. He took almost an hour, but he was so well prepared and smooth-spoken, the room was locked in attention, waiting for each word. In the end, many of the HG is in tears. Shaking breaths from the attendees are the only sounds in the room after he concludes.

He's endured much. His escape plan was risky, and I believe he deserves a hero's welcome. Most importantly he has given us vital information which we need to capture or kill our enemy. In fact, he can show us the exact location of our enemy's camp.

"Gortanik..." I see his face form the slightest of frowns and feel a twitch of sadness in my spirit. I'm sure he was taken back by my calling him his formal name instead of his nickname. I stop and start again. "Kick," this time I see him relax, so I continue, "we work with a multi-umvirate called The Alumbradai Sanctuary State. They're a power in this world who rule with a longer arm than presidents, kings, or queens. Together we're trying to make the Earth a better place to live. This group is heading the mission to erase the Horde of Barat, and its leader. Will you provide this same information to them, but in a much larger meeting, when I can set it up?"

"Yes, my queen, I will speak to them. We must eradicate this menace as soon as we can. It will take an intricate plan, and it will be time-consuming. I believe that it is possible to end his existence though."

"Clifton, please call the TASS chairman and put him on speaker," I say.

My personal assistant is quick, and the number is dialing in seconds. Everyone at the table is quiet and rapt waiting for José to answer.

"This is Chairman Brinker's office. Please hold for the Chairman," says his receptionist in her most business manner. The line goes very quiet. You know the kind of quiet where you're wondering if the line went dead. Then, a click and José is on the line.

He says, "Your Majesty, how can I help you? Are you all right?"

"Yes, I'm fine. Thank you for asking. I would like an emergency meeting of TASS set up so that the mage who had infiltrated Navan can speak and provide testimony concerning Barat. We're sure his information will lead us to the Horde and allow us to put an end to the evil bastard running it."

José replies, "I will set that in motion as soon as we are off this call. It may take a day or two. I will contact you with the specifics as soon as possible. As always, my lady, you and the Ceorfan, are welcome at Fiatrill Hall if you wish to stay until the meeting is convened."

"Thank you, chairman. I will be there around five o'clock my time Sunday. If everything runs smoothly during tonight's sting."

"I assure you that tonight's mission is well in hand. Your Firestarter will not be free after tonight. Neither will some of the slavers who run drugs and sell people in the area. That is being implemented as we speak," he says.

"I agree the sooner, the better. Alright then, if that is everything I'll see you tomorrow night. Good night José," I say and then hang up.

Looking around the room, I see that everyone is stiff and on the ready. Locked and loaded so to speak. To alleviate some of the stress I ask, "So shall we have some fun before the fight. So who wants to go for a swim with us?"

Heads turn away, others look at their feet most are shifting and grumbling. I let them off the hook. "You don't have to go. This is for fun, not an obligation. I hope to see you later tonight. Please dismiss the meeting Clifton," I say.

To Mica, I say, "Now on with the fun. Shall I send a pulse to the entire Guild?"

He nods and smiles so I send a short pulse inviting my people to swim at The Rope. They understand coordinates well, so I don't have to get into details. I feel a few light pulses back. Most are unwilling to leave the cave, but some are excited to be able to get out and have some fun.

Spar is rubbing his hands together and asks, "Are you ready to leave now."

I smile at him and say, "Yes, if Mica has gotten all of our gear ready."

I'm surprised to see Sondra and Gem with Mega. Kino's mother is looking very lovely as she stands with her daughter, Sondra. Kino's sister is smiling ear to ear, and Mega is very attentive to her. How did I ever miss that they were a couple?

I'm happy that the old grump is coming with us for fun and bringing a date at that. However, I've got an idea, it's also business. The Ducere and my general don't like to let me out of their sight, not since my abduction. That feels like such a distant memory now that I've added my grandmother's memories. I feel much more settled thinking of it now. Maybe they're comforting me in a way. Yes, I believe that's the case. My spirit is more relaxed with the horrid memories now. I shake the thoughts away. This is for fun remember? I tell myself.

Mica has divided up all the gear, and a decent sized crowd of about fifty goyles is milling around us. So, I whisper in his ear, "Take charge of the trip big-boy. Let's have some fun."

He shivers as I blow lightly in his ear. He grants me one of his sexy grins and reaches for my hand as he starts, "All right guys and goyles." He laughs at his own joke... no one else does. "This is a fun trip, but we need a few rules. We're still on the down low. For you that haven't been in modern society that's how we say we need to keep the secret of our existence from the world. You can bring blankets, towels, and food, but bring them home with you. Clean up everything when we leave. Everyone there will be adults, but the two human teenagers are very young, take that into account. Okay, let's fly."

With that, we make our way to the entrance of Navan. Excitement is high, and smiles are aplenty.

46

SWIMMING

Kendra

THE NIGHT IS quiet except for the sound of wings flapping. I feel thrilled to be out here with this many of my people. I've got to ensure we're able to do this more often and more freely in the future. I can't explain the exhilaration I feel. Words can't do it justice. It's a closeness that only teams and loyal families have. As one of us moves we all move. No wonder the bats fly this way, it is thrilling, like a synchronized dance in the air. Not that we look neat or are in order, we aren't.

Our flight is way too short for me when Kino sends Jadeite and Ore to make sure we're alone in the area. It was checked before but no sense in being lax. They pulse that the way is safe. Kino nods and pulses for us to land. The Elite warriors in the group re-con the area and set up watch stations before we get loud.

I take a moment from helping Mica set up our area to people watch. My people I think. Looking around, not wanting to intrude on anyone, I see person after person with a smile. It is obvious this is a prominent if not pivotal event for each of them.

I see Mega as he spreads a blanket for Sondra and Gem. I watch as he puts his pack on the ground and begins unloading a boatload of stuff. That nut managed to bring a whole feast, including a couple of bottles of wine and several floaties and inner tubes. He's blowing them up now... ha-ha, why I think that is funny is beyond me. Maybe, I'm just happy because this's what I wish for them—to just be normal.

Stress is leaving my body, and I'm relaxing when Jimmy and Vanessa drive up in his old beat up looking Ford truck. It seems like he's working on it. It has several areas where new metal has been welded in patching the rusty parts on the body. Ore looks over to me and pulses a question asking me if they are the young ones we're waiting for. I pulse back that they are and he relaxes and melts back into the surrounding trees.

Just then, I see a portal and watch as Dana and a beautiful brunette step through, followed by Jared and Jolie. They're already in their swimwear. Several of the Ceorfan run up to them to say their hellos.

The Pecos River runs through this area and is deep right here. Not too many people come out here because it is out of the way and hard to get to and well... snakes. I think the teens thought it would be fun for them. But when they thought they could talk us into coming, they relished the idea of giving the Ceorfan some time outside. They are thoughtful that way. Like my people, they belong with us. Jadeite is talking with them and helping them unload the ton of food and some folding tables. Vanessa is our go-to girl for parties from now on.

They also brought a trailer with a 4 by 4 on it. They might have to take off the top if they think many of the gargoyles are going to fit. I take it back. Jimmy has Jadeite on the top, and it's holding as they rev the engine and back it off the trailer. Oooh, it starts to tip up with all the weight and Jadeite raises his wings and lifts some, and it levels out—close one.

While I've been people watching my goyles have set out a blanket and food. I chuckle at them looking all proud of themselves. I notice Kick is leaning on a tree. He's looking at me... all alone. Not for long though Vanessa, bless her, goes over and hands him a sandwich and tells him she wants him suited up and she needs ropes up on the trees lining the river which have limbs that stretch over it. He winks at me in a way that seems as if we have been friends for years. I smile at him, so he'll know I saw the wink. Fuck it, I wink back. He blinks making me laugh. I think maybe his mind is healing a little like his body. I can hope that's the case.

He and Vanessa have managed to find three trees which have limbs over the river and are still high enough to swing from. Kick hangs the ropes with magic, all at one time. He turns and asks Jadeite, his friend if he'll test one to make sure it is high enough for a gargoyle.

Jadeite comes over accepting the challenge. Everyone watches his beautiful body as he walks to the rope. The trees are in a line along the river, but the river is about six feet lower than the bottom of the trees with an incline that the humans will have to climb. Good thing they're young it wouldn't be easy for someone who doesn't have some muscle, especially because it's wet and slick.

Kick hands the rope to my warrior and tells him to start running from behind the tree where it's flat and swing over the water then let go of the rope. That's precisely what my fine Ducere does. To our surprise, he hovers in the air after he lets go of the rope and never touches the water.

Vanessa and Jimmy start laughing loudly. She tells her boyfriend, "Jimmy you should show them how we do this." Without waiting for a second, he shucks his clothes off runs at the rope and grabs it while he is in full gallop. He swings high out over the water and flips into a dive before he crashes into the river, hard. He pops up to applause and blushes as he climbs up the embankment. Now everyone who has clothes on is stripping down. Thank the creator, they have on suits!

I stand at the edge of the blanket my goyles put down for me and making eye contact with each of them I start to wiggle out of my tight flying pants. I hear a breath hitch and a strangled groan. Continuing to take off my clothes with as much sex appeal as I can muster I stand in front of them in a black string bikini. And they say... nothing.

Let down, I reach for my top to cover myself up, and start to walk off. Kino stops me by reaching around my waist and pulling me to him.

He says, "Don't walk off, we were just enjoying the view a little too much for words. You are so gorgeous that I was at a loss. These other juvenile delinquents cannot even speak yet—they have been so captivated."

"Holy shit, Kendra, I'm not sure I want anyone but us to see you dressed like this. I'm so turned on it's going to be a minute before I can get up without everyone, er knowing," says Spar.

"Shut up you jerk-wad. Everyone knows we want her, pretty sure they've seen a hard-on in all their years. Kendra you sure you want to stay here we could go find a private place, and we can show you how we really feel about how you look in and out of that suit," Mica says.

That gets a giggle out of me. Feeling better I answer, "Nope, I want to play on the rope and save y'all for later. Grabbing Kino's hand from my waist, I pull him along with me to the next available rope.

Now it's my turn. I run as fast as I can I swing out and drop over the river. Instead of getting out to jump again I stay in to swim for a bit. Kino is flying through the air and does a somersault before hitting the water. I clap for him and tell him how great that is. I can see the competition starting now. All the ropes are swinging now, so I swim out of the way heading to the embankment to get in line again.

Spar yells excitedly, "Hey, watch this Kendra."

I watch as my three all run and jump at the same time. In perfect timing, they fly into the air, hover in synchronization and bump chests before plummeting into the water. I laugh and applaud for them. The whole crowd jumps and swims for about an hour when we settle to our blankets to eat a little of the feast that mostly Vanessa has supplied. Mega is still floating in the river holding claws with Sondra. I laugh when I notice the float he is using. It is one of the giant pink flamingo floaties. I guess he had to get the biggest one to hold him.

I wave Gem over to eat with us. We're talking and sharing about everyday stuff when I think to look for Kick to make sure he is eating. I glance around and see him with some of the Ducere. He is eating. I don't know what possesses me when I wink at him again. I'm rewarded with a slightly lopsided grin. *Ooo, that's sexy. Shut-up Kendra, he isn't for you.*

I feel myself relaxing and listening to stories when I hear Dana start a story from when we were much younger.

"Hey Jare, you remember that fight when we moved to Cueva Hallow?"

Jared says, "Oh no, don't you have anything better to talk about?"

"Nope!" Dana says.

"Shit."

Dana begins, "Guys, so Jared and I had just moved to Cueva Hallow. He was maybe twelve, and that'd make me eleven. Ya gotta know though, we hadn't really ever lived anywhere with other kids our age. So, we thought it was cool that there were other kids around us now. But for some reason, these other boys thought they needed to prove who was boss. So, they called out Jare."

Jared interrupts, "Not quite right! There were five of them, and they threatened to beat you up if I didn't agree to fight. So, I was trying to protect you!"

"Sure Jare, you go with that. He's right, there were five guys, and they wanted to fight. My big bro had the bright idea of fighting the biggest guy on the block in an hour. The dummies agreed. They just didn't know how dirty of a fighter this scammer is. See Jare figured that he could disperse them with some sort of repellent.– Dana stopped and made air quotes with his fingers– His repellent was us peeing in a mason jar. We did, he closed it up, and we waited...

The hour passed, and we saw them walking down the street toward our house. We're holed up in this old dilapidated garage that was next to our house. Dirt floor, big wooden doors, smelled like a sewer... you get the picture. Well with the Flimflam Five across the street, Launcher here pulls out our secret weapon. He tells me he'll throw the bomb because he's the better athlete."

"Well, at least that part's true!" Jared says.

Dana laughing says, "Jare rares back and throws... well, he tried anyway. Ya see we were standing in the opening of the garage and he was taller than he thought. As his arm came forward, it hit the top of the opening, smashing the jar of piss all over the two of us!"

As Dana's story had unfolded, most of the group had become quiet, listening raptly. After he tells the end of it, the laughter was so loud, I couldn't help but believe a little part of my goal had just been reached. Plus, where was I that they could even get away with this?

Leaning back on Mica I feel my donum start to tingle. Mica feels it too, I can tell. He looks around, and now all of my goyles are on their feet. I jump up too, but slowly so I don't startle everyone. I sniff the air.

"Smoke. I smell smoke guys," I say quietly. Mica is large and in charge instantly. "I'm telling Mega now," I tell him.

"Mega, we have a problem."

What is it, Edling?

"Smoke, I can smell smoke, and it's a lot not just a little. Mica is getting everyone to pack up."

I find Mega, he's coming out of the water with Sondra carrying the inner tubes they were floating on. I watch and listen while he's giving orders to pack up and help the kids pack. Mega tells Sondra to take charge of getting the site back the way it was and helping the young ones get home. He's also talking to the Ducere to see what's happening as well as assess the situation.

We've all thrown on our clothes and are ready to fly while Gem and the kids pack and clean. I see Jared grab Jolie and Dana's lady friend and portal out. So, I'm assuming he's heading back to Scotland and taking the girls to get them out of the way. The rest of us gather in the air where Mega gives us instructions as we fly.

47

ARRESTS

Kendra

AFTER FLYING for about fifteen minutes, I see a fire in the hills, but I can tell it's still several miles away. It looks to be near the coordinates we retrieved from the SpotOn schedule we'd stolen.

"If you don't have a respirator hover here. Your Majesty, you have no breathing apparatus. The smoke this high up can still harm you. Ore is on his way with respirators for those who need them. Everyone else, land here and await my orders," Mega commands.

My general adds, "Mica with me. Spar, you are with the queen. Ducere if you have your earbuds, start a general recon, assess the situation, evacuate any people and animals in the area, report back to me. If you don't have your earbud, you must work in a two-person team. Also, recon and evacuate. However, you must be within two minutes flying time of our queen. Queen Kendra, please call the firefighters with the location and any other hazards you notice. Also, Flint, you are with Prince Regent Dana. My prince, I would prefer you stay with our queen."

"Nope, I've got my respirator, I'm good."

"Okay, you and Flint help save a life."

Ore shows up as he finishes giving orders and passes out respirators to the rest of us. With no reason to stay behind now, we all rush forward to put an end to this travesty. I push my dragon blood to the front and am rewarded when I feel the heat on my skin.

I hear some screams and crying, so I head to where I think it's coming from. Under a large hollow tree, I find a group of frightened young people. They are huddled together, apparently at a loss of where to go. The smoke is very thick in the area, and they are coughing and generally struggling to breathe. I remove my respirator and find my dragon self can breathe just fine. Quickly I put the ventilator up to the youngest who is coughing the most, and she slumps into my arms. Spar starts for his respirator, and I hold his hand and shake my head, so he stops. I tell the people that we'll be right back and thrust several of the others into Spar's arms. I grab another of the smaller ones nodding to him we rise into the night sky. As fast as I can fly without hurting my charges I land in the area we had stopped earlier and drop them off. I tele-com Mega and pivot to return to the hollow tree. We had left five others there.

Returning to them in minutes I see one of them has a gun pointed at me. He's standing in front of several bales of what I would guess is marijuana, and some packs that I would imagine is cocaine. I remember what happened when Dana was shot, so I instantly shut my mouth, funny the way I think. The man tells me in broken English that he and the drugs go first. We must leave the others. I reach for his gun as he shoots me in the chest knocking me back a couple steps.

"Really asshat, you want a piece of this dragon?" I ask.

His eyes register that it didn't hurt me, and he turns to run. I use one of my wings to bat him into a tree, cold-cocking him and knocking out one of his teeth. Spar picks him up along with two of the others. I grab the last two, and we take them to the same area as before. There we find Kick administering aid to the ones we had previously left. *Oh, my creator, I like him... a lot.*

"Thank you Kick, here are a few more. This one," pointing to the one Spar had just dropped like a bag of fresh dog turds, "needs tied up." I hand him the gun that the shit-bag had shot me with.

He says, "Don't worry I'll take care of it."

Trusting him, I spin around and am in the air again with Spar hot on my heels. I use the power of my wings to waft a strong current of air toward a flame moving it a foot, so some deer and cows could run out of the way of the fire. That's when I see a man with a small propane torch, lighting more of the dry brush around us. Spar following my gaze nods to me and tackles the asshole before I can tell him to let me, I'm flameproof. He doesn't catch fire, but it looks like he might've been singed a bit. I launch myself at the creep and jerk the propane tank from him and extinguish it. Adrenaline is pumping through my system like crazy. I need to calm down some.

Just then, a team of soldiers in black enter the location. I'm breathing fast. My heart pounding as they take the shithead and handcuff him. It is that easy. I think the jerk didn't put up a fight because he is in shock from seeing Spar and I. They tell us they're with TASS and they'll take the man to the sheriffs who are near, so we can leave undetected. I'm still pumped. The excitement is going to take a bit for me to get over. I take a calming breath. It does nothing. I slow down enough to make sure they know where to find Kick then tele-com Mega what just transpired. I let him know where Kick is and ask if he'll tele-speak to him, so he knows what's happening and to meet us in Navan later. It starts to rain at just the right time putting out much of the fire. I think that must be Jared, so I reach to feel him with my senses, and it is him, but he's not close to me. I'll have to thank him later. Mega tells me the fires are now under control, and the Cueva Hallow firemen are doing well and not in danger.

I wave to Spar and jump to the sky. On the trip home I get close to him and glide in a current, so I can tell him what Mega had told me. I would tell him more when we get home. I just need a little comfort of having him near. It was strange to let people see me as a dragon, even if they are TASS. It is a beginning I think.

Finally, after a hot shower, we're resting in our seating area. I can still smell the smoke from our clothes in the hamper. I lean back into Kino on the couch and relax.

"Who wants to share what happened first, and did anyone bring home our stuff from The Rope?" I ask.

Kino answers, "Gem and Sondra brought everything home. They made sure that Jimmy and Vanessa made it home safe too."

We continue to share stories until torp-time. I notice how stiff Mica is and tell him I know he needs to torp and heal with my burnt Spar. Thank the creator he isn't hurt badly.

"I don't really want to be away from you guys though. I have an idea. If you can and don't mind."

Kino answers for them all, "Anything for you, beloved. Name it, and it is yours."

"You don't have to do this, but will you make me a tent with your wings, so I can crawl in and sleep there?" I ask a little embarrassed by my need to be close to them.

"That would be our pleasure little lady," Mica says, as they step up on the posing stage. They all get on their knees and wrap their arms around each other in a circle. Just before I feel the tingle of them torping, they raise their wings to form a canopy. I take my comforter and pillow off my bed and crawl in the middle of the circle. I kiss each of them and thank them before I lie down. I stare up at them and think what a lucky girl I am. Then, I wonder where Kick is. He must have his own room I decide as I drift off to sleep.

48

THE APPLE

Kendra

THIS IS the night we honor Tana. I've been trying to decide what to wear. I finally choose an amethyst colored dress reminiscent of the stone she was named for—alexandrite.

I'd texted Amber earlier asking if she knew someone who could fix my hair. She sent me the cute little guygoyle Sunny who had set my hair for Spar's honoring party. "Sunny, I like your name. But it's different for me. I thought gargoyles were named after stones, or stone shapes or other things related to rock. Where'd you get your name from?

"Well, my lady I hate to burst your bubble, but my whole name is Sunstone Carnack."

"That's a wonderful name! I just didn't know there is such a thing as a sunstone." I laugh at myself deprecatingly. "Sunny, what does sunstone look like."

"Well my queen, I have two rings with a sunstone gem in each of them." The first one he shows me is a gemstone cut like a round diamond. It has a crystal property to it, in that the fiery orange color looks suspended within it. The second was much less ornate but just as beautiful and profound sparkly blue.

Sunny takes his time fixing my hair. When he finishes, it is splendid. "Sunny, my hair is lovely. I cannot thank you enough for this. What do you do in Navan and will you please make yourself available to fix my hair?"

"Majesty, I am a beautician in Navan. I have a shop in the busy part of Navan. And I would be privileged to do your hair." He hands me his tablet, so I can put my contact information into it. "You can always depend on me, my lady. You are my first concern."

He puts an alexandrite necklace and earrings on me thinking in the same vein I had been.

"Sunny, where does the jewelry come from? Is someone making this for me?" I ask. "I really need to thank them."

"I guess you could say the Ceorfan made it for you—in a way. It was made long ago for our queens and stays in the vault. Amber chose this and asked me to put it on you for this ceremony today. I think it's a perfect choice."

"I remember asking her, and she told me that dragons have a treasure. I guess I should check it out one of these days. Is there a lot?"

"Not as much as there was; it was hidden before we moved to Navan. What is here is a treasure, but not what we had at one time. Your jewels are part of our heritage and are prized by all of the Guild. When we see you wear them, it makes us happy. It is a familiar memory. We like to say, accepting a gift honors the one who gave. That is how we feel... you honor us by wearing them."

"I wonder what happened to the rest of the treasure?"

He says, "I don't know, my lady. They say the Hewn have it."

I let the subject drop. Sunny does my makeup and chooses my shoes. Once I am ready my consorts tell me it is time for the ceremony. We're starting in the amphitheater room then we'll go to Cueva Hallow with glamours so that Dana can place a statue of our heroine in the plaza as a memorial to her. He has permission to put a statue there from the city fathers. They just don't know it is a memorial for a Ceorfan heroin.

Clifton starts the speech by telling us a little about Tana then introduces Mica who was with her when she gave her life. Mica tells us the story of how Tana died. I see tears in his eyes when he tells us how brave she was and how getting the staff from Barat has hurt the villain. His voice shakes when he speaks, making me wish I could hug him and take away his pain. After he tells of her heroism, he stiffens and tells the story she'd recounted to those who were with her on the southern wall at Troy.

Mica ends with a call for festivities, at least within the bounds of such tragic loss. "Tana willingly gave her life to save her friend Queen Leta from hanging on the battlements of Troy for another day. Tana did this out of love for her friend. She attacked Barat out of love for her people and wouldn't want us to be saddened at her fate. She'd prefer we celebrate our returning her friend to Navan as well as our victory over Barat."

After he steps down, Jared steps forward. "I knew I had to run toward the portal. I had no choice but to run in a straight line. Had she not taken the attention of Barat, I know I would've died that day. Tana saved my life and allowed me and the others with me to make it to the portal and return with Leta's head to Navan.

It is my turn. I tell my people what I knew of Tana and what she meant to the dragon queens. I remind them that I also have my grandmother's memories and explain what Leta felt about Tana. "Tana was dedicated to healing and helping with wounded, so we're renaming the medical chamber the Alexandritana Medical and Research Facility." The pulses are heartfelt and many. "She is etched in the city and will never be forgotten." The Ceorfan repeat the phrase and tell me thank you, they will not forget.

Finally, Jericho comes forward. The room stills. The only sounds to be heard is the breathing of the assembled crowd. Jericho begins singing his magic tome. As his song builds, we begin to understand her body is returning to the Earth. The goodbye pulses start. I feel each pulse singularly as if each Ceorfan were passing in front of her. Mine is the final pulse. It's powerful and comes from a memory which once belonged to Leta. In the echo of my pulse Tana's body dissolves in a flash of sparkling dust and then is gone.

I motion for Dana to come to the podium. He is last to speak. He tells the Guild that he's made a statue of Tana to place in the middle of the town of Cueva Hallow as a memorial. Everyone is invited to the placing of the statue tonight. "We'll all meet here in Navan, in the reception hall where Sis, Jare, and I first met the Ceorfan. So if we're all ready, we can open a portal now."

Jericho is there to open the portal. All of the Ceorfan, even those too afraid to leave Navan for various reasons enter the portal. This is for the family to stand together. Jericho and Kino created a spell which will make everyone appear human without a glamour stone. It affects everyone as they step through the portal.

Jared speaks for Dana as he unveils the statue. Dana never likes to receive compliments on his work. He blushes as the crowd's appreciation fills the air when the beautiful blue marble statue is unveiled. The Duke of Stone raises his hand, and we watch as he molds a red-green apple into the statue's hand. More exclamations as we see that as he molded the apple, a small apple tree close to the statue grows to maturity full of apples. Dana even looks surprised and moves to pick one and brings it to me as a gift.

I take a bite of it, and it's delicious. I tell everyone to pick some if you want, the fruit is ripe. Many do pick some, but we leave some just in case there are homeless who need something to eat here.

"Dana," I ask, "do you know the story of Tana and the apple?"

"Ya, Sissy, I do. What I didn't know, is that there was an apple tree here in the park. I also didn't know that using my gift to mold the stone apple to the hand of the statue would make it grow."

"That's crazy. Maybe just thinking of the apple and honoring her is what made it grow," Jared said.

"Yep, you are probably right."

Jared interjects, "You guys remember that today is Dad's birthday too?"

We all nod knowingly. I say what we all are thinking. "I sure miss him."

They both nod their heads in agreement.

Dana says, "Guys, I'm going to stay here and get some rest. Go enjoy the reception, and I'll see you Sunday night. I think I'll go to Scotland with you this time."

My brother gives me a hug and kisses on the top of my head. He bumps fist with Jared, then is off for his home.

The crowd's almost gone. Kino sidles up to me, and I ask him, "How did you do that trick? I didn't even know people were leaving."

He smiles and says, "That is what I do beloved. My small gift comes in handy at times."

I hook my hand in his and say, "I'm not sure any of the Guild's gifts are small. Take me home, handsome."

We spend most of the night in the reception room eating and drinking and ruminating. There's a lot of laughing even among the tears.

I tell the High Guild we'll meet before sunrise then we'll all rest. I have a lot to think about and have new questions for my advisers.

49

TERMINUS DEBRIEF

Kendra

THE TIME for the HG meeting is closing in. My head is filled with questions. I know that the HG needs new ideas and perspectives. There will be much to do and many new choices. Even so, I'm oddly at peace. So much has happened so quickly. Yet with my memories, I feel much more in control than I could've imagined before being etched.

As I walk toward my allodium, I see Clifton. "Clifton, will you please make sure that Kick is at our HG meeting. I want to ask him to take Tana's place as a High Guild member and become one of my advisers."

Clifton doesn't even register a questioning look. He merely replies, "Yes Kendra I'll do that." He's killin' it with the contractions, it makes me happy.

When I enter the allodium, it feels like home. Many of the members are already here. My consorts are spread throughout the room. Knowingly, each one lifts his head as I enter. Happiness washes over me when I see this, and I let them know I see them. I blow a kiss to Spar. I tilt my head down and look through my lashes at Mica and smile. My saucy side comes out for Kino, so I mouth, "eat me" after I make sure no one can see but him.

Kick is just entering the room and walks over to where I'm pouring myself some coffee. I'm not sure what possesses me, but I wink at him. He grins a full tooth beautiful grin. *Just a friend, he's just a friend, but a damn cute one.* After I slide into my perfectly formed, butt-shaped seat, Clifton brings the meeting to order. He starts, "We have completed a few of our previously agreed upon actions including laying Tana to rest. Jericho will etch her story into the Halls of History tomorrow."

I interject, "I want to make a motion to fill Tana's position tonight. I'd like tonight to be the night we honor her memory in the HG so that it'll be documented this way forever," I say. Everyone agrees and asks for suggestions.

"I want Kick as my new adviser. Tana allowed me to save Kick indirectly. Also, I understand everyone will not agree. However, Kick knows things that none of us do. He's seen Barat's hiding places, his tactics, and his brutalities. I need access to that information."

Few of the HG agree with my request at the outset. Yet, I continue to push forward knowing, even in the end, not everyone will be happy with Kick's appointment. I believe it was Kick who put the vote in his favor. He says, "I understand your reluctance. You fear that I may be a plant of some sort, that I'll take information back to 'my master' Barat. I can never say enough to convince you. I am left with simply telling you, Kendra is my queen. I'll die to protect her and the world from the terrors which I've dealt with for the last millennia. I'll die before I allow myself to be returned to his torture."

The vote was almost evenly split. But it leaned in Kick's favor. I also tell the members that I also want Gem as a member too. This passes quickly.

"Mega, will you tell us what happened during last night's arrests. Was the man we caught the Firestarter?" I ask.

"Yes, Your Majesty, he is, and freely admits to the crime. He's an international employee of the SpotOn oil company. He openly says they paid him to start the fires. You should see this in the human news when you are at work. His reasons for the fires are as we surmised. To avert attention from the Edomants who sell illegal drugs and slaves for the sex trade. He will not admit cartel involvement. He refuses to provide any information regarding those who he ran the drugs for or who provided the young people as slaves. The various human authorities have taken control of the case away from TASS and are tightening security in the region.

The people that you and Spar saved are with TASS now. The committee is finding them homes. Some of those who are experienced or educated are being set up with jobs. Those who are not are being trained. A select few are joining the task force working to dissolve the slave trade across the world. The fires were controlled in hours instead of days thanks to the Duke of Storms. Apparently, he arrived before we did using his portal stone. I respectfully requested he not do that again. However, he is much like you, Edling." He didn't say stubborn or willful, but I get the point and raise a brow with a cocky grin.

Mega continues, "Jericho, with the assistance of Kino and Kick altered the minds of those who saw the Duke of Storms cause the rain. Those of the group you and Spar assisted also had to have their memories modified. They now remember you being shot, but you were wearing body armor. They now only recognize you as a park ranger and Kick helping as a member of the TASS task force."

Just when I think Mega has finished his report he pauses, a worried look on his face. "Mega, go on, I can see that you have something else to say."

"Majesty, all of this is very expensive. I believe TASS will need to be repaid in some fashion. They are not organized as a humanitarian mission as we have required of them. We also may need to look at finding funding for the other people we are helping soon."

Clifton says, "We also need to address Kick's information concerning Barat. Queen Kendra has requested an emergency meeting with TASS. They want to limit our contingent to no more than five people. The meeting will take place in the UK, and I have the coordinates, so we can portal there. Chairman Brinker has also provided us a place in Fiatrill Hall to stay. This will require us to portal back and forth as needed."

Kick raises a hand, and after a nod from Clifton, he says, "Why do you not use the jump buoys for this kind of travel? It'd be much safer and would immediately bring us all back, together, if there's danger."

Many in the room understand what he just said. However, I'm not one of them. I wait while Jericho explains, "Kick, the jump buoys have all been destroyed while you were incarcerated. The only surviving buoy is a one-man buoy which I use."

"Wait." I have to ask, "What's the difference between a jump buoy and a portal stone?"

Jericho nods for Kick to answer. "A portal stone is a doorway to a destination. It's very nice to have, but you must have it in your possession to use it. A buoy is a stone which is physically located in one place. Magic words are used to operate it, and it is not physically in possession of those who use it. It can send one or many depending on the spell. The spell also controls the locations. The minute a person or group is ready to come home only one of them needs to repeat the spell. Or if there's danger, the spell instantly returns them to the home buoy. In ancient times, we used them to time warp in dire instances. But it is dangerous and the chances the party lives are, regrettably, slim."

"Can we make a buoy?" I ask.

"They were a gift from the old gods. I do not know how to make them, but we can steal some. Barat has two," he informs us.

"That is something we will definitely do when we get to his lair and put him out of our misery. It isn't enough, but I want to thank you all for sticking to our goals of helping others. You did a wonderful job. I'm sorry you don't get the credit, but I think you understand we must still maintain the secrecy of the Guild for a while longer. The world isn't quite ready to learn about us," I say.

Everyone agrees. Now, all we have left is to decide which five of us are going to the meeting in the UK. Here, the meeting breaks down. "Everyone, I will name two who will be there. Kick and me. I need the rest of you to sort it out." I decide at this point to have the balance of the evening with my goyles, so we can have some family time while I prepare for my trip to the UK. After the sun rises, I'll be free to spend it with Mica while the others torp.

Tonight, however, I feel that we've taken an incredible step forward in accomplishing our goal toward eradicating Barat. We also have another victory over the cartels. We might not have halted the whole sex slave industry, but we'll eat that elephant one bite at a time. As long as we never agree to settle with evil, we might have a chance to change the world. It's a goal. It's our goal.

The End

A SNEAK PEEK...

Turn the page to read a chapter of the next book in the
Ceorfan Gargoyle Series –

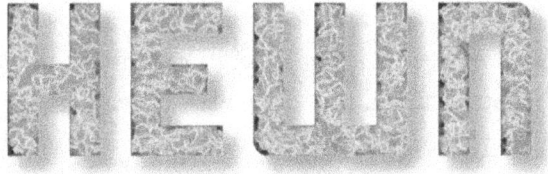

HEWN CHAPTER ONE

Kendra

Kendra

Honoring Tana took a lot out of me. I snored, I'm sure of it because I woke myself up with a big snort. Oh, that's just great, especially when I have the most gorgeous set of arms around me, ones that just happen to be attached to a gargoyle I adore. Right when I think I've gotten away with my unladylike noise...

Mica beams and says, "Your snorts are even cute," as he turns toward me and opens his eyes.

"I didn't mean to sleep all day on my day off. I was hoping to get to that alone time we want." Right then, my stomach growls like a lion.

Mica smiles a panty melting grin at me and says, "We're alone right now. If you go with me to the lunchroom, I'll make you some breakfast, princess. I don't really want to get up. I like having you close to me here. But I do have a plan for tomorrow if you can wait."

"Well, if you put it that way. Waiting isn't going to be easy, but I'm kind of excited." I jump up and go to my bathroom to get dressed.

What!? I don't have the power to dress in front of him and not start something, holding back would be off the table.

He's waiting for me by the door when I finish dressing. I grab his hand as we take off toward the lunchroom. It really is just us, as almost all of Navan is torped and will be for several more hours. I understand Jared has some of his men here taking up the slack for the Elite Warrior Guard and working while the Guild is torpified. However, I never see the guards. When the gargoyle Ceorfan torp, it's their version of sleeping, but they've turned to stone. This is also when their wounds are healed in total. Even though Mica is a gargoyle, he can choose when he wants to torp. It's his gift.

I halfway skip-run on the way to the kitchen. Mica tries to walk slow for me, but one of his steps is three of mine. I don't mind at all, though.

We make coffee when we get into the kitchen area. Then my goyle asks me if I want to cut the veggies to make a pico-de-gallo for the omelets he's making that contain bacon and eggs. He's plating our food when I finish with the salsa. He adds the cheese, and I put the pico on top. We carry our plates to the table, and he goes back and fills us a cup of coffee and brings them over. My blond, amber-eyed goyle sits across from me, so we can talk. My face heats from the joy of his pampering me. It's the little things that are special to me. I never recognized that until I had to get my own when I was alone, and it hurt me to not have the consideration I'd been used to.

My breakfast date says with his head down and a little shy, "Princess, will you go back to Oahu with me for a couple of hours. I've arranged a little outing for us before we have to be in Scotland."

I take a deep cleansing breath and blow it out oooh... that's a prescription for happiness, one that I've been waiting on.

"What should I bring, Blondie?" I ask by way of answering, looking into his dreamy eyes. I could fall into those babies.

"You will?" His face is all screwed up and serious as he keeps talking. "I was afraid that I'd messed up too badly, and you were only keeping me around because of the bond. I was worried we wouldn't have anything more than what we have now." He hangs his head as his voice lowers to a whisper.

"What! Even after that... well, that... what happened in bed with everyone? I love you, Mica. I'm not letting you go. Stuff happens in a long relationship. I'm not saying I wasn't hurt at the time. I wanted to kill you. Then when I thought about it, I knew you loved me. Especially when you came home and apologized to us all. I'm not perfect; I'll probably mess up again, and will need you to forgive me. We're in this for the long run. I often wondered before I was etched if I'm being selfish and mistreating you all by having this poly-relationship. Now I feel different with all my grandmother's experience. It's very natural for me. This is what I want. I want you."

He scoops me up and presses me close to him. Tears are in my big goyle's eyes, and he's chuckling. His laugh makes me giggle. I can't wait to touch him and feel his touch.

Sitting me on the table, he kisses me lightly and says, "Then it's forever, babe. I have everything taken care of, let's not wait and go now. If you want to, that is? You need to bring a bathing suit. Maybe, a cover-up and something to wear to an outdoor restaurant... the alert alarm rings and interrupts him. The lights flash, but not red like they did when Kick infiltrated Navan. They're yellow, and the message is blaring that there are strangers at the cave entrance.

Mica and I jump up and head for the hidden opening where we're met by several of the human guards who are training to be Elites for the Ceorfan. Mega has been calling them cadets because they want to be part of the Elites. Mica takes charge and orders them to take point and our rear guard.

On the way, he explains that the warning or danger alert is more of a doorbell. When we get to the entrance, my partner pulses out a general query through the opening. He receives a pulse back. A pulse that I understand to mean the Hewn, the nomadic contingent of the Ceorfan Guild, needs to speak with the queen.

Immediately he says, "Babe, it's safe."

"Got it."

Then using his authoritative voice, he orders a big dark-haired man, "Cadet Sanders, please notify the Combat Information Center (CIC) operators that the way is safe. Then enter into the system that Navan has seven visitors, and they're torped at the entrance of the city. The contingent will be welcomed when the sun sets and taken to the allodium to speak with the High Guild (HG)."

The cadet responds, "Yes, sir," as he turns and reaches for his comm device and starts relaying his orders.

Kick and Jericho have reached us and are getting the information on what we've discovered. Sanders is still radioing in his orders.

I step through the crowd and push my way to the entrance to reach the Hewn. What I behold, are seven of the roughest looking gargoyles I can remember seeing. They're standing in a semi-circle, torpified in place. I'm shocked, putting my hand to my chin, and yes, I have memories of torped gargoyles pulsing. It's still a surprise because without bringing up the ancestor memory I wouldn't have known. It's sort of like I'd forgotten and just remembered. I realize they haven't been here long. They must have gotten here as the sun rose when the guards were changing out to the human sentries.

"I wonder what they want," I ask.

"I know exactly what they want," answers Kick with a dismal look having just arrived. He continues when I question him with a glance. "They need your help. Barat is carving up captured Hewn to add to his Crafted army. Because we have yet to thwart him, he's upping the ante and abducting more of them."

I pinched the bridge of my nose and rub my eyes. My hatred for Barat the Rat's Ass is making me fiery angry. My dragon wants to take over. I never thought about how the bastard is carving the Crafted. I get a grip on my anger long enough to ask, "Did you have no choice at all, Kick?"

His face is tortured with pain. The vein in his neck is pulsing, and his teeth are clenched as he grits out, "No, there's no choice with Barat."

I can't stand to see his agony, so I turn and pulse to the torped

Hewn in front of me. I tell them they're welcome in Navan, and I'll see them after sunset. "We will figure out a plan to help tonight!" I vow.

My breakfast date notices my anger escalating and starts talking me down. He thinks I might do something rash. But no, there's nothing I can do right now. I'm at a loss. I stare at him with a face full of 'Help me. I don't know how to fix this.'

He says, "Princess, let's assign these men some research and go to your chambers and see if we can find anything ourselves. Answers come to me better when I stop and think for a while. Are you alright with that?"

I nod yes, instead of voice the curses that I want to spit out. He retakes charge and orders the cadets to their posts with their tablets to search for information on missing or captured gargoyles that might be on the record. Facing the guards, Mica states, "We need their locations and pertinent details for the HG meeting tonight. The meetings are usually about thirty minutes after sunset, so be ready, and in the allodium at that time."

Shooting a questioning stare at the old mage, my partner asks, "Jericho, do you have anything to add?"

"Prince Consort Mica, not really, but I do remember some reference in a document I was reading in the Halls of History earlier this week. I will see if I can find it for the meeting too. Kick, do you think that you can look up some finder spells after you give the queen and her Ducere any details you know?"

The young mage answers, "I'm unfamiliar with the term Ducere."

"The Ducere are a small team of specially trained elite warriors whose primary mission is to protect the Queen. Queen Kendra's Ducere includes her Prince Consorts, among others," the ancient wizard says.

"Thank you for the explanation. Of course, I'll search the archives," the former prisoner says.

"I know that Barat is protected, and these spells won't work on him. I have tried every spell I know. I even tried one on you when you got here, and that won't work. But we might be able to use a spell on the taken Hewn," says Jericho.

The young mage tips his head to the side slightly and nods his assent.

Mica agrees. "That's perfect. I'll keep the queen busy pulsing our visitors and gathering information until the HG meeting unless you need me sooner."

Then I turn toward my handsome goyle and put a hand on his chest. He's so smart I can't help but be proud of how he handles himself.

He wraps me in his arms and lowering his head to mine, says softly, "Babe, can I have a raincheck for our date? I promise I'll make it worth your while."

I'm going to need to change my panties.

"Believe me, I'd rather have the date. You can have a dozen rainchecks," I say.

GLOSSARY

(This short glossary is not a complete character list. More a list of terms we think you might want to remember and a few main characters.)

- **Amber** - Elite Warrior specializes in undercover surveillance. Mate to Mason.
- **Ceorfan** - (Key-or-fan) Carved or born grotesques, gargoyles and dragons. Anyone different who wants to become family and is accepted by the Guild.
- **Chiroptera** - Hand Wing or Little Wing, usually a hand with four fingers located at the top of many wings.
- **CIC** - Combat Information Center. The defense center the Ceorfan use in alert or emergency situations.
- **Crafted** - Evil mindless robot created gargoyles made from wood and magic.
- **Cursed** – The Ceorfan who were captured and tortured in the Mage Wars.
- **Dana Macbard** - (Dan-uh) Brother of Kendra and Jared Macbard. Aqua dragon, Duke of Stone.
- **Donum** - A gift, the knowing that the dragon breed has when there is a need between family members or guild. It can show up as a feeling or thoughts similar to ESP.
- **DRT** - Defense and Reaction Team of the Elite Warriors Guild.
- **Ducere** - Small specialize team of the Elite Warriors Guard. The Ceorfan Special Forces.
- **Edling** - Noble child, heir.
- **Ef** - An effigy or statue of a gargoyle.
- **Elite Warrior Guard** - The warriors/soldiers of the Ceorfan race.

- **Findare** - Took over as temporary king in the interim between viable queens.
- **Flint** - Elite Warrior undercover agent. Member of the Ducere.
- **Gortanik** - A Mage who had been held prisoner of Barat and infiltrated Navan. His nickname is Kick and he is helping the Ceorfan find Barat.
- **Grotesques** - People of the Ceorfan Race that look like what humans call gargoyles.
- **Guild** - The word is used for the race of the Ceorfan people.
- **High Guild** - The advisors to the Ruler of the Ceorfan.
- **Jared Macbard** - Brother of Kendra and Dana Macbard. Blue dragon, Duke of Storms.
- **Jericho** - Mage. Trusted member of the High Guild.
- **Kokkino Petra** – Kino - (Key-no) Mega's third in command of the Elite Guard. Nephew to Findare. Love of Kendra, Consort of the Queen.
- **Mage** - Human with the ability to perform spells of magic.
- **Mage Jar** - A glass jar of liquid lighting used and powered by the magic, in Navan.
- **Mason** - Elite Warrior specializes as a thief and undercover surveillance. Mate to Amber.
- **Megahir/Mega** - (Mega-here) Commander of the Elite Warrior Guard.
- **Mica Jacobs** - (Mike-ah) Second in command of the Elite Guard. Love of Kendra and her partner as a Federal Park Ranger, Consort of the Queen.
- **Navan** - (Nuh-van)The cave city of the entire guild of Ceorfan people.
- **Nous-fārī** - mind-speakers, Ceorfan with the gift of telepathy.

- **Pulse** - An echo pulse is a form of communication between the Ceorfan Guild. Similar to the sonar pulses of bats.
- **Resurgere** - 'Restore our family' literally, when a gargoyle has an ingot carved from his body in the seconds prior to hardening into a torpified state to sleep and heal, for the purpose of giving it willingly to another in exchange for a bone of their own body. Each party is implanted with the other's stone or bone.
- **Spar Megason** - Resurgere gave him a new life from David's body he becomes Mega's son. Love of Kendra, Consort of the Queen.
- **Torpefy/Torp/Torped** - Past tense: torpefied. Meaning: make (someone or something) numb, paralyzed, or lifeless. This is an early 19th century word from Latin [torpefacere], 'be numb or sluggish'. It is when gargoyles turn to stone in the daylight.

ACKNOWLEDGEMENTS

From **Miki** –

Thank you, our fans and readers of the Ceorfan Gargoyles Series. We appreciate each and every one of you. You are our prize. Please, if you enjoyed the books at all consider leaving us a review. It means more than you can imagine!

My family who is always supportive and helpful. Especially Robert and his wife Peggy. My husband, I love that you are in my corner. Thank you, Mom and Pop, for always being here for me. Thank you, Dad for giving me a great imagination. My son and his wife Kit and LaRay, my son Kyle, my daughter in law Callie, and my stepsons John and Jeffery, you are amazing. All my grandchildren you help me keep going. Our cousins are so wonderful! I hope everyone has people in their lives that are as amazing as you all. We are blessed to have you!

All my friends who are precious to me. Miki and Mine Guys and Goyles!!! Savages and Renegades too. Christina and Brenda, you are the best PA's ever!

Craig and Rob, you make everything in this so much more possible. What good dragons! You have always been my best friends. Garrett you really are the best co-author ever! I love you all. Thank you for your support! — Miki Ward

From **Garrett** –

Thank you fans and supporters. Miki said it perfectly above. I could repeat it here. But who'd want to read it again? I will say, thanks for giving us the opportunity to play around with your feelings for a bit.

To my beautiful wife Kathi, without you I am not a person. To my children, thanks for the pure joy, and terror, you continually provide. Because of you, I push myself to a higher standard and sometimes, near the edge of a cliff... To my adopted children, Ethan and Kasia, thank you for making my family, your family. I love you all beyond measure.

To my much older sister and my really little brother, thanks for not allowing me to follow through with my nefarious plans which I'd concocted in my youth. Still, had you allowed me, we'd all have huge houses and buffalo in our backyards!

To my Sangre de Cristo High School friends, I can't believe it's been this long. I also can't believe how amazing you are. Thank you for the fathomless love and support you've freely given me over the last four decades. — Garrett V. Ward

OTHER BOOKS BY MIKI AND GARRETT WARD

The Ceorfan Gargoyles Series

Carved

Etched

Hewn

The Ceorfan Gargoyles Novellas

My Tormented Mage

Shivers Series

We See You

Double Mirror

Elser Books are stand alone

Flesh and Bold

Stand Alone from Miki Ward

My Phantom Queen

FIND US

FB Pages

Miki & Mine, Guys and Goyles Group
https://bit.ly/2CpH3BM

Miki's FB Author page
https://bit.ly/2yMlVSG

Garrett's FB Author page
https://bit.ly/2P3USwv

Bookbub
https://bit.ly/2J3FRFh

Amazon

Amazon Author Page - Follow Miki
https://amzn.to/2Ey3qrk

Amazon Author Page - Follow Garrett
https://amzn.to/2yNYOr7

www.ingramcontent.com/pod-product-compliance
Lightning Source LLC
Chambersburg PA
CBHW071056250626

47159CB00002B/488